La Presidenta

La Presidenta

A NOVEL

Lois Gould

The Linden Press/Simon and Schuster

New York

The author gratefully acknowledges permission to quote from the following:
"El Simulacro," from the book *El Hacedor*, by Jorge Luis Borges,
copyright © 1960 by Emece Editores.

"The Sham," from the book *Dreamtigers*, by Jorge Luis Borges,
copyright © 1964 by Jorge Luis Borges. The University of Texas Press.

For support and sustenance, my thanks to the Writers Room, and to the New York Public Library, whose havens, the Frederick Lewis Allen Room and Wertheim Study, sheltered me in the course of this book; to my friends; my editor Joni Evans; and, always, to the ones who are there when the distance is traveled: Robert, Tony, Roger.

La historia es increíble pero ocurrió y acaso no una vez, sino muchas, con distintos actores y con diferencias locales. En ella está la cifra perfecta de una época irreal y es como el reflejo de un sueño o como aquel drama en el drama, que se ve en Hamlet. El enlutado no era Perón y la muñeca rubia no era la mujer Eva Duarte, pero tampoco Perón era Perón ni Eva era Eva sino desconocidos o anónimos (cuyo nombre secreto y cuyo rostro verdadero ignoramos) que figuraron, para el crédulo amor de los arrabales, una crasa mitología.

The story is incredible, but it happened, and perhaps not once but many times, with different actors in different locales. It contains the perfect cipher of an unreal epoch; it is like the reflection of a dream or like that drama-within-the-drama we see in *Hamlet*. The mourner was not Perón and the blond doll was not the woman Eva Duarte, but neither was Perón Perón, nor was Eva Eva. They were, rather, unknown individuals—or anonymous ones whose secret names and true faces we do not know—who acted out, for the credulous love of the lower middle classes, a crass mythology.

El Simulacro

JORGE LUIS BORGES

La Presidenta

FROM this angle, with her foot resting lightly on the surface of the water, you might take her for some pale ornamental giant-killer, gracefully poised on the neck of her prey. She shifts her weight, suddenly thrusting the toes down, then retrieves them with a gasp and sharp tears—since she cannot permit herself a short piercing scream. Assassins! she might cry, otherwise. But imagine how foolish that would seem under the circumstances. The gardener Miguel has merely forgotten (again) to heat the pool for her morning swim. She understands that he has deliberately left it cold, to torment her. He is laughing now somewhere in the garden, training the hose away from her favorite flowers. The bird of paradise is dying. She will shut her mind to these things; Miguel with his dirty white fedora, which he wears cocked at an insolent angle, is no worse than the others, after all. By now they are all skilled at robbing her of the small consolations; they know precisely which of her expectations it is safe to disregard, which affronts she will bear in silence. It is always a thing which the general will not notice, a discomfort that will matter only to her, and that she will not dare to mention to him. She understands well; it is because they know she is going that it is quite safe now to show their contempt. María Blanca frowns, then remembers to widen her eyes and part her lips in the little smile, a rehearsal. Her face is forever in rehearsal now. Sometimes she surprises herself in mirrors, wearing the lips this way, tilting the head back so, slightly, gazing intently as if listening to an important song.

After a moment she shrugs off the thick white robe and dives into the icy water, as a test of her strength and courage. You see? She will turn blue, still smiling. Soon they will be here, all of them, watching her, judging whether she can be trusted, whether she is worthy. Of course this is only what she imagines. In truth, they are coming for La Señora's visit, for her return from the long, terrible journey. It is fourteen years since any of them has seen her, and now she is coming here, to the house in which four months have passed since María Blanca became the general's new wife, the house in which she practices to be what they expect—or perhaps to be the opposite of what they expect, whichever is more surprising. Well, she thinks, they will see how she behaves when La Señora arrives, with what control, with what cool elegance.

In the numbing shock of the cold water, Blanca feels the tiny familiar knot of fear tighten in her stomach. Last night, lying awake in the enormous white bed, with the fine embroidered linen sheets that irritate her skin, she whispered to the general of this small knot of fear, thinking he might comfort her. The confession only made him angry. He is so often angry now, dark and silent, coiled with tension. She should have held her tongue. She had better learn to control such things, he said coldly, his massive body turning away from her, winding itself in the heavy sheet. She must know, he added, though it was hardly necessary, that La Señora had certainly never felt such a knot of fear. Blanca will not mention it again.

She presses a fist now against the place where the pain is sharpest; she will force herself to listen to other things—to fat Miguel and the sullen new maid Pina padding overhead in the narrow *cocina*, the kitchenette that adjoins the dining balcony. She begins to glide silently across the pool, kicking underwater so as not to make noise, listening to Miguel and Pina scraping heavy pots; she hears their laughing whispers as they scorch her breakfast. Always they laugh, sometimes hiding it behind their hands or under their heavy eyelids. The general shrugs; what does she expect, one never trusts servants, La Señora never trusted them, after all had she not been one herself? At eleven years of age, he would tell María Blanca proudly, La Señora had learned all the secrets one could learn on one's knees. Of course, it seemed that La Señora had been born knowing what uses one might make of such secrets, so that one would not remain on one's knees longer than necessary. María Blanca pretended not to quite understand.

Now she listens for the general's footsteps on the white marble staircase; she turns quickly and begins to swim on her back, smooth legs waving like blue-white ribbons just under the water's surface.

Often the general comes to watch her; he sinks heavily into one of the large sofas that flank the edge of the pool; he leans forward slightly, sipping his horsetail tea, which he drinks unsugared, taking it bravely like a *castigo*, a punishment for sins. He holds his thin cigar between loose fingers; it glows briefly and goes out. Eyes half-closed, he sits so, impassive, expressionless, gazing at her, exhaling in short, labored puffs, in the way of an old man running. Occasionally the pink tip of his tongue grazes quickly over his dry lower lip; one can almost hear it scrape. Occasionally he spreads the blunt fingers of one large hand across one massive knee. She goes on swimming, pretending she does not know he is there; she will arch her back and undulate slowly, dancing with the water. Her body shines like that of an iridescent sea creature, coiling, uncoiling. She has remembered to oil her skin so that it will catch the coral-gold sunlight that filters softly through the stained-glass ceiling over the pool. She has invented new movements, marvelous tricks of the limbs and spine, of the fingers caressing the water; each day she perfects another such dance, in case the general is there. They have never spoken of this.

Today the heavy footsteps are moving rapidly away from the pool, toward the general's study. Behind the heavy door there are messengers waiting. Two political friends; a dark little man from the Deutschebank, in a shiny suit; the new driver of the limousine; the general's secretary. There are too many urgent matters. La Señora's family, the sisters and the mama, are waiting in separate hotels, under different names; the priest and the doctor will be coming later, by helicopter from the mainland. La Señora will have urgent need of her famous doctor. There is no foretelling the delicate attentions she may require after all this time. Yet one may remember those glib promises the doctor himself made, and how much money they have already paid him; one may know how sincerely he believes that La Señora will not have changed; that she is still just as the general—just as they all—remember her. Still, they have had to arrange another payment of $50,000 before the doctor would agree to come to her this time. The general has made certain promises in order to get this money on one day's notice, but this is, after all, considerably less difficult for the general now than at any time in the past fourteen years. Besides, they can hardly afford not to have the doctor with them when she arrives. La Señora has been through a great ordeal—darkness and rough roads; dampness, cruel weather, and the careless hands of indifferent strangers. It is distressing to consider the possible harm that might have come to her, in spite of everything. Remember that La Señora has always been delicate. In some ways María Blanca is stronger, more of an *Indio*, with that thick mud-colored hair of hers, those solid bones. But La Señora was born with strength of another kind. Perhaps she has it still.

María Blanca feels the fear pulling at her again; she swallows a dark, sour taste, thinking she must not think so much of La Señora, even if she can think of nothing else. Instead, she will try to rehearse once more in her mind how smooth and sure her voice will be at this meeting, what expressions her face will assume when the family arrives; for example, what rushes of tenderness the general will feel for her when she faces La Señora at last, surrounded by their mutual enemies. *Sin duda*, without doubt, he understands that tonight will be difficult for her, far more difficult than the meetings with the angry officers who already despise María Blanca for La Señora's sake (as if they had ever been loyal to her). He understands well; nevertheless he will spare her nothing. In truth he regards everything as a sort of test, just as she does. Was it not a test on the first night when he cried out María Rosa's name in the darkness, while he wept into María Blanca's thick dark hair? Blanca had understood what to do then; the ways to comfort him. The next day she began the treatments to make one's hair softer, lighter, like the hair of La Señora. She began the lessons to make her voice softer as well, and the exercises to teach her body to move in new ways. All this seemed easy; she had always moved well, and changed herself to please others. One may remember how quickly she learned what to do with her hands on his body, and her soft lips and her tongue. How easily she learned to endure certain indignities, and when he could not bear to touch her at all, as more and more now he could not, how eagerly she learned to do what he wished her to do instead. Let me . . . she would whisper softly. And so? Ah. Until at last he would sigh her own name, Blanca, Blanquita, and gently touch her dark hair as it lay like a fan of feathers across his thighs.

It has been arranged that La Señora's car will arrive at eleven o'clock, just after dinner. The sisters and the mama, the priest and the doctor will arrive first, one car at a time, bringing with them everything that may be needed. The doctor has suggested that the services of a dressmaker may be necessary, but the general's security advisers have expressly forbidden this; there must be no outsiders present, the family must find another way to refresh La Señora's wardrobe for the remainder of her journey. As for medical supplies and assistance, the doctor has assured them that he can handle everything alone, if those in attendance will follow his precise instructions in any minor procedures. He emphasized the word *minor*.

The day has passed like other days, except of course that the car did not come to take them for a drive through the countryside or to one of the secluded beaches, or into the town for luncheon and shopping. Nor has Blanca been permitted to call and chat with her friend Alma Flor. Ordinarily the general has no objection to her friendship with Alma Flor. She has been well investigated, and her house servants are in the general's employ. Nevertheless, Blanca's contacts outside the general's compound have been sharply curtailed in the past several weeks, while security measures were being tightened. La Señora's arrival on the island is a secret of the most sensitive sort; knowledge of it in the village could trigger serious political reactions ten thousand miles away in Pradera, where the general's old enemies are still poised, waiting for word of his next move. In Pradera, the reunion with La Señora is regarded as crucial; if anything goes wrong, it is entirely possible that the general will not be coming home to revive his legend after all.

FATHER Padrón is the first to arrive, his black shoes caked with reddish dust, his face dark with conflicting emotions. Blanca feels an unreasonable relief at the sight of him standing in her gleaming marble foyer, holding his soft black hat against his body like a shield. He is not here for her sake, yet of them all, she believes, he is the least likely to do her harm. It was La Señora's mother who insisted that he be summoned for this occasion. For once the general had agreed without discussion, though he made a joke of it with Blanca. The mother was a fanatic, he said; not once in all her fortunate life had she done an important thing without confessing it in advance to the padre. Within the joke Blanca thought she understood the general's trust of this Father Padrón. Even if she is wrong, it is of some comfort.

From her bedroom window Blanca watches the arrival of the cars; exactly nine minutes apart they come, black and shiny, like beads of the rosary. She is not ready. The bed is still piled with dresses, the dressing table heaped with jewels. If only Alma Flor were here to say, *Por Dios!—not* that dress of green satin with drops of emeralds that dangle from the ears! Blanca tries it on anyway, just to see, but it is out of the question. The material rustles when she walks, and clings to her body, catching the light. Father Padrón would find this unseemly, and the mama of La Señora would stare at her with those eyes of stone. A gown of dark blue, then? *Puede ser*—perhaps with a pair of diamond clips? Those that the general gave her on her thirty-sixth birthday? She holds the blue dress against her body and fastens the clips so, at either side of the low square neckline; she smiles. But the clips have come from La Señora's vault; the mother and sisters are sure to remember them.

What of it? Blanca thinks with a sudden boldness; nevertheless she tears the jewels from the dress and flings them hard at the dressing table; they clatter across the mirrored surface, leaving a trail of tiny scratches.

Blanca stares now at the dress against her body; her eyes grow narrow with thinking. Without ornament, the blue seems lifeless, a color of mourning. She must not meet La Señora looking prim and somber. She imagines the sisters winking their old eyes at each other as she enters the room. No! She will wear a crimson silk brocade, with a ruff of ermine tails at the throat, like an *infanta*, like a queen. But she cannot find the crimson silk brocade. She begins to fling dresses on the floor, stepping on them, kicking at them as though they were a pack of silken dogs attacking her ankles. There! She seizes the heavy gown and steps into it hurriedly; a heel is caught in the hem; she hears it rip. *Por Dios!* she cries, and pulls at the slide fastener, breaking a perfect fingernail. Again she curses, now at the tightness of the bodice; she gasps and claws at the fabric; it will close, it must close, *there.* She can scarcely breathe, her face is flushed and damp, she is almost faint, but there before her, in the cheval glass, is the figure of a red queen.

She strokes the rich cloth, caresses the soft white fur at the throat. She turns slightly, listening to the silk move with her body like a faint musical accompaniment. Jewels . . . a rope of pearls. Yes. But now her dark-gold hair looks careless; should it not have high sculptured swirls and loops? Should it not build to a bronze crescendo at the crown? She begins to strike at it with silver brushes and a shower of golden pins, but the tight sleeves hamper her movements; she will have to take the dress off, at least the top. She struggles again with the fastener, shaking her head so that the hair falls in great loose coils below her shoulders. Now she raises her hands behind her head and plunges them into the mass of hair, twisting it, lifting it. So? Perhaps so?

Suddenly she sees a blur of white at the edge of the glass; without seeing more she knows it is the general in his white uniform. She gasps a quick nervous breath and turns awkwardly, hands fluttering to ward off his anger if it is there. She tries to inhale his mood before she catches his eyes; she is good at this. Not angry? Amused with her? She giggles tentatively, shaking her curls, knowing he can seldom resist the charm of her giggle. It reassures him, the fact that she is so much a child with him, such a toy. Carlos? she whispers lightly. I am almost ready, do you like my hair in the new way?

The general says nothing, strides toward her quietly, grasps her shoulders and turns her, roughly, toward the mirror. His hands linger a moment on her skin, she leans back against him, yielding, with a soft sigh, reaches to pull the hands down to her breasts; he often likes just to hold them like this, they are very beautiful like this, she knows, so white against the red silk and the fur; he can close his eyes for a moment and simply caress them, or gaze at her in the mirror as she arches backward, making a soft sound in her white throat like the purring of a cat; she can turn and touch him with her light hands; she can murmur against him would it give him pleasure, oh, she would, would she not, always come to him like this with her bright mouth reaching upward, twisting so that he could see her shining lips parting, tongue glistening, yes—?

They are here, he says brusquely, disengaging himself. You were to have been ready twenty minutes ago, I told you, you had all day—

Oh, Carlos, I am sorry, I wanted to look, nothing seemed, Carlos I am so frightened. She begins to cry.

Stop, he says, shaking her too hard. But then he pulls his hands away quickly, as if her skin would burn him. Fix your hair, it makes you look— He breathes an exasperated sigh and backs away from her.

Carlos, forgive me, I only—she begins again, but he raises his hand and she breaks off at once.

Close your dress, he says. And *por Dios*, fix that hair of yours! Be down in five minutes. *Five*. She nods; he closes the door firmly; he does not exactly slam it.

THEY have gathered in the general's library rather than the large salon that adjoins the pool; though it may seem small for so many, they have decided that it is somehow more appropriate, cloistered, dark and hushed, for this occasion. Blanca has had one of the large sofas moved in from the pool area, and the general's huge desk will serve well as a table. The servants were dismissed immediately after dinner; the general's aides have deliberately chosen this night for La Señora's visit because there is a fiesta in the village; the entire population will be in the streets and cafés.

At last Blanca's hair is arranged; there is nothing to do but go and face them. She has been told exactly what to say and do, except of course at the moment when La Señora arrives, when they will all find out what to do, together.

From her dressing room she can peer over the balcony and see that the door to the library is already closed; no one can look up to see her glide down the white marble stairs, crimson silk *ssh*-ing gently in her wake, exactly like the train of a royal gown. She suppresses a twinge of disappointment as she descends, remembering to widen her eyes in the look of surprise/pleasure/anticipation, to part her lips in the little smile that might mean whatever the reader of smiles wishes it to mean. She can feel the weight of her hair, massed in three great shining coils, resting upon her head like a crown of heaven.

At the door she pauses to inhale deeply, drawing the breath in, forcing it out, slowly, evenly. She can hear wisps of their voices, low and solemn as in church. There is a pause. *Now*, she commands herself, and pushes open the heavy door. An audible gasp greets her; the room is dark, and as she stands in the doorway framed in the bright yellow light of the gleaming corridor, they stare—perhaps she has only startled them, or else she has achieved the effect she wanted. Her eyes travel quickly from the weary face of La Señora's mother to the sisters' glittering eyes; to the blank round face of the old priest; to the strange bitter mouth of the doctor; and, finally, to Carlos' hooded eyes. The silence lengthens. She is satisfied; it is as she had hoped.

Good evening, she murmurs in the voice of a confident woman, a general's wife, a political figure. Padre, she adds, nodding to Father Padrón, it is so good of you to come, such a long and tiring journey. The priest's sharp eyes are fastened to hers as she speaks, she can feel the heat of them. She lowers her eyes; he nods gravely, murmuring, I am always at the general's service—a slight pause—and now at yours, Señora. María Blanca frowns at the pause, and at the mocking emphasis when he says *Señora*. But perhaps she only imagines this. She glances nervously at the general, whose attention is elsewhere; only the priest notices her glance. The general is picking at the skin around his thumb, which will soon become infected again. Blanca refreshes her smile and moves to the doctor: So good of you too, doctor, we are honored. The celebrated Dr. Salvador Ceballos, that narrow ascetic man, fiercely dedicated to his unusual specialty, had been en route to an important case in Belgium when the sudden call came from the general's chief aide. I will come at once, Ceballos had said. I wish to be paid in cash, as usual. The general's old friend and aide, Elias Rubén Caso, the one called "Chulo"—Rascal—had expressed the general's deep appreciation. Now Dr. Ceballos, bowing over Blanca's hand, says: It is I who am honored, Señora. Is there a sardonic smile now under that bowed head? She thinks there must be. A terrible man, she thinks. If only Carlos would stand beside me. But he is right, he wants me to stand apart so they will see I too am strong; they will know that with a strong wife, Carlos is ready to lead them again, that he is not old, he is Carlos still, he is as they remember.

But if only he would stand with her now, for a moment, touching her in front of them. Tell them, Carlos, *tell them who I am*. She screams it in silence, but still he sits immobile behind his great desk; its dark leather surface gleams like a stone slab, reflecting the white uniform, the bright buttons, the mass of silver hair. He is still a bull of a man, his beard more black than white, but in the dim light his face looks old, old.

One of the sisters coughs. The mama reaches toward her, offering a fine linen handkerchief. Their dark sleeves touch like a whisper. Chulo Rubén Caso motions Blanca to sit down next to the other sister. She moves slowly across the red-flowered carpet as one moves through water; the train of her gown follows with an awkward twisting, as though it had not meant to come so far. She can feel a thin trickle of sweat sliding down between her breasts; the heat of the room, of the tight, heavy gown, of the fur stifling her throat, of the silence, of her sculptured mountain of hair. She cannot breathe, it will echo too loudly in her ears, they must hear it too, rasping; she thinks, They will know I am afraid.

The ornate gold clock over the general's desk utters a faint series of tiny warning clicks, as if clearing its throat in preparation for midnight. At the same instant the sound of tires crunching stones in the long driveway signals the arrival of the last car. For another instant no one in the room moves. Then the first chime strikes, releasing them from this involuntary tableau. They stand all at once facing the door, the men gathering closer to the general's desk, like a phalanx of bodyguards; the women, all but Blanca, seeming to huddle at the side of the room. Blanca draws herself up slowly, lightheaded with panic, and forces herself to walk to the door, where she stands poised, head tilted back like a counterweight, as if to keep her from pitching forward when the door opens. There is the sound of many feet outside, of loud voices and movement; the commotion subsides, someone knocks and, without waiting, flings open the door. A flustered young man, pale and sweating, grimy hands hanging too far below the sleeves of a shabby black suit, sways uncertainly at the threshold. Behind him two workmen appear carrying a large wooden crate, much damaged. Come in, Blanca whispers. The general is expecting you.

The men move with astonishing speed, pushing aside the big library chairs, spreading heavy gray quilted blankets over the floor, setting the crate down in the center of the room, hacking it open with three sharp blows of a crowbar. Within a few minutes, the splintered pieces of two inner boxes lie neatly piled in the corner, covered with blankets. The treasure they contained lies open on the general's desk, glittering like an enormous crystal, the teardrop of a *monstruo*. They gather silently around it. The doctor speaks first, his harsh commands piercing the mood like short knives. Well, he begins. So. It is as I expected, *gracias a Dios*. But there is work to be done. We must move quickly, we must have light, this room is impossible. And I will not work with an audience, have I not told you I must have privacy, I insist on it, why are my instructions never followed?

Carlos, ashen-faced but controlled, turns angrily to his *ayudantes*. Do as he says, Chulo! *Si, general*. Rubén Caso herds the workmen out, barking orders. The mama and sisters edge closer to the desk. The mama closes her eyes and makes the sign of the cross. One of the sisters begins to cry softly. Be still, hisses the other, angrily. Father Padrón places an arm around the shoulders of the weeping sister.

María Blanca, caught like a somnambulist between sleep and waking, stands outside the circle; she cannot yet bear to move forward; her eyes are fixed, her ears tuned only to the inner sound of her fear. Suddenly she feels Carlos' voice, like a fierce whisper from inside her own head: *Señora Montero, quiero presentarte*— may I present—*la Señora Montero*. María Blanca sees her own hand reach down into the crystal coffin and grasp the tiny white hand of the body within. *Cuanto me alegre*, she whispers. How happy I am . . . Then she notices that a small piece of the little finger has broken off in her hand. She stares at it in horror. Dr. Ceballos takes it from her calmly. It is all right, Señora, he says gently, it is nothing, I will take care of it. But perhaps you will be good enough to assist me now. I will need you to fix La Señora's hair; as you can see it has become soiled and disarranged. Otherwise I believe all is well, except of course for the clothing. She will need—

Now the mama is crying. *Aii. Aii. Mi angelita*—my angel child is beautiful. She lives.

Please, says Dr. Ceballos to the sisters, with some annoyance. Perhaps you will see to your mother, we have very little time. You have brought the sewing materials, and the cloth? She will be able to follow the instructions? The sisters nod. Catuja, the elder, opens a large black leather case and takes out a bolt of heavy white wool crepe. Dr. Ceballos nods briskly. You will need to take measurements; the fit must not be too close, but I do not want voluminous folds. A pure line—he gestures with both hands, like a caress, along the body of La Señora—you understand? Catuja nods, folding the cloth back into the leather bag. The sewing machine has been set up in an upstairs room; the three women leave quickly to begin cutting the pattern.

Juan Carlos Montero has been standing motionless at the head of the coffin, gazing upon the face of his first wife in her glass jewel box. Is she Beauty? Does he seem, in his white uniform, like an ancient Prince Charming who has lost the power to awaken her? The image is his own; he finds himself wondering, as he stares at this *maravilla*—this illusion of perfect life within death—if *el buen Dios* would grant me now the power to restore her—to give one kiss for her life? He has no idea whether he would make the bargain.

Blanca reappears carrying her own silver hairbrushes. Wordlessly she stands beside her husband and begins to brush the hair of María Rosa; she brushes with tenderness, in long, rhythmic strokes. She dares not look at Carlos, nor he at her. They are both with Rosa now.

It has been said that the face of Pradera is its fortune—which is its misfortune. The land itself has always promised riches beyond dreams, always held back on the promise. And truly it could not have been otherwise. For there was too much of the land. A million square miles without horizon or interruption, so that it seemed to extend beyond all time and reason. Only the imagination of hungry men could carve such vastness into pieces of a country, calling them provinces, as though the land were a captive steer to be hacked and divided, if only to name each bleeding part before devouring it.

Even so, they could never really hope to make it theirs, to civilize it. What could be done with so much space, after all, space blank as a child's notion of forever? Emptiness sealed it in, silenced its heart, invaded its spirit like a white curse. Desolation grew in its wonderful soil like a poison crop.

Here was boundless plain, sliced by immense rivers, with desert on both sides, black impenetrable forest beyond, and beyond that, desert. Boundaries were always invisible, blurred in mist, so that no child might stand in a spot to gaze out at a clear distant line, to see a thick pale stripe of blue meet one of sharp green or white or brown. No illusion to discover, to shout, *Mira!* That is where I shall go some day. How could one dream of escape, without imagining an end of here, a beginning of there; a world on the far side of clouds? The mist, the blur, the silence were the world.

It was early afternoon in the village of Montaraz. The child María Rosa, eight years old, sat playing on the dirt floor with her new doll, a fine lady with soft black curls and a long red gauze skirt; a doll whose shiny black eyes snapped shut with a little click when she lay on her back. Rosa's brother Chepito lay watching her from his narrow cot; the two older girls napped fitfully, their limbs entangled on the straw mattress in the corner. Rosa was scolding the doll for dragging its dress in the dirt while strolling across the village square. Stupid Rósula, the child said, frowning, I warned you not to parade before those boys! So they stare at you and make remarks; for this you spoil a beautiful dress—*puta!*—slut, fool, tramp. Chepito buried his head in his mattress, stifling a laugh.

The children did not stir when they heard the voice of their father, José Andújar, calling their mother from the dirt path beyond the courtyard. Mama had said they must let him rest awhile after his long journey. Every week she said this, for every week José Andújar returned to them after the same long journey. Rosa whispered to Chepito, Do you think he has brought us chocolate? Chepito shrugged and turned on his cot so that he faced the brown curtain that divided the places for sleeping and for eating; he stared at the folds in the curtain, imagining horses. He did not want to think any more about Papa bringing chocolate. He was ten years old and now he knew where Papa came from every week, where he went when he left them the following day. He knew that Papa had another family in San Marcos, and that those children, his half-brothers and sisters, lived in a fine house with a stone floor and windows made of glass. He knew that they wore leather shoes and had a radio, and that their mama had a fine dress for church. Most important, he knew his papa belonged to those children. Chepito did not speak of these things with his sisters, although they knew too. Chepito was the one whose cheeks burned with shame in the schoolyard when other boys stood in a circle and turned their heads toward him slyly when he passed, letting the pause in their laughter touch him like the lash of a small whip.

At first Chepito thought their mama did not know about Papa's other family in San Marcos; he thought she could not possibly know, or she would never sing to herself every Friday while preparing the stew for their father's supper; she would not smile at him with her cheeks so warm and red and her eyes shining behind the little steel-rimmed glasses she wore, which made her look stern like a teacher when she talked to other people, but never when she spoke to their papa. How could she know and let him make his coarse jokes about her big soft breasts, let him lie on top of her on the other side of the brown curtain? Through the curtain Chepito had seen how he did this, grunting and shaking. How could she know that tomorrow twenty miles away he would make the same jokes and the same love to another soft round wife who would serve him another stew, and who would giggle when his big rough hands touched her while the children were sleeping?

Sometimes Chepito felt he would burst with the pain of such questions; sometimes he longed to ask his sisters, even if they were only girls. María Rosa, he thought, would somehow help him understand. But that was silly, she had only eight years of age.

Rosa was listening intently to the voices of her parents behind the brown curtain. She thought they might be arguing, though she knew their mama never scolded José Andújar the way other mothers in Montaraz scolded their husbands. The voice of Juana Ibáñez poured like sweet cream when she spoke to Papa, and she laughed often, even when he was not saying a joke, even when she was asking for something very important. Rosa always sat very still during Papa's visits; her eyes, big and dark in the thin little face, followed every gesture. It was María Rosa who knew the exact moment, just before Papa left in the morning, when he would put the money in the red clay jar above the stove. She could hear the crackling of the bills from her cot on the other side of the curtain.

José Andújar, sometimes called Pepe or Pepillo, thought of himself as a good man. He worked hard in the cement *factoría* of Don José Delgado; soon he would be made a foreman, and his wife and children in San Marcos would lack for nothing. As for his other little family in Montaraz, was he not as good to them as could be expected? Better, he often told himself, than most men he knew in similar circumstances. Had he not allowed Juana Ibáñez to use his name for the children's baptismal certificates, despite the trouble such an irregularity entailed, not to mention the additional contribution he had had to make to the church? Was he not, furthermore, entirely generous with money for these children, whose rope sandals were replaced almost as regularly as the leather ones of his own family? The good Lord knew it was not easy to satisfy most women; he had to admit that at least Juana Ibáñez did not complain much. In truth, he did not always begrudge her the money.

And she had borne him four healthy bastards. The older girls were growing round and soft like their mother; the boy Chepito was small for his age, with quick furtive eyes and a slight brown body that moved in spurts like a rabbit. José's hopes were not high for Chepito. Even now he could tell that the best of the litter was Rosa, the youngest, his little field mouse. She had eyes like his own, fierce with life-hunger, and her small hard body, so unlike that of her mother and sisters, reminded him of the first girls of his youth, the ones who could run almost as fast as he, whose little pulses beat wildly in their delicate throats when they marched holding hands across the yard, their eyes searching the corners for boys watching them. He remembered one of these girls, a light-haired one with bright darting eyes; her name too had been Rosa. He had lusted for her in her short gray school uniform and her long white socks; he remembered still his restless dreams about her white legs, the imaginings of her blond pubic triangle, an impossibly beautiful thing that in his dreams he touched with wondering fingers and found silken like the belly of his dog. Now his daughter Rosa was growing up, she too would have such silken hair there; he often imagined it. Sometimes in San Marcos, lying in bed, José Andújar would rest his hand between the large moist thighs of his sleeping wife Elena and imagine the white buttocks of his youngest bastard daughter in Montaraz.

Early one Friday José came to visit his second family in Montaraz, and found Rosa kneeling beside the well in the dirt courtyard. Rusty streaks ran down her legs from the dust and the well water. She was perspiring, wisps of her hair pasted to her forehead and flushed cheeks, and she wore only a *camisa* of thin gauze, which lay flat against her body like a wet transparent veil. For a long moment he stood motionless, holding his breath, staring at her pale wet skin in the sunlight, at her slender waist, her thin legs too long for the small narrow torso, like a baby she-mule, a *burrita*. He crept up behind her and gathered her up into his arms, burying his head into her warm little chest, inhaling her. Papa! she shrieked, throwing her arms around him, laughing. Papa! He kissed her warm neck, her chest, her shoulders; he tossed her high into the air and caught her as she squealed with fright and pleasure. He tossed her again; again she squealed. Papa! Finally he wrapped her tight in his arms and carried her into the house, where he sank clumsily into a chair, still holding her tight. She began to wriggle against him then, crying now, Papa, let me go! But now he could not, would not let her go, pretending to tease her. I cannot, look, you are locked in, I have lost the key. Then he held her still with only one hand, and with the other began to stroke her, saying, Sst, my little one, Rósula—my little Rosa—be still and I will tell you a fine story about when your papa was a boy, playing so with a little girl named Rosa, a little white *burrita* like you—

Was she so smart? Rosa interjected. Did she have dolls?

Dolls, yes. José Andújar's hand went on stroking his daughter's back, gently squeezing her arms, her legs. Rósula, he murmured, burying his face in her neck, a little smart one just like you.

Don't, Papa, the child cried, you are hurting—

Sst, *niña*, he said, lie here softly in my arms.

But—

Sst. Then José Andújar lifted his daughter and carried her gently to Mama's bed, where he lay beside her, pressing against her with his whole body. Papa, don't, she whispered, and the pleasure in her voice was gone; only the fright was there. Sst! he commanded, harshly now, and slapped her hard across the mouth. She raised her hand to stop the shock of it; he caught the hand and kissed it, then gently stroked her arm, her chest, her small flat belly. Finally he turned her over, entering her hard and swift from behind, exclaiming Ah, ahh. She did not cry out again.

When he had finished he carried her back outside to the well and washed her gently with the harsh soap. Then he dressed her in clean underclothes and a white dress. Rósula, he said softly, Papa loves thee—*te quiero*. She said nothing. He slapped her again, not quite so hard this time, saying, Answer when your papa talks to you. *Te quiero, Papá*, she answered.

MARÍA Rosa woke crying on the Saturday morning after this ordinary Friday, she would not say why. Perhaps it was only that she had forgotten to show Papa the new doll with the red gauze dress that Mama's new boarder, Señor Valdés, had bought for her in Corrientes. Next time you can show him, Juana Ibáñez said, studying her with a frown of puzzlement. Go back to sleep.

But the following Friday José Andújar did not come.

SHE was sitting on the floor, motionless in her white dress, as if she were a doll holding a doll. Her mama held a hand to her forehead, murmuring what was wrong, was she sick. Mama—the child stammered, then shook her head to dispel the urge to speak.

Chepito knew better than to ask questions. He had seen Rosa flinch and turn her eyes away when Papa spoke. He also had seen the flicker of fear in her eyes when she woke in the night sweating and crying, No, Papa! Chepito said nothing to anyone, even though he had also seen the look of guilt cross Papa's face when Rosa squirmed away from his arms. He did not know if Mama also saw these things; she gave no sign of noticing. But it was not very long

—perhaps a month—before the day that José Andújar ceased altogether to visit his second family in Montaraz.

One night Rosa crept into her brother's bed and whispered the terrible secret about what Papa had done with her. Chepito, she sobbed, it is my fault Papa does not come back, my fault. . . . And we will never have enough money for a radio! We will die.

Chepito patted his sister with an awkward hand. He did not know whether this terrible thing was her fault. Had he not heard from his friends Gordo and Chino all the ways in which a girl's body was meant to be used? Surely a man such as Papa could not be at fault for being a man in this way. And Papa was a good man —he must be, Chepito reasoned, for had he not been good to them? But why then had his eyes looked away quickly each time Rosa passed him? Why had he hurt his own daughter so that she wept now with real pain, as if from a hard belting? Surely this was a bad thing. Would the padre call this a great sin for Papa to have done? Had Rosa sinned too? Chepito could not be sure about that. He went on patting his sister's naked shoulder. Had Papa felt what he felt in touching her skin? Had she crept now into his bed to tempt him too? Would he too be at fault if he touched her in the way a man must touch a woman? Chepito groaned. What is it? his sister cried. Nothing, he said warily. Only I am sorry for all this trouble that has come.

What will Mama do? she asked.

Chepito thought. She will take in another boarder, he replied. She will divide our room in two parts again, and the boarder will eat with us every day.

Rosa sat up suddenly, her eyes large and round like black coins in the darkness. Do you think, she said, the new boarder will bring me a doll with a green dress?

Chepito raised himself on his arms and stared at his little sister's tear-streaked face. *Pobrecita*, he thought. Poor little one. And then another word came to him. *Putatita*. Little whore. He framed it silently with his lips. After a while Rosa fell asleep beside him. He lay awake a long time, watching her.

IN that summer of terrible heat, it was said that the people in the small poor towns of the northern provinces seemed struck by a sickness of sudden anger. In the streets of red dust, even the air stopped its ordinary moving, as though it waited for a signal.

In the *tabernas* the men drank more of their fiery rum than was usual, and more of the yellow gin that the *porteños* of San Luis brought inland from the great boats of the European shippers. In the heat of 107 degrees, it was wise for a man to keep his eyes cast down in the *taberna,* for to meet the gaze of another was to invite a look of knives, if not a knife itself.

Every night in the towns of San Marcos and Vasena one might hear soft cries, and sounds of rapping upon the doors of one or another of the fine houses; it was only the knocking of those poor women who came to offer a child for sale.

Even in the great port city of San Luis there were stirrings of new trouble. The sickness of anger now attacked the workers of the docks, now those of the *factorías,* now those who ran the government system of *transportes.* One could not blame the heat alone, or the yellow gin, for there were many evils in that time. One might know from the newspapers and the radio that too many rich foreigners had invaded the country. Foreigners who had made secret deals of business with the rich owners of Pradereño land. A new army of *extranjeros*—strangers from England and Germany, and the *Yanquis* of North America—who would take what they could from the fine black soil of Pradera, and from the sweat of the poor workers of the northern provinces.

From the columns of news, and the new radio set that had the shape of a small church, a *provinciano* would know that along the great curving waterfront of San Luis nine foreign vessels now floated like the ships of ghost tales. No Pradereño worker with the pride of a man would load or unload a single crate of wheat, or a carcass of salted meat, until the foreigners made peace with the new unions of laboring men. On the docks and in the *factorías,* men began to march, carrying signs of their anger, demanding more of pay and more of justice. There would be no more *esclavos,* no Pradereño slaves to be sold cheap to the foreign men of business.

When Pradera was a simple country, it was said, the poor never complained. One relieved the suffering in a simple way—by raising the palms to heaven and bowing the head to the will of *Dios.*

When the belly was full, the bow to *Dios* was easily made. When it grew too empty, there were quick ways to fill the eye and the mind of simple people. Fiestas and fierce rum; the padres of the church and the *policía* to keep order. Order was the way of *Dios,* one would know this all of one's life.

In a simple country, sounds of anger in the *tabernas* did not travel quickly through the waves of air. If anger moved at all, across the silent wastes of the Pradal, the great plain of desert, it came with little force. One scarcely heard it in the swirling red dust of the poor northern villages. Trouble was a thing of no importance; soon there would be another fiesta, a new procession in the streets, with dancing statues of saints and devils in fine gaudy clothes. The children of the poor would stare and smile; the men would drink more of the fierce yellow gin; and the pain of hunger in the belly would soon pass; it was only a part of life, and life also held *Esperanza,* the hope of tomorrow.

It is unfortunate that a country of riches and wild beauty may not remain simple forever.

It was said that on the third day of the terrible heat in this summer of anger, a local union of cement workers had struck the small *factoría* in San Marcos that was owned by the San Luisano Don José Delgado and his new partners, a group of *Inglés.* The complaints of the workers were of the usual kind—lazy men wanting more of one thing and less of another. A foreman of the plant, one

José Andújar, had grown careless and hurt his hand in one of the new machines; the foreign bosses had refused to guarantee money for such accidents.

The strike was of no importance; a band of angry men in shabby clothes marching outside a silent *factoría*. It was said that a truck filled with metal tools tried to make a delivery, and that a white van of *policía* was sent, with a blaring of sirens, to escort the truck to the gate.

The driver of the van of *policía* was hot and tired; he did not care to stop for the line of men with their signs. Instead, with a blast of his horn and a slamming of his foot upon the accelerator pedal, the van burst through the barrier of men, scattering bodies into the dirt. It was said that then the strikers assaulted the van of *policía* with a storm of rocks and dirt, with a shouting of curses.

Then from somewhere came a sudden crack of fire, no more than a handful of shots, like a shower of hail.

In the columns of news and on the radio one could find no word of who had fired the first bullet. But when the truck of metal tools reached the gate of the *factoría*, three laborers lay dead in the red path of dust. In their hands were the signs of anger, the demands for more of one thing and less of another. One of the dead men had a hand covered with bloody bandages; he was the injured foreman, José Andújar.

The funeral for the dead workers of the Productos de Concreto plant began at noon. Fifty mourners formed a thin trickle of black, to march behind the funeral coaches. It was thought later that some of those on the line were not mourners but troublemakers, who may be hired by those who would change the proper order of things in a simple country such as Pradera.

The marchers wore shabby clothes and in their eyes was the silence of blood-hatred. The procession wound like a dark rope through the hot and silent streets, past houses whose walls were made of cooking-oil cans. Past the village of Montaraz, where women with bare feet and children in rags huddled beside the road of red dirt and watched, as though this were a parade for *carnaval*.

There were no tears in the eyes of those women, not even the eyes of one who wore small round spectacles with rims of silver wire, and who had four small children with the name of Andújar, though it was no name of hers.

Juana Ibáñez watched in silence as the black coaches rolled past her house; in the first coach rode Señora Andújar of San Marcos, *la viuda*—the widow of that injured foreman. She wore a black shaw of fine lace, and her three *niños,* two boys and a girl, wore new clothes. Who are they, Mama? Rosa whispered. Juana Ibáñez made no reply. Ssst, said Chepito, the boy of the family, for in truth he could say nothing else.

SEÑOR López Figueroa was not the first of Mama's boarders to ask for a small kiss in appreciation for the fancy doll. María Rosa had never been so impolite as to refuse. She gave the kiss freely, and did not protest when they added a squeeze or pinch; nor did she pull away when they tumbled her into their laps. As a rule, Mama was in the room when these displays of affection occurred. She would wear a fixed faraway look, not quite approving, but surely not disapproving; the look of a well-trained accomplice who understands well the consequences of dissent. As it is said, one who sees much, yet says little, is one who knows which way the shadows move.

After a moment, Mama would ask with some impatience whether Rosa had forgotten to peel the potatoes for the stew, or to sweep and water the dirt courtyard. Rosa would say no or yes, Mama, gently extricating herself from the embrace of Señor García or Señor Valdés, and for his part the gentleman would have no reason to feel rebuffed.

But none of the borders had ever forced his attentions on Rosa when her mother was not present. So the child was not especially concerned on this Sunday afternoon when Chepito went with his sisters to the social club dance, and Mama stopped at the church to visit the new baby of Señora Chavez, leaving Rosa alone in bed with a sour stomach from too much spice in last night's supper. Señor López Figueroa arrived earlier than usual. *Qué pobrecita!* he said solicitously, perching heavily on the edge of her narrow cot, and began to stroke her feverish forehead, asking if she were not too warm with such a thick blanket. She said nothing when he removed it and began to stroke her neck and shoulders with a cool soft cloth soaked in alcohol. Roll over, little one, so that I can bathe your back, he said, and she obeyed. Soon he had her thin *camisa* rolled up to her shoulders, and was rubbing the cloth up and down her slender body; the cloth was cool and soothing, and made her feel drowsy, so that she barely heard him say, Now turn again; I must bathe the other side. When she did not respond, he turned her over himself. Then for a moment she felt nothing, which made her open her eyes. Señor López Figueroa was staring at her with a glazed expression, his mouth hung in a great O beneath the heavy black rope of a mustache; he held the dripping cloth now in one hand; with the other he was untying the belt of his trousers. Something about his face frightened her, so that she tried to sit up, crying, *Mama,* but he said in a sudden rough voice, pushing her back, be still, I have not hurt you. You must stop your mouth, do you hear? She whimpered and lay back. Look, he said, more gently, my cloth will make you feel nice all over, close your eyes. Rosa closed her eyes, squeezing tears. He rubbed her all over with the wet cloth, and then without it. He put the tip of himself between her legs and squeezed the tender nipples of her breasts with his rough fingers. She did not cry out again, although he hurt her very much. When it was over, he wet the cloth and bathed her again, pulling her *camisa* down like a curtain over her, and then the blanket on top as though to cover what he had done. Finally he kissed her forehead, whispering her name in a strange thick voice. She made no sound.

The following week Señor López Figueroa brought the doll with a black velvet dress and white ruffled petticoats, the most beautiful doll María Rosa had ever seen. He also brought a box of fine chocolates for Chepito, a red blouse each for Lola and Catuja, and for Mama a shawl of lace the color of a flamingo.

Rosa had said nothing to her mama about the incident, but Juana Ibáñez had wise eyes behind her round wire spectacles, and several days after the doll with the velvet dress and the other gifts, she suggested to Señor López Figueroa that he look for a larger room in a boarding house nearer the cement works. He replied that he was very satisfied with his present arrangement, and was prepared if necessary to pay a small increase in his rent. Later, Mama asked Rosa's opinion, a thing she had never done before, and Rosa looked solemnly into her mama's eyes and replied in a dreamy flat voice, Often I wish we could have a nice house near La Plata, a house with a real stone floor. Don't you agree, Mama?

For an instant Juana Ibáñez stared at her child, uncomprehending. Then she burst into tears.

The following afternoon Juana Ibáñez told Señor López Figueroa that she had been planning to move her family to a better house near La Plata, but that they would be willing to have him there as a boarder at double his present rent. Otherwise— She broke off abruptly with an apologetic shrug. Señor López Figueroa licked the bottom of his black mustache with a nervous tongue. Señora Ibáñez began again. My youngest daughter, she said, measuring the words carefully, has not been feeling well. We have the hope that her health will improve in a better house nearer the water, where the street is paved and there is not so much dust in the air.

Señor López Figueroa coughed. I am indeed sorry to hear this, Señora. Under the circumstances I will be happy to pay the increased rent. And if . . . I can help in any way with the expenses of moving, please permit me to do so.

Juana Ibáñez gave a slight nod. We are grateful for your kindness, Señor, she said in an even tone.

One week later the family moved to a three-room house near La Plata. It had a real stone floor and thick walls between the rooms, reaching all the way to the ceiling. There was a fig tree in the courtyard, the roof was sound, and Juana Ibáñez sang the words of a tango as she pumped the rusty water from the cistern for her bath. The boarder Señor López Figueroa continued to come early

Sunday afternoons, but he never again found Rosa at home alone. Often, however, he found Juana Ibáñez alone, and she always did her best to make him comfortable.

It has been agreed that La Señora must be off the island by 5:00 A.M. Her helicopter will be met by a military escort in Pradera the following night, and she will be moved directly to the loyalist headquarters, where a twenty-four-hour guard will be posted until final arrangements are made for the memorial services and the burial, both events to occur soon after the general's own triumphant return to Pradera. The plan calls for him to be ready to leave Isla de Perlas within forty-eight hours.

At 4:00 A.M. the mama has finished sewing the gown of white crepe. Dr. Ceballos has cut away the torn and stained dress in which La Señora has been traveling. He has designed the new costume so that she can be dressed quickly and easily, with few movements; though her body is pliant, it is extremely light and fragile, and cannot withstand energetic handling. The dress is made to fasten in the front, under a narrow concealed placket that runs from neck to ankle. The line is simple and tapers slightly, narrowing at the top, gently flaring at the bottom, following the body without clinging to it. The effect is unmistakably that of an elegant novitiate, even to the sleeves with the shape of soft bells. The hands are folded carefully across the breast; a delicate rosary of onyx and gold filigree is threaded through the long, delicate fingers. A fresh coat of clear lacquer has been applied to the fingernails, which have been carefully pared and manicured. The severed joint of the little finger on the right hand has been restored; there is no trace of a seam.

Finally, the general has fastened to her bodice a large jeweled medallion, a replica of Pradera's highest civilian honor. The rubies and emeralds are unfortunately of inferior quality; the general had awarded her a more valuable medal at the time of her death, but in the past fourteen years La Señora has not always traveled in the best company, nor has she ever been so well protected as she is tonight. The regrettable loss of the original piece had been reported only a week ago, when the general's Italian representatives dug up the coffin from a simple grave in a poor cemetery outside Milan; La Señora had been resting incognito there all this time, under a headstone that bore the name of Elena Antonelli.

As soon as word was received about the missing medal, the general hastily commissioned a trustworthy jeweler in Isla de Perlas to make a duplicate; the inferior stones were of the second-best quality to be found on the island. As he pins the new medal to her magnificent white gown, the general wonders idly whether La Señora can tell the difference in quality. In her lifetime, he knows, he wouldn't have got away with it.

At 4:30 A.M. María Blanca recombs La Señora's hair for the last time; it has been trimmed and shampooed, and she has arranged it, according to Dr. Ceballos' instructions, so that it resembles a pale shining helmet, smoothed straight back from the high white brow and tucked into a loosely braided coil at the back. When she finishes, Dr. Ceballos nods brusquely; she has done well.

At last the work is completed; they stand back, all of them, no longer in awe but with some pride, appraising their work. Dr. Ceballos directs two workmen as they apply sealant around the rim of the coffin, between the bronze base and the crystal dome. The sisters make deep curtsies to Father Padrón and leave the room quickly, as if they cannot bear to be there another moment. The mother, who has never stopped weeping, her heavy body wracked now with sobs of exhaustion, lingers a moment to cross herself once more. Father Padrón offers to escort her to the car; she whispers no, *gracias,* no. The general and his *ayudantes* have retreated to the upstairs study, to dispatch messages overseas. It is understood that *el doctor* Ceballos will not leave his charge alone for an instant until she is safely aboard her helicopter, shielded by armed guards and tightly packed in a new case with an armored lining. He sits in shadow beside her now.

María Blanca suddenly rushes out of the room; she must talk to the sisters and the mama before they go. She finds them at the car, and calls to them, *Wait*, stretching out a hand to Catuja. While her sister was alive, Catuja held the post of Honorary Minister of Education in Pradera. Blanca says, I wanted to say goodbye.

Catuja turns and regards her coldly. She says nothing.

I grieve with you, says Blanca. I know you do not believe me, but it is true. I hope you will trust my friendship, out of my love for your sister's memory.

Still Catuja stares, and says nothing. The younger one, Lola, lunges forward shouting, Leave us, can't you—but Catuja rests a hand softly on her sister's black sleeve. Do not say a thing we will all regret. To Blanca she makes a little formal nod and speaks finally, with difficulty. Our family is at your service, Señora. You do us all honor in honoring our memories. Then she turns away quickly and urges Lola into the car. Blanca does not move; through the rolled-up car window she sees their black-veiled heads nodding and shaking, yes and no, their pale lips framing vows of enmity, curses, plots of vengeance. The mother sits silently between them, like a great stone, staring ahead. Finally, Blanca turns back toward the house. Father Padrón stands at the doorway; only his eyes have followed her.

MARÍA Rosa entered the little chapel and knelt on the worn padded bar before the statue of La Lloradora, the *Virgen* who weeps. Rosa bowed her head quickly, not permitting herself to look just yet at the beauty of La Lloradora's face, or her gorgeous clothes. The statue stood in a circle of golden light, wearing her gown of white lace, with loops as thick as those on top of wedding cakes. Pinned to the gown were all her jewels that people who adored her had brought as gifts over the centuries: tiny candy-colored pins and medals set with real rubies and emeralds, stones that peered out from the holes in the lace like wise eyes winking in a face of sorrow. This lace, those very jewels, danced at night in the darkness of Rosa's dreams. Always in the dreams Rosa herself wore the gown, with La Lloradora's heavy gold cross on a long chain around her white neck, the medals and jewels scattered across her bosom, the gold letters spelling ESPERANZA on a scarlet sash at her waist. In the dreams she saw herself gazing at her own gold-and-scarlet image in a big mirror with a splendid frame. Last night La Lloradora had stood behind her in the dream, gazing in the same mirror. Rosa had stood very still with her eyes downcast, while La Lloradora leaned over whispering in her ear. Rosa looked up and saw La Lloradora holding out her great high crown with the long rays that shot out from its center like beams of the sun, ending in little stars like the points of magic wands. La Lloradora had taken the crown from her own head and held it out for Rosa to try on. *No!* Rosa had cried, horrified in the dream, knowing a terrible thing would happen. But La Lloradora kept nodding and smiling, *Sí*. Without her crown, she looked just like a fancy nun or a bride, with the lace mantilla covering all her hair, the lace curling down over her neck and shoulders like white smoke or the hair of an angel; and the silver tears that came out of the statue's eyes shone on her face in the dream, just like glass jewels attached to her skin, so they could never fall. The round tears lived in the corners of her beautiful black eyes and the long ones twinkled on her ivory cheeks like a magic rash, a condition that broke out from her everlasting grief, so that the rash could never go away.

Rosa was sure her dreams were serious sin, like evil thoughts; she would not confess them even to the statue itself, but would instead kneel before it trying to pray, saying a whole rosary and watching the tiny flames of other people's prayer candles, each one flickering in its little red glass like a devil's tongue whispering her dreams to God. There were not enough beads in the rosary, not enough *Salve Marías* to wash away a sin of dreaming that La Lloradora wore

Hollywood lipstick, that under her mantilla streamed hair like that of a star of the cinema, hair that glowed and sparkled like the red-gold flames of votive candles, hair that burst above her gleaming naked shoulders while she danced in the gown of white lace. Oh, serious sin, to imagine La Lloradora taking off her crown of heaven and placing its shower of sunbeams and exploding gold stars on the sinful head of Rosa Andújar. It was bad enough when Catuja had said that Santa Ana, before she was pregnant with the *Madre de Dios,* was the image of Persuasión duPre, an *estrella* of the cinema; for did she not have exactly those big round sad foreign eyes and the dark swollen lips that looked like kisses? La Lloradora's lips were full and very dark too with shining paint, but of course it wasn't Hollywood lipstick; serious sin to picture La Lloradora looking in a compact mirror painting her beautiful holy virgin mouth with a stick of scarlet wax.

Rosa looked up only high enough to see La Lloradora's slender white hand holding its pearl rosary as though it were nothing but a fancy necklace, a strand of such gorgeous expensive pearls as the husband would give his rich spoiled wife in a movie where the bedroom was all white satin with flowers in a big glass bowl, and the husband was in love with somebody else. The wife would hold the necklace he gave her, just like that, dangling it between the thumb and finger as if she didn't care at all about such things unless he really loved only her.

Rosa now threaded her own rosary in that way, between her two fingers, and tried to practice La Lloradora's expression of divine sadness, without looking all the way up at the face of the statue. She wanted to make her eyes show perfect grief, which was not like feeling poor and sad, or wishing to live inside of a movie instead of here where everything was ugly gray except La Lloradora. Perfect grief was only two tiny lines between the eyebrows, not a real frown that would make the eyes turn down or the ends of the mouth, nothing in the eyes that shone with crystal tears except sadness for somebody else, not for yourself. In perfect grief, La Lloradora's eyes made you think that a little smile lived behind the tears. The smile was ESPERANZA. If La Lloradora cried for Rosa's sadness, then maybe the inside smile meant the dream was not serious sin after all. Maybe it meant something magic instead, a miracle like the tears that grew in her cheeks without falling. *Salve María,* Rosa whispered. Four more *Salve Marías* and then ten Lord's Prayers. I have a sin to confess, evil thoughts. La Lloradora's tear-filled eyes were shining, shining, and her lips so red. I have a sin . . .

Naturally she did not hear the padre's quiet footsteps on the stone floor behind her; she never did. All the girls knew that he often came to stand outside the iron gate of La Lloradora's chapel when they knelt there; it was a thing they laughed about, it was a joke about whether he came because of their prayers, or because he too was in love with the statue, or because he liked to see the little girls kneeling down with their bare legs behind them on the padded bar, while they stole guilty wishing looks at La Lloradora's splendor. Father Padrón was old but still everyone in the town whispered about things he did to the girls who went to the nuns' school, not to the nuns themselves because they were too ugly, and their lips were so pale. But what happened when a girl was sent in to him for chastisement? Sometimes he hit her, but mostly he kissed her too, and touched her all over between hitting. Catuja didn't believe it but Lola who went to the nuns' school swore it was true. And Rosa knew such things, though she was the smallest.

Rosa, the padre whispered now. Rósula . . .

She turned a little. *Sí, mi padre.*

The fiesta of *purificación* is coming. Would you like to be *la reina* —queen of the fiesta? If you are a good *niñita* and do as I tell you. *If you want it enough—*

Rosa closed her eyes tight and saw La Lloradora standing on the platform in the center of the Plaza del 16 Enero, with the dancers and musicians in a whirl around her. The other statues bobbed up and down like excited children—a blur of saints and *monstruos,* of skeletons and animals, flowers and balloons of every color, white candles tall as men, and paper ribbons flying in the air like storms of bright rain. She sighed, a piteous sound filled with the broken ends of wishes. She tried to swallow. *La reina?* she whispered. Even if I have not yet twelve years?

Even so, whispered the padre, with a wink of sly mischief. You will march beside the statue with your white candle, so—

Rosa turned a little more, studying him.

Only if you do as I tell you, he whispered. *Niñita . . . angelita. . . .* Now she heard the heat in his voice; his breath came too fast; it was a sound she well knew. If you want it enough— *Te quiero, Rosa.*

The tears slid out of the sides of Rosa's eyes. Oh, it is not fair—

So? said the padre with a voice of righteous anger. Where is the sweet red smile of *la reina? He?* Lloradorita—my little *Virgen* who weeps?

Hola, Señora Ibáñez. Father Padrón flashed his benevolent smile, even though she had interrupted him in his study. *Permiso!* She murmured her apology, making no move either forward or back. But you have not come to make confession again, since Saturday? He rose from his high-backed chair without beckoning her. No, padre. Señora Ibáñez lowered her eyes, though not so far that she could not watch his glance as it shifted. But . . . I have come to you for help. My daughter Rosa—

The padre's eyes clouded at once, as though another person had drawn the confessional curtain between them. Rosa, he said uncertainly, testing the name upon his lips in the way one shows a great effort to remember. The youngest—?

Juana Ibáñez did not reply; she would permit him the small evasion, but without comfort. At the same time she would not suggest that by now one knew how little trouble this padre with the face of a dry apple had in distinguishing the daughters of the village one from another.

I have come to you for help, she said again, simply, taking care that none of the words should bear more weight than was prudent. Her black eyes, without blinking, kept the boldness of her meaning well hidden. Then too she had worn the new spectacles with round silver frames, which her daughters said gave her the look of a serious plump *viscacha,* that most thoughtful small beast of the desert plain, whose secrets are as well guarded as its dangerous underground cave, into which a horse or a man may stumble at his peril. There were seldom tears in the wise *viscacha* eyes of Juana Ibáñez.

What troubles the child? asked the padre, his voice now tinged with the impatience of a busy man. He gestured with his glance at the papers on his big desk, at the clock on the wall, the fat black pen in his hand, the ink stain on his middle finger. A frown now made two dark creases between his heavy brows.

'Stá enferma, said Juana Ibáñez, slowly drawing her fingers with their swollen knuckles together upon her belly, joining them like the laces of a corset. The child is— There was a pause, a small one, to conserve the strength for what had to be spoken. Puffed up, she said at last. She looks . . . encinta. Like one who is pregnant. But I am certain she cannot be.

The priest's expression did not change, though his round pink head now shook like that of a foreigner struggling to understand a native dialect. She swells too quickly, the woman went on, hurrying now. And there is always blood—

You have taken her to the doctor?

No, said Juana Ibáñez, in a whisper of shame. If she should be encinta—my daughter—

If—?

She has not even twelve years of age! the woman cried. Then she drew a breath, sharp as a sword. I have come, she said again with care, to you. Mi padre.

Father Padrón made a sudden gesture with his hands, as though to shoo the plump viscacha out of his sacred house, to make her disappear into the ground hole from where she had come. You must—he began, moving now from behind his desk, looming before her like a black cloud. If the condition— He broke off, staring at the woman. Not twelve years of age? he echoed, and fell silent.

Juana Ibáñez remained very still, allowing only the dark bulk of her presence in his whitewashed cell to disturb the peace of Father Padrón.

Then he was speaking again, now in another voice, the smooth familiar one that she heard on Sundays as it poured from the high stone púlpito of the little church. It was the voice with which he gave esperanza—a sweetness of hope to mix well with their bitterness and their fear of God the Father. You have heard, he was saying softly, the tale of Camila La Cruz, another girl of not twelve years . . . do they speak of her trial still in this province?

Sí, padre, whispered Juana Ibáñez, crossing herself. She felt a fear stirring in her body like a fever chill; it made her hesitate, as though a string of knots were tied to her words. That Camila, she stammered, who was . . .

The priest nodded. *Sí*, that one. He spoke still in the soft voice. That one who was put to death, *encinta* . . . carrying her unborn child. As he spoke the last words, he turned abruptly in his chair, as though startled by a sound outside the door. Juana Ibáñez forced herself to murmur, The padre—?

Sí, that Camila, the priest went on, pretending to search a dim memory. Was she not one who accused the padre of her village? Did she not swear it was he—?

No hay de qué! exclaimed Juana Ibáñez. Do not speak of it! Her broad, placid face had turned white as a troubled moon. She seemed to shrink from him, swaying as though she might fall backward against the door. Father Padrón nodded again, and smiled the kind smile. Well, he breathed, a long time ago, such barbarities. But now your daughter. His crumpled face creased further with a look of concern. Your little Rosa . . .

In truth, my Rosa is *ill*, padre, protested Juana Ibáñez, struggling now to keep her voice from betraying her altogether. With a pain that slices so, like a knife within. The child screams when one touches her here—she gestured at a midpoint of her belly—and here —another point high on the side. The padre nodded again, without looking. And the blood, said the woman, is so dark. *Claro que no—* she is not, it cannot be—

Of course not, he said, soothing her. *Claro que no*. But we must pray—

—and that skin of hers, always so pale, but now the whiteness—

He nodded, moving slowly toward the woman; his arm settled about her shoulders; he walked firmly, propelling her closer to the door.

—even the swelling, so quick and big, it is not—not—?

Claro que no, he murmured again. *Pobrecita*. Poor little one. It was wise that you came to tell me. . . .

His words with their singsong cadence now fell like caresses upon her ears; despite herself she felt the fear recede like a wave, calmness flooding in its place. The padre's arm lay gently across her back like a soft shawl; behind the new spectacles, a mist of unfamiliar tears stung her eyes.

Take the child, he whispered, to the Señora Doctora Restell in San Luis. You have heard—

Juana Ibáñez' eyes widened in amazement. But—

Sí, said Father Padrón, with a brisk patting. Sí. You must go without fear, but with prayer and faith; this is a righteous act; as you say, the child is ill. In truth. Señora Restell, Calle Mendoza. Mention only that you bring Rosa from Montaraz, nothing more. She will do—what can be done. With the help of *el buen Dios. Claro?*

Juana Ibáñez searched the padre's face; there was nothing of himself to read. With his beautiful white hand he made the sign of the cross between them, then withdrew the hand quickly, hiding it within the folds of his cassock, as though he feared she might steal it.

That night, Juana Ibáñez cried openly before her children, like a woman in a folk tale who has been promised evil magic. That the padre himself should speak so smoothly the name of an infamous woman. La Restell! That he should send us to such a one. Think of it.

Lola shrugged. Why does it surprise you, *Mamacita?* The padres, the *policía,* they all do what they must; have you not taught us this always? And what they must do . . . must change from time to time. *Verdad?*

Juana Ibáñez sighed wearily at the sad wisdom of her child. But he knows that Rosa is not—that she will need—

What does it matter, said Chepito. Señora Restell is not a witch—only fools believe what is whispered by fools—

But neither is she—

She is a *doctor,* Mama, said Lola.

I do not trust such a *doctor* with the life of your sister.

Catuja stood in silence at the edge of the room, holding the pile of white cloths soiled with the dark blood of her sister's *enfermedad.*

I think she is worse tonight, she said. I think—
Ssst! Juana Ibáñez held a warning finger to her white lips.

Rosa lay in her narrow cot staring up at the cracked ceiling, imagining a cinema in which *la Muerte* was a sad handsome man who fell in love with a young and beautiful girl, and once she loved him back it meant she must die to follow him. It was good to think of *la Muerte* in this way, Rosa had decided, not as an ugly big clown who danced his rude noisy dance in the procession of Holy Week. It was good because if *la Muerte* were so handsome in his formal evening clothes, with a white tie and dark gentle eyes full of pain, then when Rosa's own pain came like quick cuts of a swift blade, when she felt blood trickling inside as a slow river of life leaking away forever, it was easier to keep from crying out. She could close her hands into small tight fists and clutch the worn edges of the gray blanket in which she lay stiff as a doll; she could bite her lips and squeeze her eyes so that the tears would only slide in silence out of the corners; she could feel sadness for the girl in the *cine* instead of for herself, knowing La Lloradora was watching to see if she could. She thought La Lloradora must forgive her if she wept in this way, not crying out for her own *dolor*, her own pain, which she knew would be serious sin if she were having a bastard. That would be her fault no matter how it had come to be, and Father Padrón like a *cachadista*, one who plays sly tricks, would hear her confession without saying anything of how it was not her fault at all. If she wept in this way only for the beautiful girl in the *cine* who must die so young for the dark *Muerte* who loved her, then surely La Lloradora's painted heart would melt, and she would find a way to save the life of María Rosa Andújar and not let her have a bastard after all.

Only when the knife-pain struck so quick and deep that it took her breath—only then did she shriek *Aií! Aií!* with a cry so loud that Catuja and Mama had to come running, with their lips in a white line of fear. Then they would change the folded cloths that lay under her body to catch the dripping of blood. They would look at those dark spots, drops of poison from a wound that would not heal, and shake their heads at each other, thinking she did not see their eyes saying no, they could do nothing. How could they tell where such a wound had opened in her? Why could they not stop the blood that trickled so, as though from a rusty cup that had broken inside? Lloradora, she whispered softly, do not let me die. I am too little for so much pain. And anyway why must *I* die as a *castigo*, a penitence for sin? Rosa knew, everyone knew, there were other girls who did not die even if they had bastards from letting boys walk in the woods with them. It was not fair, but she must not think of that. If La Lloradora was so angry, she must have her reasons. Maybe she was angry with Rosa for her dreams? Especially about the crown. . . .

Well, La Lloradora would do what she wanted to do, Rosa had always accepted that. Still, she whispered to the ceiling, can you not at least let it be after Candlemas? After tomorrow? Don't you want me to stay alive for your own fiesta of *purificación? Claro que sí.* Why else would you have the padre choose me to be *la reina?* You did want me to march beside you in the procession! I know you did—in a white dress like yours. You want me beside you when they carry you from the church on the scarlet pillow. Beside you when the songs and dances start. You *do* love me best. I know it.

In the other room Catuja whispered, But if she is *encinta* with a bastard, how will they let her be *la reina?* It is a sin against—

Sst, said Lola fiercely. She is *enferma,* no one knows—

Well, but Mama will not let her go anyway, said Chepito. If she is bleeding, how can she march? Let alone—

Juana Ibáñez signaled them all to be still.

But *will* you let her? Lola persisted.

Claro que no! said Juana Ibáñez, sighing. I cannot.

Rosa sighed, a piteous sound filled with the broken ends of wishes. She tried to swallow. Did you not promise? The tears slid out of the sides of her eyes. Oh, it is not fair for the *Virgen* to break a promise!

Could La Lloradora be tormenting her as a trick? Could that be—?

Rosa frowned, puzzling this. It was true that on Candlemas the *Virgen* must answer all the prayers she had left unanswered through the year. On her own day of honor, was she not powerful enough to grant everything, even without permission from God the Father? Then might she be afraid . . . of Rosa's prayers?

Well, you need not worry, she whispered, stopping her tears. I will pray only for— And her eyes flew open again, to watch the picture of herself floating on the ceiling, a white angel floating through the film of her sinner's tears. Rosa on the ceiling could reach high enough to touch a star point of the statue's crown. Imagine: she might tear a hole in the fragile cobweb of lace that floated around the statue's feet . . . or catch the hem of that mantilla—and with a quick motion pull it down, setting free La Lloradora's torrent of glorious hair that must lie chastely pinned beneath, upon her perfect ivory scalp. If Rosa dared, could she not untie the scarlet sash and pluck off the golden letters that spelled ESPERANZA? Might she seize one of those tiny glowing jewels that winked from within the lacy bosom like secret eyes— And then Rosa gasped in horror, for the fingers of Rosa on the ceiling had darted out and snatched a tiny blood-red stone, only one, but surely it must be worth fortunes of money—even though it belonged to the dress of an old painted statue who would not even know, who could not possibly care— *No!* she cried in sudden horror. *I did not mean it!* Then she burst into real tears, of terror and guilt, of rage and pity, not for the girl in the *cine* who gave herself to *la Muerte,* but for herself. For Rosa; *Rosa.* She sobbed aloud, All right! *Bueno!* Then let me die after Candlemas, if I am so horrid. She raised a defiant fist at the statue she had just betrayed with her sinful thoughts. But you will let me be *la reina* first, as you promised! You will let me kill the cockerel for you—who else has more need to kill the *gallo* of evil? Only let me say the holy verse to get rid of it!

Solemnly she lowered the small angry fist and began to strike her own breast in the ritual way. *Me confeso* . . . I have sinned in my thoughts . . .

Then she stopped and sat up, raising both arms to the ceiling, cocking her head, smiling in the way she had to when the most important thing of all was at stake. The way she had to smile at Father Padrón, at Mama, at Señor López Figueroa and her brother

Chepito, at her papa long ago after he hurt her. . . . She smiled so now, at the spot on the cracked ceiling where La Lloradora had looked down and seen the terrible truth of Rosa's dreams. *Salve María*, she said contritely, with that magic smile that could make others do things, sometimes. I am heartily sorry for having offended thee. But you still love me best! I know it. And if I do everything just the way you want, you will forgive me. All right? *Bueno?* There was no sign from the statue on the ceiling.

In the night Juana Ibáñez stood beside her daughter's bed and touched her cool forehead. Rosa murmured, half-asleep, Do not worry, *Madrecita*. Tomorrow when I am *la reina*—

Sst, *niña*, whispered her mother, stroking the damp curls back from the child's pale face, rest now. There will be other fiestas—

Rosa sat up abruptly; in her round eyes the darkness shone like light. I will die if I do not go. I have promised. I am going, you will not dare to stop me.

Juana Ibáñez stood shaking her head; she had withstood many such tantrums, such attacks of rage, willfulness, defiance; in her mother's heart of stone she knew they always passed. Sleep now, she said in a soothing voice. Then she tiptoed away and lay wearily upon her bed, whispering a prayer of her own for the life of this child with a will so *fuerte*, too strong for either the body or the life that *Dios* had designed for her.

And in her sleep Rosa dreamed that the statue's tears of silver glass that could never fall began to rain down her painted face and splinter in the dirt of the Plaza del 16 Enero, and all the town stood watching in horror as they fell, and understood why. Rosa Andújar's shame was on their lips, behind their hands, for what other reason could it be that she was not there marching in the procession in her white communion dress, symbol of *purificación?* What other reason, after she had boasted to everyone of how the padre had promised she could be *la reina* even though she was not yet twelve. In her sleep the children of the town stood in circles and laughed, whispering her name, and the statue of La Lloradora had no more silver tears.

The morning came and Rosa lay in her bed so pale and still that Juana Ibáñez touched the child's brow in fear, thinking she would find it cold as death. *Dios*, she whispered, and Rosa stirred, opening her eyes with the dark shadows of pain like bruises underneath. I am better, Mama, she said, smiling. See—she gestured toward her belly—the swelling is less. The sleep of the night has cured me, and the blood—there is almost none.

Juana Ibáñez nodded and smiled. She had wakened her other children early, helping them dress in silence so that they could leave before their sister woke and cried again to go with them. If only one could have forbidden them all to march in that procession which meant so much more to this one than to any of the rest. But she had sighed and dressed them and let them go, quietly, to wait for her at the church. Now she must promise Rosa that she herself would not stay for the fiesta, not for the dancing or the killing of the cock, not for the fine dinner or the games. She would go only to the church, for the prayers and the chanting, and to light a candle for Rosa so that Lola might carry it for her in the children's march, high and proud for La Lloradora to see that Rosa had sent her prayers and her love.

In her bed Rosa nodded as her mother talked, and did not cry; instead she promised to rest and wait with patience until her mama came back; *gracias por todos*, she said several times— I thank you for everything. I am sorry for shouting and crying so last night. *Te quiero, Mamacita*.

And the moment Juana Ibáñez left the house Rosa got up from her bed and put on her white communion dress and ran barefoot through the woods, avoiding the streets of the town, though it was twice as far that way from their house to the church. At last she arrived, panting, to take her place among the others, making sure to stand far away from her sisters and brother so that they would not notice her until the march began. The procession was to last nearly an hour, with the children marching over a mile in the punishing sun; down one street and up another, round and round the Plaza del 16 Enero where the mayor waited for *la reina* to perform the ritual killing of the cock that must signify death to sin and evil, rebirth to virtue; a signal to the weeping *Virgen* that her purity must triumph in their hearts for all the long year to come.

After that the children would march again, back up the steep hill to the church, singing and chanting, tossing confetti and streamers, and at last deliver their bouquets of white flowers and their lighted candles to the altar before La Lloradora, who would be taken from her scarlet pillow and set in place again, far from reach, on her pedestal in the little chapel.

The procession began on a signal from Father Padrón; Rosa stepped into place at the head of the line, in front of Margarita Ordóñez, who had been hastily selected to replace her. She began to march at the left side of the statue as it rode upon the shoulders of four husky, sweating boys from Chepito's class. Pale and unsteady, Rosa held her candle high, singing louder than all the others, weaving slightly like a *borrachón* after a night at the tavern. Rosa's brother and sisters looked at each other with alarm, not knowing whether to run out of the line to find their mama, to tell her that Rosa was out of bed marching crazily in the sun.

Rosa turned and smiled at them in a strange fierce way, and in between phrases of the holy song she whispered at them, *Do not dare stop me! Do not dare!*

How funny your little sister looks, she heard one of La Lloradora's bearers say to her brother Chepito. All fat and white like—

Sst, said Chepito, and kept his eyes down and his face straight in front.

Father Padrón, marching just ahead of them, swiveled his pink head around once or twice, to make sure the boys had not tipped over the precious statue, but he never turned far enough to look at Rosa; she could not tell if he knew who was marching there; perhaps he thought it was Margarita Ordóñez. Never mind, she thought, if he does see me I will tell him the same: Do not dare stop me! *Salve María*, she murmured to the statue as she marched beside it. You hear me? See, I have come, sick as I am. Do not let me have a bastard, all right? Do not let me die, either. I love you, see what I am doing for you? *Por Dios*, give me a sign! *He!* Will you—if I give you half my life? Answer me!

An instant later she began to feel strangely lightheaded; there was a quick rush of blood inside her belly—as though some barrier had given way; and the sun seemed suddenly to press upon her shoulders like a heavy weight, pushing her down. Her knees trembled, and she looked up imploringly at the statue; were the silver tears still in place upon the ivory cheeks? *Gracias a Dios,* they had not come loose. Then as she gazed, the left hand of La Lloradora, the one that held the rosary of pearls so, between the thumb and first finger, began to blur before her as though it were moving by itself, not just from the swaying of the pillow or the bumpy forward motion of the sweating boys who carried it along the rough dirt path. *He!* The head too seemed to move, bowing a little toward Rosa as though to bend and whisper a secret; the red shiny lips seemed to part, and Rosa's ears heard a faint buzzing like the secret whisper of La Lloradora's voice in her dreams.

Sí, niña, said the voice, though the shiny scarlet lips did not seem to move at all. *Sí,* your prayer is heard.

Rosa shook her head and the buzzing stopped, but now the whorls of lace streaming down upon the statue's slender shoulders seemed to move and rustle too, a soft sighing sound like an echo in a cave. *Sí, sí,* ESPERANZA . . .

Now Rosa felt the ground rushing up toward her, but something held her and she did not slip all the way down; she stumbled on a stone, her head reeling and the pain now so sharp in her belly that she must bite her lip to keep from crying *Aii! Aii!* Do not let me fall now! she gasped. Not now! They had reached the Plaza del 16 Enero, though it blurred before her in a hundred colors. Now was the most important thing of all; now she must do what La Lloradora wanted her to do, as a *castigo.* She must wear the blindfold and turn and turn, then stand long enough in the white sun to recite the long verse about sin and punishment, evil and death. And at last she must lift up the big white sword of justice and bring it down on the head of a poor *gallo* buried up to its neck in the dirt at her feet. If she could do all she had to do, La Lloradora would forgive her. But if she failed, if she fainted or fell or forgot one single thing, then La Lloradora would send the worst *castigo* of all, she knew; for breaking her solemn oath, La Lloradora would strike her dead in the Plaza del 16 Enero, like the sinful *gallo* itself, in front of everyone.

Rosa could not remember one moment of how it went, but the others described it all to her later—how another girl helped fasten the blindfold, and two big boys buried the *gallo,* and turned her round and round; how she recited the whole long *copla,* telling in verse of all the serious sins the evil bird had committed in its short life—envy and greed, laziness and lies . . . and how it must suffer and die at once, and that its last wish was only that all the treasures it had stolen—precious stones the color of blood, golden crowns with stars, pearls and medals—all these things must be dug up and given to the children of Montaraz who could stay as pure as the holy *Virgen* herself.

At last, they told Rosa, she lifted the broad white wooden sword high above her head, and brought it down hard on the head of that wicked bird; the *gallo* shrieked an awful cry when she killed it with one stroke, and at the same time she herself fell to the ground in a heap, which made her mama scream and her sisters and brother run to gather her up and carry her home.

The white communion dress, she could see, was all spattered with dirt and dark poison blood, but when Juana Ibáñez laid Rosa gently down upon her bed, she exclaimed *Mira!* For the swelling of the child's body had gone down a little, as if something had burst inside her like one of the red balloons of *carnaval,* and whatever it was that caused the *dolor* might now go away as mysteriously as it had come. Juana Ibáñez had smoothed the child's blanket over her, and bathed her forehead with a cool white cloth, and knelt beside her with tears streaming down her face. She made the sign of the cross in silence, but even if there was a prayer for such a moment she could not have said it. Lola, Catuja, and Chepito stood white-faced at the door, clasping each other's hands. Colored streamers and bits of confetti clung to their heads and shoulders, and the shouts and music of the fiesta still rang in their ears from the streets outside.

Will she die now? Catuja whispered to Chepito.

Lola shook her head. No, she said aloud. She is too stubborn.

Then will she have a bastard? Chepito whispered.

Catuja made a funny face, like a twisted smile. If there is any bastard inside *la reina*, she said, do not dare come out. Hear me? Do not dare!

And in spite of herself Juana Ibáñez had lifted her face from her folded hands and burst out laughing.

IT was not at all as one expected. Who would have thought the *abortista* inhabited such fine rooms filled with silken cushions and patterned rugs the color of rubies, such soft chairs, polished tables, and shining bowls of silver filled with yellow fruit? Upon the walls hung paintings of rose-colored ladies in ruffled gowns, and of unknown flowers on long slender stems. La Restell herself resembled such a flower, whose petals of pale orange hair, bright as coins in the sun, lay piled upon her head in a row of proud curls like a *cresta de gallo*. She walked like an actress, with her feet strapped so, in small leather harnesses like the heads of tiny horses, and under her white doctor's coat a dress of thin blue gauze brushed against her silken legs, making sounds like the sighing of leaves.

For the examination there was a small room all of white that shone with such cleanness as one would find in a hospital; everything in it new and smelling of strong soap; everything smooth and slippery to the touch, even the sheet stretched like skin across the narrow metal cot where Rosa must lie on her back, with her feet resting high on two silver stirrups, as though to be dragged by an invisible horse. In this room, behind a black curtain, a tall stand of silver metal stood like the skeleton of a tree, hung with fruits that were small lights, cords, and lenses; a microscope of a special kind, Señora Restell explained, to show on a screen small pictures made ten thousand times larger, so that one could see even a tiny infection, a wound no larger than the point of a pin. The picture she would show on the screen for Juana Ibáñez was of something she had cut away from the tender inner skin of the child's womb, a piece of tissue scraped with a delicate instrument; it was the size of a small coin, finer than gauze; she had pressed it within a thin wafer of wax, soaked it in colored dyes. Señora Restell had done these things in her laboratory, after giving Rosa an injection to make her sleep without pain. The picture she would make must show certain things that no one could see, not even with practiced eyes and skilled hands; certain things she could not learn from touching the child so, from making her sit up and lie down, and listening and touching everywhere, just as the *comadre,* the midwife, had done in Montaraz, to discover the source of her pain. While Rosa lay asleep with her feet high in the silver stirrups, on the clean bed that was hardly whiter than her skin, Señora Restell led Juana Ibáñez into the darkened corner on the other side of the black curtain. She snapped on the light of the shiny metal stand; upon the opposite wall the screen glowed pink like the edge of a sunset. Juana Ibáñez drew her breath sharply, but Señora Restell said nothing. She only adjusted a knob, and another, until the picture grew clearer. Still Juana Ibáñez saw only a fine mesh of pink lace, a cobweb of tiny lines crossing and recrossing like twisted strands from a broken web of spider's silk; here and there a tiny mote of brown, a ragged smear of blue appeared, as though a child had passed through the web dripping tears of paint from a handful of wet brushes. At the lower right corner of the screen a larger spot glowed darker blue, like a spreading stain, as though the child with his dripping brushes had grown more careless still, in his haste to escape from the web.

Qué significa? whispered Juana Ibáñez, when she could speak. What does it mean?

An extraordinary thing, said Señora Restell; one seldom sees—

What does it mean? the mother demanded; anger and fear fought each other in her voice.

The dark shape here—Señora Restell pointed like a *profesora* with a pale polished fingernail—means only that she appears to have been pregnant—

Parece? She appears—?

Well, I see no sign of the *feto*—no tissues from the baby itself—

But nothing came out! I am sure. *Puf!* like a balloon the swelling went. No more of the poison blood. But nothing came out!

I know. Sometimes—

Then what can it mean? If the baby died inside . . . ? Despite the darkness, Juana Ibáñez' round eyes now glowed with terror; her body began to tremble. It was the same fear that had made her come to the *abortista* whose name the padre had given her.

The doctor now laid a white hand gently upon the woman's dark sleeve. Sometimes, she said again in a soft voice, *y no sabemos por qué,* we do not understand, a thing will happen, a small accident of the womb, something tears the veil of tissue, the *amnios,* that must form for the baby.

But it did not come out! cried Juana Ibáñez. If there was a baby—

Señora Restell sighed, and her hands made a small helpless gesture, a turning of the palms. Señora, I cannot tell how it happened. But there must be an *operación* now, to remove the child's womb and examine—

No! cried Juana Ibáñez in a fierce whisper. Then she stared at this Señora Doctora, at her high, careful crown of curls, at her white coat and her slender fingers. *La abortista,* she thought. Yet she did not dislike her; this was a curious thing. What if, she said, what if one does nothing?

Señora Restell frowned. Nothing is a very dangerous thing to do in such a case. The cells—

Juana Ibáñez raised a hand, as though to ward off the power of the doctor's words. Señora Doctora, *en verdad,* what will happen to my child if one does not tear out her womb?

Señora Restell hesitated. It is possible, she said then, that she will heal.

Ah.

But it is more likely— The doctor spread her fingers apart, and then closed them.

She will not die. Juana Ibáñez made it not a question.

In the darkness the doctor's eyes now glowed as brightly as her own; like two cats they stared at each other unblinking in the light of the microscope screen.

Posible, Señora Restell said again, that she will heal. But if nothing is done, some of those cells may remain, embedded there—she gestured again toward the dark stain at the edge of the pink spider-web—in the wall of the womb. They do not belong there.

But they will disappear when she grows—?

Señora Restell shook her head firmly. One cannot know this. It is not a chance one takes. If they remain, it has happened that a few years later— She broke off; a silent shrug.

But if they disappear? Like the *feto*? She will be well, no? There will be no trace of this?

No, Señora. No matter what happens, there will be a trace of this. An important one—

Ya se ve, said Juana Ibáñez quickly. She will not conceive—

Señora Restell nodded. I am sorry.

Still, she will grow, she will be well? And . . . as a woman, normal? For a husband?

That too is a thing I cannot promise. She is very young; there was much damage. You must know she has been . . . badly hurt.

When, hurt? How?

Now the doctor made a sudden impatient gesture; her eyes moved away. I cannot tell with certainty. Did she not tell you—?

No, said Juana Ibáñez. That one tells very little.

No importa, said the doctor. And Juana Ibáñez understood. Rosa's silence was the price for Señora Restell's services; and for the help of Father Padrón. *Ya se ve*, she thought. Now it is clear.

What matters, the doctor was saying, is that the child is not strong; she is fragile. That is why the *operación*—

Juana Ibáñez shook her head. That one is not fragile, she said. She had stopped trembling suddenly; there was heat now in her voice. You are wrong in this, Señora. Perhaps you are wrong in other things as well.

Puede ser. It may be so. There was a tight smile now on the pale smooth lips of the doctor. In such cases one must hope to be wrong. But of this I am sure: Without the *operación*, one risks the child's life.

Pero, Señora Doctora . . . with the *operación* one risks it too.

That is true.

And one marks the life that remains—a woman whose womb is torn out. . . .

Señora Restell sighed, with a shrug of despair. Or one who may have less than half a life to live.

Juana Ibáñez hesitated only an instant. *Bueno 'stá,* she said. Enough.

The doctor snapped off the light of the microscope and moved briskly to the other side of the black curtain. Lying still on the examining table, Rosa heard the sighing of blue leaves against silken legs and closed her eyes very tight, so that *La Señora Doctora* and Mama would not know what else she might have heard.

Juana Ibáñez stayed another moment in the darkness; she wanted to make the sign of the cross before the delicate metal microscope stand. *La Purificación de la Virgen,* she murmured, without bitterness. *Salve María.*

THE doctor has removed his glasses; he sits beside the coffin massaging the bridge of his nose with a thumb and forefinger. His head is bowed, resting against the cool glass top of the coffin; he seems almost in an attitude of prayer, murmuring to himself, or perhaps to La Señora. María Blanca approaches quietly and kneels opposite him. She would like to cry out for help, for intercession, but she cannot pray. She breathes deeply, three breaths as before, in and slowly out. I will not plead with you, Rosa, she whispers defiantly, under her breath. You still smile that smile, but it is mine now. There is a small pin in her hand, one of the hairpins left from La Señora's coiffure. Suddenly she leans forward and scratches the bronze base of the coffin; the pin bends easily but she makes a mark. Dr. Ceballos instantly springs to her side and wrests the pin from her hand. Blanca does not struggle. I have done no harm, she says simply. See for yourself.

Dr. Ceballos bends to examine the coffin but perceives nothing;

he runs his hand over the surface, but the gleaming bronze base already bears the scars of many injuries. He sighs then, and turns to Blanca, with a glance of sudden amusement. She *is* rather terrifying, he says. One cannot help that. I suppose you wish we both were dead.

Blanca shivers. I do not envy such . . . tricks of immortality.

Ah. The doctor smiles. But then what can you want with General Montero? Surely the old man has no *other* tricks—

I want nothing, she says, stiffening. It is Carlos who wants—*la nueva vida*, a new life. With *me*.

Of course, Señora. Ceballos' smile widens.

You are so arrogant, Blanca murmurs, half to herself. All of you. Carlos has no need—

Why do you think he sent for me?

Because . . . she hesitates; her face seems to fold, like that of a child who cries too much. I do not have to answer you—

He nods; he has heard the fear beneath her flat voice. Señora, he whispers, with a deceptive softness. Think of it so. If she did not exist, if I had not come tonight, that *viejo*, that old one of yours, would not be going home tomorrow. Especially not with you. Not for such a—*nueva vida* as he has in mind.

You will see! she cries. Once I am there with him—I will be vice president! I will make everyone forget. Even you—even *I* will forget.

Ceballos bows. Well. You know of course that I am to stay with you—in Pradera?

Her face drains of color; she recovers quickly. But only until she —until we have no more need of her.

The doctor shakes his head, no. To *stay*, he says again.

But—you had an urgent case. You were going to Brussels—

He shrugs. *No importa*. It does not matter; my colleagues will manage. I have told the general I am willing to stay, under certain conditions.

Blanca nods. A place in the new government—

An unofficial place. I merely wish to serve the general—and you, Señora—in an advisory capacity. We have a long relationship. He knows me. Unlike that Chulo . . . and others close to him, I have no appetite for power. Besides, I am an *extranjero*—a foreigner like you. I pose no threat to the others.

No threat, she echoes. I see.

Are you angry, Señora?

No. She does not look at him.

You do not trust me. He says this with sadness, but still smiling. My presence reminds you—his eyes dart toward the coffin, then back to Blanca's face. I may constantly compare you with her, is it not so? As if I were her lover. More than a lover, in truth. For I know more secrets of her flesh than the general ever knew, more even than the mother who gave it life. I know—

You are— Blanca shakes her head, to silence him. He touches her shoulder and she wrenches away. If the general needs you, I cannot fight you, she whispers. I am only his wife, his *señora*. The word stops her; she starts to cover her mouth, but Dr. Ceballos grasps her hand. Señora, he echoes softly, we must try to be friends. One day you may turn to me, you know. And I will be there.

Rosa Andújar could not say what she knew to anyone, but in the days that followed she began to talk of running away, of not ever returning to school, of wanting only to die. When Catuja found her weeping she explained that La Lloradora no longer loved her. I can never be like her, she said, and so she cannot forgive me, or care what becomes of me.

That is foolishness, Juana Ibáñez said with anger when Catuja told her what Rosa had said. But later, holding Rosa in her arms, she said it again in a gentle voice. A foolishness. La Lloradora is a saint; a saint is not the only thing one may want to be. In the world, La Lloradora is a thing of stone—but you are a *mujer* of flesh. A woman who may weep for her own sorrow—not only for others. For oneself and for the sorrow of life. One has both tears and *esperanza;* of all my children, Rosa has the gift for *esperanza.*

Staring at the night, Rosa thought hard of what Mama might mean by these things. A *mujer* of flesh . . . At last she decided that it must have something to do with the cinema. Women in *las cines* often cried for themselves, yet their faces never grew red or ugly. Their tears fell like the silver *lágrimas* of La Lloradora, though they did not stay forever upon the cheeks. In *las cines* women did other forbidden things, even serious sin. And still they wore beautiful clothes, hats and furs, jewels . . . Some wore pearls that were stolen, or diamonds given to them by evil men. And they puffed on cigarets, blowing the smoke out so, in long soft curls; behind the smoke their smiles looked like secrets. Mama had not wanted her to go with Lola and Catuja to see the new *cine* at the Olimpia, but at last she had relented. *En verdad,* one had read that the *estrella,* the great new star of this *cine,* was not a saint in real life. This *estrella* had the sad eyes of La Lloradora but it was from another kind of sadness, one that must come from committing serious sin and still being beautiful. In the *cine,* when she stood alone on a dark street wet with cold rain, the *estrella* tossed her head saying I am not afraid of life or death. And in her seat in the Olimpia Theatre Rosa felt her own skin stand up in small bumps, as if her body had heard; as if it wanted to cry out Sí. The *estrella* was a *mujer* of flesh who could not live in heaven; one who knew, *claro,* that she had done things La Lloradora could not forgive. The *estrella* would take her death like a penance for her sins, and come back in another *cine* to blow a veil of smoke through her smile, without caring. She was not afraid. At once Rosa saw what Mama must have meant. A *mujer* of flesh . . .

All the way home along the dusty road Rosa was silent while her older sisters talked of the *cine* and of the *estrella* in her black spangles with her hair in little waves of light. It was a strange thing, Rosa was thinking, for had one not seen *cines* about bad girls before? A German one where the girl made a man fall in love with her and then stole his money, and two American ones where the men fell in love but then repented and left the bad girls to die alone. Still, never before had she seen a *cine* in which the bad girl did not care what might happen, did not fear *la Muerte* even a little. In this *cine*, the *estrella* had known the men would kill her for things she did, for falling in love with enemies and betraying secrets, for being clever and deceiving them all. Yet she was not afraid. In truth, it was as though nothing could touch her. Not love, not being alone, not serious sin, not death. *Sí*—even *la Muerte* made her smile in that way of what is it to me; I do not care. And in the end she threw away her life, wearing the black cape of spangles and gazing into her mirror to see that she was still beautiful. When they killed her she stood so, before the men with their guns, and painted on her last red smile—not for them, *claro*, but for herself. *O*, Rosa was crying when the guns went off, but she was smiling too, like the *estrella*. That is how I will be, she cried to herself. *Mira!* Nothing will touch me.

Outside the Olimpia Theatre, the three girls stood before the new red-and-black poster in an attitude of prayer, of reverie. In Person/One Night Only/TOBAL IRIBAS! All three had seen the accompanying feature *cine*, starring Persuasión duPre as a poor girl seduced by her employer, and then forced to flee from her home village, carrying nothing but her fierce will to become an *estrella*, a star of the *cine* . . . like Persuasión duPre. Lola and Catuja had seen it once, Rosa twice. But Tobal Iribas, *en persona!* He would sing his new tango, *"Caro de Beato, Uñas de Gato"!* Nothing so wonderful as this had ever come to Montaraz. Iribas! The name alone was enough to stir up Catuja's asthma, which did not ordinarily begin to bother her until a month later, well into the rainy season. Calm down, Rosa chided her, I am thinking.

You are always thinking, Lola snapped. That is because you have only thirteen years! *I* am listening to Tobalito. I am watching his eyes close in that way of his, when he holds the guitar, so. In the best *fotografías* it is as if he is caressing it, but looking at me. He looks—as if he sees my heart through my *camisa*. . . . She shivered.

Only wait until you see my new copy of *Radio Mirror*, sighed Catuja. There is a picture of him—

Rosa made a face of impatience. Listen, I have an important thing to say. I think— She paused, fixing them with her look of authority, as though her round black eyes could pierce all their secrets. I think—it is the will of *Dios* that Tobal Iribas comes at this time.

Catuja drew a breath like that of a small horse running. The will of *Dios!* So that he will see us in the dark—and run down from that stage—and take our hands in his, and confess—that he is in love . . .

Lola covered her mouth, but the giggles escaped like a string of small bubbles.

. . . in love with my ears, and Rosa's eyes, and Lola's b—

I am serious, Rosa said. The dark of her eyes grew soft at the edges, like clouds of danger.

I am serious too, Catuja said, sulking.

Rosa stamped her foot. Sst! Do you not see—it is a sign of fate, that we are ready to carry out the plan of escape—*recuerdas?* Remember in that *cine*, where Persuasión duPre was so poor, in the terrible place with the employer who beat her—and then the *círculo* came to the town, and she made the old clown fall in love with her? Remember how she pretended to be a *periodista*—a columnist for the newspaper?

Lola shook her head. We cannot go yet. It was agreed. We need fifty dollars, and we have barely thirty—counting this week's pay, *if* Rosa does not scorch another shirt of Señor de la Cadena, and *if* we do not go to see Tobalito. *Mira!* They are charging double admission—

And besides, Tobalito is not an old clown, whispered Catuja.

Rosa was thinking again. Nacha promised she could help us find jobs in San Luis . . . we could stay with her—

Catuja shook her head. Nacha's mama did not let her go until she was seventeen—

And look at her, she is still a filing clerk, said Lola.

But in a radio station! Rosa said. If I had a job in a radio station, I would be an *estrella* in a month!

Lola made a sound of pretending to yawn. I do not see Nacha's picture in the newsreel yet—

Claro que no! said Rosa. She has small eyes that cross, and knees that point to each other. But you have beautiful *tetas*—Lola blushed at this, hunching up her shoulders so that her *tetas* would not stick out—and Catuja sings like an *angelita*, while I—I, Rosa Andújar, am smart enough to do anything. And my knees are *muy seductivo*, no?

Anyway, what of it? said Lola, still blushing. She crossed her arms now, to hide her chest. What has any of it to do with Tobalito?

Catuja sighed again at the name, which again made her cough.

Oh, why are girls so silly! cried Rosa. Why do they never think, the way I do? How does a famous singer travel, if not by car? We will make him take us to San Luis, which will save us the bus fare. And by the time we arrive he will be so in love that he will take us at once to meet his manager, his *amigos* of the theatre—do you not understand? It is exactly the chance we need, it is *perfecto*.

Catuja looked thoughtful, though still her breath came in and out like whistles. Lola was silent, frowning.

Well, Rosa persisted. Are you afraid now, is that it, *mi hermanas grandes*—my big sisters? Little mice!

Sí, said Lola, softly. Are *you* not afraid? Ever? Rosa nodded; the black of her eyes grew softer still. I am always afraid—but I do not feel it any more. It cannot touch me inside. She shrugged and smiled a small strange smile. If you let a thing touch you inside, it can stop your life. Not mine! Not here, in this village of dirt! Not ironing the fine shirts of Señor de la Cadena, and waxing the floor for his fat *bruja* of a wife. And dreaming—of tango singers!

You are mean, said Lola. We are as serious as you—

And as brave, cried Catuja. But her voice was faint with asthma.

Mienten! said Rosa. You are liars, both, as well as mice. Neither of you will go with me—ever. I can see it—

Lola and Catuja exchanged looks of guilty confession. Oh, Rósula—

Sst! Rosa said. Now I will tell you what will be, and I swear it. I am going to meet Tobal and I am going to San Luis. If either of you has the nerve to come with me, *'stá bueno*. But I am going; I swear—she turned solemnly and knelt before the poster of red and black—on the name of Tobalito.

Sometimes, said Lola, now in a voice of awe, you sound very crazy to me, Rosa. Maybe you are crazy, you know?

Puede ser, replied Rosa, in a fierce whisper. Maybe you are right.

In the small cracked mirror over the sink, Rosa's face smiled and frowned, this way and that. Good evening, Señor Iribas, she said. Then she said it again, again—in the voice now of a *coqueta,* now of a shy child, now of a woman of mystery. How had Persuasión duPre said it to the old clown in that famous *cine?* In the voice of one who did not care. *Hola, Señor!* . . . Rosa held out a small white hand. Too bold? She pulled it back and stared up from under her eyes. I am Rosa Andújar. *La periodista.* The columnist of society news. I hope I am not very late—*que?* The manager did not say I was coming to interview you for my column? *Por Dios,* you must excuse me then . . . Rosa turned and gazed at the mirror, over her shoulder. *Me siento, Señor.* I am so sorry for this mistake, but since I am here, and if you are not *very* angry, then perhaps we could chat *un momentito,* after all? *O,* you are sure? How kind you are, as well as handsome . . .

Puf! Rosa made a face of disgust at her reflection. I would not believe it for a minute! Well, but he is a man. A tango singer! She peered again at the face in the glass. Could she make her voice fall to a hoarse whisper, like Catuja with her asthma? Could her eyes glisten with a light of *el Diablo?* O, Tobalito . . .

Perhaps it was an accident of fate, or the will of *Dios,* that on Saturday, as Rosa stood ironing the finest blue shirt of Señor de la Cadena, while thinking of Tobal Iribas, of escaping, of her new life as an *estrella* of the *cine* (I knew well the magic of your voice, but, Señor—one may call you Tobal? Ah!), the heavy iron in her small hand grew suddenly hot, and the shirt of Señor de la Cadena made the sound of a snake; when Rosa looked down, it had twisted itself into a handful of brown ash. His wife came running, with shouts and hard pinches. And later Señor de la Cadena looked at his shirt and shook his head with sadness. Well, but would he still pay the full week's wages? If . . . and he smiled in the way of men that she knew. If she would scorch the creases of his *miembro* with such a heat, then—? Rosa said a thing that made Señor de la Cadena very angry; she would have to go now with no money at all, not a peso. It was said in Montaraz that she was not the first maid whom Señora de la Cadena had lost in this way.

At six o'clock Rosa packed her cardboard suitcase with two white blouses; two pairs of stockings without holes; a set of panties in pastel colors, embroidered with the names of each day of the week; four radio fan magazines stolen from Lola; three lipsticks and a feathered powder puff; one fuzzy white sweater and her favorite doll, that one with the dress of soft black velvet.

She left a note on the pillow of her mama's bed: *Madrecita,* I am going to San Luis to begin my acting career. Do not worry, I will stay with Nacha, and will send home two dollars as soon as I am in the theatre, which will be right away. Also, I will send a postcard of the Plaza Victoria, with the fountain of water! *Do not worry!* Say goodbye also to Señora de la Cadena. I hope she finds a new maid soon, and I am sorry about spoiling the shirt. Please do not worry. Mama, *te quiero.* Rosa.

Swinging the cardboard suitcase in one hand, Rosa walked carefully down the red dirt road trying not to raise the dust; after a few minutes her new sandals wore a fine coat of it. She stood still for a moment, debating. Then she took off the sandals and walked barefoot, feeling each sharp stone like an angry farewell. Goodbye to Montaraz, she muttered, gritting her teeth against the pain. I will never walk like this again. Some day I will ride back up this road in a silver car. I will be wearing fur, a great cape of soft white fur. And when we reach the top of the hill my driver will climb out to wipe the dirt from my car's wheels, and I will tell him to hurry, and to make sure they shine. The new maid of Señora de la Cadena will run out of the house to stare at my furs through the car window. Señora de la Cadena herself will stand on her doorstep remembering how I used to kneel there waxing, how I rubbed the wax with the soft rag tied to the mop while she said, Hurry, Rosa, but rub harder, make sure it shines; rub *harder*, Rosa. Señora de la Cadena will shake her head in disbelief, while her new maid stares at the back of my silver car, making dreams and wishes.

By the time she arrived at the Olimpia Theatre, Rosa had determined not to be angry with anyone, not even her sisters. She had warned herself a hundred times they would never come. By now she had almost forgiven them, though not quite. Foolish sisters; then let them stay—Lola on her knees waxing floors and ironing the shirts of men like Señor de la Cadena; Catuja on her feet behind a grocery counter, wrapping melons, smiling at her fat stupid customers in case the boss is watching. Let them both rot, she thought, tossing her head to get rid of the wish that they had kept their word, that she would not have to escape all alone. Well. She marched up to the box office. *One*, please. Her voice was firm, she noted with satisfaction. Only her knees shook a little.

The *cine* was as wonderful as always. Persuasión duPre was a poor girl living in such a terrible place that the walls shook like chattering teeth every time a train passed outside the window. Persuasión and her rich married suitor could not hear themselves over the din; they stood screaming at each other in helpless silence, she dying of shame, he dying of longing for her. Later—when she had made him want her enough—there were pale furs and satin gowns and a big ocean liner and tall flowers in glass jars everywhere. When they danced on the deck of the ship with the moonlight falling like silver coins around them, Rosa understood that they were meant to be kissing; their separate bodies moving like mirror images, together and apart, meant to be an embrace, a falling into love. One day, she said aloud to the darkness of the Olimpia Theatre, I will wear such a gleaming dress, with a jeweled dragonfly pinned to my shoulder, and I will dance in a silver night; *todo el mundo*—everyone in the world—will see me so, I swear it.

Dim lights went on and the theatre manager made a little speech to announce the next week's feature presentation and to introduce the famous guitar-playing song stylist, Tobal Iribas, fresh from his triumphant tour. Iribas came out shyly, blinking at the lights as though he had just come to life from within the dream of each girl in the audience. He bent his head to one side, listening to the sighing of his name. Rosa saw tears streaming down the face of one girl she knew; a sea of handkerchiefs waved, wrinkled and damp with tears; a moan of passion rolled softly from somewhere in the back rows to somewhere in the front, gathering intensity. Iribas adjusted the microphone, setting off another ripple of emotion at the sight of his long pale fingers; a dozen girls thought, *Mira!* How tenderly he would touch me, that could be my skin, see how he loves me. Finally he began to sing, caressing the guitar, the microphone, the cord of the microphone, the air. His pauses came like surprise kisses. Rosa thought he seemed to know exactly where to place them so as to cause a moist shiver at the base of the spine, behind the knees, between the thighs. Two girls near Rosa sat shaking, chilled and feverish, their faces splotched with the grief of the tango. It was an orgy of heartbreak, everyone was happy.

Ten minutes before the end of the performance, Rosa left her seat to stumble out of the theatre and calm herself. Then she walked around to the back entrance. A sleepy guard sat slumped over a green table, flipping the pages of an old sports-photo magazine. Rosa said, *Perdóneme,* and flourished a piece of paper upon which she had written a polite message: Please admit Señorita R. Andújar, who has agreed to interview Tobal Iribas for the social column of this newspaper. Sincerely, F. de la Cadena, Editor, *El Tiempo de Montaraz.* She had used the typewriter of her employer's husband so that the letter would look important, even with mistakes. Rosa hoped the guard would not notice the mistakes. She smiled confidently at him, glancing at the clock over his head as if she were in a hurry; tapping one foot lightly, as she remembered Persuasión had done in this part of the *cine*.

The old man looked up at her: dusty shoes, hair curled with irons, a mouth of red paint, a flash of high round whiteness within the open blouse. He shrugged, passed the note back across the table, and pointed with his chin in the direction of the dressing room. Second door, he said. Do not blame me if he kicks you out. That one—

Mil gracias, she murmured, striding past him swinging the cardboard suitcase. You see how simple? she thought. Another sign of Fate.

Rosa had pored over Lola's old radio fan magazines, searching for stories, gossip, shreds of information, rumors, lies about Tobal Iribas. Aside from the *fotos*, there was not much to find. Still, there was a story of his first success—with a tango about a foolish boy who buys a fancy car for a blond girl, and lends the rest of his money to a friend. Soon he sees the blond girl driving off, with the friend and the money, in the fancy car. They wave to him, *Adiós, muchacho.* In the song, the poor boy lies dying of his broken heart, on a dirty cot in a cheap room, in a bad hotel on the poorest street in town. Only his mama sits by his side, weeping. . . . It was a tango of despair. *Sin esperanza . . .* without hope.

Radio Mirror explained that Iribas wrote the song when he was eighteen years old, and more or less in love with the daughter of the assistant manager of a small radio station in the village of Santa Clara. The girl friend wept over the song and persuaded her father to let him play it on a Saturday afternoon program of amateur love songs and poems of the *vaquero* life. The station received over two hundred postcards from girls asking about the poor dying boy and the singer who had made them cry for him.

Iribas was a sensation overnight; his career on the Santa Clara station lasted nearly four months, until the daughter of the assistant station manager fell in love with a boy who wrote a poem of the *vaquero* life. By then there were Tobal fan clubs in four neighboring towns, and a talent agent from San Luis suggested a concert tour. After three weeks of one-night-only in the small towns such as Montaraz, the agent promised, Tobal would have an excellent chance for a recording contract. For Tobal there was not much choice: a concert tour or a temporary engagement in a San Luis café as one of a trio of strolling singers, playing for three dollars a night plus tips.

Montaraz was his last stop on the tour. Tomorrow he would be back in San Luis, in his own room on the Avenida Florida, where, with any luck, seventeen-year-old Nelly de Saavedra would be still waiting for him with a sweet red smile and a warm kiss. Just before his performance Tobal had thought about Nelly, while gazing at his profile in the dirty mirror, slicking back his long black hair with glistening fingers dipped in pomade. He had turned to one side, then the other. He had lowered his eyelids, then ducked his head while raising his eyes. This was the Iribas look. Tonight, Nelly, he whispered. For you, Tobalito will give the girls of Montaraz something to remember.

Rosa pushed open the dressing-room door and set the cardboard suitcase beside it. She settled herself primly at the edge of the canvas cot, crossing her legs, then uncrossing them. She smoothed her red skirt, folded her hands, jumped up, fixed her hair, searched for a towel to wipe her dusty shoes. Then she stared at her face in the mirror framed by a necklace of round lights. *Hola, Señor,* she said. One may call you Tobal? Ah. Tobal . . . *dígame*—tell me, how does a man feel knowing that the moment a girl hears him sing she will fall in love?

Puf! She made the face of disgust. So. You ask which song is my favorite? You will never guess. It is your first. *Sí,* that one of such sadness. Such *desesperanza!* The heart of it is like a poem. Rosa closed her eyes and hummed a fragment of the verse. Should she have tears? She would think of something sad. Not that silly song! She would think of the face of poor Mama, reading Rosa's note of farewell. Or of poor Rosa, with that brute of a Señor de la Cadena. Well, she would have no trouble making tears.

She frowned. But what if he has enough of sorrow from that music of his? Easy tears from too many foolish *muchachas?* If he prefers laughing? If he is looking for one who never weeps, for eyes that promise only pleasure, good times? She tossed her head, shaking her ironed curls, forcing a laugh of gaiety. No, *por Dios!* How did Persuasión laugh, like a shower of bells? *O*, Tobalito . . .

At first he did not see her. He had kicked open the door, sweating and cursing, seeing only a cardboard suitcase, which he kicked aside. *Bastardos!* he said. He had just lost an argument with the theatre manager, who insisted that he perform three extra songs to please the crowd—since they had been charged double the usual admission, a fact which somehow had not been discussed in advance with the booking agent. Tobal had been hoarse for the last twenty minutes, his throat on fire; he was sure he had a fever; the heat in the theatre was unbearable. Screaming little *putas*, little whores, he had a headache from them too.

He collapsed into the hard chair at the dressing table, took a small flask out of a drawer, and held it to his lips for a long time.

Rosa, making herself very small, sat behind him, half hidden in the shadow at the edge of the cot, studying him in the glass. No tears, she decided. Then she stood up and held out a small white hand. Congratulations, Señor Iribas, on your brilliant performance tonight.

Who—what in hell?—who let you in?

She withdrew her hand, expressing dismay. But surely they told you I was here, Señor! Oh, dear—I am María Rosa Andújar, society columnist for *El Tiempo.* Did no one tell you that I was coming this evening? I cannot understand this—

Iribas stared at the small creature before him. Very thin, and with enormous hungry eyes, brown hair of no distinction, very white skin and little round knees like a child's. He decided to look at those knees another thirty seconds before throwing her out.

. . . society columnist, she was saying, very fast.

Society? he laughed. She winced. *Perdóneme,* he said, and how old are you, fourteen? Look, whoever you are, whatever you want, I am tired. I need a shower, and my throat—

Rosa caught her breath. *Por favor,* she prayed in silence. I cannot go back; let me do what I must. For my life! Then, in a voice of Persuasión . . . a voice of no breath, but only of passion . . . she

said, Señor, it is true that I have only eighteen years. But I am *the*
Rosa Andújar, whose column you have no doubt read in San Luis.
It is syndicated everywhere. Her pencil made a thoughtful tapping
upon the blank page of her notebook. She watched his eyes watching her; they moved to the rhythm. Well, but I see I am wasting my
time here. She shrugged and held out a small white hand. *No importa.* It is of no consequence . . .

Three hours later Tobalito Iribas was driving north toward San
Luis on the Valverde Highway. Would his girl friend Nelly still be
waiting? Or had she skipped out, taking his table radio? Well, his
guitar and three suitcases, two leatherette, the other cardboard, lay
neatly stacked in the back seat. And beside him, with her fragrant
brown head resting lightly on his shoulder, was the former society
columnist of *El Tiempo de Montaraz.* Her eyes were closed, but she
was wide awake.

Nelly, this is Rosa, he said, making his voice sound like an
offhand shrug. She is here to become an actress, like your sister
Emilia. She does not know a soul in San Luis. I told her we could
introduce her to some people . . . He trailed off.

Nelly's eyes rested briefly on Rosa, on her clothes, her skinny
figure, the traces of red dust on her shoes. She gave a small nod,
then flung her arms around Tobal. Oh, I have missed you so, she
exclaimed. You cannot imagine how lonesome it has been, all the
girls at La Mosca kept asking when you would be home, and—her
voice dropped to a whisper—I spent every night alone, just as I
promised. And you? She glanced at Rosa. Tobal laughed. Of course
I did, *querida,* what do you think? I have been so exhausted, nothing but driving and singing, I tell you I am sick from it, my poor
voice is gone, it is a *maravilla* that I even finished the tour.

Nelly picked up his suitcase and carried it to the bed; she

snapped it open and unrolled the red satin shirt, the green one. Sst, she said. How did you two meet, anyhow?

At a session of *fotografías*, Rosa said. In Montaraz. Señor Iribas heard me say that I might come to San Luis some day. He was so kind, he told me all about you, and your sister, in fact he talked so much of you that I begged him to introduce us. I know it is a terrible thing, to come so, without warning, but my cousin Nacha, who was supposed to be home when I arrived—I planned to stay with her until I found a place—she was not home, and I cannot imagine why, but Señor Iribas, seeing I was upset and had no place to go, was so kind offering to help, and—well—here I am.

Throughout the speech, Nelly kept her eyes fastened on Tobal's guilty face; his eyes went back and forth between them like eyes of a man with fever, with fright, with a sinful pleasure.

So, he broke in finally, his voice a little too loud, here we are.

Shall I make some coffee, Nelly said, without conviction. Unless Rosa would like to phone her cousin again? What if she were home by now, worrying?

Rosa glanced at Tobal. Ah—

Ah?

The truth is, Tobal murmured, I told Rosa she is welcome to stay here with . . . us tonight—I will sleep on the sofa.

No! Rosa protested quickly, I would not think to disturb the two of you. I will call my cousin, who must be frantic, you are quite right.

Why not relax? Tobal said. She will just assume you're coming in the morning. Besides, the nearest phone is in the *farmacia* on the corner, and it is closed.

Nelly said, I will leave you two then. I should go home and get some sleep, since I promised Emilia I would go shopping with her before work tomorrow. She needs some high-heeled shoes for her audition.

Audition? Rosa said. Nelly smiled. Oh, yes, my sister is trying out for a part in a new play. It is about a scandal in a girls' school, Emilia said there were several small parts open for young girls.

Can anyone go . . . to this audition?

Nelly shrugged. Why not? But they ask about your experience.

I have experience! Rosa said. Comedy, drama, musical. I have played all the heroines—Joan of Arc and Juliet. I have also, she added with a coy laugh, played a housemaid and the plaything of a *viejo rico,* one of those old rich men who make fools of themselves.

Really? Tobal looked impressed. Nelly did not.

Of course, Rosa went on, they were only small-town productions. But the directors had very high standards, I am sure I could qualify for—

Nelly was doing rapid calculations in her head. Why not come with me in the morning and meet Emilia? In fact I know where she is now—at a fancy party. She asked me to come but I wanted to wait for Tobal—I could just take you there and introduce—

Tobal said, Rosa is too tired now, tomorrow is soon enough.

I am not so tired, Rosa said. If Nelly thinks it's a good idea—

Oh, definitely, said Nelly smoothly. This party will be wonderful. Filled with stars of the theatre, producers; only *personajes* of great importance, celebrities—

Tobal looked sullen. Nelly put her face against his shoulder, nuzzling. Oh, Tobalito, don't be angry, *I* would not stay one minute at such a party, I would only take *her* and come right home to you. I want to hear all about your trip, I have already heard what a *maravilla* you were. Do not say no, it would be so good for Rosa to get a head start. That is what she needs us for, you said so yourself, to help her get into the theatre, no?

Tobal gave them both a sulky look but said nothing. Rosa gave Nelly a big excited hug and went into the bathroom with her suitcase. Nelly gave Tobal a sweet red smile and a long, warm kiss, exactly like the one he had thought about in the dressing room at the Olimpia Theatre in Montaraz.

Rosa emerged from Tobalito's bathroom wearing a mask of heavy orange make-up, through which her lips and eyes gleamed like holiday candies. Her hair was swept up on her head in a pile of fat sausage curls. Nelly groaned and pulled her back into the bathroom, where she set to work scrubbing, brushing, and repainting with pastel colors, until she had not only restored the original thin, large-eyed child, but had somehow succeeded in making her look even younger. Finally she took a big scissors and snipped off the sleeves of Rosa's fuzzy sweater, transforming it into a soft little bolero that left her slender arms and shoulders bare, adding to the air of vulnerability. There! she exclaimed, standing back. *Mira!* Look at yourself! Rosa gazed into the mirror at a waif with shining hair and an innocent pink smile; she touched the artful blush that filled in the hollows of her pale cheeks. Those round dark eyes still overpowered the narrow white face, but now, within the lights and shadows Nelly had supplied, they seemed softer, more likely to flash than to burn and consume. Even that small sharp nose looked less like the beak of some little scavenger bird; it seemed designed to sniff the air, like the nose of an aristocrat. Am I interesting? Rosa asked Nelly, giving the hair a doubtful pat. *Cómo no?* Nelly replied. How else could it be? Directors like Amado Nervo have *señoritas* with red mouths and black pompadours so, filling the waiting room like rolls of carpet. A little white mouse, on the other hand— She shrugged.

In the thirty-minute bus ride between Tobal's place and the Nervos' fashionable apartment on the Ocampo, Rosa skillfully drew from her new friend, as a fine needle draws a silk thread, all the background material she would need for this party. Nervo was directing the play *Las Angelitas,* for which Nelly's sister Emilia was auditioning tomorrow. Nervo was married to Soledad, the celebrated actress who would be playing one of the two leads in the play. However, Nervo had discovered Emilia, who had recently done a small walk-on role in another of his plays, a comedy, and Nelly thought her sister was sure to get the third-best role in *Las Angelitas*—playing a frightened schoolgirl who tells terrible lies about her teachers. Rosa listened carefully, memorizing the important details. She wanted to know all about this play, and all about Emilia, and which other plays Nervo had directed, and what the critics had said about his work, and what Soledad was really like, and how old, and how openly Nervo carried on his well-known affairs. . . . Nelly gossiped happily. The better she coached Rosa, she reasoned, the faster Rosa would be out of her life—and Tobal's.

Rosa felt a momentary pang of regret that, from Nelly's description of the play, there was only one part she could imagine herself playing—and that was the role Nelly seemed so sure would go to her sister.

And this is my little friend, Rosa Andújar. Nelly winked at her. Young as she is, she has spent a whole year acting in repertory in Córdoba, and she's just come to the big city to give up acting and find honest work.

The laugh of Soledad rippled upward in silver waves from deep inside her spectacular throat. She was a woman of luxurious proportions, and when she laughed, the entire milk-white top of her quivered, causing little lights to dance at her jeweled throat. It was considered a captivating experience, Soledad's laugh. *Querida*, she said to Rosa, no girl with eyes like yours can be thinking of giving up the stage.

I agree, Nervo murmured politely. Rosa offered a shy smile to the famous director and the famous wife to whom, according to Nelly, he was so flamboyantly unfaithful. If I could be, she replied, in a low passionate voice, if I even *thought* I could be a great actress like Señorita Soledad, or ever work with such a brilliant director as Señor Nervo, then indeed I would not dream of giving up.

Well said, replied Soledad, with the bubbles of musical laughter in her throat. You are familiar with my husband's work?

Oh, yes, Rosa breathed. The films, of course, and the plays, every one that has toured the provinces. *El Círculo* was my favorite—I see it in my dreams still. Although the play itself was nothing—the magic was all in the way Señor Nervo staged it.

Soledad glanced at her husband; an oblique look. The child is a charming liar, said the look; can you tell? But Nervo did not look amused; instead, Soledad concluded swiftly, he seemed quite taken. Whether by the lies, the charm, or the child herself, there was no telling. But in eleven years of marriage, Soledad had seen that particular look of his often enough not to be alarmed. Rosa Andújar was not especially attractive, except, she realized, for the intensity that shone out like a shameful secret from under the ingenue costume, the soft wispy curls and the feral little face. Like most *pobrecitas*—most poor little things—Soledad figured, with her usual astuteness, this one was, *al fundo*, a *matador*.

The actress shifted her gaze to Emilia Martinez, the ambitious

little minx whose sister had brought this child to the party—out of
malicious mischief or simple stupidity, one could not be sure. On
the one hand, Soledad was well aware that Nervo had been toying
with this Emilia. She also guessed that he had half-promised her
the role of Nona, without asking Soledad's opinion (probably because he knew what Soledad's opinion would be: Emilia was
clearly an adequate little actress, as well as much too pretty; therefore she couldn't possibly have the part). Now it suddenly occurred
to Soledad that this—Rosa Andújar, was it?—would make a fine
Nona, which would neatly solve the Emilia problem, with less
blood than usual. The only question was whether the fierce little
Rosa might present a more significant problem in the long run?
Soledad studied the girl through narrowed eyes, sifting her in-
stincts.

Rosa Andújar's sensitive antennae began to quiver; she adjusted
her smile a quarter-turn away from Nervo and toward his wife.
Señorita Soledad, she whispered shyly, I wanted to confess something to you.

I know, said Soledad. You are here because you have no inten-
tion of looking for a job outside the theatre.

To be honest, I am not sure, Rosa said boldly. But that was not
what I wanted to tell you.

Ah, well, go on.

Once I saw you in a *cine*, I think it was your first one, *La Fiesta
de Amor*. I promised myself that night that one day I would meet
you, and when I did, I would confess what I felt seeing you in that
cine.

You liked *La Fiesta?* Soledad's eyebrows lifted with disbelief.
The picture had been such a resounding failure that only her con-
nection with the producer (her first husband) had saved her career.

Well, it was my first *cine* too. I did not know enough to like it or
not like it. And now—she laughed a tiny, self-mocking laugh—I still
do not know enough. To me, any *cine*, any play, is still more real
than life. But shall I tell you what I felt that day? That is the confession.

The actress nodded. *Claro*, this child already knew her seductive
powers; Soledad approved.

I felt I had had a vision of the Madonna. I believed . . . you could hear prayers.

Soledad gently stirred her champagne cocktail with a slender finger, considering Rosa over the rim of the glass. And how old were you, she said, when you stopped believing in this fantasy?

Rosa lowered her eyes. *Válgame Dios,* she murmured, now that I meet you I realize that I have not stopped.

The actress reached out with the finger that had stirred her drink, and gently twined a lock of the girl's hair. I have a feeling, Rosa, that your true faith lies in one Rosa Andújar. She also hears your prayers, and listens well.

Sí, Rosa replied with a sweet little smile. But most of the time there is no answer.

Soledad laughed a soft silver peal. You must learn to project better; one day a powerful friend might be sitting in the balcony. Practice reciting the prayer in front of interesting company—such as tonight's. What do you pray for at this moment, for example? A good job—in a doctor's office? A shoe shop?

Rosa shook her head. You know.

Ah, well, then don't tell me. You are coming tomorrow to audition?

I am not sure. Rosa gave a helpless little shrug. Emilia said I could come with her. I know I could not hope for more than a silent part. But it is a wonderful play, so powerful. Even with a silent part, I would have a chance to watch you work. It must be the way my papa—he was an artisan—worked with a piece of precious stone. Carving a figure, as though it were hidden inside the stone, waiting for his touch. I imagine it is that way for you, shaping the unhappy teacher you play in this drama. I know it is a most difficult role, a person so unlike you—someone who is not beautiful, not graceful. I think if I could be there to see you carve such a figure, I could begin to see how much I must learn.

Oh, not *so* much, Rosa, said Soledad. You already know a great deal.

Rosa cast a long, adoring look at the older woman, and chose to ignore her mocking tone. I know, she stammered, that I would die for the chance to have you be my teacher.

Soledad smiled.

Both Rosa and Emilia read badly at the audition. Not that it mattered. A hundred girls had shown up at three o'clock to read for the handful of small parts. Forty more were turned away. The director, producer, associate producer, and stage manager sat clustered in the first three rows of the darkened theatre, determined to pass the next four hours as painlessly as possible, nodding and sipping terrible coffee from paper cups, trading mean jokes about the ages and weights, the knees, breasts, buttocks, and thighs, the lips and probable sexual skills of the miserable flock of hungry birds up there chirping and displaying their little feathers. No one but Amado Nervo was certain which girl was Rosa Andújar; the others knew only that a *chiquita* by that name was going to get the part of Nona, after this charade of an open audition had mercifully ended. Eight other girls would be selected for smaller parts, those with a few lines, those with none. Someone called Emilia Martinez would not be selected for any role in the production.

These decisions had all been reached earlier in the day, after a tense meeting in the office of the producer, Pancho Miguelete. The tension had begun when Pancho's wife stormed in brandishing a clipping from the morning paper; it was in the column of gossip, *Un Momentito*, an item linking Pancho's name with that of an aspiring starlet, one Emilia Martinez. According to the item, the girl was being cast in the coveted role of Nona, in Pancho's new play, *Las Angelitas*.

Dolores Miguelete was, among other things, heiress to a fortune of tin; it was her money that financed most of her husband's theatrical ventures. For this reason he had always been very circumspect about his more private enterprises; it was, in fact, a point of great pride with him that he had never broken off an affair with a member of the cast of any of his plays until after the play had returned its investment.

Hence, although it was highly unlikely that this scurrilous paragraph was true, there seemed no safe way to pacify Dolores Miguelete, or to dissuade her from telephoning her trustees to arrange for certain financial sources to become unavailable.

Ah, Dolores, Nervo had said, patting her arm. Can you not tell the item is a stupid lie? Pancho doesn't even know this lady, I swear it. *I* invited her to the party last night. I introduced her to the two of you. Would I *do* that if they—?

Of course you would, Dolores retorted. Why not? Anyway, I don't want to discuss it. I came here merely to say one thing; either this *puta* has no part in the play, or there is no play. *Claro?*

Soledad had been sitting quietly near the window, gazing at a group of ragged boys hustling tourists for coins. She seemed bored, holding her gold-tipped black cigaret quite still, allowing the ash to grow an inch or so before tapping it lightly into the crystal ashtray on her lap. She hated the taste of these cigarets, but she adored their color, and paid thirty dollars a carton to import them from a tobacconist in Montevideo who had them specially hand-rolled for her. She burned about three packs a day, considering the long curl of platinum smoke an essential part of her costume, like a jewel.

Of course she was not really bored, she was simply waiting for a lull in the festivities. At last she heard one, and turned her marvelous face toward them. Really, I don't understand why there is such a discussion over this. Nervo had never considered casting a ripe twenty-two-year-old slut in the part of Nona. The girl is supposed to be twelve, no? Flat-chested, skinny, plain—

'Stá verdad. That is right, Dolores, Nervo said. In fact there was a kid at the party last night who seemed just fine—ugly little thing, Rosa something—

Oh, Amado, Soledad said wearily, not *that* one.

Why not? Nervo retorted. She was lively, at least. Had a tense, unusual energy I liked.

Soledad rolled her eyes. I doubt if that child has ever been near a stage.

Nervo's famous hackles rose two notches. Even if that were true, he said evenly, I could make a spectacular Nona out of her, and you know it. But as a matter of fact, I made a small investigation this morning. He shrugged, to make it a thing of no consequence. You remember José Hirojosa in Córdoba? This . . . Rosa? said she had done some repertory work up there with him? And he said she was . . . a *maravilla*. That savagery leaps right at your throat from the stage—

Soledad gave a supremely bored shrug and turned back to the window, hiding her smile. She would bet the balance in Dolores Miguelete's checking account that Nervo had never talked to José Hirojosa. She would have doubled the bet that if he had, Hirojosa would have had no recollection of a young actress named Rosa Andújar. Soledad allowed herself a tiny satisfied sigh. Sometimes, she reflected, it was almost too easy to rearrange the furniture in a man's mind.

THE rehearsal of *Las Angelitas* had been stalled at this scene since yesterday morning. Nervo, in a state of cold fury (the state in which he functioned best), was wrestling with the will of that little Andújar girl, the one playing Nona. The trouble seemed to be that no matter what the director said, this child could not bring herself to dissolve into terrified tears. It was not that she had not been trying; in truth, with each attempt, her thin body heaved with violent, awkward sobs—as real as those of a child in a tantrum of rage. But there was not an ounce of fear in it; she seemed more likely to kill than surrender. And surrender was the point of the scene.

Nervo had explained it a hundred times; she simply could not—or would not—see it. The fight of a butterfly, Rosa, he would tell her calmly. You are the *mariposa*—caught in the other girl's net! Have you never seen a butterfly in the net, Rosa?

It was such a simple scene, really. The play's villain, a child called María, had ordered Nona to give up all her money—two dollars of hard-saved allowance. Nona did not owe María anything, and hated her besides. Still, the play called for Nona to scream, to cry and protest—and to give in. The scene was to show that María always won.

Queridas! Nervo had said to them all, the very first day. Nobody refuses María. She has the way of winning everything she wants. *Claro?*

But why? Rosa had demanded. I do not see *why.*

The director had stared at this skinny child for a full minute, and then had stalked off the stage.

But why? Rosa had whispered to another girl in the cast. Juanita had whispered back, Because the playwright says so. And because Señor Nervo says so.

Oh, Rosa had said. And the first time they rehearsed this scene, the only one in which she, Rosa, had to bow to the will of María, she had screamed like a *pescadora,* a fishwife, defying the other child as though she had a loaded pistol pointed straight at her heart. I will *not!* she would shriek. *I* will not.

Rosa! Nervo would shout at her. Sst, Rosa!

And she would be silenced, but her body would still tremble, as though in an echo of rebellious rage. Rosa, he would plead with her then, listen to me. Do you not understand? María is never shouted at that way! Not by anyone, least of all by you. Even the teachers are afraid of her, remember? And her own grandmother?

Sí, Señor. But—

Not—one—more—*but,* Nervo would shout finally, biting off each word as though it were a piece of her. Not—one—more—explanation.

She would stand there then, still as a little doll, saying *Sí, Señor,* I will try. And he would shake his head. Strange child, obedient as a lamb in every other scene. Sweet—and *Dios* knew, docile when she wanted to be. Especially backstage, whenever he beckoned to her. All he had to do then was point, or snap his fingers. Without a sound she knew what to do. A *maravilla.*

So her resistance in this scene was a kind of craziness. It mystified him, the way she fought him—all that wild energy. Electrifying, it was. Still, he had played the game with her too long. If she did not catch on today, he sighed to himself, he would have to get rid of her.

For the love of *Dios, querida,* he was shouting at her now, exhausted. The famous voice had a hoarse, almost ragged, edge. You are terrified, remember? You are not angry. You are not defiant. When you scream "I will not!" we all know well that you will.

We've been over that, have we not? Let us have it once more. And I mean that. *Once* more!

But—Rosa shook her head—*me siento* . . . I am sorry, Señor Nervo, but—

Querida, he said, reverting to icy calm. I will attempt to summarize for the last time. When this child yells "I will not!" it is merely a cry of pain, no? Nod your head, *querida.*

Rosa nodded her head.

She could just as well scream, "I want my mama!" No?

Rosa nodded again.

She knows she will do just as she is told. The rest of the cast knows it. The *audience* knows it. So—he drew a deep breath, letting the thunder pour back into his voice—why are *you* still fighting *me?*

The child bit her lip and made her way to the front of the stage. She peered blindly out into the darkness where he stood, fuming at her.

I want to do it right, Señor Nervo, she said, pleading. You must know. I have told you how much it means. But Nona, she is the poorest girl in the school. She has less than all the others—she says this. It's not like the other girl, Concha, who stole the bracelet. María can frighten that one with blackmail. I understand why Concha obeys. But Nona—she *must* fight for the little she has. She has no reason for fear.

Nervo groaned. *Jesucristo,* he muttered. You know why this play is the great hit of North America? Because it is true. In life it is the lie, the cheating, the meanness—it is the power that counts. You think power has something to do with reasons? By the way, Rosa Andújar. He looked up at her suddenly. His voice was very cold. You want to be in a play, *niñita.* How much do you want it? Enough . . . ? He glanced at his watch.

Rosa stared into the blackness until his words seemed to hang there, assuming the dark shapes of echoes. Her throat closed.

Soledad's laugh rang across the stage. Let me have two minutes with her, Amado. I think I can help.

Nervo exhaled loudly. *Por Dios!* All right. Everyone else, a break. Except . . . His eyes swept the stage and lighted on a plump little blonde in a tight middy blouse. Evalina! You come backstage with me a minute. I want to work on that . . . lisp of yours. It is coming out comic; we do not want comedy . . . distracting from the tension.

Soledad shot a quick glance at the bucktoothed Evalina, noting only the fourteen-year-old breasts under the schoolgirl uniform. Nothing serious, she concluded. Still, she too would have to do something about Evalina's lisp.

Rosa Andújar stood silent on the stage, her thin arms folded across her body as if to ward off blows. *Me siento,* Señorita Soledad, she said, not sounding at all sorry.

But— Soledad reached for the child's hands. Look at me, she commanded. What do you make of the bad girl in the play, of your enemy María?

Puf! Rosa said, making a face. She is *puerca.* A terrible creature. But no one can get away with such nastiness all the time. That is what makes me so angry—she is not real.

Well, said Soledad gently, why do you think the writer of the play allows her to get away with it?

I—I do not know. It is not explained. That is the trouble.

Oh, but it *is* explained, *querida.*

Rosa frowned. She . . . she finds out other people's secrets, you mean? Like the stolen bracelet?

Yes, that. And—?

Well, and then she threatens to tell, but that is—

That is only one of her tricks, said Soledad. It is not the main one. Not the one *you* need to understand if you are Nona.

Rosa gazed at the older woman, her small chin still raised in defiance. I do not know, she said.

Soledad reached out and smoothed Rosa's hair. Her hand lingered for a moment. María's main trick, she said slowly, is knowing that everyone has a guilty secret. Even if she has not found it out, everyone knows she can. María's power is their fear. That is all. It is all she needs.

Quía! How can that be? What should I be afraid of? What can she do to me—to Nona?

You are not listening to me. Soledad grasped the girl's shoulders and gave her a small hard shake. I tell you that doesn't matter. *All* that matters is the fear. And in life, everyone has it. Even I. Even you, *mi amiguita.* My little friend.

But—

Soledad smiled. This María, she said slowly, was born understanding that fear. She must never care if everyone hates her; she must know it has a use; it is part of her power. Ah, Rosa. My little waif. *Pobrecita!* How much do you want, Rosa? Enough to beg? On your knees? You do understand. It was not a question.

Rosa lowered her eyes. *Sí*, she murmured. *Basta*. Enough.

Nervo and Evalina had emerged from backstage; the director's face bore no expression. There was a sly smile at the corners of Evalina's mouth. Soledad did not miss it. All right, Nervo began shouting. Let us take it . . . from just before María twists Nona's arm. Ready, Rosa? Soledad gave her a little push. You are ready, she whispered.

Rosa walked quickly to her place. Ready, she said.

Go upstairs, María commanded in a cold little voice. And bring me all your money.

Rosa backed away slowly. She seemed almost to fold into herself, as if she had suddenly grown smaller. Her eyes darted back and forth; her whole body seemed to wince. I will not, she cried, a thin, piteous wail. Real tears seemed about to spill inside her spiraling voice. I will *not*, I will *not*.

Nervo's mouth dropped open; it was perfect.

María! he shouted. Grab her arm—twist it hard. *Bueno!*

Rosa gasped; a small piercing squeak—mouselike—burst from her throat. Where are you, Evalina? Nervo yelled. The little blonde rushed forward and grasped María's arm, trying to loosen her grip on Rosa.

Hit her, María! Nervo yelled. Hard! No, the other hand—hold on to Rosa! *'Stá bueno!* Back off, Evalina—*bueno*, touch your face, there! You have her, María, hold on—

Dígame—say when you have had enough, María said with an icy calmness.

Rosa stopped struggling. *Basta*, she murmured. Enough. Her voice was filled with a new emotion, a kind of awe that seemed to have nothing to do with the twisted arm, or the slapped face of her friend. *Basta*, she repeated. I will do . . . whatever you want.

Beautiful! Nervo shouted, applauding. María, show us your victory—just a little smile, so, just a little nod of the head, this way, *bueno!*

Rosa, rubbing her arm, slowly crossed the stage. Her face seemed lit with a strange glow, like that of certain religious pictures.

Curtain! Nervo cried. *Brava!* He was on his feet, still applauding, racing up the steps onto the stage and into the wings. Soledad! he shouted. Where is my genius wife? *Querida!* Darling! What *maravilla* did you do with that impossible child?

Soledad laughed, extricating herself from his arms, lighting one of her black cigarets, shrugging. One had only to assure her that she was born to be María.

And?

Nothing more. Soledad inhaled deeply, looking bored. One must let her discover the rest for herself, no?

Nervo waited for her to go on. Soledad exhaled and crushed out the cigaret.

Discover what? he demanded.

He? Whatever she needs to fulfill her *destino!* Soledad laughed lightly, touched her husband's face with the back of her hand. Dear Amado, she said kindly. What does a María need to know? Only how it must feel to get in María's way. No?

Nervo stared at her curiously. So, he sighed, you are in love with her too.

But of course, *querido. Claro que sí.*

The morning after the play opened—to wonderful notices in all the newspapers—Soledad invited Rosa out to luncheon in a fancy restaurant with fresh yellow flowers on the tables and waiters who talked in whispers, as if they were embarrassed to discuss such expensive food aloud. Soledad waved the menu away and ordered a delicate white fish, and wine to match. Rosa could hardly speak, but Soledad seemed not to notice, so it was all right. The restaurant was filled with people who recognized the great actress: some nodded across the room to her and blew kisses from where they sat; others rose and bowed with slight flourishes; a few came over to the table just to kiss the air next to her cheeks, murmuring *querida,*

querida, querida. This delightful child, Soledad would say to this one and that, is Rosa Andújar. She is Amado's great find, you must come and see her in the play. Rosa blushed and lowered her eyes; the kissing friends murmured kindnesses; Soledad whispered in their ears and they looked at Rosa again and nodded, smiling. Rosa said nothing, but went on eating the delicate white fish and the little salad of pale green leaves. Soledad motioned to the waiter, calling him *mi hijo,* even though he was not nearly young enough to be her son.

After the luncheon Soledad insisted that they go shopping. You must have two new dresses, she said, with an imperious frown at Rosa's white ruffled blouse and shiny black skirt. You look—well, she said, shrugging, we will fix it.

Just outside the restaurant she took hold of Rosa's shoulders and spun her around in a circle, like a toy. With one long finger she tilted Rosa's chin, gazing at her with narrow thoughtful eyes. Dark blue, she said at last. And very . . . She glanced down at Rosa's long, slender waist. Very close-fitting. But never mind, we will find something. She linked her arm through Rosa's and propelled her toward a shop with glossy black awnings, like hooded eyes over its windows. Oh, no, Rosa cried, not there! I have heard—it is much too—I cannot—

Nonsense, said Soledad with a brief burst of musical laughter that caused people in the street to turn and stare. When they saw her they went on staring, marveling at the way she walked. It was not that she moved like an actress or a mannequin, not swinging the hips so, in deliberate curving arcs. She moved with a boldness, a precision, as though nothing in the path ahead could surprise her, or make her pause to measure the risk. Rosa longed to walk that way, holding her small head high, with such careless bravery. She would have given anything to have such a crown of bright hair rising and descending with her movements as she floated through the crowd. Rosa hung back a little to study Soledad's walk, one foot always set so, precisely before the other, like the spring of a cat; it might have been a dance step performed to the song of her laughter. Even from behind one could guess there was a tiny smile on her face, the sort of smile that was not for anyone but herself.

What are you thinking, *amiguita?* Soledad said, turning suddenly.

I was admiring— Rosa stammered. I—

Me?

Well, how you walk. You walk as though your papa's servants had just set the stones in the street.

The laugh emerged, low and secret now, like the simmering of water on a blue fire. The arm that linked her to Rosa exerted a quick light pressure, like a hug. Rosa blushed. I admire your blush, said Soledad. You must teach me how you do that.

In the fitting room at the dress shop, Soledad sat smoking her peculiar cigarets in the wasteful way that she did, heaping the long ends in a crystal ashtray. Crossing and uncrossing her endless legs in their dark silk stockings. Oh, not that one, she would snap wearily. *Por Dios,* take it off, *querida,* it is dreadful. She would sigh and shrug at the frantic sales clerk, waving her off with a flick of white fingers. Have you nothing simple, nothing pure? This child must be very pure—can't you see? She touched Rosa's waist lightly. The line here, just this, is perfection. Rosa held her breath. The clerk whirled away, all frightened nods and curtsies, backing out of the fitting room. *Sí, Señora.* Soledad's cool fingers remained where they were on Rosa's skin. Perfection, she repeated, drawing out the word.

Señorita Soledad, Rosa murmured, feeling two spots of high color rising in her cheeks. Soledad's other hand reached up and touched them. The salesgirl edged back into the room, arms heaped again with dresses. Soledad waved her cigaret toward the pile already discarded.

Never mind, she said, we will take the violet one, there. And the little green one, there, yes. She glanced quickly at Rosa's feet, and kicked off one of her own shoes, a cobweb of delicate black strips, set high on a heel shaped like a weapon. Try that, she commanded. Rosa slipped it on her naked foot.

Perfect?

Rosa nodded.

Good. We will buy shoes next time. Not now or I will have a terrible headache. So we will go to my apartment and try on shoes. *Bueno?* She did not pause for a reply. Have the dresses sent to me.

No, wait. She will wear the violet one now. And bring her some proper underthings. She made a disapproving face at Rosa's *camisa* and panties. Like this. She raised her pleated hem to expose a flash of peach-colored silk and handmade beige lace. The girl nodded. At once, Soledad snapped. Can you not see that the child is exhausted? She has a performance tonight.

Will this do, Señora? Soledad took the handful of pale silk, shook it free of its delicate tissue wrapping, held it out to Rosa. Put it on.

Rosa's blush now covered her throat like a pink veil. She stood frozen for a moment; the salesgirl waited, poised for flight. Soledad lit another cigaret. Well?

Rosa removed her slip and cotton panties, her eyes carefully avoiding the mirror. Soledad seemed amused; her wonderful eyes swept Rosa's body briefly, from her throat to her feet. Her lips parted; a thin curl of cigaret smoke floated between them like a message in a foreign tongue. Rosa took the handful of silk, with the little white tag that declared its worth to be more than she would earn for three weeks' work in *Las Angelitas*. She slid the silk up over her legs and into place, shivering at the way it felt, like the soft caress of a woman's hand. She gazed first at her reflection in the glass, then at Soledad's eyes, watching her. Finally she pulled the narrow straps into place on her shoulders. The silk clung to her in a way that made her want to cover herself, as though she were more naked than before. Will that be all, Señora Nervo? the salesgirl asked in a timid voice.

Sí, Soledad murmured, without taking her eyes from Rosa. Wrap the green dress and send it. Oh, and remove those tags. The girl's small gold scissors flashed, and she was gone.

It is very beautiful, Rosa whispered. Thank you.

You are very beautiful, said Soledad, crushing out the new cigaret.

It was not true, of course. But that was of no importance. That Soledad had a need to say this—whether or not even she believed it —gave them each a certain power, and a certain expectation. Rosa could not have guessed how she knew this.

So, are we ready? Soledad asked, touching her.

Rosa covered Soledad's hand with her own, but in the mirror

where Soledad studied their reflections, Rosa's eyes darted like small birds. Soledad whispered, Look at us; Rosa smiled instead.

IT was predictable that Soledad would demand more obedience from Rosa, and closer attention, than Nervo had. After all, Nervo was now nothing more than her director. He had had to stop sleeping with everyone in the cast once Dolores Miguelete had taken a propretary interest in him. Dolores' jealousy was notorious. The only escapades that ever seemed beyond her control were those of her husband, and even those, it was generally assumed, got that way because she preferred them to.

In any case, Nervo had abruptly stopped summoning the little girls backstage. And for a while Soledad commanded Rosa's full attention. It was not at all clear how Soledad really felt about this latest protégée; most of her friends assumed it was just another of Soledad's little things. A woman of such passionate vitality, such juice, had to have a great many little things in the course of a play's run. Otherwise she grew bored, and it showed in her performance. If Rosa was anything special, no one close to Soledad sensed it.

Of course there was that ravenous hunger in the child's face; Soledad clearly loved feeding that sort of need. She had a fine slender body too, with long bones so delicate they hardly seemed capable of supporting her. Soledad had always been an *aficionada* of delicate young flesh. Now in her forties, she had a positive craving for it. In Soledad's case, it was not innocence that she sought; it was only and purely the feel of the flesh. That famous tongue of hers would linger over the crook of an arm, the delicate curving ridge of an ear; she liked to travel erotic routes that the girl herself had never before discovered. It was whispered in certain quarters that when Soledad and a young female lover lay joined in a circle, with Soledad's own lush body arched and echoing silent cries of pleasure, she would hold her lips lightly against the silken warmth of the delicate child's open body and murmur gently inside her, Sweet, oh, sweet. The tenderness of that interior skin was known to be the only sensation Soledad considered exquisite. And Soledad was a woman of exquisite taste.

The Nervos' white living room had a hidden movie screen behind the wonderful portrait of Soledad that was painted by a famous French artist. Rosa loved the portrait; it showed Soledad in a high-collared black dress with ruffles, very tight fitting with little buttons all up the front, so that she looked like a lady of the last century. She even had on a little straw hat with flowers, and her tiny hand, with a white kid glove tight as skin, held the carved handle of a black parasol. The picture showed her standing on a little yellow bridge, and she was wearing a sweet pale smile. Everything around her had a kind of green-gold color, which Soledad said was the color of the light in Paris. Some day I will see if that is true, Rosa promised herself. And an artist will paint my picture so, standing on that little bridge with the shape of a rainbow.

At night when the Nervos had guests, Soledad's portrait would rise at the touch of a button, disappearing into a hole in the ceiling, and then the huge movie screen would come down so they could watch any picture in the world they wanted. The machine to show the movie came up out of a door in the floor. All of it seemed to Rosa magical, more magical even than the movies themselves had ever been at the Olimpia Theatre in Montaraz, when she and Lola and Catuja had sat staring at the actresses' shining gowns and jewels, at the men's black dinner clothes and white pianos, the mirrors and the soft couches, and most of all, at the pale hair and dark glistening mouths of the beautiful ladies who were all La Lloradora come to life.

The first movie Rosa watched in the white room with Soledad

was the story of a poor Spanish girl who worked in a *factoría*. She was so beautiful that a rich old *militar* fell in love with her and gave her shawls and veils, gold pieces and hats with great brims like waves that dipped in the center so that only one eye showed, and shadows played on her white skin as though it were a game of hiding. In the picture the old *militar* gave the young *estrella* all these things even though she was very cold to him and teased him terribly. What do you think? Soledad whispered when the film was nearly over, and the old *militar* had almost died in a duel so that his *querida* could leave him for a dashing younger man, and then the girl tricked everyone by deciding to stay with the old one after all. Oh, said Rosa excitedly, I love the black dress, and the white lace one too. And oh, the way she pasted that little curl so, in the center of her forehead, in the shape of an S. Like this—look, have I done it? But—she paused, frowning—I don't know why he loved her so, she was very silly really, shaking her shoulders all the time like tambourines. And why did she go on making him think she didn't love him, when she did?

Ah, said Soledad, laughing her laugh that was a descending octave. You are the very silly one. Why do you never notice what is important? Could you not see that the director was the one in love with her? He was telling his own story! Just the way he photographed her—the way he lit her face! Soledad clasped her long hands and threw her head back, sighing. How marvelous he made her look! Believe me, she never looked so marvelous; I saw that actress once, she was a cow, her brows and lashes so pale and eyes so light they expressed nothing. This man made love to her with his camera. *Por Dios!* Even the actor—the old *militar*—the director made that man look like himself. Even to the shape of the moustache, the sorrow of the eyes.

Well, then, Rosa said thoughtfully, it is a wonderful story. But did the director really risk his life for that *estrella?* And did she choose him? Did they stay together always?

Soledad leaned across the white sofa and kissed her. Rosa's lips parted, and Soledad's tongue traced a delicate circle inside. Of course not, my darling, she said. If she had loved him so, if they had stayed together always, why ever would he have had to make such a silly movie?

NINE British officers of the new steel *factoría* had assembled inside their executive board room. The square gleaming table was set with nine fresh pads of crisp yellow paper; with chairs of soft dark plush and with men in fine suits, trying not to sweat.

Five minutes after the meeting began, there was an explosion of thunder beneath their window. What is that? said the chairman of the board. The strikers, whispered the secretary. They say the *policía* attacked—

Two immense carts filled with garbage crashed against the bolted gate of the *factoría*. Then two more. My God, whispered the chairman, without a glance toward the window.

There was a scraping of chairs, a rolling of pencils. It was said that the men in fine suits then rolled their sleeves and grunted like laborers, like low *trabajadores*, as they pushed their great conference table against the door for protection.

What now? whispered the head of production; his deep voice had the tone of a frightened old woman.

A message! cried the manager of advertising. A message of urgency to the President—

The director of accounts licked his dry lips. We sent it yesterday, he said. No reply.

The Ambassador, then? Sir Neville—

Sir Neville . . . has left town, sir. No one seems to know—

Left? The Ambassador?

The chairman of the board took off his coat. In that case, gentlemen—I think we had better move the chairs, too. . . .

A small group of union marchers had clotted together, gatherings of two men or three, exchanging glances and fierce whispers. Suddenly one of these clots had broken out of the silent line and gathered around a fine black foreign car parked outside a restaurant. The men had begun to rock the car back and forth, crying Death to Foreigners; five or six others had left the line of march to join them; in seconds the fine black car lay upside down like a monstrous shiny corpse. The pace of the marchers had quickened then—as though the men had found a mission beyond grief.

The marchers filed past the old market, past the tracks of the British-owned Ferrocarril del Sud, past the wide *avenidas* that led to the Plazas Victoria and Constitución, tree-shaded streets with their splendid buildings designed in Second Empire style, elegant façades of apartment houses in which the rich sat complaining of the heat, of the high price of imported butter, of the makers of trouble in the street.

It was clear now how the march would go; the next block would yield another symbol to be destroyed, and another. Automobiles and buses, streetcars and shops, a church, a convent, a railroad station.

It took the San Luis *policía* less than fifteen minutes to catch up with the demonstrators at the Plaza de Once Febrero. By then enough damage had been done to warrant an order to fire at will; at least that was the view expressed later by the *Comisionado*. In any case the guns of the *policía* made the brief official response to a wanton destruction of property.

Two blocks away, in the Plaza de la Constitución, Congress was in session. The luncheon recess had ended, and deputies who had dined at their clubs and favorite restaurants in the neighborhood had walked back to the Chamber in a state of near-panic. Have you seen—? Did you hear—? they called to each other in whispers, heads shaking in disbelief. Everyone had seen; everyone had heard. Most had walked several blocks in the fierce heat—past the burned-out hulks of cars, their feet crunching on shards of window-glass that littered the pavement.

Within an hour the many angers that smoldered in San Luis had burst into flame, as though a master arsonist had set a single match to a thousand heaps of oil-soaked rags. A mob gathered at a bus station, overturning buses and setting them ablaze. Vandals broke into a sporting-goods store and carried off rifles, shotguns, boxes of ammunition. Looters scurried through the shopping district with armloads of radios, mattresses, crates of tinned food. Armed rioters were scuffling on the Calle Florida—over a pair of stolen boots, a bottle of whiskey.

But what is to be done? What if—? In the Chamber of Deputies no one dared finish a sentence. Deputies began shouting at each other; a lapel was seized, a fist was raised. One said the President should call out the troops. Another demanded mass arrests, a curfew, armed patrols. The deputy from Cortena pleaded for a meeting with the union leaders. The deputy from Corrientes wanted to declare a state of siege. In angry confusion, the deputies from Corrientes and Cortena threw their pens at each other; the deputy from Pavon hurled his notebook and had to be restrained. It was said later that obscenities and shocking insults flew through the chamber; these were later deleted from the *Diario de Sesiones*.

A messenger arrived to report that the Vice President and several other government officials had gone on sudden holiday. Government offices were closing for the day—and would remain shut until it was safe to reopen. Alarm spread in official San Luis like the fires in the streets.

In the chamber, someone in a uniform had begun to speak. At first no one could see who it was. *A mob,* said the voice, in a commanding tone. *A mob, gentlemen—*

Who is that? whispered the deputy from Pavon.

Looks like Montero, said the deputy from Corrientes, releasing the coat collar of the deputy from Cortena.

Montero? What is *he* doing here?

The President just gave him the Labor Ministry—

Promised him, said the deputy from Pavon. Didn't give—yet.

I hear, the deputy from Corrientes put in, that he is pimping for Brigadier General R—

The deputy from Cortena snickered. Well, at least he isn't sweating, like you.

Tst, said the deputy from Pavon.

—A mob, gentlemen, Montero was saying, *will not be ruled by a mob. It can be reached—these workers can be reached—but only if we move with precision, with control. . . .*

Where does Montero stand on labor? whispered the deputy from Cortena. The deputy from Pavon shrugged. He stands where he can see the shadows move.

Control . . . like the well-disciplined militares *we are.* Montero glanced around the chamber with an ironic smile. The disheveled deputies began a straightening of collars, a mopping of brows.

Montero stood at attention in the rear of the chamber, his spotless white uniform gleaming at them like a reproach. The polished brass buttons marched smartly across his chest; even the part in his thick black hair seemed to be following orders. *It is no trick to restore order!* he was saying. *But can we not promise them justice? Can we not understand?*

Jesucristo! said the deputy from Corrientes. The man is insane. We should have five army units rolling in the street right now. Has anyone talked to the President?

Seated on the wine velvet banquette at the round table nearest the window, las Señoras S and R and Doña Margarita Delgado, the distinguished ladies of the distinguished *Sociedad de la Benevolencia*, waited for their friend Dorothy Milgrim, wife of the American Ambassador. She arrived, flustered and charming, blowing kisses and apologies. . . . Disgustingly late, but I tell you my car simply could not move through the street. Have you seen what is happening out there?

Por Dios, I wish I had not, said Doña Margarita with a fervent little sniff. Señora S shuddered. More and more impossible, said Señora R, glancing at the menu. Did you see the white Rolls-Royce they attacked across the Plaza? Such a beautiful car, whispered Dorothy Milgrim, I wonder whose.

Señora S snapped her fingers; a waiter hurried over and bowed as if nothing at all were unusual. I hate to ask, Luis, it must be chaos in the kitchen this afternoon—Señora S's voice dropped to a conspirator's whisper—but I have a sinful craving for oysters. . . .

Truite fumée for me, said Señora R crisply, craning her neck to see who had just arrived in a flutter of lilac chiffon. Some actress, no doubt. And then maybe the bass, she said. No, the *contrefilet*.

Isn't it wonderful? Mrs. Milgrim chirped. Everyone's so brave to come out for luncheon. Considering—

Me siento mucho, Señora, said Luis. But the oysters, unfortunately— His shoulders rose a quarter-inch, indicating despair.

Hm? Oh, never mind then. I'll try the *truite*. If you are sure it's fresh.

Gracias a Dios that this place is able to maintain some order, said Doña Margarita. But I will have only the lobster. And some fruit. I cannot bear to eat in this weather.

Señora S nodded. Nervous stomach, with all these disturbances—
Have you heard about the *militares?* asked Mrs. Milgrim.

No, what now?

Plots, said Señora R, gazing into her compact mirror, touching the corners of her lips with the point of a curved scarlet nail. Boring plots. Colonel this and General that.

One hears nothing but the vilest rumors, sighed Doña Margarita.
Señora R laughed. As though it made the slightest difference which of them was in charge of robbing us with the taxes.

And which, Señora R said, of clearing the ruffians off the streets.

Mrs. Milgrim sipped her ice water and held her tongue. Tony had advised her to be careful at moments like this—after the last time.

Sst, said Doña Margarita with a frown. We ought not to talk about the government's troubles. But you remind me of something, what was it? Oh, yes—did anyone see what the President's wife wore to the opera Thursday?

Not those yellow ruffles of hers, I hope, said Mrs. Milgrim, making a face.

Señora R snapped her compact shut and sighed a bored little sigh. When will she learn how to put herself together, do you suppose?

Never mind her dress, said Doña Margarita, gesturing. It was the necklace that I noticed.

You and all the world, said Señora R. Diamonds the color of last night's coffee; I never saw such stones.

Where do you suppose the money came from this time? murmured Señora S.

Well, not from the orphanage fund, said Doña Margarita, smoothing her hair.

No, *querida*, said Señora R. They say that disappeared into their *casa de campo*. In *La Opinión* I read that la Señora Alvear had crimson damask put on the bedroom walls.

Grotesque, sighed Señora S, with satisfaction. Like the walls of a brothel!

Porqué no? said Señora S. Everyone laughed.

Mm, your lobster looks delicious, Margarita, said Mrs. Milgrim. What's everyone doing about the theatre?

Too dangerous in that neighborhood, said Doña Margarita, chewing delicately.

Can you imagine—and we had tickets—

Well, but even in the Calle Posado, where the Jews—

Oh, I heard—practically next door to you—

Some ruffians in the middle of the night—

Por Dios, what did you do?

We—? Señora R shrugged. *Querida*, we had the servants put up the chain on the outside door. What on earth else?

Well, in our building, thank heaven, there are none.

No? What about José Dreyfus?

Oh, *they* are not—

But of course they are, *querida*. His father—

Well, but he married—

Doña Margarita laughed. Well, but they all married! Try telling that to the Liga Patriótica!

Señora R patted her chin with the corner of her pink napkin and and glanced at her watch. Do you think it is safe to shop this afternoon? I need—

If I were you I would wait till I got to Paris. You and Alberto are sailing—?

Well, I am not venturing outside for anything—straight into the car and straight home. Can I drop anyone?

A sudden explosion, like a clap of thunder, stopped them for a moment. Eyes darted to the window, then quickly shifted back; one could hear the drawing of breath.

Mrs. Milgrim shifted in her seat. Thank God the doorman here is armed. Did you notice—?

I too, said Doña Margarita, patting her alligator purse. Enrique bought me a little pistol yesterday. Mother-of-pearl.

Señora R laughed. Well, let us hope it is all over by the next time we have luncheon.

Amen, said Mrs. Milgrim.

SOLEDAD stared at Rosa with a look of ice. I am never treated this way, she said, not even by men.

Rosa looked contrite. But I did not—

No importa, snapped Soledad. It does not matter. Only do not imagine that you can lie to me too, after all the rest.

I never lie, Rosa whispered. You know I do not! Oh, please, there is nothing between Amado and me, I swear it. She reached out to touch Soledad's shoulder, to embrace her, so that Soledad would feel her trembling. How could you imagine—?

Stop, said Soledad shortly, and turned her wonderful face away. It was not possible to allow Rosa to see her cry. Not that she hated to show emotion; it was only that she had studied herself in mirrors, weeping, and she did not like the look of her eyes, the Chinese way they narrowed. After a moment she spoke in a low voice; the words came slowly, with effort, as though through cloth. Rosa thought she recognized the tone from one of Soledad's scenes in *Las Angelitas*. It was very moving.

Listen to me, little idiot. It is not that I care what you permit some *bufón* like my husband to do with your body. I care only what people say about you. Perhaps that is a fault in me, a selfishness. The perfect shoulders gave an eloquent shrug, a resignation. Perhaps you think I care only because your reputation involves mine. That it is for my sake I suffer over such vile gossip. As if I deserved it. *Dios,* how you have used me.

Oh, Soledad—

Never interrupt me, it makes me crazy. I have only a little more to say, then you can protest all you like. I am not such a faithful person myself. You may say that; possibly you are right. Another shrug. *No importa.*

Soledad, please let me—

Soledad's hand fluttered like a white handkerchief. She sighed. If we part over this, and we may, she said, I leave you with only one more gift—and that is my wisdom. Never permit more than one lover to be known. And be certain the one who is known is the one you want known. Otherwise, *querida,* you will end up on the streets of San Luis, like all the other little girls of *Las Angelitas*—all those *estrellitas* who disappear behind the stage!

But—

Did I say not to interrupt! I will explain, though you don't deserve it. You already know too much for a nervous hungry girl. Sometimes it is good to be talked about. Sometimes even the false rumor can be useful. But one must be more careful. A rumored lover is very dangerous. Let us say for the sake of argument that my poor Amado is a rumored lover. You have done nothing. Yet you risk everything. You risk losing my friendship, yes? Another time perhaps a rumored lover may be just what you need. Someone powerful whose friends—whose enemies, perhaps—would be interested in your affair. This can be useful. Of course I would not know about such things. Well. Soledad sighed deeply, turned, and presented her famous profile. Her eyes, however, fixed on her own reflection in the mirror behind Rosa's head. I am finished now. If you have anything to say.

I have, Rosa murmured, two questions. The first—is whether you are telling me that it is over between us.

I don't know yet. What is the other question?

Well, I don't see how one can permit a rumor that one has a famous Señor So-and-so for a lover. If in truth one does not.

Soledad turned and smiled a wicked smile. *Querida,* she said, tracing the delicate line of Rosa's jaw with one scarlet-tipped finger. If the rumor was that *you* loved him, why on earth would any famous So-and-so deny it?

Rosa began to giggle, then bit her lip. Soledad moved closer, still pouting, but with a playful tilt of the head. Why don't you kiss me now, she said, while I decide whether it is the last time.

That night Soledad introduced Rosa to the shipping magnate Elias Rubén Caso, who, it was said, planned to produce an extravagant musical film next year, with a projected budget of five million gold pesos. Rubén Caso had shot his wife to death six weeks before. He had explained to the police that it happened while they were sleeping peacefully in their bed. He had had a terrible nightmare in which his wife, in that very bed, was fornicating with another shipping magnate, an English one. Rubén Caso wept while he told his dream. In his sleep, he said, he had taken the small pistol out of his nightstand drawer and performed a husband's duty. Out of respect for the honor of his family and his country. No charges were pressed.

This is the child Rosa, said Soledad sweetly. Rubén Caso peered at Soledad's white bosom; his expression did not change. I have told you, Soledad went on, linking her arm through his, that she wants to appear in my next film. It will be amusing to help her, no?

Rubén Caso's heavy eyelids fluttered slightly, as if with some effort. He stared at Rosa, allowing his eyes to remove her charming green taffeta dress, the necklace of little black hearts, and the vulgar silver shoes. She stood before him in her sheer black stockings; he imagined her nipples red and erect. Why would it be amusing? he asked Soledad.

Well, my darling, because of all the amusing people who find her interesting.

He sneered. Who, for example?

Oh, this one and that; you know. Soledad's eyes flickered restlessly around the room; her foot tapped, indicating displeasure; this conversation was taking too long.

Let me think, said Rubén Caso, ignoring her warning signs. Jorge Oleas, the fat *cochon* from Radio del Estado? Amado Nervo of stage and screen, taking time out between boys of the chorus? And possibly . . . he yawned . . . possibly the beautiful Soledad herself, no?

Soledad shrugged. Amusing, she said. You are always so. She turned one gleaming shoulder toward him and began to move off. In any case, let me know when you want to see the child for her screen test. Rubén Caso laughed. You are promising that Amado will direct *Amor, Amor*. Why did you not say so?

If you like. She hesitated, without turning back.

And you will play the role of Martina, at something less than your usual outrageous fee?

She turned now, took out a black cigaret and held it toward him while he fumbled for a match. I will play Martina as agreed—for my usual fee. Which has gone up only thirty percent since the last film you produced.

Soledad, said Rubén Caso with a loud laugh. You must still think I am crazy.

She blew a gentle stream of smoke toward him, then waved at it, making no serious attempt to dispel it. Chulo, my darling, I stopped thinking you were crazy the first time you married a shipowner's daughter, when you were in love with me. Would Thursday at eleven thirty be convenient?

His lips parted to speak; she leaned over and kissed him, breathing the rest of her puff of smoke into his mouth. He coughed. Make it eleven forty-five. His massive arms went around her and held on for exactly three seconds longer than she would have permitted.

THE feet of Elias Rubén Caso, in pointed shoes of black-dyed lizard skins, were set so upon his great empty desk, like ornaments. He kept them crossed at the ankle, so that a visitor could see and admire precisely four inches of sheer black silk hose with a discreet pattern of scarlet diamonds. So, he said, peering up at Rosa from under those puffed eyes of a frog, the lids of which seemed far too heavy to go up and down by themselves. The cinema awaits yet another *estrellita*. He?

She nodded, feeling the two familiar spots of color in her face, as though a warm finger pressed there, and there, upon each cheekbone. Soledad says you are a natural talent, he went on; she does not say at what. Señor Rubén Caso's eyes were trained like guns on a point midway between her throat and her breasts. She remembered now that he was called Chulo—Rascal—by his friends. She shifted in the chair; it was of smooth black leather, very soft, so that any movement caused a warm, and not unpleasant, sensation upon the backs of one's legs. A natural talent, he said again. I am sure we will discover it in no time. He smiled.

One had heard of course that Chulo Rubén Caso was one of those who maintained a small private studio in which certain well-known actresses had got their start in his pictures. It was good that, at Soledad's request, Rosa's screen test was to be held here in a real studio; still, it was odd that in two days Soledad had not answered her telephone calls. Her eyes roamed warily around the producer's huge office, all lustrous black and luminous white like the jealous husband's suite on a luxury ocean liner, in a movie about love and dishonor. The husband, played by Chulo, would be one of those who killed both the wife and the other man, and got away with it in the end because the lovers had, in fact, sinned. Tell me, the producer was saying, in a voice of oil, as he uncrossed his ankles and recrossed them the other way. What do you think we should have you do first?

I suppose, she answered shyly, you will want me to read from the script? I have brought it—

What a splendid idea, he said. I shall do just that. Exactly. He cleared his throat then, as one clears the palate between the fish and the meat at a fine dinner. First, however—

Ah, she said. First. Her smile curved, not unsweetly, and she made a demure motion with both hands, as though to close a button that was already closed.

He shook his head.

No . . . ? She looked at him without expression.

Niñita, he said, swinging his feet off the desk and rising; he sounded hurt. We had thought only that first we would ask you to perform another sort of scene . . . a brief one. He made a dismissive gesture. Ten minutes. Fifteen.

A scene, she said.

A love scene. Love. Scene.

With clothes off, she said, without expression, in the way of one who has memorized the words.

Of course not, *querida.* What did you think! You will wear a pretty costume. He laughed then, and touched her shoulder with the back of his hand; he slid the hand slowly across her chest. The hand was warm and moist; she did not pull away.

Well then, he whispered. If you are ready?

She said nothing; he picked up the receiver of his white telephone. Has Señorita Soledad's party arrived? We'll meet them in Studio C. *Bueno.*

Soledad? Rosa stared at him, bewildered.

Hm? he said. Oh. I forgot; here is the costume. Soledad had it sent this morning. He slid open a drawer of the sleek desk and removed a slender package of lavender tissue; he shook it so that a handful of sheer silk, the color of cream, poured from it into Rosa's lap. The *camisa* was familiar; her first gift of intimacy from Soledad.

Problema? he said.

She shook her head, no.

He raised an eyebrow. You are sure.

She hesitated then. *She* wants me to—?

Nothing you haven't done many times. A scene and a costume, you know by heart; *she* assured me.

No, Rosa said then, and her voice came out in a whispered squeak, like that of the mouse in the trap.

He glanced at the watch on his wrist, scowling. *Querida mía,* he said, one has very little time in this business.

I will take up no more of it then, she said, lifting her chin.

He laughed. Don't be silly, you are not a fool, or a child. You have been in this city how long? Two years? Three? Soledad is your *amiga*—she wants to help you! You have worked as a waitress at the Café Tortuga? And elsewhere?

Some . . . radio work. Rosa thought quickly, but her voice was not steady.

Sí. Some . . . radio work. He smiled. Well. He sighed. I am not here to persuade a hungry girl with no breasts that she wishes to be a movie star. I only agreed to do a small favor for Soledad. He reached across her, resting a hand on her thigh, and held a finger over the black button on his white telephone. I imagine you know how angry Soledad gets when one . . . disappoints? Shall I press this, or do you want another five seconds to think about it?

No. Wait. I only . . . it is only that I do not understand. Why *she* would want—

Why not? he said, pleasantly. If I were in her place, I know I would. He sighed then. *Es lástima.* Pity. Well—

I—what will you do with this film? Photographs of me with—her? Wearing this? Doing—?

He shrugged. I? It goes straight into Soledad's vault. And no copies. He held up his hands in the way of a magician, to show his sleeves are innocent.

If. If I do this, she said, I will have a featured role in *Amor, Amor?* Seventy-five a week . . . ?

He nodded, the heavy lids dropping over his eyes. One might have expected them to make a sound as they fell. His fingers drummed lightly on the telephone. My photograph, she said, on the billboards? My picture alone—not even hers?

But of course! he said. Yours alone. Soledad *insists* on it. I told her this was a craziness, but— He spread his fingers now in an elaborate helpless gesture. Who am I to question a lady in love.

Rosa stared at his hands; he wore two platinum rings, each with a pale star sapphire, on his little fingers. She gazed at the milky stones, then at Chulo Rubén Caso's blue eyes under the thick brows. The rings were a perfect match.

She drew in her breath and smiled at him then, with a toss of her head. He admired the gesture; the *puta* was much too skinny for his taste, but she had spirit. He touched her hair; a proprietor's touch. Charming, he said. *Puede ser*—it may be a shade too dark. We will fix it.

LAS ANGELITAS had run nearly two years, a record for a straight drama in Pradera, and especially noteworthy for a play imported from North America. Even so, Miguelete, the producer, had not wanted to risk mounting a new production to tour Mexico and Argentina. His wife Dolores was tired; she wanted to take another trip to Europe; she needed some new clothes. Then perhaps if he wanted to make a new *cine* she might let him do that—if her new lover Amado Nervo directed it. She knew that would be all right with Soledad, as long as there was a wonderful part in it for her.

As for Rosa Andújar, Dolores had no worry about her any more. Nervo seemed to have no interest in her, and Pancho was still busy chasing a boy of the chorus from his last musical comedy.

Rosa's performance as Nona had been described by the critics as "filled with *pasión*." One review had noted that the droop of her narrow shoulders, at the moment of surrender to her enemy, had said all there is to say of those who lack power; "she is all the *pobrecitas* of the world."

ARMED with her bouquet of clippings and a cheap leather portfolio filled with photographs of herself from *Amor, Amor*—laughing, serious, and in profile, her lips dark and shining, her hair done in three different colors—Rosa now belonged to the battalion of girls who patrolled the streets outside the massive gray stone Palacio de las Artes. She hung around the actors' cafés and make-up shops, reading theatre want ads. She made the rounds of the producers and agents. And she shared a small furnished room with Juanita Ortiz, who had played Concha the thief in *Las Angelitas*. Juanita had been in the city five years; she knew where to buy cheap sexy clothes and how to alter them for the best effect. She helped Rosa cut a high slit in her tightest black skirt, so that when she sat for an interview she could cross her legs in a more profitable way. Juanita also knew how to make little beads of black paint on the ends of her lashes; this made the eyelids look heavy, it was the latest thing. Juanita could put green triangles around her eyes, and draw on lips that were twice the size of her own. She taught Rosa how the actresses made themselves more glamorous for pictures, with a grease to make the shoulders shine, and a wire under the breasts to push them up. She even took Rosa to a *centro de belleza* where a hairdresser named Guy would cut her curls in front like the curls of Persuasión duPre. Fluffy curls around the face like this, Juanita told Guy, showing him a picture of Persuasión, and nothing in the back. Like a boy's hair in the back, with a little point in the middle, because it shows off the neck. Juanita paused and stood back, appraising Rosa from behind. She has a quite pretty neck, she said, squinting her eyes. Guy began to cut.

Rosa believed every word Juanita told her, even when she suggested that Rosa ought to do something about her breasts. My friend Lupe, Juanita explained, had it done; it is just a little *operación*, not just to make them big and round, but to make them stand up all the time, like this. She gestured, holding her own generous breasts. They will point straight out all the time, even when you lie down. No sooner had Lupe done this to her breasts, Juanita explained, than she found a fine job dancing at one of the new cafés where girls danced with the breasts naked. Men sometimes tucked twenty-dollar bills between them, or between their thighs, and if the girl could roll up the bill very tight, she could keep it as a tip. It was an easy trick, the way a dancing girl in the East could roll a man's cigar for him; men liked the way a girl's perfume mingled with the tobacco, there was nothing like it. Juanita laughed. Men everywhere would spend money for a girl to do such tricks.

Juanita said that Lupe made a hundred pesos a week, and the tips extra, for dancing in this café. But the owner would only hire girls who had the *operación* to make the breasts stand up pointing straight forever. Rosa had saved half her salary from *Las Angelitas;* with little gifts from Nervo and Soledad, she had managed to send home ten pesos a week, so that at least her brother Chepito could go to the *universidad*. But since the play closed, Soledad had found new diversions, and Rosa had had only one job at Radio del Estado, after her old friend Tobal Iribas introduced her to the manager there. This manager interviewed her privately in his office, and she wore a very sexy dress, borrowed (stolen) by Tobalito for the occasion from his girl friend Nelly. The dress was bright purple and shiny, cut very low on top. Rosa leaned forward only twice during the interview, and once she leaned back, crossing her legs in a certain way. Señor Jorge Oleas had come around his desk and stood very close to her chair, so that she could see clearly the effect she had on him. She pretended not to notice. When he touched her finally, she blushed and stood up so fast that she almost lost her balance, falling against him. Somehow he got the impression that she had nothing on under the purple dress. Anyway, she got the part of a naughty girl in one of the daytime soap operas that her mama listened to. The part lasted three weeks, until the wife of the man she was supposed to seduce (in the play) received *informes* of the affair and forced her husband to end it. Señor Oleas had promised Rosa another part in another soap opera soon, but it was clear that this time she would have to do more than fall against him in Nelly's purple dress. She still had thirteen pesos, which was not quite enough for her share of the rent, and Juanita had already lent her money for last month's. The landlord had warned them that he would not wait again this time; he had a brother-in-law waiting to move in. There was also not enough to buy food for the nights when she and Juanita could not get soldiers at one of the cafés to pay for more than a glass of cheap wine. Certainly there was not enough for the *operación* to make her breasts point out straight enough for a job like Lupe's.

Whenever the young lieutenants and captains bought dinner, Rosa saved the bread, wrapping it discreetly in a handkerchief as Juanita had taught her. Sometimes there were nuts in a bowl; these too could be saved. Once Rosa managed to bring home most of the meat from her plate; it was enough for three meals in a thin soup.

Juanita said nothing, but there was not the need to speak. Rosa knew the time had come to make an appointment with Señor Oleas at Radio del Estado. Perhaps it was already too late. After all, Rosa knew how many other hungry girls were now hanging around the Palacio de las Artes, waiting to be discovered by the manager of the radio station. Such a man could have his way with all of them, for a promise of half a chance to play a naughty girl on *Todas las Mañanas*.

She could have held out for perhaps another two days, waiting for a call from one of the agents who had said *puede ser*, perhaps tomorrow. But then in the night Juanita woke up with a terrible pain. Are you sure you're not going to have a bastard? Rosa asked her. I am sure, Juanita said; she was crying with the pain and her body was covered with sweat. Maybe you are only a little hungrier than usual, Rosa suggested. Maybe the pain will go away if I can get a little meat? Juanita moaned, shaking her head; she looked a bad color, blue-white, like one who is already dead.

Do not worry, said Rosa, but she was frightened. It was no use calling an old friend like Tobal Iribas at this hour; that one had finally proposed to his girl friend Nelly. If they were getting married, it would be a long time before Rosa could call him in the night for a new favor. Juanita's friend Lupe had said she wished she could help, but, despite her valuable breasts, she had no money right now. The thing was, she had not yet paid her hospital bill. If Rosa and Juanita could wait until the next payday, she might let them have ten dollars, but by then, Rosa thought now, Juanita would surely be dead.

In spite of the hour Rosa got dressed and went out alone, to the Noches de Ronde Café on the waterfront. This was a thing which she had never done before. A fat young captain bought her two glasses of wine and took her to his sister's room, at least he said it was his sister's room, where he gave her twenty dollars just to put her red lips on him there, without even taking off her dress. He said he only wanted her to kneel down in front of him, with even her little hat and her shoes on, just as if she were kneeling in church. He did not even touch her with his hands. Ahh, he cried, at the moment when he spurted on her white dress, and pulled away as if she had caused him pain.

Afterward Rosa called the doctor for Juanita, and paid for a stomach medicine, and bought meat bones for a soup. Juanita did not ask how she got the money.

ONCE again the country lay trapped inside the summer, as though in a sealed white chamber. On the airless streets of San Luis, people moved slowly, pushing against the heat like exhausted swimmers. On the streetcars, when a stranger's arm collided with that of another, a curse would be muttered and one would wrench away, as if a blow had been struck. The anger and despair of laborers, those slow fires that had simmered for years, seemed now to have ignited and burst in the night. The new mobs were different; some magic had changed the ragtag groups of workers into an army of *asesinos*, professional bands who could be hired to destroy property, shouting, Death to *Extranjeros,* Death to Foreigners, Death, Death . . .

Now there were leaders, experienced directors of riots, men who knew how to organize such hatred. The Liga Patriótica had always been skillful at turning random anger into useful action. Systematic raids began in the Jewish sections; people were dragged from their homes and beaten or shot in the street. Wherever an "incident" occurred, fire trucks filled with armed police sped to the scene. But no arrests were made. Instead, the rescue squad mowed down passersby, thus setting off another storm of protest, another mob besieging headquarters, another official reprisal.

In the meantime, San Luisanos were also running out of food. With the strike of transportation, no supplies could reach the markets; whatever had been in food stores at the start of the rioting disappeared quickly; milk or eggs that sold for a few centavos on Friday morning were fetching three or four pesos by midafternoon. But at the fine restaurant on the Calle Florida, fresh seafood salad was still being served—to regular customers only, and behind locked doors. The icebox was amply stocked with eggs—and with fresh butter and cream. Miguel, the doorman, was also well prepared—with a new .38 revolver tucked inside the handsome black uniform with the gold epaulets and the stripes on the sleeves. Miguel also had the usual orders.

Outside the hushed and elegant dining room, many killings went on. One knew now that the *policía* were doing most of it. Not the workers, not even the *asesinos* of the Liga Patriótica. On the corner where an incident occurred, the *policía* would shoot anyone poorly dressed who happened to be caught in the vicinity.

The lists of dead and wounded now appeared every day in the newspapers and on the walls of public buildings.

Messengers in black suits raced back and forth from the Chamber of Deputies to the Casa Dorado. The emergency line of the telephone at police headquarters was out of order. A general alert went out to all military bases within a ten-mile radius of the city.

That night the powerful union of federal workers met to consider its options—and its divided loyalties. Fifty thousand government workers whose jobs were controlled by the bureaucrats who were issuing, and obeying, orders to gun down *trabajadores:* anyone in the clothes of a workingman. A general strike would paralyze the city, but it would also endanger the jobs of all the members, from radio announcers to postal clerks, telephone operators to bus drivers.

Manuel Quiroga, the *Federación's* burly boss who had been brave in his youth but now was only rich and cooperative, sat pondering a telegram from Colonel Montero promising the Labor Ministry's support for the strikers and sympathy for their demands. A deal—if Quiroga's union voted not to strike. Quiroga would have liked to make the deal; it would have made him look good in many important places. But he already knew he could not risk it; the mood of the rank and file was too ugly; too many men in the *Federación* were already watching him, waiting for him to make one more false conciliatory move. He frowned, drumming his fingers. Then he summoned the waiting messenger. Tell Montero I can do nothing, he said. We strike tomorrow. Wait—

The messenger paused; there was no expression Quiroga could read. Tell him— Quiroga's bulldog face creased into his famous grimace. Nobody had ever called it a smile. Tell him, Next time.

The messenger saluted. I'll tell him, Señor.

Quiroga swiveled his big chair around to the window that faced the Calle Florida. Tomorrow morning, he said, there will be nothing out there. No papers, no radio, no telephone. Have the lines cut tonight, as soon as it is dark. No transportation out of the city. He sighed. Nothing.

Quiroga's bodyguard had been standing motionless at the door. Now he spoke in a gray toneless voice. There will be troops, he said. There will be dead men.

On Friday the suffocating silence of the city had deepened. Stores, hotels, markets, and bars stayed closed. Quiroga's orders had been followed; there was no civilian movement of any kind.

But the bodyguard's prediction had also come true. All night the troop trains had moved through the countryside, bristling with guns that stuck out of their windows, guns that fired in the darkness at anything that moved. The streets of San Luis were filled with soldiers and sailors, all heavily armed and prepared to follow the same order as the *policía*: Shoot to kill.

9

ROSA walked with quick light steps along the Avenida de los Angeles, counting the new beggars. Every day there were more. Old women in fine clothes who would lean toward a stranger, looking oddly puzzled, as though to ask directions, then suddenly clutching with thin hands, thrusting their faces close, whispering, *Ayúdame!* Help me! As if it were an accusation. And the children with flat black eyes, with full red mouths that turned down at the corners even when they smiled. The boys, everywhere the little boys, learning to place themselves so, in their tight military uniforms, hips thrust out at provocative angles, in the poses of girls, leaning against the doorways of cafés and elegant men's shops. The girls wore high boots and angry mouths, the boys wore attitudes of swagger. Everyone touching the helmet of polished hair, everyone with a gesture suggesting salute, to catch the sidelong glance of a fat, well-tailored gentleman from out of town. Smiling then, in that downturned way. *Sí, Señor.* You are looking for a friend?

A woman of no age sat before a bank, her filthy once-red skirt spread around her on the pavement like a magic circle, a territorial flag. Her three children squatted within the circle, gray-faced and still as phantoms, awaiting the end of the working day, the thinning of the crowd. Soon the mother would shake the few coins out of her cup and count them, sighing. She would call the children as though she thought they were off somewhere, playing. As though they were hopping in the street on their skinny legs, shouting and kicking at the tops of soda bottles. The mother would scold them, shaking them off the skirt that must now serve as a table for the evening meal. Rosa would not look at the meal; she could taste it with her tongue's memory. Later, in the dark, she knew, the skirt would be smoothed again, to be made ready for the night. The children would sleep there, rolled together like a litter of stray mongrels, squabbling and tearing at the ragged hem to cover their small calloused feet. The mother would sleep sitting upright, her back propped against the wall of the Banco Federal de Pradera.

Rosa hurried past them, fixing her gaze on the reassuring glances of passing men. Juanita had told her there were two young officers visiting the radio station yesterday; they had promised they would be back tonight to take her and a friend out to a café. A café, Rosa had whispered to herself, as though it were the start of an old song. She was lucky to have such a friend as Juanita, who did not forget favors.

Now her own red skirt, short and full, brushed against her bare legs, making kissing sounds. Not me, she called silently to the beggar woman and children, repeating it all the way down the block like a psalm in her head, syncopating it to the rhythmic click of her high thin heels on the pavement. Not . . . me. She quickened her step. Not—me. At the end of the block she stopped, waiting for the green light. She turned her head, not really wanting to see them again, but the faded red skirt flashed like a spot of dried blood. Without thinking, she ran back to where they sat, clutching a coin in her fist like a holy medal. One of the children looked up as she came toward them; she pressed the coin into his hand; he said nothing. Rosa spoke to the mother. *Dígame, por favor . . .* how old are you? The mother did not raise her eyes. Seventeen, she said. Rosa backed away from them and ran again down the block. This time she kept on going, straight into the street, against the light. Horns blared; a policeman's shrill whistle pierced the air; people stared. She kept running. Not me! she screamed at the cars, at the drivers sealed inside them, blaring their horns to cover her voice.

Tell me how it is that actresses are always so pretty, Captain T said, yawning through his clipped black mustache. The tiny hairs surrounded his O of a mouth like a jaunty eyebrow. Always so red-cheeked, he went on. *Sí sabrosa . . .* so juicy. Rosa's painted smile widened appreciatively; the little gay laugh she had learned to float, like a child's toy, streamed from her throat in delicate bubbles. Captain T's fingers gripped her smooth bare knee. Oh, Captain T, she said softly, trembling a little under his touch, it must be the flattering light from those white uniforms. On such an arm, the cheek of any girl has no choice but to glow. She touched his shoulder lightly, the gesture of a shy child.

This one talks like the lyric of a tango, no? Captain T's elbow nudged Captain F's ribs. Captain F laughed; he signaled the waiter for more wine. In the powder room Juanita whispered to Rosa that Captain T had an important new job in the Ministry of Labor. The boss of his boss was that Colonel M, the handsome one who, it was said, had powerful friends in the government. *Verdad?* said Rosa, sounding bored. And what does yours do? Oh, mine, Juanita said, drawing a shiny purple outline above her upper lip, then kissing a tissue. I think he works in the Ministry of Education. She shrugged. A nothing.

Rosa's eyes twinkled mischief. Want to trade? Juanita hesitated, studying her plum-colored fingernails. No, she said carefully. Mine has sexy teeth. She smiled wider with her new shiny mouth.

Rosa pondered this; Juanita was not a graceful liar. Was it not so that the Education Ministry was to be put in charge of the radio station? On the other hand, Rosa had heard of that Colonel M. His picture appeared almost every day in *La Opinión*, always on the front page. She sighed; clearly, these were two young officers with sexy teeth. It would be very hard not to fall in love with both of them. Or, more precisely, to have them both fall in love with her.

When they went back to their seats, the small firm tip of Rosa's warm left breast accidentally grazed Captain F's right shoulder, which caused him to lose the thread of his sentence. Captain T did not notice; nor, when his fingers moved slowly upward from Rosa's round knee to a soft spot several inches above it, did he perceive the interesting glance she exchanged with Captain F over the rim of her wine glass. Juanita's high giggle played a musical accompaniment to the dance of their eyes; she had had too much wine. Perhaps that was why she was listening only to the bolero the orchestra was playing when Captain F mentioned something about a new program of historical dramas that the Ministry wanted Juanita's boss to put on the air next season.

In the afternoons! Rosa exclaimed, blushing. Oh, you must have it in the afternoons! Captain F said they were thinking of a midday hour, for the women at home. There would be love stories of famous ladies of history, queens and such. Oh, said Rosa, but the children must hear them too! Think of history lessons with the voices of real queens and—she permitted herself a glance of mischief at both captains—their military conquerors! The officers chuckled; Juanita tried not to pout. But I am serious, Rosa went on timidly, one small white hand on Captain T's sleeve while her eyes locked with those of Captain F. To learn the *historías* on the radio! With the voices of our country's great heroes . . . She bit her lip then and looked down. A shivering of excitement? Of shyness?

Captain F was enchanted; his gaze fixed on the charming indentation in the center of her lower lip, where her little teeth had just rested; it was all he could do to keep from reaching across the table to put a finger there. Instead, he coughed into his wine glass. At the same instant Rosa felt the moist thumb of Captain T's right hand tracing a small arc high on the inside of her thigh. She shifted gracefully in the little chair, as if to keep time to the rumba; somehow this motion permitted the other fingers of his hand to slide easily beneath her. She heard but did not acknowledge the sharp intake of Captain T's breath; in fact she was arching then, turning her smile just to the left, lifting her chin so that Captain F's eyes could feast now upon the long white curve of her throat, with the little black satin ribbon she had tied there; it was, she knew, a very fetching sight, especially in the smoky blue column of light that had just drifted across their table. If Soledad had taught her nothing else in the time Rosa had spent watching her, she had at least taught her how a star moves with the light.

She has a way—Captain T rolled his eyes—of planting her kisses. His friends made extravagant gestures of understanding. No, I swear, Captain T went on, each kiss takes root; one can feel it inside the skin for days.

It was true that she made love with great care, pressing her soft parted lips into place here, and just there, and exactly so, as though to draw out a man's pleasure to hoard like a jewel.

Where did you learn such tricks—in the woods of Montaraz? he asked her lightly on the third or fourth night.

Certainly not, she retorted. I never made love with anyone there. I have learned everything just now—she kissed him softly, on the neck, under the ear—and just here (another kiss, more passionate, on the mouth). And I expect—she drew back, playful—a good mark in the course.

I will give you the best mark, he said, with my teeth, here. So?

Oh, yes, she moaned softly, her body flowing against him as though the warmth of it would fuse them.

Rosa, you are a witch, I swear it.

She shrugged. Witch, whore. I am none of the terrible things you call me. I am only a skinny, flat-chested girl. And she would smile that smile of hers, the teeth so startling white and even, sparkling like smooth hard candy in a red velvet heart. Such a smile could persuade a man of her innocence. Fortunately, thought Captain T, I am not one to be fooled. What innocent would use her mouth in this way, tracing such a slow path of moist heat around one's ear and neck, down one's chest, kiss by kiss, and oh, with such eloquent sighs. When the lips parted she would use the tongue like the small pointed flame of a laboratory torch. Applying it deep inside the pit of one's arm, and around the nipple of one's breast, and traveling in endless circles through the whorls of black hair across one's belly, one's groin. So that a man less in control of himself would scream aloud with the weakness of such pleasure.

How could she have become so adept at it, in just those few nights with him? How could she have learned every one of his body's secrets, timing her movements to his breathing and sighing, as though she were a spy posing as an ordinary tourist with a book of foreign phrases? How far to . . . ? And oh, please. I will take that . . . and that one too, yes. Oh, thank you, Señor. It is perfect. You are . . . oh, yes, Señor.

You taste of me, she would say to him, like a pleased child, running her tongue around her own mouth, appraisingly, after he had kissed her everywhere.

Nice?

Mm. You know, your beard tickles, especially—she pressed his head back down—especially there.

Nice?

Mm. Is your boss, that Colonel So-and-so, going to be at the studio party?

Mm. Don't know. Why?

Oh, I just want to tell him . . . She reached down to entangle her long fingers in his black hair. He groaned, as if her touch had set a low current running inside his scalp. To tell him, she whispered, what a fine captain he has—serving under him. She underlined the little joke with a silver laugh.

Captain T did not reply. Instead he parted her, entered her with his mouth. Very dark, she tasted. A sweet sharp darkness.

Why not, she murmured. I'll tell him how . . . your beard feels there. She moved to the rhythm of his tongue, like a dancer. He opened his eyes to watch the sharp little bones of her hips raised above him. Her body would twist and arch backward like a delicate bow pulled taut; he could feel her grow tense under him, quivering. Won't the colonel . . . she gasped, won't he like to know that?

He raised his head higher, to look at all of her, the white slenderness spread before him like a delicacy. He could not answer her.

Querido, she said. I am talking to you. She raised herself coyly on an elbow and peered down at him. From this angle her small round breasts seemed to him immense, as if he could hardly contain them in his hands.

What? he said. Oh, I don't know. Anyway, why are we talking about colonels? He reached up to hold one breast; the flesh of it seemed to press blindly against his palm, as if it had a will. Colonel M is a fool, he murmured, squeezing. His eyes closed. The breast answered his hand, silently.

Why a fool? she persisted.

His eyes flew open again. He frowned impatiently. Because he does not know his power. He drew himself up now, alongside the breasts, as though they had summoned him. Be still now, he commanded, and lowered his head. She suckled him gently, sighing.

With her fingers she traced delicate circles on his shoulders and back. But she said nothing.

Colonel M, he murmured against her, with sudden anger.

Mm?

If he were half as smart as he thinks he is . . .

Sí? she said dreamily. What would he do?

. . . get rid of his enemies. Put his friends where they could help him. We control all the job assignments.

She sighed, counted two, then murmured idly, why do you not tell him so? He shook his head against her; his mouth tightened its grip upon her breast. She winced but did not pull away. Instead she stroked his hair. Then you could be his friend. He would owe you a great favor, no?

He sighed and rolled heavily away from her. Favors. One never collects.

She sat up, seized his great head in her two soft hands, gazed at him solemnly. *You* would, she said. Her fingertips played with the lobe of his ear. *You* would know how. You would have loyal friends, smart ones. They would learn the colonel's best secrets, no? She paused. Then a tiny mischievous smile. And his worst ones. Does he have a wife?

I think she died.

A girl friend then?

He shrugged. Very young ones now. Two or three, I think. Little whores.

Ah. He is not sure of his power?

Why? Captain T scowled at her. They are very pretty whores. With enormous— He gestured.

She made a face. Of course, enormous. But *estúpido*. If he were sure of his powers, he would have a woman.

He laughed. Like you? A woman of seventeen, like you?

Well, she said, pouting. I am full grown.

Full, he agreed, suddenly aroused. Turn over, I want to—

No, wait— She struggled, a half-hearted push.

I said, Turn over. He shifted, seizing her. She lay half turned; he gave her rump a light whack, and another. She twisted in his grasp, her eyes blazing indignation. No; don't do that.

I will, he said. He delivered another slap, harder than the others.

His fingers tingled; the sensation excited him. Suddenly she leapt from the bed, shaking with rage. Her face flushed; she stood before him, trembling. Delicious, he thought. Look at that! I swear to you, she was saying, her voice high and almost shrill. You will not do that to me.

He lit a cigaret, his hands shaking now. She looked like a shivering child, though he suspected she was not really frightened. How adorable she was, thin, white, naked, raging at him. Her skin in little bumps, the nipples of her breasts red and pointed, like tiny weapons. She had never seemed so pretty. Rosa, he said, his voice thick. I am going to take you from behind, like the little bitch you are. You will whimper and say oh, oh, and you'll put your bottom high in the air. And I'll do it quick and hard. *Now*.

Rosa hesitated only a fraction of a second. Then she did as she was told. Oh, she whimpered. Oh.

The following morning, Captain T and Rosa went to call on Jorge Oleas at the radio station. It was arranged that Rosa Andújar would star in the new weekly series of historical dramas, at a starting salary of $150 a week, with a one-year contract. Her first role was to be Cleopatra; after that, Queen Isabella, Carlotta, and, for Navidad, the Virgen María.

Oh, I do want you, he whispered.

Oh, and I want you too, she whispered back, sighing gently into the center of his ear. But not now. He was holding her so tightly that she was certain she could feel the talons of the carved eagles on the buttons of his tunic; perhaps they would leave impressions on her skin, like imprints of a royal seal. She felt him swell against her, pressing her against the whitewashed wall. She murmured something indistinct—*Por favor*—but that could have meant please do or please do not. In any case he did not choose to hear it. Rosa, Rósula, he merely breathed against her hair, inhaling Noche en Paris. We do belong together, you see; in the middle we fit so—like the cigaret to the match.

She struggled free then, with a playful glance upward, through the black-beaded fringe of eyelashes which had cost her four whole pesos, but which made her look very dangerous. Then you must be careful, she warned. If you ignite me, I am hard to control.

He laughed in the way that told her he did not like it that she had pulled away, that she was playing *la coqueta*. I can always control such things, he said. A little witch burns fast.

Then promise me something? She said it light and quick, breathlessly, in the way that they liked it. Taking care to make it sound as if it did not matter so much whether he said *sí* or *no*.

Let me guess, he said.

All right. A small giggle to take the edge off. The ruffled white top of her blouse had slipped, so that one splendid shoulder gleamed in the darkness like a moon. His fingers reached for it; cool to his touch. He made a low sound in the back of his throat.

You want, he said, a better contract for the radio drama.

She tossed carefully tousled curls so that the tender crescents that lay coiled, like parentheses around the small face, performed a delicate little dance on each cheekbone. Kiss-curls, they were called. No? The fingers on her shoulder slid an inch or two before tightening their grip; she seemed warmer now, unless it was his imagination.

It is not a better contract, she said. I want to do another show, a serious one. I want to talk to the people . . . about you. She let it all tumble out at once; her lip trembled and she looked at him with her eyes round and very soft. Please.

Out of the question and you know it, he said, trying not to show his pleasure at such a request. He slipped the ruffled collar down with a short, decisive gesture, so that now her perfect small breast rose from it like another moon. He caught his breath.

Out of the question, she echoed, with a little catch in her voice. At the same time she gave a small, nearly imperceptible shrug, just enough so that the blouse slid back into place.

What is this, he said, frowning. We are not going to begin playing this sort of game, you and I.

No, she said simply. At least *I* am not. She began to slide one foot into its pretty silver sandal. She stretched out the leg, arching her toes, and slid her fingers slowly up the new silk stocking, smoothing it, though this was hardly a necessary process. He watched it all carefully, trying not to. She pretended not to notice him watching.

You have decided, he said slowly, huskily, to behave like a little whore with me. *Moza de fortuna!*

Her face registered nothing. If so, she said quietly, lifting her small sharp chin, if that is what you choose to think. Although really, if I *were* what you say, she added, allowing a trace of careful mischief into her tone, I would certainly never let you cheat me of my fee.

Aha. So you admit it—a fee! *Extorsión!* He sounded hurt; perhaps he only meant to hurt her. Was it not so? he murmured then. Was it not that we meant something to each other?

But we do, she said softly. *Claro!* Perhaps he really was hurt? But you know you mean everything to me, whereas I—I mean only a few good things to you. Is that it? She leaned over suddenly and kissed him, a very long moist kiss it was, reaching inside his mouth with the tip of her tongue, as though she were looking for something she had misplaced. At last he grasped her shoulders and held her away from him, though it meant fighting his own body to do so. She gazed at him, expressionless. So?

Well, he said. I will see what I can do. But it is Oleas who decides such things.

Ha, she said. You control Oleas. He does what the ministry tells him. She shrugged and slipped the other foot halfway into its sandal, letting it dangle like a bright toy. You will put in a word! What self-respecting *puta* would settle for a fee like that?

All right, then. *Bueno.* What will satisfy you?

Tomorrow, she said, draping both soft white arms around his neck. Tomorrow, we go together to the studio. You will tell Oleas that I am to have the second program—in the evening—with my name announced in the newspapers. And a new picture, with my hair in the new way. And of course a new contract. I will want—she frowned—how much will I want?

Hm, he said, pretending to think. Five hundred dollars weekly?

Seven, she said. *Sí? Sí, 'stá bien.* That sounds right. And the contract—for two years. She did not need to wait for his replies; he was smiling. And tomorrow night—she fastened the second shoe and stood up swaying against him, clinging as though she could not quite balance. Then she took his hand, held it to her lips, kissed each finger, and led him to the door.

. . . And tomorrow night, we shall celebrate. In all of the ways that you like. *Sí, querido?*

He laughed and swept her into his arms. *Moza de fortuna!* You drive a hard bargain for a girl with such small breasts.

On Wednesday a delegation from the Ministry of Education was to meet in Señor Oleas' office. Rumors flew through the studio on wings of panic. It was said that the ministry wanted the five o'clock tango hour replaced by a discussion program, featuring government leaders and important men of business. It was said the serial drama *Vidas y Pasiones* was not catching on in the provinces; perhaps it would be moved to another time of day, perhaps it would be dropped at the end of the month. A news announcer who had made an unflattering joke about the Vice President would probably lose his job, although the fact that his wife was now sleeping with Oleas might save his skin. The betting was that it would not. Rosa Andújar overslept that Wednesday morning and woke up with a sick stomach. Juanita thought her face looked an ugly color, a sort of greenish yellow; she admitted she had felt dizzy and faint for two days now. It was clear from the way her dress hung that she had lost weight—perhaps five pounds. Here, Juanita said, making a terrible face at the reflection of her friend in the mirror. Put on this belt, at least you will look not so much like a starving mouse. Pull it tight—no, tighter! This way it will also keep you from feeling hungry. There, and put more rouge on, your cheeks are the exact shade of last night's soup.

By the time she reached the studio, the newspaper photographers who had come to take pictures of the important meeting were already disconnecting their flash bulbs. The meeting was over; the visitors were shaking hands and flashing big smiles at Oleas, who looked very sad. Rosa whispered quickly to Oswaldo Diaz, the young station manager; I am not feeling well. I need something at the *farmacia*. I will be right back.

Diaz frowned, looking pointedly at the big clock behind the sound engineer. I wanted to go over the scene where—

Please, Rosa begged. I am really sick. Oswaldo peered at her. She did look a little off. Five minutes then, he grumbled. He did not like Rosa much, but she was still pretty thick with Oleas. She fled out the door and was waiting for the elevator when the colonels emerged, flanked by two security aides and a male civilian secretary. She smiled shyly at them and stepped into the elevator first. By the time they were all in, the car was very crowded; it stalled only once between floors, which was better than usual. Rosa turned slightly to get a good look at Colonel Montero. Dark, handsome, like his pictures. Tall, massively built. He felt her staring at him and half turned; she was about to smile when she slid slowly to the floor. She had not felt dizzy; it was very odd. A moment later there was a crowd around her helping her to her feet. The colonels had left the elevator and were climbing into a long black car just outside the door. Would you like some water, Señorita? a woman asked. Are you all right? Sí, she murmured. I—I think so.

Outside, in the car, the *militares* were talking about the meeting. Oleas, they agreed, would give no trouble about the program changes. The announcer who had made the unfortunate remark about the Vice President would be suspended for six months, a decent interval. Then the case would be settled, depending on the Vice President's wishes at the time.

But who, said Colonel Montero, was the girl who fainted in the elevator?

What? Oh, said Captain T, just a girl. Actress, I think.

Actress, you think. Has she a name?

Captain T shifted uneasily in the black leather seat. Rosa So-and-so. She is on that awful serial drama *Vidas y Pasiones*.

Um, mumbled O. My mother listens to that.

Is she good? Montero asked.

Rosa? said Captain T, feigning boredom. Good at what, acting? Colonel O snorted.

Of course acting, Montero snapped. What did you think I meant —fellatio?

Colonel O laughed again; this time the others joined in, all but the secretary, who kept his eyes straight ahead, hands primly clasping the handle of his cowhide briefcase.

Captain T had a face of red splotches. Was that not what you meant, sir?

No, said Montero, flashing a smile at Captain T; it was not a smile of good humor. But since the subject comes up, is she?

Is she what? Captain T's eyes avoided Montero's. Now the others shifted uneasily, all except the secretary. Montero sighed heavily. Here— He tapped the secretary on the shoulder. Give the captain a hundred pesos. The secretary's briefcase snapped open with a discreet pop. There was no other sound in the car, except for the faint rustle of paper as the note changed hands, and the briefcase snapping shut. Montero smiled again at Captain T. Have the girl—Rosa, was it? Have her hair made yellow, and tell her the party starts at seven tonight.

What party? said Captain T tonelessly. Sir.

Montero said nothing while the car idled at a red light. When it started to move again, he said, very quietly, Captain, I have been meaning to tell you there is an order on my desk concerning your transfer to . . . Fumarola. It lacks only my signature. Montero sighed, gazing out the car window. He nudged the shoulder of the secretary. Is it not so?

No, sir! the secretary replied quickly. That is, yes, sir. He fumbled in his pockets for a pen, a note pad; he scribbled hastily without turning his head; the briefcase opened and closed again, like the jaw of a crocodile. The other officers stared busily out their windows.

Seven o'clock, Montero said. *He*, captain?

Sí, murmured Captain T. His voice was almost inaudible.

He?

Sí . . . mi coronel.

Rosa Andújar did not attend the party of Colonel Montero. At exactly seven fifteen, however, a long white envelope was delivered to the doorman of his apartment house on the Calle Orilla. The envelope contained the hundred-peso note, folded inside a sheet of delicate gray notepaper which smelled faintly of Noche en Paris. The note said: Dear Colonel Montero, My hair is still brown—with regret. It was signed Rosa So-and-so. Montero laughed and went out to a *confitería* for his usual evening vermouth. The doorman could not recall who had delivered the envelope—not even whether it was a señorita or a señor.

On Thursday an order was dispatched directing the transfer of one Captain T to . . . Fumarola.

MANUEL Quiroga had been studying the new lists of casualties; it was necessary to call another emergency meeting of the leaders of his *Federación*. Montero had called him at six o'clock that morning. *Por favor*, was all he said. Quiroga grunted. *Bueno*.

The leaders of the *Federación* wanted no part of the blame for another wave of killings. We will have to issue a statement, Quiroga said. No one spoke. And we will have to call off the strike. He studied the faces around the table. The others exchanged glances; still no one spoke. *Bueno?* Quiroga barked. Estanislao? Bernabe?

All right.

The city stank of the garbage that had lain uncollected since the start of the new strike. Pieces of electrical cable lay everywhere, like severed parts of great dead worms. And everywhere were burned-out hulks of cars and buses. Again no trains ran, no ships left or entered the port of San Luis.

On Saturday at noon, communication was restored; telephone lines began to hum at once with wild rumors. This time the border police in Paraguay announced to the San Luis authorities that they had uncovered a massive plot of Communists; that armies were about to seize both sides of the Rio Bravo—and from there advance and take over the capitals of Paraguay and Pradera. On Saturday night, San Luis police issued a statement to the press, announcing that a raid on a private apartment had uncovered a nest of Russians meeting to establish a nationwide network of *espias*—spies for the Communists.

The press ignored these reports.

On Sunday, for the first time, the list of dead and wounded contained fewer names than the day before.

By the end of the week that was later to be christened *La Semana Negra*—Black Week—most of Pradera knew that the government deserved most of the blame. The *policía* had been brutes; the Chamber of Deputies had panicked. The workers had only behaved like children. There had been no need—and no excuse—for the excessive show of force by the authorities.

Colonel Carlos Montero wrote a letter to *La Nación,* in which he said, "We are all guilty. The dead cry in our dreams."

Montero's aides, who had begun to appear with him in the Chamber of Deputies, had managed to leak his most recent speech to two columnists in *Hoy* and *El Diario.* It was reported that the colonel had risked his own base of power in the government to plead for humane treatment for the angry workers. It was said that Montero alone had kept both his head and his heart in the crisis. It was whispered that Pradera would hear more of this man. Manuel Quiroga read the papers and permitted his face to crease in the famous grimace which no one dared call a smile.

PAUNERO Stadium was filled with a capacity crowd of twenty thousand, victims of *La Semana Negra* and *Amigos de las Victimas*, who had paid fifty pesos each to see *los políticos* and *los personajes* of show business embrace the weeping women whose husbands had died in the rioting streets of San Luis. Embraces for the victims whose brothers and fathers and sons had been robbed and beaten, whose shops had been destroyed, whose livelihoods had vanished in the terror. *Mira!* cried the audience. See the actors and actresses of stage, screen, and radio, standing on the platform in formal clothes, in dinner jackets and spangled dresses. *Mira!* The *estrella* of the screen bestows a kiss and a smile upon the man in a wheelchair—and on one who shuffles like a fool or a drunkard, whose life blurs and vanishes before him. We have suffered an earthquake of politics. The masters of ceremonies spoke of it as a kind of natural disaster, like the temblor, the eruption *volcánico*. We have survived the darkness together, they said. We have come through, into the light. They spoke of the rally as a *vendaje*, a great bandage for the mortal wound of a nation. They called it historic, this moment of *esperanza*, this surge of hope and pride in the future of Pradera.

In the press, *La Semana Negra* had already passed into history. The tragedy that was over. It had become the sort of cataclysmic event that everyone, save the victims themselves, could use for some profitable end. Finite horror—a single violent upheaval that destroyed lives and fortunes without threatening one's own. Horror to contemplate, to study, to fasten one's gaze upon; was it not a good thing, in the end? Could it not make people forget—at least for a few weeks, while the dead were being counted, the injured nursed, the property repaired—that there was still a gnawing within one's own belly, still a look of pain in the hollow eyes of one's own children, still a fierce anger in the heart of those *pobrecitos,* those poor ones who labor without *esperanza.*

And so there was a frenzied gaiety about this fiesta for the relief of those who suffered. As if the organizers, the *personajes,* the collectors of money, feared that a pause between prayers, a silence of thought, might bring back the causes of the horror. The music was very loud; one could scarcely hear the speeches. And the lights were very bright; they danced over the spangled gowns of the young *estrellas,* over the yellow hair and the white teeth and the sweet red smiles.

Scarlet bunting swirled around the bandstand. Everywhere enormous banners proclaimed ESPERANZA!

In the center aisle of the orchestra tier, a young woman stood holding a small portable microphone, from which trailed a cord five hundred feet long. *I am here today,* she was saying into the microphone, *to describe for you the mending of our country's broken heart.*

On the platform at the other end of her aisle stood a phalanx of *militares* in splendid white uniforms. The actresses in their gaudy evening gowns laughed up at these colonels and linked their arms. The girl with the microphone described this to her listening audience.

At the center of the *militares* stood *el coronel* Carlos Montero, the new Minister of Labor who had come in person to deliver an official message from the President to the victims and their friends.

Like rays of a sun, the girl was saying into her microphone, *our leaders have come to comfort us. We are all* lloradoras *today; we weep for each other. And here are the strong shoulders for our weeping. This is our* maravilla—*our miracle.*

Montero stepped forward to greet the crowd. He held his arms high and wide apart, the palms of his hands facing each other, as though he were holding aloft a great package. The girl whispered into her microphone. *Atlas,* she said, *who lifts the weight of a broken world.*

There was no breeze in the stadium; the sun beat down upon the crowd. But its light played on the white uniforms as though directed by an unseen technician.

He shines, sighed the girl into her microphone. *But listen to the cheering.* . . .

He had begun to speak; at each pause, the shouts of the crowd grew louder, stronger. He promised swift help; food and medicine; clothing for the homeless, shelter for the orphans.

And all of this, he said, is only a beginning. The money one may give today—

The crowd burst now into a frenzy of cheering. Montero gestured with his outstretched arms. His strong face broke into its endless white smile. *The smile,* said the girl into her microphone, *which Pradereños have begun to see in our dreams; the smile of* esperanza.

The money we give today, he went on, cannot be enough. No matter how much, it must not be thought enough. What we pledge here is our heart. Our strength. And our spirit.

The girl moved slowly down the aisle toward the platform; the cord of her microphone uncoiled behind her. *Listen,* she commanded her audience. *This is the man whose words stirred the deputies. Now they stir us.* . . .

She moved closer still, studying him. The close-cropped black hair that made him look so much younger than fifty-eight. The square jaw that might have been chiseled in stone. How immaculate his uniform was; the other officers looked hot and rumpled. Montero's heavy gold-braid collar lay high and close on his strong neck, yet he seemed cool; he seemed totally unaware of it. The gleaming visor of his cap cut across his brow like a black salute. She described it so to her listeners.

She had seen him only once before, in an elevator. And she had not noticed then that his face was deeply scarred; the marks of some ravaging disease. She wondered idly if his photographs were retouched; the marks never showed. She studied the scars now, reflecting how odd it was that they did not disfigure him in the least. In a way, they saved him from his beauty; the rough marks were of *virilidad;* they made him seem more of a man. Even with scars, it seemed to her a face of the cinema hero who wins the *estrella* in the end. She smiled to herself but said nothing of this into her microphone.

She moved closer still, the cord uncoiling in her wake like a charmed serpent. She had read that this colonel could hypnotize a crowd with that gesture of a *salvador,* savior and conqueror in one, with upraised arms and a great white smile. She had laughed when she read this. Hypnotize! Not me. Now she realized with a start that she felt a kind of tremor at the base of her spine, like a shiver. In this heat. Whatever it was, she did not like the feeling. There were *cines* in which people talked of such a sensation. If a woman felt it, it could cause her to forget what she wanted of the man who made her feel it. Well, she thought, it will pass.

The crowds roared again. He was shaking hands with a man in a wheelchair. We will rise together . . . he was saying. We will march.

The girl held the microphone high, to catch the cheering. Then she lowered it to her own lips. *Listen,* she whispered. *They are shouting his name.*

He was not much of an orator. Even as he spoke, as he paused to let the crowd's emotions build, he seemed withdrawn, inward-turning, almost sulky with self-absorption. As though the noise disturbed him or made him feel afraid.

Yet he held one's eyes—including hers—the way a dark color draws and consumes light. It was said that he used this power in his private dealings with people. That, in fact, he refused to meet with groups or committees, but would talk with only one person at a time. In such talks, one understood, he could win over anyone. Cynical union leader, shrewd *militar,* sophisticated radio star . . . whoever it was would emerge from such a meeting visibly shaken— as if he or she had survived an encounter with some mysterious natural force. Like the temblor.

Montero had begun to descend the platform steps; he would pause to hear the personal stories of petitioners as he made his way through the crowd. The girl moved forward quickly.

One has heard interesting warnings about this colonel, she said into the microphone, raising her voice as she approached him. *Some say he is a dangerous enemy. Or*—puede ser—*perhaps a dangerous friend. But in the salons of the rich, in the humble* chozas *of the poor—indeed, everywhere—it is said that soon he will be the man . . . of our future. A brilliant soldier. . . .*

She stood just behind him now; her voice played counterpoint to his. An old woman stood weeping before him; he touched her shoulder, saying, There will be help for you, a place to stay—

Hear this man, said the girl into her microphone. *His voice lights our country's dark hour.* . . .

She was speaking louder now, loud enough now to distract him. *Montero!* she cried. *The man of this hour. Of all our bright hours to come. Montero*—

He turned sharply; she cupped the microphone between her upraised hands; for a moment he thought she might be praying. Tears in her eyes, and his own name, like an anthem, on her red lips. Then he saw the microphone. *Montero!* she cried again.

Quién es? Who—are you?

She smiled. I am the girl who fainted in the elevator.

With the tumult around them, he scarcely heard the hasty introductions of his *ayudantes.* Not that it mattered. He bent over her hand with a stiff little bow, like that of a courtier in a pageant. She heard him murmur the words "beautiful" and "pain"; the rest of his sentence vanished in the storm of voices. She favored him with a curious half-smile but said nothing. The microphone was dead, her broadcast over. Of course you know what I mean, Señorita Andújar, he murmured.

I am not entirely sure, colonel, she said, blushing. But I thank you.

No importa, he said with a short laugh, showing his even teeth in the familiar smile. It does not matter. Enough that you have a great talent. Understanding its uses will come in time. She smiled back then, with that small sudden toss of the head, that gesture of the *estrella;* she had learned it could take a man's breath. She studied his face discreetly, reading it now for clues. Would an ordinary charm be enough for such a man? What a misfortune it was that he had such a preference for blond hair. She resisted a defensive urge to touch her own dark curls, to stand straighter, to wish with all her heart that she had worn a dress of pale blue, that she owned a saucy hat with a veil of lace.

He asked if perhaps she were free after the rally; if she cared to join him for a glass of wine. *Me temo que*—she murmured shyly. I am afraid— O, you must not be *afraid,* he replied, laughing. We could have a coffee instead. She paused a fraction of a second, considering. My secretary would have to apologize for me at the studio. I am scheduled to give an interview at five. She shrugged then, to make it seem important but unimportant. A columnist for *El Mundo*—

Me siento, he said. I am sorry—

O, you must not be *sorry,* she answered smiling, mimicking his tone with precision. We could have a coffee instead.

His eyes flashed something like surprise; he laughed, delighted. Come on, then; I know a way to dodge admirers. He whispered to an aide, who quickly dispersed four others to arrange a narrow path through the crowd. Montero took her hand and led her to a narrow exit at the rear of the platform; from there they raced to a small *confitería* on the opposite corner; in less than five minutes they sat facing each other across a small table, breathless and laughing. He admired her ability to run in such dangerous high heels. She admired his ability to disappear while twenty thousand admirers clamored for a chance to touch his hand.

What I meant before, he said, as they sipped vermouth from slender glasses, was only that a lovely actress—an *estrella* like you— shares some of the miraculous powers of doctors, or priests, or magicians.

Perhaps they are all the same, she suggested. But you were saying something about pain.

About the power to cure it. That is the best of a magician's talents, do you not agree? Yet even the corpse of a child can do it.

Now you are teasing me, she murmured.

No, he said. I have seen it myself. There was a surprising sadness in his voice; he seemed suddenly different from the powerful figure that had stood smiling before the stadium microphones. He seemed . . . vulnerable. Shall I tell you? he asked.

She nodded, resting her chin on clasped hands, in the way of a child begging for a story. He told her then about his brother's death at the age of two, when he himself was barely five. It was the only wake for an *angelito* he had ever witnessed, though he knew they still celebrated such things in the provinces.

It was held in the tavern, of course. All of life was held in the tavern. And sudden death as well.

One had only to drag one's poncho across the dirt floor, daring

one of the local *vaqueros* to step on it. A poncho wrapped around
the left arm would do for a shield. If the enemy killed you first,
well, such a death was at least a brave way out of one's wretchedness.

In the tavern a man could wash his dark thoughts down with his
fierce gin, with his fighting; one could gamble away the corn or the
goat on a throw of the *taba*. And one could hear the talk of the
vaqueros, the cowboy adventurers who rode free in the wilderness,
without fear or the noise of women's complaining. One could imagine one's self such a man, with the *cuerpo* of his enemy sewn into
the bloody hide of an animal; a man who could ride through village
streets with the head of his enemy on a pikestaff. For a poor *provinciano* such tales were the meat of life. And so was war.

So many white candles, Montero was saying. For the wake of an
angelito the room blazed like a church on fire—only of course the
smell was different.

He would never forget, he said, that amazing stink of grease, yellow gin, and strong cigars; it had stung in his nostrils like a sharp
pain. At the time, he said, it seemed the smell of *purgatorio* itself,
the place where the soul of a little brother must pause for the
nights his elders needed him.

The colonel gave her a sudden wicked grin, it flickered across his
mouth like a bright flag, signaling danger. Rosa smiled back, an actress' salute, containing the usual promises. You cannot imagine
how he looked, he said. My two-year-old dead brother sitting high
above us in his best clothes. My mother had dressed him in the way
of a small *vaquero*—a cowboy with a soft white shirt and loose *bom-
bachas*, a fine new woolen poncho over his shoulder, a high soft
chambergo on his head. They had propped him up in a chair made
of the skull of a small horse. And the chair was set upon a stack of
rum crates, and the crates in turn set upon a table. *Mi hermanito*—
his eyes staring out into the darkness, his arms hanging so at his
sides—my little brother! He ruled . . . like a small dead bandit
leader. So fierce, he seemed to frown with the shadows; I thought
he glared at the guitar player and the drunken dancers whirling
around his pedestal like barbarians. Laughing *borrachos*. They fell
in heaps on the floor and made the ugly kind of love one makes in
purgatorio.

The colonel paused and studied the face of Rosa Andújar. She gave no sign of what she felt, but reached out and touched his hand, so light a touch, as though to say she would follow where he led her. He drained his glass and signaled for another vermouth. They were both silent for a time. Then he continued, frowning, as if it had now become an effort to remember.

The old ones did not dance, of course. They only sat in the shadows with their cigars; they sat and talked of their horses, of their politics—of the price of hauling yellow gin all the way from San Luis.

She leaned toward him. And your mama—?

Sí, he said. And my mama. She sat so, straight up, facing the guitar player, and her shoulders moving in time to his music, and her eyes on the face of my dead brother. She would nod to him now and then, as though to say, *Bueno, mi niño,* I am glad to see you behaving yourself. And with her arms she made the cross in her dark lap. All night she sat nodding at him so, with her arms crossed. During the day they took him down and kept him in a cold room, where the flies would not bother him.

And then they buried him?

He laughed, a short bitter sound like a blow. No, after that night my mama rented him to another family. The celebration went on three days more. It was good for business.

Were you afraid? she murmured.

He pondered this briefly, then shook his head and laughed. Jealous, he said. I envied that power of my dead little brother. Montero stared fixedly into his glass; Rosa shivered. Of course, he said after a moment, by the time I was nine I had learned how foolish that was. The one I should have envied was the tavern owner. Like the priest, like the beautiful woman. He had the magic to cure our suffering. A little corpse, a little more of yellow gin. . . .

Rosa nodded. Sí, she said. He gave the power to your brother, and it made him rich.

The colonel looked at her. Did she remind him of someone? He could not think of who it was. Sí, he said then. I have lived half a century since. But I have never seen a stronger magic. Joy was in it, and crazy faith, and most of all, terror. From this a whole village could be shaken out of wretchedness.

For one night only, Rosa whispered.

He shrugged; another menacing smile. *No importa,* he said. How long never matters. The power to do it for even a moment, that is the miracle. Don't you agree?

Rosa nodded. The *maravilla,* she knew suddenly, was that Colonel Carlos Montero was smiling at her here, telling her this story.

THE announcement on the entertainment page of *La Verdad* was brief, though the picture of Rosa with her new upswept feather curls was very pretty. I look fat, she said, making a face. You do not, he said. You look . . . *muy seductivo.* He began to read aloud:

Señorita Rosa Andújar, who plays the role of Camila in the popular daytime serial drama *Los Ricos También Lloran* (The Rich Cry Too), has signed a contract with Radio del Estado to do a series of special evening broadcasts called *Los Manos Ayudantes* (Helping Hands). A spokesman for the station explained that every evening Señorita Andújar will select the true-life story of one struggling family whose case has been brought to the attention of the Labor Ministry. The program will tell how the ministry is helping the family in its time of trouble; interviews with officials of the ministry and with the selected "cases" will be conducted in person, on the air. Señorita Andújar, nineteen years of age, has appeared . . .

Idiots! cried Rosa, snatching the paper from him. Not a word about you! I am going to call the newspaper—

No, *querida,* he said, laughing. It is better so. Do you not see? Our names cannot be linked.

She stopped still, staring at him. But why? Are you so ashamed to have such a nobody talk about you to the people?

Rosa—he reached for her—you know it is not—I only— Remember what happened when we appeared together at the theatre— He trailed off, looking uncomfortable.

Ah! she said, tapping her foot. Disgusting gossip, such as that, bothers you. Not me.

Well, but we have to be careful. *Querida*—especially now—I cannot afford—

You cannot? She glared at him. His eyes evaded hers. *We* cannot, he amended. You know it is one thing to be—well—you are not such a private person.

Ha. *El coronel* Montero, the great Minister of Labor, seen in public with his *moza*, his little whore from the world of entertainment. Is it not scandalous?

Sst, Rosa. Stop.

No. Her eyes blazed at him, glinting from within the bright arrowheads of paint that now shadowed her eyes, gleaming like an idol's jewels set in the whiteness of her face. If it is such a scandal, *we* will stop. I will do nothing to harm your career. *Por fin*—after all—what is *my* career? Nothing at all. Yours—you are the important one. You, *querido*.

Do not do this, he pleaded. This is—

No, she said again, marching away from him. You are going to be —some day, not so distant a day—

Rosa, Rósula, I am not going to be anything without you.

El Presidente, she said. You are.

He laughed. Foolishness. The old man wants that *vicepresidente* of his—his creature, his puppet.

Well, she said, crossing her arms and inclining her small head in that way of a child, to please him, you know what happens when puppets begin to dance by themselves. The master cuts a string and—? But it has nothing to do with me. We are—she lowered her eyes—we are not connected. I do not exist.

Rosa, he pleaded now. You know well how I feel.

No, she said shrugging. I do not.

He stood in the doorway now, ready to leave her, dressed in his black dress uniform, her favorite, with the white garrison belt and the medals, the boots of gleaming black. She liked this moment best, when he would want to kiss her goodbye, and she would grow more passionate so that he could not go. She would breathe such short little breaths the way that a child does, gasping. And she would reach up to tug at the center buttons of his tunic, with a playful little gaze, a tiny wistful smile. Irresistible, she knew. An eyebrow arched, so, lips parted. And the little girl's whisper—I want to—*Oh*, do not leave me yet, *un momentito* . . . just one more minute . . .

He would try to loosen her fingers, whispering, Not now, I must go—

And she would pout, only a little. But you always—and by then her cool fingers would have found their way inside the tunic, would be stroking the hair of his chest as though playing a familiar chord. And in another instant—his belt opened, his trousers loosed, and her hair shaken free of its careful actress curls—she would be there before him, on her knees, *Permítame*—

Jesucristo, he would say, touching her head as if in benediction. And her mouth would be on him, her tongue. He would glance down at the little bones of her pale shoulders, slim to the point of evanescence; at the gold curtain of her hair swinging, catching the glints of the fading daylight—so late it was, *por Dios!* he would think, they are waiting—yet here he stood rooted to the spot she had chosen, with his carefully pressed trousers huddled around his knees and with this . . . this fierce warmth on him like the glow of a small red sun. *Por Dios!* he would murmur, and let her . . .

At Radio del Estado two of Rosa's fellow actresses from the cast of *Los Ricos También Lloran* were gossiping in the elevator; one could read their faces; they were not saying the words of friends. But what does she need a costume for, anyway? whispered Pita.

Carmen made a face of contempt. That *putatita,* she said, always needs something special.

I do not know, said Pita, how she wangled an evening program out of Oleas in the first place—

Boring! Politics! I guarantee that nobody will listen—

But now she is bossing everyone around as if—

Ya lo creo! Did you see how she helped herself to my red silk flower— I was saving it—

No! As if anyone were going to see it!

Well, I heard they invited that columnist from *La Opinión*—

Who did?

Pita shrugged. Must have done it herself.

Carmen frowned like a dark cloud. No, she must have made Oleas—

She certainly has him wrapped around—

Well, do not worry. She is going to fall flat on her sharp little—

They burst into giggles, then, just as Jorge Oleas got on the elevator, accompanied by his protégée, Rosa Andújar, with her hair pinned loosely up in a careless little knot at the top of her head. She was wearing a man's cast-off dinner suit, shiny with age, two sizes too big, and from what one could see, nothing at all underneath. Pita's red silk flower was stuck bravely in her lapel. Carmen gasped and poked Pita in the ribs. Pita shook her head and pointed to her eye. Carmen's head swiveled again for a better look at Rosa's eyes. Two glistening teardrops were there—paste diamonds, fixed somehow in the center of each lower lid. The effect was startling, especially when she smiled.

Hola, Rosa, said Pita in a voice of ice.

Oh, Pita, said Rosa. I hope . . . do you mind my borrowing— She gestured at the flower and smiled.

De nada, said Pita, with a bored little shrug. Not at all.

Good luck tonight, Carmen murmured.

I need it, Rosa said.

I doubt it, Pita mumbled under her breath.

Oswaldo Diaz, the station manager, was to introduce the public service program, *Los Manos Ayudantes,* with a brief description of the Labor Ministry's new projects for helping the poor. There was not much to tell about Rosa, so Oleas suggested he talk about what she was wearing. The idea had really been Rosa's—both the costume and the description—only, she said, to add a little color. "She comes to us," Diaz said, "dressed like a beggar in a rich man's old clothes. And in her eyes shine the tears of the *niño perdido*, the child who is lost. . . ."

On the first night's broadcast, Rosa had wanted to start with a little song. Oleas thought that was a fine idea, even though she was not a singer. She managed somehow to sing in the voice of a tearful child, which added to the effect of identifying her with her audience. This song, Rosa whispered into her microphone, is a sort of love song, but different. You will hear why. *I love a man,* she sang, *who will gaze into my eyes, and see tomorrow. I love a man . . . who sings of* esperanza, *but whispers* revolución. *I love his strong arms that will hold me, and set me free . . . For in his embrace I am more than myself. I am the* madre *who weeps; the child who is lost. I am . . .* todos. *I am everyone.*

I dedicate this song, she said, to Colonel Carlos Montero, the wonderful new chief of our Ministry of Labor. In a moment I will tell you why.

In a darkened office in the Labor Ministry, Carlos Montero sat listening to his radio. The ministry staff had left for the day at five o'clock, but Montero had come back to place certain papers in a cabinet with a special lock. Now he sat on in the darkened room, mesmerized by the sound of a woman's voice.

The door opened; Captain H, his secretary, stood uncertainly in a narrow shaft of yellow light. Quickly he closed the door again, making no sound.

Years later Captain H was to confess what he had seen in the great Montero's office that evening; what he had discovered there in the narrow shaft of light. Tears were streaming down the colonel's face, he wrote, and the trousers of his white uniform were open. The colonel's hand was upon himself, and Captain H had seen it moving in time to the rhythm of the woman's song. He recalled thinking how fortunate it was that he had shut the door at once, so fast that he was sure the colonel had not seen who it was who had intruded upon this very private moment. Nevertheless, the following day Captain H and three young civilian employees of the Labor Ministry received yellow notices in their mail, informing them that they had all been transferred.

The following day's newspapers carried photographs of Rosa Andújar in her outlandish costume, singing "I Love a Man . . ." into her microphone. The program was described as a sensation. She had told the story of a poor family in Santiago province; of how their application for relief was handled with care and speed by the great Colonel Carlos Montero himself. Each week, she said to her audience, *todas las semanas*, I will bring you another true story. *Una historia* of suffering and of hope. *Esperanza!* So that you will know someone . . . cares.

The following Thursday evening, all of Pradera stopped what it was doing at seven o'clock and turned on the radio. Rosa Andújar again was introduced . . . the lost child in the rich man's suit. Again she wore the brave crimson flower in her lapel, and again Oswaldo Diaz told the audience about the diamond tears. Again she sang "I Love a Man . . ." and again Montero sat alone in his darkened office, making love to Montero, the hero of her song.

Each week the columnists in the newspapers mentioned *Los Manos Ayudantes*—the case that Rosa dramatized, the small touches she added to her costume. Once a red feather duster, when the *pobrecita* of the evening was a housemaid from Mar del Plata. Once a bowler hat and a cane when the subject was the cruel mistreatment of a metal worker by his English boss.

One night she took off the dinner jacket, baring her slim shoulders in a spangled black *camisa*. The *pobrecita* of the evening's case was a garment-factory worker paid a starvation wage for her piecework on glamorous clothes. Rosa looked, said Diaz the station manager, even hungrier than the girl she described. Like a waif from the streets, locked in the closet of a rich señora.

The studio engineers took to playing with pink, blue, and green spotlights, for the benefit of Diaz' descriptions, and those of the newspaper men who often dropped in for a few minutes, just to

pick up a line or two about what Rosa Andújar was doing tonight—
what she was wearing and how she looked, and how she sang her
love song. Her skin, with the different-colored lights, was variously
described as alabaster, marble, crystalline, ivory, satin, and cream.

Best of all were those diamond tears. In interviews she explained
that they had been inspired by La Lloradora, the Madonna in the
poor little church of her childhood. La Lloradora, she would say
shyly, always heard my prayers. I hope she sees me now, wearing
these tears for all the Rósulas who still kneel before her tonight—in
their sorrow and ours. It was—Rosa was—as the *periodistas* said—a
wonderful *historia* all on her own.

I SWEAR to you . . . the singsong voice of María Blanca floats like
a caress . . . I swear to you that I will give my life, as La Señora
gave hers, to you, to Pradera, and to Montero, for they are all one
and the same . . . just as she and I are now one . . . and the same.

Like the cry of a monstrous wounded animal, a strangled shout
rises from the throat of the crowd in the street outside the cathedral. Señora, Señora, Monter-o, Mon-ter-o. The chanting, like a
magic incantation, grows louder and faster until scalding tears fill
her eyes; soon they overflow, coursing down her pale, shining face.

Carlos, she whispers, turning from the microphone, help me, it is
frightening, their love, it terrifies me. Calm yourself, he snaps. Control your voice; the radio audience cannot hear your tears, they
hear only a voice of trembling, the sound of weakness. Have I
taught you nothing in all this time? It is strength they love, your
name is Montero now. He breathes it into her ear like a benediction. Help me, she murmurs, forgive me. Be still, listen to me, he
says. He would shake her if he could. This love—this cry you hear,
the helpless, frightened calling—it is like the love of a woman or a

child; it must be mastered. Learn to master it, Blanca, or I promise you it will destroy you.

By now she cannot hear him; his words are silenced by the mystic chanting of the crowd—Señ-ora, Señ-ora . . . Blanca chokes back her tears and answers as though in silent prayer, moving her lips. Mon-ter-o. Then she turns her face toward Carlos. His own lips are parted, his breath comes in short harsh spasms. As if, she thinks with a start, as if he were gripping her head against his body, moving her back and forth against him. Carlos, she sighs, knowing he cannot hear her. *Te quiero*. I love you.

In the afternoon, Blanca sits before the microphone in the center of one side of the huge table, flanked by deputies and secretaries. The table is littered with telephones and heavy leather-bound volumes containing lists of names. Beside her right hand, the one with the famous square diamond ring, rest the packets of crisp new bills, neatly stacked and bound with white bands. One secretary counts out the bills, and then jots down the case histories of all those who receive them from the cool white hand of the Señora. Upon a signal to the outside corridor, the room fills with petitioners who have been waiting for this audience, often for many hours. A name is read aloud from the leather-bound volume, the petitioner steps forward to recite the specific nature of his or her desperation. Blanca sits here for two hours, hearing these stories, dispensing these bills, just as she imagines Rosa did, and with the same patient smile. Sometimes she forces herself to listen, but mostly she thinks of other things.

What is your name?

Manuel Velásquez, Señora. I have come to ask your assistance in the matter of my job.

What is it you need? she says. Sometimes her fingers drum restlessly on the pile of bills.

I am a laborer, he says. The chicle factory has laid off a hundred men, and I have urgent need of a job. My wife expects our third child in a few weeks.

Blanca turns to the deputy at her side. Find him a job. Meanwhile—she nods to the secretary—we must give you something to buy clothing for the child. A bill is peeled off the top of the pile. What will you name the child? Blanca asks, smiling.

Juan Carlos Montero Velásquez, Señora. And if a girl, María Blanca.

Blanca turns her smile deftly toward the flash of a news camera. "And if a girl, María Blanca . . ." will be the caption that appears under this photograph in the news of tomorrow.

BUT why does the President not make *you* Minister of War? Rosa would demand. Have you not told him you could do both jobs?

He would shrug. Because the Vice President has the inside track, I have told you.

She would turn her pale listening face up at him, propped upon a hand, that small face that tapered like a heart, in which the dark round eyes took up far too much space, crowding everything except the Hollywood mouth, that marvel of wet red paint that seemed always to hint at a valuable secret. She smiled at him now, her thinking smile. Did you not tell me once about all the money the Vice President borrowed from that German bank?

He sighed. They all did that, everyone who was here at the time. Unluckily for me, if they had not sent me overseas, I could have made a fortune. The Germans were so eager to make friends then, especially with the younger officers. And *sabe Dios*—God knows—

Sst . . . she interrupted, still thinking. And now it is not so good that they did, is it? I mean now that we are against the Germans, it is not so good for Mendoza and the others? It would be . . . she smiled again, and reached up to touch his mouth, running a finger gently down his jawline. An embarrassment? *Escándalo?* If everyone knew about all that money? None of them paid it back, *verdad?* Did they?

Mm, he said, frowning. But nobody knows it, I have never—

Well, she said, extending her arms in a careless stretch. The bank knows, *sí?* There are still papers?

He was alert now. What are you—?

Nothing, she said, shrugging. *Nada* . . . I was only thinking; would it not be—

What?

—only thinking about my friend Juanita. You remember?

What about her?

You remember, the pretty one with the big pompadour—she gestured—who is in love with that German banker?

Ah yes, he said, that Juanita. He smiled at her.

I was only thinking how it would be nice to have them over sometime. Do you not—

—if he could get that information—

—copies of the papers that say how much money—?

Rósula, he said huskily, stopping her mouth with his own. *Querida.* Such a brilliant little—

She drew back. Little what?

Thing, he said, allowing her hair to brush across his chest, his belly, his thighs. You may, he said, folding his arms behind his head, do what you will with me. She hesitated for a fraction of a second, studying him with eyes of black diamond. Then she closed them. I love you, Carlos, she murmured. *Te quiero.* . . . What she meant by it at that moment neither of them cared. Which was as it should have been.

IT was the night of the President's reception for the English prince and his cousins the Dukes of York and Sandringham. They were very young boys really, insufferable boys born to their arrogance and carefully trained to the uses of it. The President studied his visitors through gold-rimmed spectacles, seeking signs of acceptance. There were none, unless one counted ceremonious nods of the blond royal heads, ignoring contempt in the blue royal eyes. Arteaga felt no anger; at the age of eighty he knew that anger was an emotion he could no longer afford. Besides, he had learned long ago that all emotions are pointless when one is dealing with princes of foreign states. It was after all important only that they had come, these arrogant young men; that England had asked to send them on this formal visit as an expression of restorative good will.

The truth was that England had recently acquired a taste, not to say a passion, for Pradereño beef and grain. British leaders would therefore find it prudent now to forgive the President's rudeness in seizing the railroads of Pradera and nationalizing them. Railroads built by Englishmen, owned and run by Englishmen for nearly forty years—on cheap Pradereño labor, for immense English profit. They understood, the *Inglés*, that this President had seized their valuable property with some reluctance, to appease his angry workers and his *militares*, to keep his Casa Dorado safe from *nacionalista* mobs and his throat safe from ambitious colonels. They had understood it all immediately; not until now had they felt a need to pardon it.

It was unfortunate—the President himself could scarcely deny it—that the *Inglés* had run the railroads so well, so much more profitably than the Pradereños could do. Unfortunate, even he would say (in friendly company), that his people, raised in the warm climate of sloth, might never be taught to care about such details as efficiency. The railroads were losing time and, more important, so was he. Still, the system of *transportes* now belonged to the people, and that was supposed to keep the *nacionalistas* quiet for a time. For how long a time the President had not much cared to speculate.

Your highness, he said, bowing from the neck. The prince clasped his hand and together they faced the photographers, smiling blindly into the flashes of light. Each of the splendid young men bent to kiss the jeweled hand of the President's lady, murmuring *mucho gusto* in Oxford accents that made the phrase seem a quaint sort of foreign slur.

At that moment, three miles away at Campo del Cuerno Grande, the seventh artillery division, the third infantry, the ninth cavalry division, and troops from the schools of arms and for noncommissioned officers had assembled to await a signal. General D, mounted on a charger called Rebelión, was to lead the first column from the post barracks into the center of San Luis, and from there to the Casa Dorado.

According to the plan, it would be forty minutes before the President and his two hundred guests, including the ministers of Culture and the Interior, were seated at the long banquet table in the state dining room. The first course, a superb *terrine de faisan aux pistache*, would then be served and cleared away, and the gold-rimmed blue service plates set with shallow golden bowls for the *velouté dame blanche*. The young prince would rise to propose a first formal toast—*al Señor el Presidente, y la Amistad de nuestras naciones*—raising his crystal goblet filled with French champagne. At the conclusion of the toast, according to the plan, precisely sixty minutes from the English prince's kiss upon the hand of the President's wife, the *militares* would take over the country in a coup without blood.

It had started, as such things do, with a rumor—true or false—planted in a political gossip column, the day before the coup. President Arteaga, whose custom it was to wait for his aides to prepare a summary of the day's news (and then ignore it), happened to be sipping his coffee and paying inattention to his fretting wife, when his eye caught an item on the back page of the newspaper she was reading. It was in the column of Jorge F, the liberal editorialist.

Dios! the President exploded, spilling his coffee.

What, dear? said his wife, safely hiding behind her paper.

The Radicals are going to draft General D—run him against my man—they will kill us!

Señora Arteaga lowered a corner of the paper and peered at her husband, to see if he was already out of control. *Querido,* she murmured mildly. Calm—

The President's face had begun to turn an alarming color. He stamped his foot four times before making contact with the floor buzzer. *Asesinos!* he shouted. *Asesinos!*

Aides and secretaries scattered through the Casa Dorado; calls were placed; cars dispatched; telephones of red, black and white brought to the President, with the Vice President and two cabinet officers on the other ends of the lines.

The Vice President held a white cloth to the razor cut he had just inflicted on his neck. Have you seen the paper? the President's voice crackled in his ear. The Vice President winced. *Qué significa?* What do you make of it?

The Vice President did not know what to make of it. He shrugged. *No importa.* Probably means nothing, he said, concealing his fright.

On the red telephone, the Minister of the Interior disagreed. It means *revolución,* he said.

The Vice President's white cloth was saturated; blood had begun dripping onto his shirt. *Mierda,* he muttered.

Somebody has to find out where this piece of . . . came from, who is behind it. A damned plot—

Sí, said the Vice President, but what if they—

If they—said the minister on the black telephone—we've got five million tied up—

Eight, muttered the minister on the red telephone.

Only, said the President, if everything goes—

Well, but what can we do about General D?

Get him! shouted the President. I want him in my office in half an hour. All of you. General D will resign at once. *Claro?* The President hung up all the telephones and turned to his wife. Two months to go, he said, everything arranged, and now— He punched at the newspaper with his fist, closed his eyes, and pinched the fold of flesh between them. *Por Dios—*

You are upset, *querido—*

He said nothing, but gazed at her as if he had never seen her before. Then he got up abruptly, knocking over his coffee cup, and left the dining room.

If the President was old and tired, the Vice President was still young enough to sweat. Six months ago the old man had promised him the presidency, without strings. Well, hardly any. All he had to do was promise to keep a friendly eye on the old man's foreign investments. And of course his own. It should have been *una cosa segura,* a sure thing.

General D, wearing his black dress uniform, stood at attention on the blue-and-white carpet in the President's west-wing office, exactly twelve minutes after the old man had shouted, Get him! General D did not bring a signed resignation.

Can you tell me, said the President, in a voice of ominous calm, about the "news" in this newspaper column? Where it came from?

No sé. I have no idea, sir, General D replied, not glancing at the paper, nor meeting the President's eyes.

Well, is it true? What do you mean, you don't know? How can you not know?

General D gazed directly at him now. Not true, sir. And I was not informed of it.

How did it get in there, then?

No idea, sir.

The President drew a breath, counting slowly according to his doctor's instructions. It did not help. D, he said, pushing the name out as if it had a taste. You are a liar. Always were. This is a stupid conspiracy; you are a fool to let them use you—Montero and the others. All fools. He stopped, as if he had been running. Suddenly his fist shot out and slammed the polished desk. I want your resignation.

I do not understand, sir. I had nothing to do with this.

You mean you refuse— The President leaned heavily across the desk. Two little veins on his high smooth forehead began to throb dangerously. You refuse?

No, sir, said General D, smiling. I mean I fail to see— Two of the ministers stood up. One whispered to the other.

Let him go for now? said the Vice President, uncertainly.

We have no choice, the Minister of Commerce agreed.

Twenty-four hours, suggested the Minister of Finance.

Twenty-four hours, said the President. In the meantime we'll look into—

Señor F will print a retraction, said the Minister of the Interior.

Then we will talk again? murmured the Vice President.

But you will submit your resignation—

General D did not reply.

—and if we find—said the Vice President—

—we will be forced, said the President, to accept it.

Claro? said the Vice President.

General D smiled.

The President stared at him. *Claro?*

Muy claro, Señor el Presidente, General D replied carefully.

Get out, said the President.

The general saluted.

As soon as General D had left the room, the President began pacing the blue-and-white carpet, hands clasped behind his back. His shoes left indentations; in the four years he had been in office, the tracks of his pacing had left a clear dark oval path slightly longer than the desk. The Vice President had noted it often; as soon as he took office he planned to replace the carpet. Its flattened pile suggested too many old crises.

He won't resign, the President muttered, almost inaudibly.

He will, said the Vice President, but sweat was already trickling between his shoulder blades.

Of course he'll resign, said the ministers of Commerce and Finance, neither of whom believed it.

General D climbed into the gray suede interior of his limousine; the little red and white flags fluttered gently above both front fenders. Back to Cuerno Grande, he said to the driver.

The army chiefs of staff had scheduled a secret meeting for 3:00 P.M. to discuss the feasibility of *revolución*. They had not expected to vote on the question today. Each of the chiefs in favor of *revolución* wanted it for a different reason. Even those arguing against it were for it—they simply didn't want it yet. General D began making telephone calls, which were intercepted as usual by his secretary, who relayed the relevant details to the Casa Dorado through the customary channels. The messenger who delivered the transcripts of selected calls had copies made—one for himself, one for Colonel Montero, one for Señorita Rosa Andújar at Radio del Estado, one for Señor F, the liberal columnist of *La Verdad*, and one for Manuel Quiroga, chief of the federal workers' union.

What do you think, the President asked the Vice President, after leafing through the transcripts.

They will never agree. The Vice President sighed. Not one of them knows what he wants.

Except Montero, the President replied.

The ministers of Commerce and Finance shook their heads. That *fanático*, they said. D and the others cannot afford to listen to him.

Incorrect, said the President. Correct that he is a *fanático*. Incorrect that the others will not listen. *Los fanáticos* have a way of forcing the others to listen. Even when they cannot afford it.

I would not worry, said the Minister of Commerce, without conviction.

You are panicking, said the Minister of Finance.

Somebody has to, the President retorted.

Thirty-six hours later, General D, mounted on the black charger Rebelión, led the first column of troops from the barracks at Campo de Cuerno Grande. Fourteen thousand men marching or riding in columns would converge at the Plaza de la Constitución, and then fan out in a sunburst pattern to surround the Presidential palace.

The city knew nothing of troops, or of trouble. Only the banks had been notified, so that officers might make the necessary calls to important depositors. But from the columns of news and the radio, one would know only of the royal visitors, of the fine food to be served them, of the gown of yellow ruffles to be worn by the President's wife, of the smiles and speeches of *amistad* to be made by the ministers.

In the *centro* of San Luis, stores closed at the ordinary hour. The broad *avenidas* blazed with white lights; the black cars of the *po-*

licía rolled in silence through the streets, insuring the *seguridad* of the Royal Inglés.

At the Casa Dorado, the festivities ran more smoothly than the train of a nationalized railroad. The cream soup had been ladled into the golden bowls; the prince had raised his wineglass, offered his toast, and resumed his seat. General D then entered the room, bowed and saluted the President. Excellency, he said, smiling, I regret to inform you that you are no longer President of Pradera. . . . I am.

The troops had surrounded the palace; two Cabinet ministers had left in haste through a side door, driven to the port, and boarded an armed naval vessel.

On the radio, the voice of Rosa Andújar was describing the soup, and comparing it to the color of Señora Arteaga's diamond necklace.

At seven twenty, a special edition of *La Verdad* appeared on the street near the Plaza Victoria. It cost three dollars and bore the headline REVOLUCIÓN! in giant letters. The story said only that a coup had occurred, followed by an orderly transfer of power.

By nine o'clock, crowds of curious San Luisanos had gathered in the plazas. People were shouting *Patria! Libertad! Esperanza!* Little red-and-white flags were selling briskly on the corners of every street.

No one seemed to know who was in; only that the President was out.

In fact, he was halfway across the Rio Paraña, on the naval vessel bound for Uruguay, along with his ministers of Commerce and Finance. It was said that in the haste of departure, Señora Arteaga had somehow missed the boat. It was later reported that she was seen, still in her diamonds and yellow ruffles, boarding the British royal airplane in the company of the young prince, his cousins the dukes, and enough French champagne to ease the pain of a turbulent crossing.

At ten o'clock, scattered acts of violence occurred in the streets of San Luis. There were the usual burnings of streetcars, a demonstration of protest against the Corporación de Transportes, and the burnings in effigy of President Arteaga, his Señora, his vice president, and Sir Neville B, the British ambassador. At midnight, the light of the Plaza de la Constitución was red with a dozen bonfires, the air redolent with the smoke of *Yanqui* gasoline.

The new government issued a fine proclamation vowing to stamp out fraud, corruption and immorality; an end to all forms of tyranny by *extranjeros*. Pradera for Pradereños! *Libertad! Esperanza!*

The following morning, General D was out of office and Colonel de L was in. There was a rumor that D had been ousted because he wanted the Vice President and the Minister of Culture executed by firing squad in the Plaza Victoria. Colonel de L had argued that public executions would not look good in the foreign press; it would be enough to throw the rascals into jail, on the usual charges of fraud and embezzlement. The Vice President's management of the President's illegal business activities was outlined in detail in the newspapers. The Minister of Finance was said to have stolen six million pesos, deposited in his wife's name in a numbered Swiss bank account.

On Monday the Supreme Court of Pradera gave the new regime *de facto* recognition.

On Wednesday Bolivia, Argentina, Brazil, Paraguay, and Chile issued cautious statements of approval.

On Thursday Italy and Germany followed suit. And on Friday the United States and England expressed relief that order had been restored in Pradera. Vows of friendship were delivered by the new ambassadors of every country.

Inside Pradera, all expressions of opinion were enthusiastic. The democratic press called the army leaders courageous, wise, experienced, and temperate. The fascist press called them heroes. All political parties approved, except for the Communists, who called the new regime fascist and whose newspaper was immediately suspended. The editor was jailed on unspecified charges.

Nobody had any idea what the official polices of the new regime might be.

Only one man had a clear picture of what he wanted: uncompromised *nacionalismo* at any price. In the new government Juan Carlos Montero, now promoted to the rank of general, would retain the Labor Ministry, and would also serve as Minister of War. It was said that, at the moment he assumed office, he had a locked file containing the signed resignations of three thousand officers. The file was said to be in a safe in the apartment of that mistress of his, the radio actress Rosa Andújar.

On the morning General Montero received his new appointment, Señorita Andújar went to work as usual; however, she arrived at Radio del Estado in an official limousine bearing a license plate of the Ministry of War.

Within an hour of her arrival, the director of Radio del Estado, Jorge Oleas, had agreed to renegotiate her contract. From now on her salary would be $1,500 a week.

That same afternoon, two actresses from the cast of *Los Ricos También Lloran,* Carmen Ruiz and Pita Vallejo, were suddenly dismissed without explanation. Their parts were combined and rewritten for a new actress named Juanita Ortiz, an unsavory little *puta* of no particular talent who, it was said, had once done a favor for Señorita Rosa Andújar.

The American Ambassador's party was held, as always, on the embassy's green velvet lawn, where tropical birds stood about in formal poses mingling with the guests and only occasionally spread their fanciful tails to make a political point. The women guests hovered over the flower beds like iridescent dragonflies, those slim, long-nosed, high-strung insects which in Pradera one calls *los caballitos de Diablo,* little horses of the devil.

Doña Margarita Delgado was there, of course, and so were Señoras S and R. It was a party for *todo el mundo* to honor the *militares* who were now running the government, in their handsome white and black uniforms, with their sashes and bits of gold, their colored battle ribbons and their high boots polished like black glass.

For a hostess, the new leaders were pure delight—they adorned a garden party like a new species of exotic animal. Today the colonels and generals stood about in their crisp dress whites, escorting decorous society ladies covered with feathers, trailing ribbons and streaming laughter that bubbled with expectation. General Montero had had the impertinence to bring that *querida* of his, that radio girl. Ordinarily an unpardonable effrontery, to sport one's *ra-mera*—one's little friend—at a formal diplomatic function, but Montero was such a charming general, and it was said that he was going to be one of the very big ones in the new leadership. So if the Milgrims objected to his bringing that . . . *muchacha* of his, in her flamboyant actress clothes, dripping scarlet fringe, well, one chose not to raise an eyebrow of displeasure over the welcoming smile.

For Doña Margarita and the Señoras S and R, however, there was no diplomatic restraint. And so it came to pass that sometime during the sultry evening, when Rosa So-and-so slipped into the powder room of pink marble and gold, of mirrors and satin benches and white flowers in crystal bowls, Doña Margarita and the others happened to follow, and Señora S, standing at the mirror, chose the moment to admire the little fancy comb of ivory, studded with tasteless little colored stones, with which Señorita So-and-so had fastened her streaming yellow (outrageously tinted) hair.

Is that real? Señora R inquired, in a pleasant tone.

The comb? said Rosa with a nervous little laugh. Oh, yes! Too eager by far to please. Did she think perhaps Señora R had meant the color of her hair? Señora R coughed delicately to stifle a small laugh. Those imitation ones always break, you know, Rosa went on. But not real ivory—

Verdad? said Doña Margarita, edging closer. May one touch?

Rosa obligingly removed the comb from her hair and held it out, like an offering. *Irrompible!* murmured Señora R, in a tone of wondering. Unbreakable! She edged closer to inspect. But are you sure it *is* the genuine ivory?

O sí, Rosa said again, smiling at them. Carlos—General Montero—paid so much for it—

O, querida, said Doña Margarita, I am sure that he did.

The laugh of Señora S burst at last, behind her feathered powder puff. It caused a little cloud of pink powder in the air. Señora R handled the comb of ivory, then passed it to Señora S. *En verdad,* it looks quite real, does it not? said Doña Margarita, smiling. Her long white hand, flashing gold and diamonds, reached out and plucked the comb from Señora S's outstretched palm. Unfortunately it fell to the pink marble floor, where it snapped, so that its white teeth and colored stones flew in every direction.

Ah, said Doña Margarita, trying to look sad.

Señora R finished powdering and gave Rosa a sympathetic pat on her shiny crimson sleeve. *Querida,* she whispered, you ought to make the general take it right back to—wherever he found it.

Señora S held the door open and turned her sleek dark head just a little. *Me siento,* she whispered lightly. I am sorry—that he did not give you something real.

Rosa said nothing. After a minute alone in the powder room of pink and gold, she swept out into the garden again, her hair now brushed loose, cascading sunshine upon her shoulders. She moved quickly toward the elegant crowd, her small chin tilted high, placing one foot precisely in front of the other, in that brisk bold gait that she had learned from Soledad. By the time she reached Montero's side, the pain had vanished. *No one touches me,* she said to herself. *No one stops me. No one dares . . . not me.*

THE rumor—unconfirmed, of course—was that the *Yanquis* were about to recall Ambassador Milgrim and create a diplomatic furor of astonishing proportions. The day the rumor reached the handsome dark-paneled men's grill at the Jockey Club, agitated members were lined up three deep at the famous brass bar rail with its fanciful hand-carved brackets shaped like the heads of polo ponies. Pablito the bartender already knew about Milgrim; he also knew all the details of the impending furor. Pablito knew more secrets, and passed them along earlier, to more important ears, than any of the gentlemen whose whiskey-sodas he had been pouring for twenty-three years. It was said that Pablito was also a millionaire, whose fortunes had risen discreetly with the fall of each administration he had served. Nobody could ever tell with assurance whose side he was on, which was perhaps the only secret he had ever kept entirely to himself. *Buenos días, Señores.* Whiskey-soda?

When the news about Milgrim broke, all other talk at the bar stopped abruptly—even the latest gossip about General Montero and that radio girl. It wasn't that any of them would regret Milgrim's departure from San Luis. *Al contrario;* if only the fellow had gone quietly six months ago, as Señor R said, they might all have raised a farewell toast right here at the Jockey, and forgiven him almost everything.

But it was not Tony Milgrim's style to go—to do anything—quietly. Whether he was merely a fool or a *mala pécora*—one who is truly wicked—was still a matter of heated opinion in San Luis, but at least everyone agreed that he was brilliant at stirring up trouble. This latest, however, was outrageous, even for him. The rotter had gone and printed up a confidential little green volume filled with important names—every *personaje* in Pradereño industry, banking, politics, and high *sociedad.* The list was said to reveal scandalous secrets about new friends and old enemies; or who was involved with whom in the latest *negocios sucios*—dirty deals—with the Germans.

Milgrim had had the green booklet privately printed in the States, and then had copies sent to the entire press corps in Pradera. A stunning blow, considering how desperate the new Pradereño leaders were for money—*Yanqui* dollars—to foot the bills for their new army. All those tanks and fighter planes they would need, not to mention the tailoring bills for the new tunics, and the boots; Colonel Montero alone seemed to wear out a fresh pair every hour.

Anyway, Milgrim had certainly spoiled any chance for the *Yanquis* to dash off the check for fifty million that Pradera was counting on. One would guess that *puede ser*—perhaps the *Yanqui* President had unofficially put him up to it? And now the Germans had made it clear they were not only busy but broke. So it began to look like serious trouble for the *militares*—though they had been in power so short a time that none of the newspapers had got it straight as to which *militar* was sitting firmly in which office.

But did you hear who the man said was laundering the money? Lord I was saying, in a horrified whisper, to Señor R.

I thought he said we all were, called Señor J from the other end of the bar. Even old Dreyfus was in there. Imagine! Whiskey-soda, Pablito.

Señor M shook his head. The man could have waited till he got home—

What would have been the point then? said Don José Delgado. A serious arsonist stays to watch the flames, no?

But fifty million worth—

Never was a chance we would get that loan, anyway, said Señor R, sighing. Why would the *Yanquis* trust a pack of *burlones*—?

Then why were they so quick to recognize them?

Don José chuckled. *Quién sabe?* Even I do not recognize the President yet. Of course they keep him in bed signing pronouncements; only Montero seems to get up and dressed for the photographers.

Well, said Señor J, there is no need to recognize any of them now. The whole lot will be gone in a fortnight—

What do you think, Pablito?

Pablito smiled. Another whiskey-soda, Señor?

That Montero, said Don José. One has to admire—never a false move. The way he goes after—

Amazing! I hear the union fellows are all in love—

Not quite all, said Lord I. Still, I can tell you how he does it. Sits them down and says, Now. Only tell me what you want for Christmas. Do not be shy. Pretend I am Papá Noel—Santa Claus.

Señor R smiled; Don José laughed aloud. Santa Claus! Ho ho ho.

At first, Lord I went on, they say nothing. They sit so, shifting their eyes at one another; they cough; they light cigars. Sliding their feet on his new carpet. What is this fellow about? they think. And then—? And then. At last one brave lad pipes up with a magic wish. I would like—a twenty percent raise. No, forty! cries another. Ten paid holidays? Twelve for me, says a bold one. And suddenly they all speak at once—*los pensiones* and the sick pay; *aguinaldos*, bonuses for the year-end; a sharing of the profit! *Seguridad social* . . . Lord I waved a hand, indicating the world.

Don José laughed again. And he only sits, so. Smiling, nodding?

Sí. Sí. He says then, *Bueno, Señores.* Only sign here; I will do the *negocios* for the new contract. Trust me. You will have everything. *Todos.* On Christmas morning!

Ah, said Señor R. Quiroga will not sit still for government favors. He knows what they cost.

Lord I shook his head. This time it will cost him more to say no —he knows this too.

Ya lo creo, said Don José; his voice had dropped to a whisper. They have arrested Garcia, of the transport union. . . .

Lord I nodded. He was one who preferred not to sign. . . .

Pablito! Another—

Is it true Montero has a money deal with Rubén Caso—?

Chulo? No! Well, maybe only a small one. Perhaps a gift for the general's lady friend? One hears—

I hear he has her sit on his lap when he negotiates—

Verdad? Lord I's pale English eyes lit with pleasure. Like the American puppet, Charlie McCarthy?

Sí, said Don José. Only with her, it is said, no one can tell which is the *muñeca* and which the *maestro.*

I have heard she does not say a single word. Her mouth works too hard in other ways.

Oh, I like that! said Señor R. I must remember that one. It reminds me—something about her servicing him on the air—

Lord I made a face of mock disapproval. Dreadful, he murmured, chuckling.

Well, said Señor R, in any case the man is too clever to be hurt by that—

Ah, but those clever men are just the ones—

You speak from experience, *he,* Roberto?

Whiskey-soda. . . .

Guess what I heard about you today at the studio? What is that green book? Are you not coming with me tonight? You can wear a white tunic—Carlos, you are still reading!

He looked up at her, darting around him like a bird in purple feathers, chirping at him. Hm? he said. Just rereading this—collected speeches of Il Duce. He slipped the other book—the little green one—into a pile of magazines.

Oh! Il Duce! she cried, and made a face, and executed a smart salute, mocking him.

What I heard— She paused, raising an eyebrow, teasing.

He said nothing then, but sat marveling at the way she moved. She was always moving, it seemed; always stirred up, unsatisfied, looking for something. Even when she stood quite still, something fluttered, like the beating of a heart.

What you heard—? he prompted.

They said, someone said, that your first toy was the skull of a man—a famous bandit; that your grandfather killed him in a duel.

His face broke into the sudden mischievous grin that was her favorite of his smiles; it meant that he liked the situation, whether or not he trusted it. Sí, he said. The skull of *El Despachador*, the last *vaquero malo* in Santa Fe province. Very fierce, he was. *Muy violento*.

And your grandfather—?

The grin widened, revealing another inch of gleaming teeth. He shook his head. My poor grandfather . . . I think he won the skull from a peddler, in a toss of the *taba* at some bar. You must not tell your friends at the studio—I prefer the story as they have told it.

You would! She gave him a playful, teasing kiss, with the round tip of her tongue curling inside his mouth; one fingertip traced a careless circle in the hollow of his ear. Carlos—

Anyway, he said, stroking her feathers, her lovely throat, the soft crimson ribbon of her mouth. My *first* toy was a sharp knife with a blade as long as this—he held his hands so, cupping her breasts. My mother would wrap me up inside a bullock's hide, then tie the bundle with long thongs, to two trees, so that I would swing . . . She would leave me so for hours. The knife was my friend, my playfellow. He never let me weep for boredom; he never wounded me.

Truly? Her eyes were round with the need to believe, like a child's. He laughed. By the time I had one year of age, I knew how to attack and slice a branch, so—as it moved with the wind. By then too I could throw a lasso of twine well enough to catch a small bird —he crooked a finger round her slender neck—like this.

Ah, *no lo creo*. I do not believe you. One year of age!

He stared at her, astonished. But it is true—

All right, she said, shrugging. Then it does not matter whether I believe you.

What does, then? His smile had vanished. Was he angry with her? She was suddenly still, studying him with her head tilted in the listening way, her body quivering like an animal to the scent of danger.

In this same way she listened well to the talk of him at the radio station, at the next table in the café, in the chatter of her girl friends who flirted with the younger officers, the jokes of journalists who came to take her picture with the new hair style (swept up to the side with an explosion of ringlets over one ear). Your handsome friend, the general, they would say. So refined. But in his eyes, have you noticed, always the hard glint of steel?

She had heard the remarks of some clever men—her boss Oleas, even her brother Chepito, for whom she had found a fine job at the radio station. They too, speaking of this hardness in Montero, explained it in ways that she thought must be so. A strength, a coldness, they said, of the kind one acquires with easy victories. Winning at games of sport. Making quick money. Skills that would give a man an early sense of power. Over one's horse, or a woman; over men who were clumsy, hungry, afraid.

It was said that Montero had never been seen drunk or tired; and that he never fell in love. Such things must lead to a melting of steel. Or else he thought they must. And so he polished his tall boots every day and stood erect in his spotless white tunic, watching the drunkenness of others, the nodding and the reckless passions. And when they sat together talking of what must be done, he would sit so, listening, laughing at their jokes, watching their hands. His own hands seldom moved, but when they did it was a quick motion, always at a surprising moment, which caused someone else to let down the guard.

Rosa would hear these things and think, *sí*, this I understand, and this. It was a way she admired, though it would never be hers. She could never lie in wait so, she would never learn to pounce; she must always be moving, prowling, always testing the water, tapping the wall, fingering the chain for the weak link. They were, she decided, perfect opposites—large and small, dark and pale, cold and hot . . .

She wriggled off his lap now. What matters, she said lightly, is that we are going to have fun tonight! A new night club—my old friend Tobalito—*recuerdas?*—Iribas, the tango leader? He owns this place, gorgeous, with lights and leopard skins, a casino, I am dying to go. Everyone goes—all the *personajes*, and the beautiful women, Carlos! Tobalito promised us the best table—

I cannot go, he said shortly, not looking at her. It sounds exciting. But we have an emergency meeting. Colonel T and the others—

Her eyes blazed. An emergency meeting, why not? In some dreary bar, to invent some dreary new crisis. The President forgot this and now Colonel L can't do that. And Ambassador Milgrim, *el cochon*, says we are all German spies so we can't have any American money for new uniforms, and now who will pay for the tanks? *Dios*—

He began to laugh. How—how did you know about Milgrim?

She shrugged. Well. You are not the only ones with German spies! But I also know how that green book—the one you just hid from me?—yes, there—I know how it may be good for you, and bad for the others. But why should I talk to you? I am just a stupid *chica*—

But I do listen to you—even when I should not!

No. You only want to sit in your dreary café, with those— And what will come out of it? Tell me. Eight more big pronouncements? Ten? She made two small fists of her hands and began to strike her chest. *Pronunciamento! El Presidente* says—no more slang on the radio! Hear this! A law against sexy tango lyrics! And those foreign movies—SINFUL! SIN must go! More *Dios* in the schools! Longer skirts on the *muchachas!* She dusted her hands. See? It is no wonder all your new laws are so mean and silly—look at the places where you sit dreaming them up!

How do you know so much about where *militares* sit and dream?

He was still laughing; she gave him a pouting look. Everyone knows, she said. The hideouts of your *amigos* are on the front page. *Los militares!* Fools—how I detest them.

Aha. Well. Know what I heard about you?

I do not want to know. What?

Now he laughed, making it sound like her own cascading, breathless trill. It made her stare at him; had she caused this lightness in him? Her eyes danced. A sporting game in which she, undeniably, was the *maestra?* She laughed with him, fitting it to him; a lovely harmony.

I heard, he said, teasing, that you have not always hated *los militares*. In fact—

What is that supposed to mean? Who said that?

The tongues that wag, he said. *No importa.* You are not upset—

Why should I be?

But you are! Crying!

Of course. She turned away from him. Is it not what you wanted?

Sí, he admitted. But now I am sorry. *Querida*— He reached for her, turning her face around, holding her small chin in gentle fingers. It is only—

But her eyes refused to meet his. She would not settle for his apology. I want you to come tonight, she said sadly. I want to show you off . . .

I know. But the others need to talk—

Well, let them! I have an emergency too. Tell them you have a pronouncement—

He wavered. Well. I'll come for an hour; *los militares* can wait an hour. All right?

As he hung up the telephone, she watched his face change; hard and handsome still, but the jaw had relaxed; somehow the line of it softened, so that now it was only a strong sharp line, rather than a weapon. She smiled at the idea of that, thinking *puede ser*, it could be, that he no longer felt he must be quite so much the general with her. At least not in the face. So, he said, clasping his hands in the way of a man who has dined well. Quiroga is finally coming. He'll be here at ten with the others. It means— He broke off abruptly, noticing her smile, her scrutiny of him. As though she had caught him exulting. What use could she make of it? Still . . . When his eyes met hers, his expression had changed again; it was now the startled blank of a stranger who has just discovered a lady in the dining room of his club. You had better— I will call you when they leave. He rose as though to escort her out, pausing to shuffle letters at the edge of the desk, with a busy frown. *Bueno?* he said, with that formal engaging smile of his, the one he practiced for newspaper men.

But—she scowled in the pouting-child way that she had learned he found disarming—not always, but often enough. I thought . . . you wanted me to stay.

His glance fidgeted now from her eyes to her hair, the flight of a *tábano* who senses the breeze from the horse's switching tail. It is not—

I see, she said with a careful softness. Not that *you* suddenly don't want me. Only that now they tell you that you do not. Did he say it, Quiroga? Just now? Did he say, *We* do not want that . . . She dropped her small chin to her chest, so the voice came out in a deep growl. That . . . little—that friend of yours—eavesdropping on us.

He smiled, in spite of his agitation. She sniffed then, indicating disdain. He preferred disdain, she knew. Her other feelings, the hurt pride, the hunger—oh, especially the hunger, which he called her *voracidad*—made him uncomfortable still.

Querida, he said, resting his hands now on her shoulders, as though to restrain her. Do not make me say—

Why not? she snapped, disengaging herself. She turned away, a quick shrugging off, as one spurns an unwanted suitor. Marching resolutely toward the door, she looked so pretty, he thought, with a sudden perverse stab of pride. Her small head set with such grace upon that lovely slim neck. It made him want—

Just tell me this, she said, simply, without any anger at all, Was I not, did you not, find my presence useful yesterday? With your idiot *grupo de militares?* Not one of whom you trust—and with good reason!

Well . . . He began to pace in his new black boots; they slid on the new white carpet, which gave him a feeling of unsteadiness. She was right. She was—and it was not even important that her being there made the others uneasy. One had to admit, though not to her, of course (did she suspect?), that this very unease could be useful; it gave him an unexpected weapon, sharply honed. The question was only whether one could be certain that one's grip, one's hold on things, permitted the use of a weapon with two sharp edges—one forever curved against one's own throat. No one else would have dared—no one else had ever dared. This made him smile. Well—

So? Her voice echoed his like a tap of the foot. He could not tell if she was even a little afraid. How sure could one be of such a creature? A dangerous thing, allowing a woman to stand so close. They would all tell him that. Close enough to learn one's heartbeat? *Claro que no;* he of all men would never trust a woman with so secret a code.

Finally he spoke. They do find you disconcerting. Even when you don't say a word. *Verdad.*

And you? She glanced backward toward him, over her shoulder; only a quarter-turn of the head, and the gaze itself unreadable, for her eyes seemed half-closed. It was a captivating look—almost sly, so that one might have thought it merely flirtatious in another woman, at another moment. Carlos, she said softly, think of it. *They* come to *you.* They know they must, finally. Already they see how you move. How you can change a whole system, when they can no longer settle the simplest of their disputes! You alone; they *see* it. You have made them see—and the workers are not *estúpidos,* they are not like your soldiers. Hungry men always know at once who has power to help them and who has power to hold back . . . to help their enemy instead. The poor—she looked at him now in the other way, the soft way—it is worth their lives to perceive such things at once. Have I not seen this—have you not?

Sí, he said gently, it is exactly the way I planned it.

Ah, but the plan did not include me? Is that it? How quickly the softness had evaporated; it took his breath.

Querida— He sighed again, as though he were now the petitioner. *Por favor* . . . It is only that I don't know yet how far they can be pushed. How much fear they have—or how much trust.

Talk your secrets with them then, she said, allowing only a hint of impatience to color the words. But—she hesitated, as though to think a new thought—if you do not begin now to test them, how will you know? And when?

He said nothing to that, but stood contemplating her in that bold pose—half *coqueta*, half reckless youth, offering him an invitation or a dare. It occurred to him now that whichever it was, he had, all of a sudden, no desire to refuse her. *No quiera Dios!* Let God forbid such a weakness. Could she tell?

Carlos, she whispered again, caressing the sound. I will only sit at the table, with my hands folded so, in my lap, like a good girl. I will say not one word unless you signal me. Remember when I sat so, during your first talk with the union men? Remember what I heard, and what you said later—

He nodded. *Sí, sí.* It had been an excellent idea of hers, the visit to the women needleworkers in Mendoza. The publicity, the front-page photographs in all the papers, and now they were already organizing those women, a thing that had been thought impossible.

Still he wavered. What do you think of Quiroga?

She shrugged. They still call him El Tiburón, no? But I think he is a very old shark now; his teeth are blunt from too much chewing of small soft men.

He smiled; he favored her with an indulgent shake of the handsome head. She saw it and tilted her chin toward him a fraction more, warming to his invitation. A dance. It was as though she had tricked him into watching her seduce him; yet the truth of it was that this was his favorite of all their intricate games. Quiroga's men, she was saying, how long do they hold out in their strikes? My sister in San Marcos wrote to me: Do you know what the shoe-makers' families are eating? Cats. *Sí*—and have they strength for fighting? *'Stá claro*, he needs you more than he admits. They all do, but he knows it. I am sure; that is why he is coming. Carlos—the color was rising in her cheeks—do you not see, it is a fine thing, a miracle for you—

He laughed, a short harsh sound like a shot. They do not yet believe in this miracle. Especially Quiroga. That one still fights like a shark; you are wrong.

She shrugged again. Then we must persuade him to stop struggling so. He has no real choice, has he? Did you not tell me—

"We" must persuade him, *he*? He echoed her, enchanted now, in the way of a proud papa whose fearless six-year-old wields his wooden knife like a born *vaquero. Me gustan mucho*, these dreams of yours! They are always so much bigger than one imagines. But—he tilted her chin—how do you think "we" will persuade El Tiburón to do business?

Well— She hesitated, studying him as he teased her. Then she spoke slowly, picking the words as carefully as a child choosing important gifts for a temperamental papa. Did *you* not say . . . were *you* not thinking . . . about meeting with those *locos*, those hot-heads who fought with him in Santa Fe? They have broken away from *La Fraternidad*, no?

Sí. El Tiburón threw them out—he knew they were spying for the bosses.

Well, and did you not think you might help them start a new *grupo*—to do the bargaining? A sort of *sindicato*? And the bosses could fire the others if . . .

He grinned at her, shaking his head with delight. In truth, she was a fine listener.

In truth, that is what she wished him to think.

And then—her voice rising now with excitement—everyone would be happy to let you—to let you help them. They will see you are the key—

Well. He began to pace again, stepping more firmly now to keep each boot planted precisely where he set it. Quiroga is still too strong; the men know him. He would destroy them . . . He made a slicing gesture, the quick finger across the throat.

She smiled and shook her head, no.

Querida. He waved a dismissive hand. You know nothing of how such men work.

She gazed at him, silent for an instant. Then she said softly, you are right. I know nothing . . . but what you teach me. But I learn well, no? Have I not the best *maestro*—

His full laugh rang out now like a deep cracked bell; he opened his arms wide and she ran to him, softness flowing around him like liquid.

ROSA had insisted on watching the parade from the terrace of her new studio apartment on the Avenida Posada; the apartment was directly underneath Carlos' penthouse, which would surely make exercise for the tongues that wag, but what of that? Carlos had said. In the first place, those tongues will go no matter what we do; in the second place, the apartment is . . . more suitable than where you live now. *No te gusta?* He made a wink of sly mischief. Do you not like it?

And she had nodded, *sí*, for it was beautiful. Exactly the room she had imagined on the night she had first arrived in San Luis, on the reluctant arm of Tobal Iribas. She had imagined it while trying to sleep on Tobalito's musty sofa with its smell of cheap wine and stale love, while all night the flashing red sign of the Hotel Reina Isabella across the street throbbed on and off like a beating pulse; in her ears the horns of the night struck a single shrill chord, like a thrill of fear. If she closed her eyes now she could see the flash of that night still, red as a danger signal. Yet here she stood in a room the color of cream; sunlight skipped on the walls like handfuls of gold coins. There was a sofa that sighed with pleasure when she sat down; cushions like the bellies of rich old men, and a crimson-patterned carpet like one she had seen in another dark dream, or was it real, the house of a tall lady with fiery curls and a dress that made the sound of leaves, while Rosa lay with her feet bound by silver stirrups. She frowned, trying to remember, or not to remember.

Here on the wall was a yellow painting of a little arching bridge; she had seen it in a window—oh, Carlos!—and he had bought it for her, just like that. Best of all, there was a great square closet, as big as the room in which she and her brother and sisters had slept, separated from Mama and the boarders by the ragged brown curtain that hung from a rope. A closet! To fill with dresses and hats and shoes, so that when it was filled it would look like a party of beautiful laughing guests, a rich *cine* full of gauze and spangles, stiff white lace like the loops of a wedding cake, scandalous black like the scales of a dangerous fish, the kind of dress that Soledad had worn as though it were her skin. Fur, thought Rosa suddenly, and laughed again. White fur! And with the tips of fingers in her mind she reached out to touch it there, a cape of white fur, so long that it hung to the floor, sweeping the carpet like a great soft broom. And this cape began to turn slowly, fanning out like the tail of a bird, while a voice behind it, the silken voice of a salesgirl in a famous shop, whispered, Will that be all, Señorita Andújar?

From the terrace Rosa gazed through heavy binoculars, down at the broad white *avenida* dancing with people in the sun, and the columns of shade trees shaking their green hair as though to dry it in the breeze. The trees beneath my terrace, she said aloud. It made her giggle, and she put a hand over her mouth. The parade would not begin for another hour, though the sidewalks had been seething like this all night, alive with noise and flags, all tied with little black knots of policemen at the corners. It was to be the biggest military show anyone had ever seen. Marching forests of men carrying guns, sunlight striking them like showers of stray gold bullets, here on their polished helmets, there on their buttons, boots, swords, even the stiff braid that coiled like fat golden snakes around their necks and arms, then uncoiled in sudden streaks down the sides of their marching pants. Between the columns of men, there was to be a motorcade of long black limousines, the best German limousines, rolling in regal silence, each with a single important *militar* who stood tall in the back seat as though he were astride a horse. Carlos would be standing so, with his smile of perfect teeth, his arm in a fixed salute, suspended as though on a string from heaven.

Rosa sighed; his smile would be very tired tonight. This parade was *muy importante,* she supposed. With the faces of children turned up like small suns, and the young soldiers with their short haircuts like rows of military brushes, and the President with his tight straight line of a mouth under the tight straight line of a mustache; his smile like a line that shot up, and his frown like a line that shot down, as in a drawing by a child. From where she watched they would all be neat blocks of sticks, dark and white, moving like parts of a machine on the belt in a *factoría.* A parade was always pretty, all the square parts moving together that way, like a dance of dominoes. But it was boring too. Rosa yawned and put down the binoculars. It would go on for hours and hours, marching into the night with torches and special lights, and speeches of who we are and what we will become, and none of it had anything to do with more bread in the mouth of a poor shoemaker in San Marcos whose daughters had had to eat the meat of their skinny orange kitten and what would they have after that. Well, she thought, at least Carlos had listened to her about Christmas. At least he had done the smart thing she suggested, done it in a fine clever way that the others could not criticize—they were always criticizing him! It was only jealousy, she knew, because his picture was in *La Opinión,* or he went with her to Tobalito's and sat a big table, and *todo el mundo* came to say hello. It was not fair that they should hate him for these things; he had worked so hard, and had she not worked hard too, did they not deserve what little they had? She walked slowly around the room, touching things with her fingers, with the back of her hand, soft as a caress.

Anyway he had done it well this time, she thought. It would cost the others not a peso for the shoemaker's daughters to have something sweet for Christmas. She smiled; a fine thing Carlos had done. She thought of all the bosses in the land, sitting at their fine big desks, with their mouths dropping open when the secretaries brought the telegram. This has just arrived, sir. Collect. From the

Labor Ministry. Shall I open it, sir? *Sí*, the bosses had said, looking very busy and nervous. It says,

POR FAVOR. PAY ONE FULL WEEK'S WAGE TO EVERY EMPLOYEE, COMO AGUINALDO. A BONUS FOR CHRISTMAS. ALSO ONE BOTTLE MENDOZA CIDER AND ONE SWEET CAKE. COMPLIMENTS OF LABOR MINISTER, CARLOS MONTERO. EXPECT FULL REPORT ON WORKERS' RESPONSE TO THIS GESTURE. FELIZ NAVIDAD. C. MONTERO, MINISTER.

Carlos had had his staff figure the cost of this "gesture," and it had come, he said, to twelve million gold pesos. Think of that! But the bosses would have to pay it, they did not dare refuse. They would have to pay—even for the telegram! And the people—oh, was it not a fine thing?—the people would know that Carlos had done it. Every worker in the country! Rosa smiled as she gazed through her binoculars at the columns of perfect troops, beginning to march now down the wide white ribbon of the *avenida*. Row after row marching crisp and sharp like tiny wound-up soldier dolls. Bursts of cannon fire and brass music. And the rolling *militares* with their palms upraised, as though to hold the sky; horseback-riding in their open cars. Around them swirling paper snow, and flags of every color, and the drums that beat like hollow hearts and tanks that made thunder and horns that shrieked like animals in a storm. She sighed. Tonight in the mud-and-tin house of the shoemaker in Corrientes province, they would hear Carlos' New Year speech on their radio. They would open their bottle of Mendoza cider and drink a toast to ESPERANZA, to the hope that rises when one may believe in the sweetness to come. *Sí, esperanza* was with them; sweet cake in their mouths, and in their hearts the name of a new *salvador*—Montero. Tomorrow the voice of Rosa would tell them again, on the radio whose shape was a tiny cathedral. She would tell them of how Montero had begun this year for them, how he had sent them his love. Cider and sweet cake; money and ESPERANZA.

Colonels L and J, and Brigadier General R—whose men called him El Negrito, the slave driver (with affection, though not to his face)—stood side by side before the wall of streaked white tile, in the men's room of the Café del Mar. He is always late, muttered Colonel J, tearing at the stiff buttons of his new khaki *calzones*. El Negrito gave a grunt of assent, though one could never be altogether sure. Colonel L said nothing, concentrating instead upon the high strong arc of his urine, which he was trying to direct with force to a spot precisely one tile higher on the wall than the spot El Negrito had hit. General R's stream, already losing force, had begun the descent in slow tears toward the filthy stone gutter at their feet, where Colonel J's modest contribution had run its course, trickling into the drain.

It is only one more sign, Colonel L went on, over the sound of his own liquid music. The others tried not to show an excessive interest in the continuing force of that high yellow arc, but indeed it was as though the man had not pissed for a week. El Negrito made an elaborate show of the shaking of his long and well-formed *miembro* before tucking it out of sight. El General Montero, he said in an important voice, is in some danger of becoming a playboy. He placed a careful emphasis on the word *danger*.

Colonel J buttoned up hastily and began to speak very fast and loud. Did you see his face again today in *El Tiempo?* At some tango palace? I prefer *that*, said El Negrito, to the one in *La Opinión*, where he sits at yet another bargaining table playing *el buen Dios* now to the *peones* of Santa Fe.

Colonel J's head bobbed up and down as though it had been activated by an emergency pull cord. Did you hear, sir, what the business leaders say of the Christmas escapade? I have had three calls at least from the *presidente—*

That is odd, said Colonel L. He never mentioned them to me—

I meant the president of the Banco Federal, said Colonel J, expressing his anger on behalf—

As I was saying, the President is concerned—

So are we all, said El Negrito, putting an end to the game. He struck the swinging door with his fist and drew a breath like a gasp. *Dios*, what a stink in this place. I think we will begin the meeting at once; if Montero comes—

—he will think—

El Negrito scowled. It is time he did, no?

That Christmas business, whispered Colonel J, one hears it was *her* idea. A publicity stunt—

Really, said El Negrito, feigning lack of interest. His eyes swiveled to Colonel L. Did one happen to mention that to the President?

Colonel L calculated quickly. I did. Sir.

And—?

Colonel L smiled. He . . . shares our deep concern, sir. That the army, the government, not be used—

El Negrito waved an impatient hand, like a slap. Without the *floreo*, colonel. Did you find the President, ah, amenable to our ideas of how to solve this problem?

There was a pause as they settled in their chairs, lit their cigars, ordered their beer, swept the room with their eyes. Colonel J stole a brief glance at the front door. Colonel L watched only the eyes of El Negrito. If I may say, sir—? Colonel J began uncertainly.

What?

It was a mistake to let Montero take the labor job in the first place. At the time, of course, who else would have touched it?

Colonel L looked thoughtful, though in truth he had had the same thought. We could reorganize the ministry, with one of us—

El Negrito's index finger spread the wet ring on the table before him into a larger circle. Too late, he said. Too late for aspirins.

If it is to be surgery, said Colonel L softly, it will be a very delicate *operación*.

The, ah, *Semana Negra* Funds? Colonel J blurted, without thinking. The others went on smoking in silence, as though he had not spoken.

I hear Señorita Andújar has recently moved? said El Negrito in a casual tone.

Colonel L nodded. I believe—

El Negrito shook his head. Your investigation, colonel, is taking longer than we anticipated.

Colonel J was watching the door again. He is here, he said, with a visible twitch. El Negrito's expression did not change, except for a slight curl of the lip. Colonel L turned slowly in his chair and waved. *Hola,* Carlos! We were just beginning to worry about you.

ON their first night in the Casa Dorado, Blanca sits at the edge of the enormous bed. Is it the same one? she asks. The same bed he shared with Rosa?

Carlos touches his brow with a gesture of weariness. He cannot remember, he assumes it is a different bed. Since the night of his sudden flight into exile there have been eight upheavals in Pradera; eight regimes established and deposed; eight *presidentes* residing in the Casa Dorado, each with a señora of dramatically different style, age, and taste in decor. The last one, he understands, had occupied the yellow bedroom on the third floor of the residential quarters; it was said that her husband, General Esteban Paz, had never set foot in it.

But this bed, Blanca persists, touching the coverlet of scarlet damask. How is it possible that he cannot remember if this was his bed?

Blanca, he says, in the tone of irritation one must take with a perverse child, one who delights in the sly attack of innocent questions. *Blanquita mía,* he says; I have said that I do not remember. Then he adds, as though to erase the anger in his voice, I seem to recall a lighter shade of wood, a blond wood, and not such an ornate carving of *angelitos* at the head and foot. Well. He shrugs. I am not sure. But you look tired, *querida.* The work is hard for you?

No! she says quickly. But there is so much—I must learn everything at once, so that they will trust me. Your *militares.* Yet I know . . . they will never trust me. They do not think me capable. A gypsy dancer—a *puta* . . .

Sí, he says, with a smile. But they did not think Rosa was capable. And Rosa could have ruled the world. With her tongue of fire, and her brain. A *genio* of politics.

Still you need to say that! she says, with a start of sudden tears. I cannot bear the way you caress her name. Especially when you are talking about me! Carlos— Now she hesitates. He does not encourage her, but she must ask; she must always ask. Do you love her still? No—do not answer! Her body twists; she turns her face from him, hides it in the soft pillows.

Blanquita, he sighs. Once it was enough that I had found you, that I wanted you. Once you confessed that you loved Rosa too, had always loved her. You no longer say it. . . .

But I do! I only meant—

Sí, he says. Perhaps you meant something else. In any case we are here now, you and I. You have my name, my country. You are vice president! I give these things to you as another man gives his wife a trinket, a coat of fur. If I die you will lead the country, think of that! In all her life Rosa never dared think of that! Yet her dreams were larger—and more beautiful—than the dreams of ordinary women. Can you not see it so? She has left them to you to make real. He pauses; Blanca does not respond. He touches her shoulder. It is not enough, he says, with bitterness. I see it.

O, Carlos, she whispers. *Me siento.* I always disappoint you.

He bends over her and bestows a kiss upon her smooth cheek, tasting the tears. I am not the one you will disappoint, he says, and then leaves her.

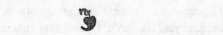

AMADO Nerbo, the famous director whose films and plays continued to be somewhat less famous than his other ventures, had jumped or fallen to his death from the window of his suite at the Hotel Playa del Sol in Atlantida. It was said at first that he was despondent over his losses at the casino, which, *en verdad,* were staggering. It was also said that he had stolen money from his actress wife Soledad, to cover the equally staggering losses of an old friend, a certain young officer who held a high place in the government. Colonel L? Colonel J? While these things were being investigated, a tango recounting the tragic story was introduced by Tobal Iribas at his popular new night club; the tango was an instant sensation, and was promptly banned by the Ministry of Culture.

Iribas' night club was closed by order of the Department of Sanitation, on a charge of inadequate ventilation in the ladies' room, an unacceptable level of filth in the storage pantry, and rodent droppings found in the kidney stew.

That weekend Rosa and Carlos accepted an invitation from Chulo Rubén Caso to visit his *casa de playa*, just outside Atlantida. Chulo had prefaced the invitation with a small but exceedingly thoughtful gift to Señorita Andújar; it was the *negativo* of a certain film that the Señorita would undoubtedly prefer to have in her own possession. Chulo had no need to explain how he came by this *negativo;* it was to be assumed that he acquired it in a forced sale of valuables by an unfortunate widow, someone famous, who had recently booked a one-way passage on one of the luxury liners bound for the South of France. It was said she had left in a hurry, and would be gone for an indefinite time.

Carlos Montero understood that Chulo Rubén Caso's expression of friendship had only the most delicate suggestion of an attached string, a matter merely of the hope that Carlos' personal attention might be called to an application currently on file with the Ministry of Transport. A routine matter. Should the application be promptly approved, however, Rubén Caso's shipping company, in partnership with the government, would own and operate Pradera's first commercial airline, with facilities in a choice location at the military airfield twenty minutes from downtown San Luis. It was understood that, should Rubén Caso's new airline be permitted to commence operations at once, without the usual delay for approval from six regulatory agencies, there would be certain further, even more generous, expressions of Chulo's friendship for the general. Needless to say, these things would be arranged in due course, and without any needless discussion that might be misunderstood, thereby provoking embarrassment, at some future time.

Meanwhile, it was to be a splendid weekend.

There would be carriage rides in the pine forest, where the horses' hooves sank so deep in the carpet of needles that it was like riding in a dream where even the most furious action made no sound. There would be dancing on the terrace; Rosa would wear a green dress with fringes, and Carlos his black dress uniform. Unless the white. In the morning Carlos would play golf with the *personajes* at the country club; they would meet for cocktails and roulette before dinner. There were no big noisy night clubs in Atlantida, only elegant little bistros with upholstery the color of jewels, music as light as the white Chilean wine. On Sunday everyone would gather for tea at the famous *confitería* on the Plaza; one would sip vermouth and nibble at the sinful chocolate truffles of which, everyone said, a single bite would spoil your teeth forever. One would even watch the scandalous *espectáculo* in which a prize of money was given to the prettiest señorita in the shortest of *los shorts*. In truth, the clothes that one saw on the Plaza were an outrage; and the gambling too. One took nothing seriously at Atlantida, which was, *sin duda*, why the serious rich Pradereños loved it so. Rosa closed her eyes and pictured a small *cabaña* on the sugary sand of the Playa Brava, a terrace where luncheon was five courses long. She would order a small green salad, and talk, frowning, of the heat, of the sunburn, and of poor Amado Nervo. Was it true there was a young colonel mixed up in it? And had one heard that Soledad fled to the Continent for a lifting of the spirits—or of the face? *Quién sabe!* who knows what such women do when they disappear? Rosa would wear a look of interest or of boredom like a señora of high *sociedad*.

By Saturday afternoon, Rosa had changed her clothes so many times that Carlos laughed at her, at the chaos in the mirror, the room littered with images she had discarded like skins of a snake. She would emerge crowned with iridescent feathers, shoulders streaming with ribbons, her face flushed brighter than the paint on her mouth, wisps of curls pasted to her cheeks like question marks, her limbs dancing to tunes in her head. *Niñita*, he would reproach her, shaking his finger with mock disapproval, frowning to hide his excitement. He could not have said why he loved her best when she was dressing up so in her colors of flame. When she turned to him, trembling in her gypsy rags, her movie-star *esplendor*, with her eyes of a child pleading for love—or some other answer—a warmth would stir the coldness in him, in the way that a man who is numb can be stirred by strong drink. Not too fine a brandy; the trick is better done by a swallow of fierce cheap rum made from the crude sugar cane of one's own province.

Sí, he would reassure her. You are beautiful. And she would shake that stubborn head of hers, no.

I THINK we have got what we need, sir, Colonel J said, suppressing a smile. He held out the folder, hoping for a slight flicker of satisfaction in General R's eyes. There was none. The President is aware—?

Yes, sir. The President was informed this morning.

Where is General Montero now?

In Atlantida, sir. Weekending with . . . friends.

Bueno. You are sure this is—complete? He opened the folder, fingered the pages without looking at them. And the press?

Colonel L has prepared a statement.

General R let the folder drop to his desk and cupped his hands together; the fingertips met and parted, suggesting an ingenious trap. I do not think a statement, he said. A hint will do. '*Stá mejor.* One of the columnists—Jorge F perhaps. Anyway one of the liberals. It will seem less—ostentatious.

But it will take longer. Sir. Colonel J's gaze dropped to his boot tips.

We can afford a day, said General R. It is a long weekend.

Yes, sir.

And—

Sir?

For the moment I would keep it simple. The girl's apartment

rental. The fur coat? We will hold back on the rest of this—he flicked at a corner of the folder—till we see how it goes. We do not want to overdo, *verdad?*

No, sir. Colonel J's heels clicked only a fraction of an instant behind his salute. He had been practicing.

There was an urgent call for General Montero; the page had traversed the white and gold lobby of the Nogalo Hotel twice before a lady directed him to the cocktail terrace. The lobby was filled with those who enjoyed the sight of each other more than the spin of the wheel in the gaming rooms. At a small table in the corner, Señora R, Señora S, and Doña Margarita Delgado sipped vermouth *y soda,* and shook their heads at the *Americanos del mal tono*—the vulgar *Yanquis*—who harassed the waiters in loud voices, demanding their Scotch-on-the-rocks.

Did you see *her?* Doña Margarita hissed, nudging Señora R.

How could one miss? Señora R replied, sighing. In white *fur.*

And did you hear that she was mixed up in that Nervo business? No!

Well—

Señora S waved a hand, causing her bracelets to collide with the sound of a small dismissive bell. *Mas importante,* she whispered. Did you hear about the burglary in my building? *They* have hushed it up—

You mean Dreyfus? *Es verdad,* he was beaten up, *el viejo,* the old man?

Sí—and they emptied the safe. The whole family fortune, puf!

Well, said Doña Margarita, peering into a large round mirror, pressing her lips together, adjusting her hair, glancing at Señora R's new spray of yellow diamonds. It is true that the Jews never pay their taxes—

Still—

Señora R shrugged. I have trouble working up sympathy—

Yo también, said Doña Margarita. I have shed all my tears this week for poor Soledad.

Oh, no, laughed Señora R. Not that—

I loved her in *Gran Casino*.

But how did you see it? I thought it was banned by the new regime. Too much of Soledad showing in it, no?

Of course, *querida*. But Chulo had a print—

Chulo has a print of everything—

So one hears. Look—is that not Montero himself?

The others swiveled discreetly; Doña Margarita merely held her mirror so that it would reflect the entire room behind her. He is in a terrible hurry—

Qué hay de nuevo? What is new about that? The three laughed together, a cascade of musical notes.

General Montero? The voice of Pablito, the bartender, had a tone of urgency. I regret to disturb—

It is all right.

Trouble, sir. *Asunto de gravedad.*

The newspapers? But how? Never mind; I know. Montero drew a breath. Pablito. One telephone call. *Por favor.*

Yes, sir.

To Baron von M at the bank—*le conoce? Bueno.* Only tell him that I . . . that we have changed our minds about his kind offer. Tell him I will call.

Montero replaced the white receiver in its golden cradle and stood in the glass booth, weighing alternatives. Then he strode back to the cocktail terrace, smiling. Rosa heard his footsteps before she saw him; without quite knowing why, she turned her head only a little. It was as though an electrical signal leaped between them; she could almost see it. *Dímelo!* she would have screamed. Tell me! But she only went on nodding at the story Chulo was telling. As though she did not know, as an animal knows, that everything in the world hung on the wind of some fearful distant storm. On a piece of news that Carlos had just received in an unexpected telephone call that had lasted less than a minute.

He held the receiver pinned to his ear with a shrugged shoulder; it was clear that he needed both arms free, to make the gestures of a man striking at phantoms. He had begun to prowl the room, hugging the walls in the way a newly captive animal takes the measure of the cage. Even the black cord of the telephone trailed from his collar like a leash. For once, his movements had a randomness; he might thrust at the air with his fists; at the telephone with his voice; but there was no clarity, no form, to the attack. Rosa sighed; it would be no use to argue with him now; he would do it his way. With a snarl of long-distance orders—or pleas—to lieutenants whose loyalty might be in doubt, to troops that might have other instructions, to allies—Quiroga? Colonel J? Pablito the bartender? Could he guess what new alliances had been forged since that first warning telephone call from the bar at the Jockey Club—or perhaps before? There were things he could tell by their voices; she studied his mouth, the muscles of his jaw; here was a sign of assurance. Of reassurance.

She gazed at the pile of his uniforms, heaped now upon the smooth white bed like fallen soldiers. He would pack them and go, leaving her here in Rubén Caso's cool guest room the color of a moonlit beach, with its crystal bowls filled with white flowers, its delicate curtains at the French windows, floating out toward the sea like veils. He would leave her so, in this playground crowded with toy people and musical games, as a child is left to play while Papa attends to the fierce business of life. He had said that she must appear tonight at the costume party Chulo was to give in their honor; she must go and charm their host; that was the best thing she could do for him. It was true, she could not deny it, they could invent no plausible excuse for her to run away with him now; it would only provoke more wagging of the tongues, such a fleeing in the night like a pair of thieves. And in any case, what would she do in San Luis while he fought with his fierce *grupo de militares?* Stand at the side wringing her hands? She would only be in the way, as they said she always was. War, especially civil war, is no place for a woman, *por fin;* this was what he had to tell her. *Por fin,* he believed it.

Still he had not told her what she needed to know. What is the weapon they have pointed at your heart? With whose bullet is it loaded? At first he had simply lied to her, swearing he knew nothing. But tomorrow the papers would have it; he had told her this; therefore he must know what they would say. At last he had shouted at her, Money! Hurling the word with an upward thrust of his arms, as though to fling a tainted fortune into the air at her feet. There! Take it! Some . . . missing funds, he said. They have arranged a charge of theft. El Negrito and the others. The Labor Ministry is to be denounced for fraud . . . for mismanagement. He trailed off, his mouth twisting as though *she* had struck him. Lies, he said, shrugging. Of course.

But then how? She flew into his arms, trembling. Carlos, *dímelo!* How?

It seems, he said, they have some . . . bits of paper. Still his eyes avoided hers, like the eyes of a boy with his first woman. I do not know what they have. The lease. On your apartment.

The spots of color had begun to burn in her cheeks, as though he held a match to them. I am the bullet, she whispered. They use me to destroy you. And you let them—

He raised a hand to silence her. No. I have told you the truth.

My apartment—

The rent is paid by the owner of the building. The favor of a friend. *Nada.* It is nothing; it is done all the time.

She shook her head. And the rest? The other . . . bits of paper?

Well. A few things. That fur coat—

No! She was still trying to control her voice, but it was escaping her, flying thin and high like the cry of a lost child. He put his hands on her shoulders, resting them only, without pressure. At last he looked at her. They will say I used certain funds. *Recuerdas—* you remember the relief rally? For the victims of the street riots. You were there—

La Semana Negra! Six million pesos! Carlos—they collected six million pesos.

His eyes were flat, without light. He kept them steady as he took a cigaret and lit it.

All of it? she said, in a tone level as his gaze. All missing? No? How much? Carlos—how much?

He said nothing, only inhaled his smoke, deeply, holding it down.

She began to weep without any sound. He spoke then, gently, as though from far away. I will be forced to resign, that is all.

Por Dios, she sobbed. They are going to arrest you.

He smiled. *Puede ser*—it may be. But I do not think so. I think they will be satisfied only to shoot me here, in the legs. The President will spare my head, I think. He may yet need it—

But the money? What happened to it?

He frowned, irritated. What happens to money! he shouted. *Se fue.* It goes. Families were helped, orphans. Medical treatment—we have records . . .

Six million pesos? Carlos—*dígame.* How can you not trust me now?

His eyes glittered in a way that made her think of the things they said of him. He let go of her shoulders and began to speak in words of ice. They are right—you understand nothing. What do you know of money? Of how funds are managed? You are a woman. Not even that, a child!

She wanted to shout back at him, No! But her throat had closed. She had felt this fear often enough. Once, when her father . . . And when Señor López Figueroa . . . and the others. Father Padrón. Once on the table, hearing the terrible whispers of her mother and the Señora Doctora with the hair of flame. Once in the theatre when Amado Nervo had said only the simple words, How much do you want it, Rosa? Enough to beg? On your knees?

She gazed at Carlos, as though at an image of herself. Each of them was seeking a truth; any truth. In his dark eyes the glittering light seemed to flash like a dangerous cold fire. Once he had told her of those strange spreading fires of his youth on the Pradal, the great desert plain. Farmers setting the torch to their own lands to burn off the grass that had died of thirst. Seven hundred miles, a thousand, burning all at once, like an endless dream of hell. For once a single flame began to dance on the face of that dry flat country, nothing human could stop its course. In the night, Carlos had stood near an old *estancia* in the midst of such a storm of fire. He had stood surrounded by a red blanket of death, watching the black shadows of horses fleeing for their lives. The sky itself, he said, had burst red above him, and in his ears the only sound was of crazy laughter, the crackling of black plants twisting like devils in the flames.

Recuerdas, Carlos, she said aloud, remember what you told me of the animals, those you saw that night in the fire near Misiones?

He shook his head at her with a sudden tenderness. Horses hiding in the woods, at the water's edge . . .

And the single steer that was trapped—

Sí, querida. The crazy *novillo* went back through the fire, and survived.

There were tears on her face now; she could taste them, but she did not know what they meant. Carlos, which animal am I? The frightened horse or the crazy steer?

You? He held her tilted chin in his fingers and studied it, as though it would tell him the answer. He touched the tears with a cautious fingertip, in the way one touches mysterious things. You, he said, are the *caballo de arcabuz,* the horse that stands fire.

They stood for a moment touching, with the sense of heat and danger rising between them like a new part of themselves. I am afraid, he whispered, that I am beginning to need you.

But that is not a thing to fear! she whispered back. It was a brave answer, and both of them had the wisdom to doubt it. Still, for the moment it was true enough. It was what they were looking for. When he kissed her goodbye, it was there.

CHULO was wearing ordinary evening clothes, except for the enameled studs that matched his remarkable mask—a sorrowful white porcelain replica of his own face with black eye holes in the shape of crosses, and a small open O in the center of its crimson-painted smile. Rosa wore tights the color of her skin, with a handful of sheer white netting, strewn with silver stars, draped lightly across her breasts and pelvis. She had copied the costume from a new *cine* about the rise and fall of a showgirl who, at the end, died beautifully, wearing diamonds and dragging a fur coat down a splendid curved staircase.

Chulo's mask surveyed his guest of honor with a slow approving nod. Charming! cried the voice behind the painted smile. You look like a wicked angel. But then you always do. Come and meet everyone. Unless you prefer to run off with me at once, and do wicked angelic things behind General Montero's back? He paused as if waiting for a serious reply. Rosa smiled at the little black crosses in the mask. Chulo, she sighed. You too are always the same.

Well, then, whom would you like to meet? He began to point with a white-gloved finger. We have two Arab sheiks; that one came with a harem, the other brought only an oil well. There are far too many American cowboys, though that one in the black hat has a real Indian's scalp in his belt. And *mira!* Did you see the black Snow White? Can you imagine how she found seven real dwarfs in this town, off season? Oh, and a marvelous Adolf Hitler—there she is, with the Jewish slave boy! Oh, but here is my personal favorite, the blond Negro in black lace panties and gold chains, can you see him? But everyone is beautiful, do you agree? Champagne?

Rosa nodded, blinking. Who is that, the Chinese empress in the wonderful silk robe?

Where?

The porcelain mask swiveled to follow her gaze. Ah, that is one of your admirers! Chulo squeezed her arm. Go and talk to her, she will be thrilled.

But who is it?

Chulo laughed. What would be the fun of this party if I spoiled everyone's secrets? Go on. He gave her a playful push, and the mask turned away to greet a dancing sugar skeleton on the arm of a man dressed as Queen Victoria in her declining years. *Maravilla!* Chulo exclaimed, moistening his gloved finger to sample the sugar.

Rosa made her way to the red silk empress. Your Majesty, she said, executing a half-curtsy. The empress held out a hand with scarlet talons two inches long; a diamond ring in the shape of a serpent crawled from knuckle to wristbone. Señorita Andújar! The voice poured like clotted cream from behind the cruel Chinese features. She wore no rigid mask, only caked white flour and glistening paint, but the effect was eerily the same. Señorita Andújar! she exclaimed again. But how perfect for you to come as a queen of tarts. The red silk robe whirled about like the cape of a *matador;* the empress was gone. Doña Margarita! someone called. *Hola, querida . . .*

No one touches me! Rosa forced herself to say it aloud, in a fierce voice against the gaiety of the music. Dressing upstairs, fastening a turban veil to her head with a spray of shooting stars, she had felt the rhythm of the tango inside her. Now the inner music had stopped; only the shrill cries of old pain and fear echoed in her limbs. She pressed her feet against the floor of polished marble, feeling the coldness through the thin soles of her silver shoes. Hard and real, the coldness pinned her feet to this spot so that she would not run, or faint, or weep. Out of the corner of her eye she saw a dark shining smile, like a smear of blood, blurring toward her, turning away. Someone carrying drinks edged past, pushing her forward into a pair of naked arms. Above them smiled a rubber mask with the features of the American President. It wore a white Homburg with a rakish tilt; a cigaret holder was clenched in its famous smile. *Perdóneme Vd.,* Rosa murmured, struggling against the naked arms; they tightened their grip. But this is our dance! The voice inside the American President spoke with a heavy German accent; a blue plume of sweet marijuana smoke drifted out of the cigaret holder. Have you forgotten? the voice persisted. Rosa drew a breath and smiled. Of course not, *Señor el Presidente.* And she began to dance. All around them, hemming them in, danced nightmare figures from her childhood. La Muerte and La Lloradora, both in the arms of men painted gold. A beautiful woman, dressed as an ape, embraced a pretty boy wearing only a wig of long blond hair, wisps of it pasted discreetly to his body. On a mirrored table in a corner of the room a young girl, perhaps ten years of age, danced naked except for a small red satin heart that swung from her neck on a string. The heart was a purse; from across the room one could see that it bulged with money—pesos, dollars, Deutschemarks. Chulo stood at the child's feet with his mask upturned, silent pleasure poised in tribute within his dark smile.

Raw oysters were being served on trays of carved silver; coins made of paper drifted from a mirrored ball in the ceiling, as though a bored hand were dispensing largesse. Laughing girls dressed as slaves passed among the guests, shooting ether from little silver guns. And in certain corners people gathered to make various kinds of love, without removing their masks.

Are you having a fine time? She felt a sudden cold kiss on the nape of her neck; Chulo. It is a very interesting party, she said. He laughed. You hate it, *verdad?* Come, we will go and have a civilized talk somewhere. He seized her hand and began to lead her through the crowd, toward the cool terrace that faced the harbor. Tiny lights winked up like trusting eyes from the yachts that lay anchored at the marina. Rosa followed her host, silent as a captive Eurydice, without the slightest illusion that he might show her a pathway out of his underworld. She followed him because she had planned to; she had urgent need of this man—or rather Carlos did. Which was now the same thing. True, Carlos had not said this in so many words. Still, he had left her here, and at last it was understood between them that he would not leave her now to play the games of a child. This game was dangerous; he had said it himself. He had said it was the most dangerous game of all. He had not smiled when he said this, but she had. Indeed, she could have replied—though she did not—that it was the game of all her life.

I am glad of this moment, said Rosa, choosing the words with care. I wanted to thank you for your kindness. It was a very thoughtful gift.

What? Oh, the *negativo.* Chulo laughed. 'Stá nada. I only wish I could also erase the memory of your pain on the day we filmed it. Such a frightened *pobrecita* you were! Are you still? Under all that worldly . . . veiling?

Sí, said Rosa; she tried to gaze solemnly into the small black crosses that hid his eyes. I am frightened still.

Not of me, *todavía!* But perhaps I can allay some of your other fears?

That was what I wanted to talk to you about.

I thought so. You may— He slid an arm around her bare shoulders. She shivered and moved only a little. Chulo . . . I cannot joke with you about these things. You are a powerful man, and I am only—

—a poor showgirl? The sweetheart of a soldier? Come, Rosa, you and I can write wonderful dialogue for this scene. We did it once—

Sí, but now you are wearing a mask. And I am not.

A woman like you always wears a mask. Disguised as—how did the red empress say it? Oh, it was good, I thought.

You heard what she said?

Querida! It is my party. I hear everything.

What else have you heard, *por ejemplo?*

Well, I have heard why General Montero sent his regrets this evening. Why he left the seaside in such haste, preferring the heat wave in San Luis. *Pero . . .* I have not yet heard why the beautiful Señorita Andújar was left to the tender mercies of this pack of *salvajes*.

Rosa would not permit him to know that he had surprised her. Who told you why Carlos had to leave? There was a lightness in her voice. Perhaps he would not notice that she was trembling.

But everyone has heard it! he exclaimed. Tomorrow your general will be torn apart by another pack of *salvajes*. Not so gaily dressed as these. All in dreary uniforms. It is too bad. Chulo sighed. But was that what you wanted to talk about, *querida?* Is it why we are standing out here in this air full of perfume and music—I in my mask of sorrow, you in your seductive veil of stars—when it is so clear that you dislike me?

Chulo . . . she began, and then stopped with a sigh. What is the use; my wits will never match yours. And the truth is you are right about almost everything. I need your help. I am willing to do . . . whatever is in my power to do. But . . . I do not dislike you. That is the only thing you have said that is untrue.

Chulo's mask glittered in the moonlight. He kept his head very still, with only the profile turned toward her. The breeze ruffled his black-and-silver hair, so that wisps of it rose and fell against the smoothness of the porcelain cheek, creating a strange liveliness. Like the haunting beauty of *la Muerte* in evening clothes in that old *cine* . . . the beauty that made the young girl give up her life. Thinking of this, Rosa trembled again. This time Chulo saw or felt it, and drew her closer.

Then in what way can I help you? he asked. His voice was soft; it held no menace now, which somehow frightened her more.

I need thirty minutes on Radio del Estado tomorrow night. You can arrange it with Oleas . . . so that all the other stations carry it too. Radio Federal; El Mundo. All of them.

He said only, Is that all?

No. If I speak . . . if the whole country hears me, there could be a big demonstration. Workers, Women. *Provincianos*. Carlos' friends will help, Quiroga and the others. But someone must take the responsibility. It must be done in the right way. There— Her voice faltered; she recovered it quickly. There is some money . . . I have new friends who will help. And I have old enemies who can be persuaded.

Chulo said nothing for a moment. Then: Has the general appointed you? To make me his, ah, finance minister? Or, *puede ser*, his production manager?

You must know, she said, that he has not. He would not—appoint me, as you say.

Ah. Then suppose one agreed? To assume "responsibility" in this critical moment. Let us say, a temporary finance minister? It would be understood, then, that one would hold such a post, on a more official basis, after the crisis?

Rosa hesitated only an instant. Long enough for a breath, but not a thought. I can say this, she began, threading her way as though through a small opening, such as the O in Chulo's smile. I know Carlos would trust you. If I do.

Chulo grunted, whether with doubt or satisfaction she could not tell. Then Carlos trusts *you* more than one had thought.

I do not know about that, she said. I know only that he trusts me. . . .

Well, said Chulo, with an expansive sigh. I will think about it.

There is no time to think. She rested a delicate white hand upon the sleeve of his expensive coat, silken to the touch. He turned suddenly and leaned against the stone balustrade with his back to the sea. Shall I remove my mask?

She smiled then. Not if you think I am wearing one.

CHULO Rubén Caso was the kind of man of whom it was said, with both envy and derision, that he had many long thumbs. Until now his grasp had been wide but clumsy; he produced bad movies and good business; he pursued the right men and the wrong women; he built fortunes and lost them as a fool loses coins in the street. His life was, like Chulo himself, a thing of considerable bulk but no particular form. It could be said with fairness that the thumbs had now grasped the thing he most desired, which was a base of personal power.

On the night of his fancy-dress party, therefore, Chulo was awake to the stroke of rare good fortune, the *choque* of opportunity, when it appeared in the unlikely person of Señorita Rosa Andújar, that young woman of no special grace or talent, whose charm he had previously found limited and hardly novel, and whose wits were sharper than her delicate bones, a condition which, in his eyes of a weary frog, rendered her utterly sexless.

So it was when the *chica* began to speak of her sudden—one might almost say desperate—need for his friendship that Chulo discovered to his amazement that she was a thing of beauty, and that he loved her. Perhaps to no one else in the world could this *maravilla* have happened in quite the same way. For only Chulo could have perceived at this moment that the *puta* had now the makings of a *personaje*. It would be necessary to proceed with more than his usual caution. One must do what one could to protect the Señorita, and her friend the general, from too much knowledge about one's production plans. These had already begun to take shape in Chulo's mind, but they must rest for a time without disturbance; at all costs one must restrain one's impulse to jab at them with a long, clumsy thumb. For the moment Chulo needed only to gain the Señorita's perfect trust; *entonces*—then—one must gain that of *el general*. There was a way to do this with a single stroke; one shivered with the boldness of the thought, but it was exactly the way in which one must think. Chulo Rubén Caso had not produced a string of bad romantic movies for nothing. The plot would call for *el dios del amor,* the god of love; *el Señor Cupido*. The general must be made to see that Rosa risked her honor, her career, her life—to save his. Would he then repay her in the way that a man of honor must? *Claro,* the idea was outrageous. And *claro,* it was the only way. Chulo himself would play the god of love; only this would guarantee the success of his most ambitious production. With a shrewd *militar* for a hero, one who would never for a moment think of marriage to such a woman; and the woman in question, such a bad one! The shrewd *militar* knew too well that a bad girl is not a wife, and vice versa. Accusations of theft and corruption were *cosas de cajón*—matters of course; arrest, disappearance, cowardice, desertion, even a temporary loss of *poder*—all these misfortunes one could survive. But marriage to a *puta?* A radio actress with a dark red smile like a stain of sin? She was, as one has heard it said, no better than she should be. For an ordinary *militar* of advancing age, the taking of such a wife would mean political ruin. For a man within reach of the presidency—*suicidio*. It would take a *genio* to produce a success of such a plot. A *genio*.

Chulo had many telephone calls to make. To Jorge Oleas at Radio del Estado. To Baron von M at the Deutschebank. To the President. To Lady I, the wife of Lord I, who would surely tell him company secrets her husband would prefer that she did not. To Señor F, the liberal columnist, for an exchange of breached confidences; to Don José Delgado for an exchange of dangerous favors. To Colonel J, who, one had heard, had little to lose by accepting the offer to become a double agent within the *grupo de militares*. And, *por fin,* to Pablito the bartender at the Jockey Club, who would know which of the others was lying, and also why.

When he had done with this night of telephoning, Chulo would have money and information enough to begin work on his production; Rosa Andújar would have her radio broadcast; Carlos Montero would have his *demostración* and the restoration of his *poder*. Chulo would have a toe, as well as a number of his long thumbs,

inside a great door. And a marriage of love would be arranged between a new leader of Pradera and a half-naked *puta* with stars on
her breasts, some of whose previous acts of love Chulo himself had
been privileged to record on film not long ago, and of which he had
thoughtfully kept copies in his studio vault. Chulo emitted a sigh of
happiness behind his porcelain mask; it had a cool, precise sound
which pleased him.

In the bar of the Jockey Club, Pablito had turned on his radio to
hear the special broadcast of Rosa Andújar. The volume was low;
one could scarcely hear it over the tinkling of glasses and ice, the
voices of *los señores* gathered for their *aperitivos*. It was the usual
early-evening crowd; soon they would disperse for their homes, to
join their wives for the theatre, for a dinner of el baby beef at the
Ambassador or the elegant new night club on the Calle Florida.

Is that the general's lady? said Señor R. Turn it up, Pablito!

No, said Lord I. Turn it off.

Imagine letting that *puta* make political broadcasts! How on
earth do you suppose . . . ?

Porqué no? said Don José Delgado. One hears Oleas is the new
lackey for Montero.

Not for long, said Baron von I. Did you see the papers today? F's
column?

Sst! said Señor R. Listen!

Why do the rich men hate Carlos Montero? said the voice of
Rosa Andújar. *Because he cares about you and me! The poor and
the powerless! Not the Yanquis who order us around. Or the Inglés
who grow fat from our industry—while we grow hungrier still! Why
do the rich fear General Montero? Because he does not fear them!*

Por Dios! exclaimed Lord I. The woman is a menace. Is it possible the President knew about this speech? I cannot believe—

The enemies of Montero are desperate men, said the voice on the radio. *They tell lies to discredit him.* . . .

Whiskey-soda, Pablito! said Don José. Double.

We must show them we do not believe such lies. We must go . . . into the streets. To shout the truth!

Think she can actually do any damage?

I doubt it, said Lord I. These people . . . I mean—

The truth—is the bread that Montero puts into the mouths of our niños.

Turn that thing off, Pablito. *Basta!*

The truth—is the new peso in your pocket. The peso Carlos Montero wins for us. From the Inglés! From the Yanquis! From . . .

In his office at the Casa Dorado, the President sat at his mahogany desk, immobile as a statue, supporting his head with both hands. Across from him, seated in carved armchairs, were Colonel L, Colonel J, and Brigadier General R, El Negrito. They were listening to a woman's voice on the radio.

Montero needs us now. Tonight! Wake up, amigos! We must march together. In the streets of San Luis. In the Plaza Victoria. We must shout the truth . . .

But who is responsible? The President was trying to control his voice. Thirty minutes! On every station!

El Negrito was striking one hand with the fist of the other. She will be cut off any minute. They are preparing a program of tango music . . .

She has been on for ten minutes! shouted the President.

. . . *A general strike of workers!* said the voice of Rosa Andújar. *Todos los hombres. Todas las mujeres. Together! In the streets! For Montero!*

Dios, murmured Colonel L.

I want him arrested, said the President.

We cannot risk that, sir! said El Negrito.

I listened to you, said the President. His eyes were very bright, like those of a man in fever. Now I am listening to this.

It will be worse, sir, said Colonel L. It is always worse to make a political prisoner.

—not a time for panic, said El Negrito. Why do we worry about this? This— Nevertheless, he continued to strike one hand with the fist of the other.

—not going to start a *revolución,* said Colonel L. This whore who performs in soap operas.

I want him arrested. And I want her fired. *Claro?*

A mistake, said Colonel L.

A serious mistake, said Colonel J.

In a new house of white stone, in the city of San Marcos, Juana Ibáñez sat at her new dining table, with her hands at rest in her lap, one curled upon the other with the palms turned up, so, like two pieces of a broken cup. She sat in the fading light, as had been her habit in the days before there was enough money for a lamp to be lit in each room. With her were Catuja, Lola, and their husbands; they all sat in silence around the new table, listening to the voice of Rosa Andújar on the radio. Juana's eyes glistened; she kept her head bowed and her gaze fastened upon the hands in her lap, so that the others would not see her tears of pride. Of course she knew well the power of her youngest child's voice raised in anger and pain; it had moved her often enough. Still, what a thing of pride and wonder it was to hear this power now, full and sure like a *trompeta,* a *clarín* of heaven. To know with a sureness that such a sound, from the throat of one's child, could lead men to do one thing instead of another.

This man, Carlos Montero, said the voice of Rosa Andújar, *has rich and powerful enemies.* Militares. *Bankers and* políticos. *Foreigners. . . .*

Juana Ibáñez began to nod, as though to the rhythm of an old song.

But Carlos Montero also has friends. Who are they? Workers. Hungry children. Poor women and provincianos *who are paid the wages* of esclavos. *Slaves in the* factorías. *On the* estancias. *Slaves of the rich and powerful men. . . .*

I am a worker. Like you. I am his friend. Are you? Are you one whose wages rose twenty percent last month, because of Carlos Montero?

Catuja turned to her husband and took his hand, holding it with a gentle pressure. He smiled at her, murmuring, *Sí.* Thanks to the personal interest of Carlos Montero, Juan Bautista Saldias was now an important *hombre* in this village. He sighed with the satisfaction of it.

. . . Are you one whose niños ate raisin bread on Christmas Day because of Carlos Montero? . . .

Rosa completed her radio address without suspecting that her closing words had been supplanted by a new tango about a poor soldier who wins a national lottery, deserts the army, and then loses everything, including his honor, because of a blond *puta* who betrays him with all the men of his regiment.

Whether the choice of this particular song involved any sort of deliberate slander upon the characters of Señorita Andújar and General Montero was never clearly established. Still, two newspapers made a sly joke of it the following morning, one in an editorial cartoon and the other in a small article that ran in a box alongside the leading story of the day, which was of course the financial *escándalo* about *el general* Montero, chief of both the Labor and War ministries and reputed leader of the powerful *grupo de militares* surrounding the President.

The news of Rosa Andújar's "resignation" from her job at Radio del Estado, and the cancellation of her popular evening broadcasts, appeared in a separate article in the entertainment pages. The brief announcement mentioned that her role in the soap opera *Las Ricos También Lloran* would be assumed by an unknown young actress— a new discovery and protégée of Jorge Oleas, the broadcasting executive. There was a photograph of the new *estrella;* she had a sweet red smile.

On the radio and in the newspapers the whereabouts of General

Montero were first reported as unknown, or for the moment not revealed, pending the *investigación* of the charges against him. Then one columnist speculated that he had fled to Uruguay with ten billion pesos of missing relief funds, stolen from the victims of the *Semana Negra* riots. Another said that he had been arrested and was under heavy guard on the prison island of Santa María. *La Voz* reported that he was aboard a German gunboat bound for Europe, and *El Tiempo* had exclusive photographs showing him hiding out in his mistress's lavish apartment on the Plaza Victoria, sipping green tea from a silver gourd and surrounded by ill-gotten treasures. *Sin duda,* the photographs were three months old. Finally, Radio del Estado and Radio Federal reported in the evening news bulletin that General Montero was in critical condition in the military hospital at Campo del Cuerno Grande, suffering from *un postración de las fuerzas vitales*—a prostration of the vital processes; that mysterious collapse which so often befalls a hard-driving *político* who undergoes a sudden loss of power.

It was three o'clock in the morning when the startled doorman of the sleek white-and-silver building, in which Juanita Ortiz had recently acquired a small terraced studio, reluctantly pressed the buzzer to her apartment and announced in a voice of sleep, *Me siento mucho, Señorita,* there is a lady here who says you expect her—*ahora?* *Sí,* Pedro, crackled the voice of Juanita; it is as she says.

Rosa, with a face of dry chalk and deep shadows like bruises beneath her eyes, appeared at Juanita's door; they embraced in silence, and Juanita felt the trembling of Rosa's body. I am sorry to come so, seeking a favor, Rosa whispered. Juanita stared at her. Between us, she said, there are no favors. Come in—

Is he here—Rudi?

Juanita shook her head. The baron spends Tuesdays with his wife.

Rosa glanced only briefly at the yellow room; she smiled without saying anything. Juanita nodded, smiling in return.

Rosa touched the sleek yellow sofa, and then sat, listening for the sigh of the cushions. Tell me, she said. What Rudi thinks of what has happened. What he says of Carlos.

Juanita sat beside her friend, and hesitated.

I promise, said Rosa, it remains between us.

Cree que—he believes that Carlos will triumph. He is—you must know he is a friend. What he has done today—

Rosa placed a hand upon the arm of her friend, to silence her. Do not tell me, she said. In the afternoon there had been a break-in at the office of the Credito Industrial y Comercial de Pradera; it was said the police had aided the *asesinos*, but the reports were in conflict. It was certain only that Josef Lieb, the banker, had been forced at gunpoint to open the company's safes, and that the *asesinos* had found stocks and bonds in piles that reached to the ceiling; government securities, shares of Union Telefónica, private stock of the Corporación de Transportes, bars of gold—enough to fill the national treasury? to build a new army? to free a political prisoner? It was the sixtieth birthday of Josef Lieb. *Feliz cumpleaños*, the *asesinos* had cried as they left him on the floor of his secret vault. Happy birthday. Rosa rested her hand now upon the black silk sleeve of her friend Juanita. Do not tell me of Rudi's friendship. She paused to draw a breath, as though it caused her pain. I want to know only that Carlos is safe.

Juanita frowned. You do not trust me. Me! You have no cause—

Rosa sighed. It is too late to talk of trust. There are terrible things of which we cannot speak, not even you and I. We have kept our silences before. And now there are things I hate, things I fear. And I am *impotente*. . . . But never mind. I have come only to say goodbye. I am leaving tomorrow—after the *demostración*.

Juanita gazed at her friend with astonished eyes. Leaving? Now? But he will be free—!

Rosa nodded and looked away. That is why I must go. My family, *mi madre*—we may take a voyage. I have wanted to travel, you know . . . The gaiety in her voice trailed off as abruptly as it had begun. You must say nothing. Not even to Rudi. Promise me.

But you love him. Juanita spoke in the soft voice of wonder, but it was not a question.

Sí, said Rosa, with a small shrug. *El amor.* As we know, you and I, that is a thing of smaller consequence than life. What happened yesterday—what will happen tomorrow—these are what I know. What will happen if I stay with him? They have made the price too high, these *amigos* of his, these *militares;* and the others, all of them, his rich enemies. I have no more weapons to fight them; they have arranged that. Yet he will defeat them. And who will care that it is my victory? Mine—but only if I surrender, if I go. He will be safe. It is so clear now, suddenly. Only if he is free . . . of *me* will he be what he must be; only then he will have everything we fought for. *Verdad?* A simple *historia*—she laughed a short harsh laugh, filled with pain—like that of the prince and the peasant girl. *Recuerdas?* Remember when I played that role on the radio? And was the same not said of her? A common woman cannot win a crown of power in that way. She can win a man, perhaps. A marriage ring. But not a crown of power. Not—

Juanita reached for the hand of her friend; a cold hand. She covered it with both of her own. He will not surrender you, she said in a voice of sureness. Carlos is not a weak prince; Pradera is not a pale white country of men with thin lips and no courage. *Por Dios!* Where would Montero be this night, if not for you? Do you believe he denies his need for you!

Rosa withdrew her hand. *No importa,* she said with weariness. I cannot think about that; I must think where he will be tomorrow. And where I will be. She reached into her purse and drew out an envelope. I have written a letter. I want—I need for you to ask Rudi to arrange . . . I want him to receive it after—after they have released him.

Juanita took the envelope; still she stared at the exhausted white face of her friend. Rosa, she said softly, we have known each other well. Better than we have spoken of, *verdad?*

Rosa said nothing.

I will do what you ask; only promise me that you will not go before he answers.

No! The dark eyes blazed now with a fierce light. I cannot sit so, in that apartment—that *regalo de amor* that they say he stole for me! Wait there like a spider? For him to come and tell me that we can go on. Just as before! As though nothing had happened? I . . . I will not play *soldadera*—camp follower of the resurrected hero!

No, said Juanita, with a little smile. You will be his wife. This *I* know.

Nunca! Rosa began to march across the yellow room, one foot placed precisely so, before the other, and her head high, so, like a small *militar*. I will never—and *they* will never—and *he* will never . . .

Juanita shook her head. *Sí*, Rosa. Juanita is never wrong in these things. *Recuerdas?* That Juanita who first cut the high slit in your black skirt, that you might cross your legs so, as you do now with such an easy grace? That Juanita who taught you how to make those little black beads on the ends of the eyelashes? *He?*

Rosa smiled, remembering. *Sí*. And at the *centro de belleza*, that Juanita who chose the style for poor Rosa's hair—cut it so, she said, here and here, like this, *mira!* She has a quite pretty neck! But then, *mi amiguita*, was it not the same wise friend who said one must have a certain *operación?* For the breasts! This I remember too. I was going to get a fine job, dancing at a café—

Mm. Juanita laughed. All right. I was wrong that time. But that time only, you will admit, no?

Ah, *mi amiguita*. Rosa ran to her friend and embraced her. I do trust you. You will deliver my letter—

Juanita nodded. And you, she whispered, you will see. That I know what will be.

GENERAL Montero had been informed of his options by two armed guards, during the short ride from his apartment on the Calle Orilla to the waterfront, where a navy gunboat lay at anchor, ready to transport him to the island of Santa María, midway across the Rio Verde between San Luis and the inland coast of Uruguay.

Except for its small staff of armed and well-trained guards, its watchtower with two machine guns, and an imposing tall fence of electrified iron filigree that ringed the island like a deadly collar of black lace, one might take Santa María for a modest fishing resort; a handful of small wooden cabins, sparsely furnished, and without barred windows. A prison designed for officers and gentlemen, *en verdad*, although there had been moments in its history when reputedly it had been used by secret police for certain extreme forms of interrogation. There were barracks for the guards and a central dining facility where a prisoner might dine with his jailors, or alone, depending upon his rank and the gravity of the charges against him. The grounds were scrupulously maintained by inmates serving long terms at the neighboring prison island of Esteban Tomas. On Santa María a prisoner might roam the gardens at will; guards with cocked rifles maintained a respectful distance. No one had ever escaped.

There was no telephone on Santa María, but letters were delivered daily by naval launch, and radio communication maintained at all times from the island post commander, to the President's office at the Casa Dorado, and to army headquarters at Campo de Cuerna Grande.

It was understood that General Montero's stay on the island would be brief. No one was yet certain of his scheduled departure or his ultimate destination, but it was assumed that he would be permitted to leave Pradera within forty-eight hours of his arrest, provided that he acceded to certain conditions set by the President and the *grupo de militares*. These conditions pertained to money, a signed confession, and a promise to remain in indefinite exile, with no attempt to participate in politics of any kind, anywhere. The moment *el general* provided his jailors with the assurances they sought, he would be escorted to a naval vessel bound for Uruguay; from there he would be free to sail or fly to Mexico, Panama, Argentina, or Spain. All charges would be dropped; the official *investigación* would be concluded with no evidence of wrongdoing by *el general* or any member of his staff. As to the missing money, it was suggested, the general would be permitted to make full restitution to the people of Pradera; some of it, undoubtedly, would find its way back to the national treasury.

Late Sunday afternoon, upon payment of one thousand gold pesos, General Montero was permitted access to a small radio, which he listened to in the privacy of his cabin. One of the guards claimed later to have seen him weeping as he listened to the words of his *enamorada*, pleading with the people to save him. A letter was delivered to him later that night, upon payment of another thousand gold pesos; the letter informed him that his *enamorada* had been dismissed from her job, shortly after being cut off the air, and that she was in hiding. The message was unsigned, but it made clear that Señorita Andújar had known she was in danger prior to the broadcast. Certain friends were now trying to arrange for a safe passage for her out of the country. Money had been furnished by the federal workers' union, the *Federación* led by Manuel Quiroga, El Tiburón. That one had also organized the nationwide *demostración* which would occur tomorrow. In the meantime, Baron von M was attending to other details.

On Monday morning the courier delivered two additional messages, this time with no charge. One was from the President; a brief announcement that the prosecution against the general had been dropped, that Montero's ministerial post and titles had been restored, and that the President personally extended a cordial invitation to the general to appear with him tomorrow in a ceremony expressing the solidarity of the government; this occasion was to occur at noon Tuesday, on the balcony of the Casa Dorado. All press and radio stations promised full coverage of this historic event. The favor of an immediate reply was requested.

General Montero smiled and opened the second letter, the one from Rosa. *Querido*, it said. I am going away. Do not try to follow or find me. I know this is best for you now. I rejoice that I have done what I have done, so that all you have wanted will be yours. *Te quiero.*

Montero folded the letter and stood silent for a moment, gazing out at the black water of the Rio Verde. Then he turned, nodded to the orderly, and marched with resolute steps to the office of the post commander. Messages were dispatched: to the President, to Manuel Quiroga. Within an hour El Tiburón and a small party of union leaders arrived on the naval launch that was to take Montero back to San Luis. It had been arranged that *el general* would arrive in secrecy, as he had left; he would be admitted to the military hospital at Campo de Cuerna Grande. An official bulletin would be issued in the evening, stating that he had been in the hospital since yesterday, undergoing routine tests for a recurrent complaint of *cólico*.

On the launch, Montero sat with El Tiburón, drinking whiskeysodas. They were silent for a time, and then Montero said in a quiet voice, Find her. Tell her I want her to stay. Ask her . . . if she will marry me.

El Tiburón's face creased into the smile that no one dared call a smile. Are you certain, he said. They could do this again, you know.

Montero shook his head and gazed out at the black water churning past them. He sipped at his drink and made a face at the strong bite of it. He said, There was something I had forgotten until last night. I remembered it in my room, with the sound of boots outside my door, and the sound of metal that was not mine to command. I had a radio, a poor one; it barely worked. There was a broadcast—ten minutes before it broke off—and it cost me a thousand pesos to hear it.

El Tiburón said nothing; his black eyes beneath their heavy brows searched the face of the general for a sign of weakness. He scarcely heard Montero's words; only the sound of his voice. Still he nodded as though what the man was saying made sense to him.

Montero sighed then, a startling heavy sound. Power is a *cosa relativo*, no? A relative thing. Like fencing—the art of touching and not being touched. Whereas *el amor* . . .

El Tiburón laughed then, that bark of a laugh that never suggested a lightness in him. He too had heard the broadcast of Rosa Andújar, and knew something of the power—*relativo* or no—that her words had come to have over men. Even men like El Tiburón himself. But marriage . . . He shrugged and downed the rest of his drink. There was no sign of weakness in the face of the general.

. . . love, said Montero, is *de especie diferente*. A game of another kind.

But of equal danger, said El Tiburón. One would not marry a

woman if the cost was greater than one could pay? If the cost turned out to be—*puede ser*—everything?

Montero hesitated only an instant. Then, still gazing out at the black water, he said, To fence well is to calculate correctly, as we have seen this day. As to the other, one cannot know the cost. One knows the woman. One knows oneself. *Basta*—it is enough.

El Tiburón nodded; the smile that was not a smile had left his face. He said nothing, but to himself he thought two things: That the general was not a fool. And that the woman was his match.

Meanwhile, two hundred special trains filled with *peones* from the outlying provinces, south, north and west, had begun the journey to San Luis for the *demostración*. Families unable to fit into the trains piled by the thousands into *colectivos* and buses, bullock carts and the cargo trailers of giant trucks that had been hastily made available by certain German-owned *factorías*. Bands of students were marching on foot or riding on bicycles from the universities, and five hundred parish priests were leading their flocks in a *procesión* of automobiles generously lent by the church, upon the suggestion of the bishop of Corrientes province. Extravagant promises had been exchanged in the night, and vows of useful friendship. In some cases it had proved necessary for the knowledge and proof of damaging secrets to be whispered into the ears of important *personajes* whose help was needed and slow in coming.

Sin duda, there was also a great movement of money. A spontaneous *demostración* is a very expensive thing. Money to pay for the special *transportes*, for the telephone calls, for the new friendships and the extravagant promises. Workers reluctant to make a long and uncomfortable journey to express loyalty to a stranger must be persuaded in one way or another. And so it was arranged that in certain cases free lodgings would be provided, and food for the *niños*. One also heard that several big *sindicatos* were kind enough to send representatives in the night, to collect the working papers of all their members. These papers would be returned, it was made plain, as soon as the worker reported in person to the headquarters of the *demostración* in San Luis. *Claro,* if he did not appear to collect his papers, the man would never work again.

Por fin, it did not matter why the *peones* poured into the city, million upon million of them, to shout in the streets for the return of General Montero. It did not matter which role in the production was played by the Baron von M, by Chulo Rubén Caso, by Manuel (El Tiburón) Quiroga, or by Pablito the bartender at the Jockey Club. It did not matter which of them had had the charge of certain arrangements, or who had given the orders from a hideout in Uruguay, or from the prison island of Santa María, from a lavish apartment on the Calle Orilla, or from a hospital bed on the *borde* of the city. In the years to come, it would be whispered, and at certain times published, that *she* had somehow done it all, with her smile of promise, her tears of rage, that brief shrill cry with her *clarín* of a voice that was broadcast, alas, to too many idle *peones* in too many poor *pueblos*—and *sin duda* with the temporary use of her celebrated tongue in certain other ways—on the night of the *negocios sucios,* the dirty deals that so altered the course of the handsome general, and of his country. *No importa,* as it was said on the following day, the day of the *demostración,* the day Carlos Montero was appointed *vicepresidente* of Pradera. *No importa* how such things come to be. Three million in the streets! Shouting, *Viva Montero! Viva Patria! Libertad y Esperanza!*

'Stá maravilla. In truth, was it not a miracle? In truth, it was not.

DoÑA Margarita dialed the number of her friend Señora R. Had one heard? Montero was married yesterday—*en secreta, sí!* To *her!*

Señora R had heard. One would have thought, she said dryly, that after all that had transpired, the *bufón* would have had the brain to get rid of the *mujeracha*. But *puede ser* he could not shake her off, a creature with such a bite—

It will be the end of him after all, said Doña Margarita, with the excitement she ordinarily reserved for important tragedies. And to think the man had come back from the dead!

Claro, he has dug the grave again. They will never let him run for President with a *ramera* wearing his name—

—for once those fools may have the sense to kill him—

—one may have to pay them to make sure! But what do you imagine she did to the poor man?

Did? Señora R laughed lightly. She must know where he has the money hidden—

O, it cannot be that! He has spent it all on that horrible fur coat—

—and the dress of saffron feathers—

—and the orchid made of pink diamonds, had one seen?

Perhaps she has threatened to tell Chulo Rubén Caso what the *vicepresidente* does in bed? Or what he does not?

I have heard that Chulo already knows that secret. It is he who arranges—

O, Rosita, said Doña Margarita, you are a wicked tongue!

Not so wicked as some. But if it is true what one has heard over the years—

That *el general* prefers *los niños?* The little boys? But they all prefer *los niños;* one is so bored with that—

In any case it is not enough to explain—

—he has her dress like a boy when they—?

Sí, but still, what kind of fool marries a *marquida* for such a service?

For what reason, then? She is surely not *encinta?*

Válgame Dios, can one imagine the bastard of those two! But she cannot be; all those *putatitas* fix themselves in the country before they come to town, so that—

O, *querida*, sighed Señora R, it is probably just a simple story. Like that of the simpleton King of England and his *moza de fortuna*. The poor *vicepresidente*—perhaps he is in love.

Love? Doña Margarita laughed a long silver laugh. *Basta!* she cried. Can one persuade you to come shopping after luncheon? One hears the new collections from Paris—

—with the skirts so tight one can scarcely move—?

Sí, meet me at three o'clock . . . Doña Margarita trailed off into another burst of silver laughter. *Love! O, querida,* she said. You always find the joke to cheer me up!

María Blanca is reading a story of how it was on the day Carlos returned as if from the dead. The crowds in the Plaza Victoria, shrieking his name. The bowing of the President, all courtliness and smiles. What did she wear, Blanca says, when you stood on the balcony, waving? She holds up the book. See? There is not a word here of how she looked.

Carlos closes his eyes and pinches the fold of flesh between them; he is very tired today. Come, he says, signaling. She still knows how to soothe him in these times, but now it can take nearly an hour, and even then there is no assurance that his mood will lighten. Besides, she was going to have her photograph taken with her hair in the new way. Well, the photographer will come back tomorrow. Carlos, she says, lifting her head once. Afterward will you show me again the photograph of her with the cardinal, on the night when she wore the golden gown with one naked shoulder?

He does not bother to answer this, but for a moment she has stirred his memory. Did I ever tell you, he says, with a sudden laugh, of the time when the men from the *sindicato de transportes* came, and she was doing her exercises? She used to do this funny thing with her legs up, so, as though riding a bicycle upside down.

I know that one! Blanca exclaims. She did it in front of them?

He smiles; then with a gentle push makes her head bend again to its task. I think . . . he says, breathing faster now . . . Rósula never enjoyed that exercise until that moment.

Rosa no longer walked with quick light steps along the Avenida de los Angeles; she was always a passenger now, in the back of the long black limousine with the license plates of the new Ministry of Labor and Social Welfare. She had an office there, as well as one at Radio del Estado, the station which Chulo had bought and given to her as a wedding present. Jorge Oleas worked for her now; he called her Señora, and had to ask her brother Chepito for an appointment to see her. Sometimes she said yes—after all, he was trying hard to make up for firing her in that terrible time of Carlos' trouble. The moment it was all over, and she became La Señora Rosa Andújar de Montero, he had made a grand apology, offering to serve under Chepito as assistant manager of the station at half his former salary. Her brother had urged her to accept; Oleas knew many useful things and could behave very nicely if he wanted to. He would want to from now on.

The little red-and-white flags mounted on the fenders of the limousine fluttered in the hot breeze as the car threaded its way through the traffic. The uniformed driver never turned his head, but his eyes sometimes caught the reflection of La Señora's eyes in the mirror that was meant only to help guide him between the buses and the *colectivos*, around the beggars and the peddlers of cheap carved animals, through the clots of dirty children kicking bottle caps under the wheels of trucks, so that the streets of San Luis would glitter as if they had been paved with Coca-Cola and Naranja Crush.

When it happened that the eyes of the driver met hers in the mirror, Rosa would look quickly away, as though he had caught her at some piece of mischief which he would report to the authorities. There was a panel of glass between them, which rendered her movements silent to him, as his were to her. This sometimes caused Rosa to feel strange, as though one of them were not real at all, but only a statue on display in the window of a shop. When she could gaze at the motionless back of the driver's head, with its florid neck and little black hairs; at the stiff band of black uniform collar; at the backs of the square hands in black leather gloves moving silently upon the steering wheel, she felt reassured that it was he who was the *modelo*—the mannequin. But when the blue-gray eyes met hers in the mirror, she grew frightened; for then she felt it must be the other way; it must be that he was real, and she was not.

Sometimes on these rides she would keep her head turned sharply to the side, fixing her gaze upon the people in the street— the beggars who never moved, and the thin quick girls who darted among them like bright hungry fish. There were so many people, a blur of faces red with anger or white as *la Muerte,* the anger burned out. So many faces; yet they no longer frightened her in the way that they had once, in the days before she could move so swiftly past them in a great black car. Today as they passed the Banco Federal she cried to the driver, Stop, here! But he could not hear her through the glass. There was a telephone beside her so that she could have signaled him, but she never liked to do this— perhaps because he always looked into the mirror when he answered the signal. Instead she rapped upon the glass between them. *Aquí! Deténgase!* A woman of no age sat before the bank, her ragged skirt spread about her on the pavement like a magic circle spread to catch the brilliant sun. Her children hunkered on their thin legs inside the circle, pale and silent as *angelitos.* Rosa reached into the soft white purse that lay beside her on the leather seat; her fingers closed upon a crisp bill. She did not look at the denomination. Stop! she shouted.

Sí, Señora, he said, touching his cap; his eyes in the mirror mocked her; she had shrieked like a *pescadera*—a fishwife—and he had replied in a low voice so that she could not hear him. The car glided to a halt; she jumped out and ran to where the woman sat with her *niños.* There was a new baby, and the small boy, the one to whom Rosa had given a coin once, so long ago, had grown tall and hard; his eyes had the look of one who is old. But one of the little sisters was not there; she would have been six or seven years old by now. Rosa stood before them holding the money in her white-gloved hand. Where is the other girl? The blond one? she asked. *Donde 'stá la rubia?* The children looked up at the lady in her white dress, with her golden hair. The mother did not move. *Muerta,* she said. *Espero que 'stá muerta.* I hope she is dead.

Rosa said nothing more; her fingers opened so that the money floated down upon the woman's skirt. One hundred pesos. The mother raised her eyes then, and Rosa saw that she was not the same girl who had sat here before, not the one who used to sleep here with her hard straight back propped against the white stone wall of the *banco.* Not the same one. Rosa shrank back, frightened; an old whisper sighing within her, like the voice of a child. Not . . . me. Around her people moved and whispered; she sensed rather than saw or heard them, blurring colors and sounds. Some of them pointed at her clothes, murmuring, *Mira! Mira!* She felt a hand upon her own skirt; perhaps it only brushed against her, but she pulled away. *Por favor,* she whispered to the mother who sat before her. I wanted to help you. The mother said nothing; it was as if there were a panel of glass between them. At last Rosa turned and made her way back to the car; the driver stood at attention, holding open the door of the passenger compartment. She felt his eyes following her; they seemed flat and dark like the eyes of the *niños* hunched together within the circle of their mother, waiting for the night.

In the car Rosa saw a smear of black upon her white dress; she removed her glove and held a finger to her tongue; then she began to rub at the mark. Once she looked up to see if the driver was watching, but she could not find his eyes in the mirror. The little red-and-white flags on the fenders fluttered gaily; the car had picked up speed.

In the mornings he wanted her to come to him as he slept, while he was still unconscious; he explained that she must kneel so, with her body astride his, balancing so that she would hover over him, suspended. He would give no sign of waking, of wanting her there, of knowing she had come. She must wait until his body made its own involuntary sign. She would fit herself to him then like a soft sheath closing upon a drawn blade. He had told her that in Italy the little whores of nine learned to do this, lowering themselves upon a man in this way, balancing so with their small thin haunches bent like twigs; silent; scarcely daring to breathe. But if I want to embrace you? Rosa had said at first, with a pout of playfulness. And then, what of the times *I* would wish . . . ?

Sí, he had replied, looking away. Not yet, *querida*. Or not now, not this time. He wanted only this, for her to come upon him so, as a stealthy dream of mysterious warmth, a darkness descending like a moist sigh, so that, in his half-sleep, he might imagine himself a rod of golden iron, rising and bursting like a sun held fast in a soft ring of night flesh. She must utter no sound to dispel the dream; she must not move in a way to remind him of herself, of the fact that it was only she, Rosa, his wife. She came to understand that otherwise he could not bear for any part of her body to touch his. Not this time; not yet; not today.

After the first several weeks they did not speak of it again; she ceased to protest, but would do as he asked. In time he would grow to expect it more rarely, and then more rarely still. One morning, some months after they had been married, he would cease to want even this.

In the nights it was different. He would come to their bed armed with work, with reports and proposals of the day, with schemes and schedules, political secrets. These they would share; of these they whispered with tremulous excitement, like children or lovers—exchanging political gossip like endearments. He carried folders against his body like shields, and she would disarm him gently. Is that the speech for the meat packers' strike? Did Chulo tell you about the trouble Tobalito is having, reopening the night club? Remember you promised—

Sí, he would tell her, and what of her day? What of her new column for *La Voz:* Women Want the Vote. Had Chepito found a writer to help? And what did Juanita say of the actors' quarrel with the producers? Did one truly think there was a chance they could be made into a union? Actors? He did not believe it. They were like women—one could never organize them.

She would look at him in that way of a child, with her hands so upon her slim hips. So! That is what you think? And am I not an actor—besides?

She too brought him secrets, reports from her new friends, her new confidants—she found them in all sorts of places: the fitting rooms at smart shops, the ladies' rooms of fine restaurants, the servants' quarters in the households of certain *personajes.* She would bring secrets to him like offerings of love, piling them up between them on the great white bed with its smooth sheets of linen, embroidered with pale blue flowers and their initials entwined in silken threads. She would stroke the raised letters of their names while they whispered in the darkness; her fingers would trace the stitches in the way of a blind child learning to read. And they would speak of what must be done tomorrow in Corrientes province, in Catamarca and Rosario, at the meeting of El Tiburón and the new steel *sindicato.* . . .

And in those first early days, after the night of secrets, after the morning when she had moved over him like an angel without a body, he would breathe, *Vidita!* my life! and spring from the bed exulting like a prisoner released. Charged with force as though she, with her secrets, with her silent ring of magic fitted to his body, as though she had given him—or had let him draw from her—a kind of potency, a new *poder.*

Carlos, she would say with a bright smile, as though the thought had just come to her. What would you think of setting up a *fundación*—for charity, I mean.

A government *fundación?* He would frown.

No, she would say quickly, with a little shrug. Just . . . something unofficial. *Sabes*—a private *sociedad,* for good works. You know, like the one those ladies have—those fancy ladies with their luncheons.

Ah. He understood. You want to compete with Doña Margarita and her *amigas* of the smart black hats, *verdad?* The ladies of the little furs—with the heads so, biting the tails?

She would make a face. Do not tease me! I do not want to be one of those *brujas*—those witches! What I want—and she would whisper then, like a conspirator—is to do what you did with the shoemakers' union. Make another *sindicato*—another *sociedad,* a better one. A serious one. Those *brujas* have their luncheons, but what do they do for the mothers in the streets, with their *niños?* What do they do for *muchachas* in the garment *factorías?* Carlos—could we not make a better *fundación,* you and I? Would it not help the unions? El Tiburón says—

He would laugh, stroking her. *Claro,* El Tiburón says you would make a better *fundación* than anyone. I think the shark is afraid of your teeth.

Still you tease me, she would cry. And then force herself to be still, to study him with her listening face. He wanted to talk of other things. She would nod, and say the important thoughts after him, nodding. Like a wise echo, turning the words in her mind. The train journey to Tucuman, where the students had begun to cause trouble. *Sí,* she would go with him; she would make a special radio broadcast from the *universidad.* She would remind the students of who it was who had caused the easing of their examinations! And after he had called Pablito, the bartender who was now director of the new federal *policía*—after they had decided what must be done about the troublemakers, the protesters, then, *puede ser,* she could try again to speak of the *fundación.* Carlos. . . .

Cariña, he would sigh with weariness (though he had already decided what must be done), it would not do for the Vice President to run a private charity *fundación.*

Well, but you would not have to—Chepito could help me, and Chulo. I could bear all the *responsibilidad,* and only make it clear that you direct me. That it is your wish for me to help the people—

Mm, *puede ser.* He would yawn. Chulo thinks—did he tell you?

Sí, he thinks as you do. For you always seem to know the right way! It must be unofficial. And to bear my name only—because it is I who will—

And that one must find a way to finance it, without—

Sí! She laughed, clapping her hands like a child. Remember how the Christmas cakes were paid for? And the cider for the workers? Carlos, you are always so clever—

He smiled; she had a fine nose for how a thing was done. And she was quick to see when he agreed that a thing could be done, if it were good to do. She knew he had spoken of this *fundación* with Baron von M, and with Quiroga. She knew there were many ways to extract the voluntary gift from a businessman. *Verdad,* he reflected, these things a woman always knew! There could be no tax imposed for such a purpose, but one might suggest to the *personajes* what was expected of them, and how much. It need only be made clear that careful records would be kept—of those who gave freely and those who refused. There were always small ways to persuade the reluctant ones. And in truth, a *fundación* in the name of Señora Montero would have a great usefulness for the election campaign. All of his advisers had agreed to this. Still, they had warned, one must exert care about the use of La Señora herself in such a venture. A matter of *dignidad* and restraint. A matter too of control over the money. Chulo had pointed out that a system must be devised. One could never be too careful about such things when a woman was involved. But what of that. El Tiburón had agreed that a children's hospital in the name of Señora Montero would be a fine thing in San Diego province, where the new *sindicato* had been having trouble recruiting the women workers in the metals plant. And had La Señora not expressed a wish to establish a home to care for pregnant girls? Surely the bishop of Córdoba would be

pleased with such a thing for his area—one had understood that
there was some trouble winning support from his parishes?

Sí, querida, Carlos would say absently. We will talk of it again
tomorrow, if you like. But first why not offer your services to the ladies of the *Sociedad?* If they accept you, I will buy you a little fur
with the head and the tail. *Bueno?*

> *My dear Doña Margarita,*
> *It is with great pleasure that I write to you as wife of the*
> *Vice President, to offer my services to the* Sociedad de Bene-
> *volencia. In accordance with your gracious tradition of per-*
> *mitting the wife of the chief cabinet officer to serve as honorary*
> *president, I am prepared to assume my duties immediately,*
> *and to extend through you an invitation to the señoras of the*
> *board of directors to hold the season's first meeting in my new*
> *office at the Ministry of Labor and Social Welfare. A light*
> *luncheon and refreshments will be served. Please honor me*
> *with the favor of a reply at your earliest convenience.*
>   *With respectful wishes,*
>   *María Rosa Andújar de Montero*

Doña Margarita called her friend Señora R and read her the letter over the telephone. Señora R hooted with laughter at appropriate intervals. Can one imagine? they both cried. A light luncheon and refreshments! But one must be careful in the reply. What
on earth can one tell the creature? She could have him set the dogs
of the *policía* on us!

Por Dios, said Doña Margarita. There must be something in the
constitution that says no *putas* may serve on the board of directors!

O! shrieked Doña Margarita. How I would love to write her that!
But it is a serious thing, one must do nothing to offend the husband. José would kill me!

Well, Paca will have to think of something. She is the secretary,
after all.

The following evening, Señora S found just what they needed in
the bylaws of the organization. Doña Margarita was so pleased that
she sent her friend a box of Swiss chocolates, which was very
wicked of her; she knew very well that Señora S had been on a reducing diet for a whole week. Nothing but el baby beef and *ensaladas* of rare plants.

My dear Señora Montero,
It is with deep regret that I must write to decline with thanks your charming offer to assume the duties of honorary president of the Sociedad de Benevolencia. *It has been called to my attention that the bylaws of our constitution state clearly that no officer of the* Sociedad, *including the honorary director, may be under thirty years of age. In view of Señora Montero's youth, she is thus rendered automatically ineligible to serve the* Sociedad *in any official* capacidad *whatever. May I assure you at this time of my own disappointment over this matter; I am certain that we would have benefited greatly from your participation in our programs of aid to the less fortunate citizens of Pradera.*

> *Very truly yours,*
> *Margarita Delgado*

The letter was read over the telephone to all sixteen members of the board of the *Sociedad de Benevolencia,* who agreed unanimously that it was a brilliant solution to a dreadfully embarrassing problem.

My dear Doña Margarita,
In view of the unfortunate technical regulation regarding the age of honorary presidents, may I respectfully propose that my mother, Doña Juana Ibáñez of San Marcos, be invited to serve in my place? She is over thirty. Doña Juana has graciously agreed to assume the duties of office at once, should this be agreeable to you and the other señoras. My invitation for the meeting to be held in my office at the Ministry of Social Welfare is still extended. Kindly let me know if this arrangement meets with your approval.

> *Very truly yours,*
> *María Rosa Andújar de Montero*

Again Doña Margarita called Señora R and read her the letter over the telephone. The creature was more brazen than one had supposed. You answer this one, Rosita, said Doña Margarita Delgado. I am out of stationery.

My dear Señora Montero,
The Sociedad *has received the kind offer of your mother's willingness to serve the* Sociedad *in your place, but must de-*

*cline with regret, in accordance with our constitution. It is
with great pleasure that I inform you of the recent appointment
of Doña Margarita Delgado as our new honorary president.
Our first meeting of the season will be held privately at her
home; unfortunately we cannot extend an invitation to
outside guests who wish to attend the business meetings.
However, we are planning a number of public events for
the coming season, and we would be honored to have you
and el vicepresidente attend these, as your schedules permit.*

With every good wish,
Rosita R
President-elect
Sociedad de Benevolencia de San Luis

Four days after this letter arrived at the Ministry of Social Welfare, the *Fundación María Rosa Andújar de Montero* was established with formal ceremonies in the Casa Dorado, attended by
the President, members of the cabinet and their *señoras*, and the
press. The event was reported on the front pages of fifty newspapers; it was broadcast over all radio stations, and in the newspaper Rosa now owned, *La Voz*, there was a centerfold section
filled with photographs of La Señora dispensing money and food
baskets to needy petitioners, and receiving checks from twelve
leading businessmen representing the steel, transport, meat-packing, and shipping industries.

It was reported that four major private *fundaciónes* which had
previously contributed heavily to the *Sociedad de Benevolencia*
had voted to transfer their gifts this year to the new *Fundación*,
and also to double the size of their usual gifts in order to assist the
new *Fundación* in setting up its ambitious new programs of aid to
needy women and children, to homes for unmarried pregnant girls,
to a children's hospital in San Diego. . . .

One month later the *Sociedad de Benevolencia* lost its tax exemption, by order of the Ministry of Finance, on the grounds that several of the *señoras* on the board served also on the boards of church
groups, which was decreed a conflict of interest. Without a tax exemption, the *Sociedad* could not hope to raise money from private
contributors, and within a month the organization was dissolved,
after one hundred and four years of service by elegant ladies to the

poor and needy of Pradera who could not afford Swiss chocolates or reducing diets of *el baby beef* and *ensaladas* made from delicate wild plants.

SHE had burst in unexpectedly, and in her voice was a note of fear that she had never let him hear. Carlos—

What? He was reading a report of the tar bombing in a theatre at Santiago del Estero. A Jewish group performing. Casualties—did one wish anything done? The *Asociaciones Israelitas* had asked if a delegation might be sent to discuss—

What? he said again, but did not look up. I have not wished to cause you concern, she said. I am—there is blood. More blood.

From—? Still he would not shift his gaze from the page. An editorial in *Cabildo* attacking the *Asociaciones Israelitas* for demanding protection. Demanding! By what right—

Probably not serious, he said. It will stop, as before—

She shook her head. *Creo que no;* not this time. It has been so for a week. First a spot; then another. Finally it is a river that runs . . . I am weak. Yesterday—

Pain? he said. His voice had an edge. If she were unable to travel—

No—yes. *Poquito.* A little pain.

Ah. Well. Let Ceballos have a look at you once again.

Once again, she said, he will ask questions.

About our habits in bed? Tell him we have no habits in bed. God knows it is so.

My past habits, then. He will—

At last he looked up at her, with exasperation. You need not answer—

He will say that now I must. He will insist that now—that he cannot be responsible otherwise. Carlos, you know this. We have talked of it.

Yes, and what we agreed is still what must be. One cannot afford now for outsiders to know . . . certain things. You will tell him he is a brilliant doctor; that this was why we had him sent for, paid his passage from Italy; is it not so? Since he is brilliant, he should have no trouble solving a small mystery, as he assured us. On the other hand . . . Carlos made a quick gesture of dismissal. Then with two fingers he grasped the deep fold of flesh between his eyes, pressing it as a man who wears heavy spectacles seeks to relieve discomfort.

He held his fingers so, shading his eyes until he was certain that she had left him. Then he resumed reading.

Outside the door she turned suddenly and went back. The *Asociaciones Israelitas* have asked me— I talked with Pablito; why have those *policía* of his not tried to stop these things?

It would be better, Carlos said with coldness, if you did not talk to Pablito without asking me. And you are far too busy to meet with . . . such groups. You must reserve your strength.

Her face grew whiter. Does Baron von M talk to him? Is it Rudi's *amigos* of the Deutschebank who pay those *asesinos?* Who buy the *bombas asfixiantes* and the handguns? Carlos, *dímelo!* Do I anger your supporters? Because I say you are stronger than this? That you do not need such help!

You know so much of politics, he said, and his lips formed a smile that was not of laughter.

I know only what you teach me, as always, she said. But you have real enemies to set dogs upon. Real ones who do not sing and dance for pesetas in the provinces!

There are certain things of use . . . he began, but she was gone.

Rosa placed her feet in the cold silver stirrups and read the eyes of *el Señor Doctor* Ceballos. You are not going to tell me the truth of what you find, she said.

He smiled. Señora, how is it that I have not earned your trust? It is you who withhold information.

She turned her head to gaze out of the window; there was a bird, hungry and trembling. It pecked at the glass. I have learned, she said quietly, to trust no one— She broke off, drawing a breath; his fingers had begun to probe inside her.

That is a mistake. He spoke with an ordinary lightness, smoothly, as a doctor does with an uneasy patient. Surely one is never so alone as that!

Al contrario. She gasped again, a quick sharp sound, to prepare for the pain that was to come. On the contrary, she said again. One had better be as alone as that. It is what one must do to survive.

The doctor's fingers had moved sharply upward; she stifled a scream. In this case, he said in the gentle tone now of one who often inflicts pain, with regret. If one may suggest, survival may depend on the Señora's abandonment of that belief. For if you cannot trust me, you rob my power to help. The *poder* is yours, either way.

The Señora spoke then in a very even voice, knowing that the effort to keep it so would help to distract her both from the pain and from her hatred of this cold man with the long white face, who dared to know more than he would tell her. You have the confidences of my body, doctor. Should you demand any beyond that, *puede ser*, one might begin to doubt your skill.

I understand, he said slowly. Still, I must know—at least—at what age, *por ejemplo*, at what age you became a woman?

She resisted a sudden urge to laugh, even if it should cause terrible pain. At the age of eight I became a *mujer*, she said. *Ocho años*. A sudden flash of anger cut through her voice, twisting like the knife of his probing fingers. She turned her head more sharply toward the window. The bird still perched upon the sill, pecking at the glass like a messenger with an urgent secret. Eight.

Eight years? said Dr. Ceballos, affecting a tone of ordinary interest.

She made no answer. I see, he murmured. I understand.

But of course you do not, she said, with a sudden icy fury. Of course you cannot. At eight—*ocho años*—an assault by one's father? And then, at eleven, by one's father confessor? And in between, by many men in the house of one's mother? *Claro*, you cannot understand. One knew them by the sound of their footsteps in the dirt road. And by the weight and smell of their bodies. One knew, *también*, the rhythm of their breathing. And the colors of the dresses of those pretty *muñecas*, the smiling dolls which they sent afterward—together with the money they owed *mi madre* for their board. Each *muñeca*, *Señor Doctor*, was named Rosa, *sabes?* For her pretty red smile that never faded. Even when its dress was torn, and the *muñeca* itself lay broken in the dust—

Señora, there is no need—

Rosa smiled. I have never had the *reglas*, doctor—the woman's courses—not since the age of eleven, after the father confessor . . . Not since the *maravilla* which spared me the child I might have had. The *bastardo* of the padre. I had no *operación*; I had no child. And until now I have had no—

Por favor, whispered Dr. Ceballos in a shaken voice; in truth, he did not want to hear more, though he would soon need to know everything.

It is what you asked, is it not? She gazed at him calmly. So. But still I have no answer to my question. The bleeding—

Permítame, he began, recovering the smooth tone. Allow me first to say—

She waved a hand. No. Only tell me the truth. Now one has the right to know, *verdad?*

He made a gesture of helplessness. But I cannot, he said. One must await the reports . . . from the laboratory. He had withdrawn his gloved hand; she turned sharply, in time to see the dark blood. You are lying to me still, she whispered.

He busied himself washing. I can tell you only that in a woman so very young, but who has, whose *historia* . . . It is *muy difícil*. A difficult case.

Mil gracias, she said, now with a tinge of bitterness. The visit is over, and you have learned all you need. Only I have not.

I regret, he said, touching the white sleeve of the stiff cotton gown they had made her wear; she had made a joke that it was a dress for a child's first communion. For a moment when his hand touched her, he thought she might weep, but no. Nothing touched La Señora, it was said.

I am going on a long train journey, she said. I assume that you have been informed. The campaign—

Sí, he said. It would be wise if I accompanied you; with the general's permission?

I will need treatment? Needles? Killers of pain?

He shrugged. We will see. When the reports—

Ah, she said. The reports.

IT has been said that a Pradereño relieves the suffering of bad government by raising the palms to heaven—for in this way one makes a bow to the will of *Dios*. It is always true that when the belly is full, the bow is easily made. But when it is empty, ways must be quickly found to fill the eye and the mind—lest the people leave off their bowing to *Dios*, and raise their fists against the bad government.

In the shops along the Calle Florida there were stockings of silk, smart gowns, and small hats to wear off the face with a saucy tilt, so, and a wisp of veil across the eyes. *Qué seductivo!* And for the *caballero*, el Homburg of straw, the very latest.

But in the province of Córdoba there were many arrests of persons who did not wear the latest fashion, and who complained that one thing or another of the new regime did not suit them either. The new *policía federal*, directed by Pablito the bartender, now had a power over the whole country. All crimes were of interest to the *policía federal*; it was a matter of national *seguridad*, the maintaining of law and of order.

One might hear of laborers who refused to join the new government *sindicato*. A stubborn and ungrateful thing, when one considered all that would be gained by giving up one's *independencia*.

How could one not be satisfied with the new paid holidays, and the bonus for Navidad, and the envelope of pay that seemed twice as fat as before—though one could buy only half as much food with it? The leader of a union who pointed this out—in a way to keep his *poder*—went to a certain prison. And after that, the men were eager to join the government *sindicato*.

The army had swelled double in its size, and it was made a crime to report any news of which colonel was promoted to general, or which businessman received a military contract, or where the garrisons moved in the nights. Yet one might see the new white military roads unrolling to the borders of Paraguay and Brazil. One might watch the military parade on the day of *independencia,* and cry, *Mira!* when one saw the new war planes made in Pradera, and the new airborne troops in their white uniforms, and the mountain units and the tanks that could travel at speeds of forty kilometers an hour, laden with cannons and machine guns and men. *Mira!* Silver planes flew over the route of the parade, and over the heads of foreign diplomats who stood transfixed upon the reviewing stand surrounded by the smiling military leaders of Pradera, all in their new uniforms with their shiny boots. *Mira!* The foreign diplomats were not smiling; they had nervous faces and stains of sweat on the backs of their diplomatic suits.

From the sky came a white rain of paper *bombas* saying, Pradera for the Pradereños!

On the radio *el vicepresidente* Montero was heard to say that war was a natural social phenomenon, and any peaceful nation such as Pradera must begin at once to arm itself with very big tanks and planes and guns, and many more men in new uniforms, so that other, not-so-peaceful nations would not mistake the love of peace for a loss of *poder.*

On the first anniversary of the new administration, a new law was passed to dispose of all political parties. Puf! In the news one saw fine photographs of the smiles and handshakes. The *Presidente* and the *Vicepresidente* smiled and shook hands over the good news that they had made with this law. Next to the photographs were editorials that bore the headline *El Año del Esperanza*—The Year of Hope. Soon there would be a single state political party—a *partido del Estado.* This would make it easier to vote in the free election, *no es verdad?*

The editor who wrote the strongest anti-*Israelita* editorials for *Cabildo* was selected to serve as the new Minister of Public Instruction. His first announcement was that tighter control was needed over public morals and teaching in the schools. Daily religious instruction was to be given in the new curriculum, and certain textbooks would be replaced by others. The church leaders spoke with care from their *púlpitos,* praising this good sign that the country would soon return to a state of moral health. A very good sign, *en verdad,* the *restauración* of compulsory bowing to the will of *Dios.*

There were certain sounds of anger in the left-wing press and the universities. But the new federal *policía* sent troops to restore order. Certain newspapers were closed, and others were fined heavily for improper toilet facilities and failure to install safety tires on their trucks. The universities changed certain policies so as to keep a sterner eye on student activities, so that the authorities could prevent rowdy groups from forming, and others from holding meetings. Enrollment procedures were adjusted so that certain applicants would not be accepted at all by the universities; finally one heard a rumor that certain student leaders had gone to certain prisons. This was not reported in the press or on the radio. In all such matters the Ministry of Instruction issued lines of guidance, to make the transition easier, and to cooperate with the *policía* in the matter of *seguridad.*

In San Luis the *porteños,* the people of the port city, dressed up all the time and looked very smart. There was a boom in real estate and even the price of el baby beef was high. A beautiful new subway tunnel was built by the Germans, with Spanish tile murals on the walls. *Avenidas* were made wider for shoppers and strollers. Everywhere one found new little shops like jewels such as one used to see only in Paris. Everywhere there were new cafés with gaslights such as one used to see only in Vienna, and sleek *confiterías* such as one saw only on the streets of New York. One might go out for tea or ices, or a small hat with a wisp of a veil, and feel the excitement in the air of the street; one felt it in the limbs like the new dance tunes.

In the provinces there were the traditional holiday fiestas in the streets; the old statues of the saints still marched in their rich gaudy clothes. On the radio one heard popular new tango singers— for the popular old tango singers had suddenly left the country; it was said the government had not cared for some of the tunes they carried.

In the cinema there were popular new stories of women who tasted forbidden pleasure, who wore smart dresses, whose cheeks were full and round from the fine food they ate, and whose lips always shone like bright ribbons of silk.

Such *cines* had always been most popular in the provinces, where bellies were the most empty, where the bowing to the will of *Dios* now seemed a thing of the past. In the provinces the *Fundación María Rosa Andújar de Montero* had begun to do good works, distributing small gifts and announcing large plans for the hospital and the school and the nursery. This too was a very popular *cine*.

And so it was that a fine new idea began to form in the mind of Chulo Rubén Caso, the Finance and Culture Minister, who now met with the chief advisers of Carlos Montero to plan the campaign for his election as *Presidente*. Chulo had begun to whisper his idea into the ear of Chepito Andújar, the brother of Rosa who now was the manager of Radio del Estado, over the head of her old boss Jorge Oleas. Would it not be a fine thing, Chulo said, if Rosa were made the *estrella* in this great *cine* that is the Year of *Esperanza*. Should we not see that a photograph of her sweet smile appears on the campaign banners and posters, alongside Montero? It is Rosa that they know in the provinces. Rosa's voice on the radio. Rosa's *Fundación* . . . In truth, those who are angry with him are not angry with her. And vice versa.

Chepito saw at once the wisdom of this idea. And the next day at a meeting in the campaign headquarters Chulo looked at Rosa and smiled in the way he had smiled on the night of his fancy-dress party, the night she had come to him with a plea for his friendship, and a promise of hers.

After the meeting Chulo rode beside her in the car, back to her office on the Plaza Victoria. I know what it is you really want, he said in a quiet voice. I am the only one who does.

Rosa stared at the back of the neck of the driver. Carlos knows, she murmured. He—

He knows the face one reveals to him. Chulo permitted himself a short laugh. Carlos knows the mask of Rosa you have created for him. And it is very beautiful. He turned slightly, gazing at her hair arranged in the new way, with two swept-back rolls of a sausage on top, and a small explosion of curls at the bottom. His eyes rested briefly on the smart white hat with the little feather, and the smart white jacket with embroidered green leaves on the shoulders. She was wearing trousers; it was the latest style in Hollywood. She squirmed under his gaze, shifting in the seat, crossing her legs. Two spots of color appeared on her cheeks, like stains; one hand began to flutter like a bird to her hair, her collar. In spite of herself, even now, Rosa was never certain; never the *mujer* of the world that one saw in the *fotografías*.

Very beautiful, that Rosa, he said again, now in a tone of reassurance. But one can always be more *a la moda, verdad?* It is Chulo who knows the way. And you know that I do.

And what is it that you think I want, she said, still staring at the neck of the driver.

Not more than anyone, he said. To be immortal. Such as the saints, the great *estrellas* of the cinema. He laughed softly. Or, perhaps, the great leader of one's country. *Mira!* He reached over and rested a hand, very lightly, upon the knee of her white trousers. *Todavía*—already you have the white trousers for it!

She smiled wanly and removed his hand, but said nothing.

Is it not an odd thing, he mused, that our political tongue has no form *feminina* for such an important word. *Presidente? En verdad, la Presidenta* is only the *wife* of the President.

And that is what I will be, she said softly. If Carlos is elected.

You know he will be elected—

I have no other ambition. Carlos—'stá mi vida. He is my life.

Sí, claro! said Chulo, but in a way to make her frown. And after Carlos? What then?

She laughed then, a sad small sound that surprised him; it seemed more like a cry. It is of Carlos you must ask that. After Rosa? What then?

Now you joke with me, said Chulo. You, who are too young even for the *señoras* of the *Sociedad*. A *muchachita en la flor*—the bloom of youth.

Sí, she said. *En la flor*.

When she had left the car, and he was going on to his own office at the Culture Ministry, Chulo picked up the black telephone. *Sí, Señor?*

What did I tell you, Frasco? Chulo burst into laughter.

The driver smiled a tight smile into the rear-view mirror.

What did I tell you? Chulo said again, shaking with his laughter. *Que quiere la putatita?* The little whore wants—to be President.

ON the day that Rosa came to Corrientes province with a train-load of gifts for the needy children of the shoemakers, it is said that eleven people died trying to touch her hand. The newspapers and radio mentioned nothing of this; no photographs ever appeared, although it was admitted that a brief stampede of *peones* had occurred near the railroad station of Santiago del Estero. Too large a crowd, and the train was thirty minutes late; the *policía* had difficulty restoring order.

It is said that this was only the first of such small tragedies that began to follow or precede La Señora whenever she visited the *pueblos* in her jewels and furs, with her gilded hair piled high like a nest of feathers, and carrying a treasure chest such as one sees in *cines* about pirates. The chest was filled with money which she held out between white-gloved fingers as a Madonna holds the *rosario*.

Outside the railroad station at Santiago del Estero, a mother held her crying child high, so that she might catch a glimpse of La Señora. The child grasped one of the white-gloved fingers. *Mira!* Blanquita! the mother cried. La Señora gives you a gift. The child grasped the white finger and would not let it go. *Déjelo!* said the mother. But the child held fast, as though she thought the finger must be the gift, not the coins. At last they pried her loose, and she resumed her crying.

La Señora suffered a painful swelling of the finger, and after this it was decided that the touching of hands, the passing of money directly from her fingers to those of the *peones* was too dangerous a practice, despite the value it had for the photographs. In their zeal, in their need, these *salvajes* and their *niños* would tear her to pieces.

So it came to be that the gifts would be showered from the open windows of the train; the hand of La Señora would reach out to them still, in a gesture of greeting and benediction. But with care; she would no longer reach far enough to touch. Instead there would be men to distribute the packages of sweets, wrapped in the paper that bore her likeness and that of her husband, both of them smiling and fat-cheeked, both of them wearing clothes of dazzling white. *Mira!* the *peones* would cry to their children. *Mira!* La Señora! And in the rush to see her, it was an unfortunate thing, a few *peones* would somehow fall and be trampled upon; a few would suffocate. One would hear the splinter of glass or wood, and the crying. Within minutes more *policía* would come with their rifles, and order would be restored. The train would move on and the *peones* would go home to their mud houses, in their hands a coin of silver or a package of sweets, and a bright photograph of two smiling faces which one might place upon the table, or fasten to the wall beside the *crucifijo* of Jesús and the *imagen* of the *Virgen.* In a mud house, one draws comfort from a new article of faith.

Mira! they would whisper to one another, admiring the photograph. How like an angel she looks. How like an *estrella* of the cinema. And he, in that white uniform. Like a god of war. Yet he comes to us and takes off the uniform, rolling the sleeves of the shirt, so, saying, *Mira!* I am *un trabajador,* a worker, like you. What does it say on the paper with the photograph? *Carlos y Rosa. Esperanza!*

FROM the columns of news and the radio, one would know that the grand reopening of Los Pájaros, the elegant night club owned by that tango singer Tobal Iribas, was the most important event of the season. More important, one well understood, than the rioting of students or the disturbances in the provinces. What of the arrests and savage beatings of troublemakers in dreary clothes? One turned the page to see famous *personajes* preparing for the gala party, choosing a tiny jeweled hat with the tail feather of an osprey for the moment when the voice behind one's photograph in the newsreel described the way one had looked, laughing over the bubbles of champagne, nibbling an egg of the devil with a stuffing of el caviar, posing beneath Tobal's new chandelier of forty thousand Austrian crystals which rose or descended at the touching of a button, to facilitate cleaning.

One had far better think of these important things than of the inflation, the swift changing of certain laws, or the sudden goings of certain old friends. Goings where? and *por qué?* Old friends who only last week were *personajes* too, with their photographs in the newsreel smiling in the way that new friends would smile tonight at Tobalito's club, shaking one another's famous hands and toasting the high life of this year of *Esperanza*.

One understood that Tobal's serious sins against the government had been forgiven—after a certain payment of gratitude to the favorite *fundación* of La Señora Montero. He had been thick with her long ago, no? One understood, with a wink of the left eye and a tap of the finger beside the nose, that those of whom one whispered were engaged in dirty dealings of this kind or that. The finger always tapped at the nose in this way when one mentioned the name of Tobalito and the *personajes* of high *sociedad* and low who would smile for the photographers every night at Los Pájaros, over the champagne in silver buckets, at the tables of black mirror, along the walls of ivory and pale-gray satin in the room of wonderful lights.

In the way that Pablito the bartender had once performed his service of value beyond the mixing of whiskey-sodas for the *señores* at the Jockey Club, so Tobal Iribas had become the *centro de informes* for La Señora; the unofficial center of her network of mouths that whispered unofficial secrets one had better know of one's old friends and new enemies. For how else can one tell them apart from one day to the next?

It was, *por ejemplo,* Tobal who had informed La Señora that her old friend Soledad would soon return from the Continent for a brief visit, at the invitation of Chulo Rubén Caso, with whom the actress had some new business. It was Tobal too who predicted that Chulo might soon be not quite so trusted an *amigo* of La Señora as perhaps he once had been. Certain messages had gone in recent days from Chulo to the new *grupo de coroneles* of the army— whose simmering hatred for La Señora now brewed with the concentrated strength of a poison tea. The driver of La Señora's car had been replaced many times as a precaution. Still, when she rode alone she would stare at the shoulders, at the back of the neck, at the eyes that by chance would meet hers in the rear-view mirror. She would stare so, knowing well that this one too would soon—if he had not already—file his *informes* to one enemy or another. *Los espías*—such spies as this—were everywhere. I am too small, she had said once to her brother Chepito; too small for so much hate. Still it grew around her, like a shadow lengthening at her heels, following as close as the accidental deaths by trampling and suffocation that always occurred when she appeared in public; close as the troubles in the provinces; as the prescriptions of Dr. Ceballos, for the newer and stronger killers of pain.

As a favor to an old friend, Tobal volunteered to hire a small private army of *espías* to find and remove the writings of filth about La Señora that grew like a slime on the walls of public toilets in certain cafés and government buildings. There are, as it is said, a thousand words for a whore in the *lengua* of Pradera. All of them began to appear on the walls beside the name of La Señora, and in the streets beneath the new campaign poster that bore her name and likeness now as large as those of Carlos—as though she too were a candidate for office. Chulo had had to persuade the Vice President of the importance it would have for the voting in the troubled provinces, where the name of La Señora was a word of magic, and where that of Montero himself might cause a feeling of fear. There were many meetings until at last the decision was made. And Chulo helped to design the poster, selecting the new style of hair for Rosa, a simpler arrangement with not so much *sensualidad*. It was Chulo too who directed the camera to show the tilt of her chin, and the long lovely line of the throat, so as to draw the eye quickly to the sweet shining smile that one might still imagine held secrets of a certain kind.

It was here, across those parted lips and upon that long lovely expanse of throat, that the writers of filth scrawled their messages. An army of cleaners moved in the nights to remove the signs of disrespect for the general and La Señora; a law was passed to make a crime of writing certain words on the walls or on posters hung in places exposed to the eye of the public. Still the words continued to be written so, with thick bright letters, in indelible colored chalks and inks that could not be washed away with an ordinary soap. Everywhere the name of La Señora continued to be written, followed by a thousand illegal words.

Every night from the elegant office above his elegant night club, Tobal dispatched the night army of *limpiadores*—the censors—and *espías* to remove the new public offenses with strong chemicals and whitewash. And every night in the club itself, the new *personajes* danced to the daring new tangos, and Tobal reserved the largest and best of the round black-mirrored tables, along the wall of ivory satin, for Chepito Andújar, the brother of his old friend Rosa; it was said that from now on Chepito had better keep a watchful eye on certain unofficial activities.

Chepito had developed a great fondness for the high life—the hee-lee-fay, as one said in Pradera. He was happy to make Los Pájaros his unofficial night headquarters, the place where he would come to entertain his business friends and also certain young ladies of the stage, the screen and the radio. Often he would present each *muchachita* with a favor of the evening—*un recuerdo,* a souvenir.

He would summon the girl who sold cigarets and select from her tray the small packages of surprise. Inside the packages each of the girls would find a jewel for her wrist or throat, a real one like something she had seen in photographs of La Señora herself. Chepito had had the copies made and sent by the jewelers to Tobal's night club, where they were stored in a safe that bore Chepito's name. In the evenings, when Chepito came, he would take from the safe the packages he would need, and a thickness of new bills, to be pressed with a flourish into the palms of the young men with perfect smiles and polished shoes who were in the employ of Tobal Iribas. The headwaiter and the waiter, the captain and the *maître d'hôtel*, the bouncers and the squadron of others whose duties were not so clearly specified, but who would greet Señor Chepito with a perfect smile and a reverent whisper of his name. Some of the young men, it was said, served a tour of duty in the night army of *limpiadores*—the unofficial censors—before moving on to certain other private armies with other unofficial duties, following the intricately crossing tracks of old friends and new enemies.

And seated at his table Chepito would summon the young men, calling each one by name and asking of the health of his family. Chepito would sit so, stroking the bare shoulders of the *muchachitas* on either side, and order fancy *cocteles* and dishes that were not on the menu. Everything must be prepared in a special way, as a treat for these young girls who had never heard of such *cocteles* or tasted such food. They must try everything, for soon—he would explain—they would surely all be great *estrellas* of the stage, the screen, the radio, and it would be their names one must whisper with the bow of reverence when they graced the table of Chepito at Los Pájaros. His left eye would wink at the waiter and the headwaiter; his finger would tap at the side of his nose. The young men of perfect smiles would serve with a discreet flourish the fine special dishes and fancy *cocteles* that only Señor Chepito could command, with a clap of the hands, from the bar and kitchen of Los Pájaros.

For a poor *provinciano*, it was said, Chepito had learned well the manners of a *niño bien*—that sort of playboy who has no thought of the bill for such an evening, or for such jewels at the throats of young girls, or, for the matter of that, for the young girls themselves. It was said that Chepito now handled with ruthless skill the business of radio stations, newspapers, and film studios controlled by his sister and her husband the general; that he also handled well the fiery spirits of his sister, who—*por desgracia*—had too much of fire and far too much of *poder* for the comfort of anyone in Pradera —except this *niño bien* of a brother.

Finally, it was added, in the low voice of secrets, Chepito performed still another important duty for his brother-in-law the general. This was the matter of liaison, as it is said, between the general and certain young *muchachitas,* younger than those to be seen on the arm or at the table of Chepito himself. And there were other liaisons with certain young boys, even younger, it was said, than the girls. It was whispered in this low voice of secrets that the general called these children of the night his *angelitos,* his little dead brothers, and that with them he played certain unusual games. One would understand that a powerful man such as this must have the need of unusual games, to release the mind from the troubles of his office. One would shrug the shoulders, adding with a smile that the general had need too of a release from that troublesome wife of his, that *bruja,* that witch of too much fire and too much *poder*.

Tobal Iribas had the *informes* of these matters, but it was not yet a thing that had passed from his mouth to the ear of La Señora. In the meantime he kept a narrowed eye upon this *niño bien* of a brother. And he kept his own counsel, in the way of a man who knows the value of certain secrets.

On the night of the gala celebration for the new success of Tobalito, all the *personajes* dressed themselves in fine new clothes and drove up the Calle Florida in polished new German limousines, each driven by a Negro chauffeur with skin of a color to match exactly the soft interior of the car; it was the latest thing.

Some *señores* of high *sociedad* brought their *amiguitas* instead of their wives, since the party was of a sort, in a place of a sort, that the very highest of *sociedad* would not wish to be seen attending. Especially if *she* were there, with that unspeakable *niño bien* of a brother, at the largest of black-mirrored tables on the ivory satin wall in the room of wonderful lights.

Baron von M of the Deutschebank would surely come with that longtime *querida rubia* of his, the blond Señorita Juanita Ortiz, while the dark-haired baroness smoldered at home in the *casa de campo*, with the sallow children and the whispering servants and the baron's ancient mother in her high-necked gown of black Spanish lace. One understood that the Deutschebank had recently bought a major interest in Los Pájaros. Certain ladies of not quite the highest *sociedad* had arranged parties before the party, and ladies of the show business and other not quite the lowest *sociedad* would arrange other sorts of parties after the party, and in between Tobalito would pour music and champagne enough to float all of the new ships and airplanes of all the fleets of Chulo Rubén Caso, from San Luis to Paris. And the bill for the evening would be paid without a thought by certain associates of Baron von M at the Deutschebank of Pradera.

A hundred photographers flashed their lights with a noise like that of the corks from the wine, and the smiles of the *personajes* opened and closed according to the same rhythm. There she is! someone would hiss into a microphone, trailing its cord along the sidewalk like a tame black snake. Señorita . . . ! And the little lights would pop, sending a shower of illumination upon the field of upturned faces with the mouths open like the mouths of baby birds. *Peones* in dreary clothes lined the broad *avenidas* in every direction, and those who were closest strained against the ropes of scarlet velvet that marked the passageway from the limousines at the curb to the gleaming entrance doors of the club Los Pájaros. Thousands of eyes bright with a fever of love watched the Señorita this or that, as she alighted from a car the color of night, in a gown the color of stars. The faces of *peones* would shine with pleasure, as though that señorita in her starry gown, whoever she was, had the power to lift one over the rope of scarlet velvet and carry one into the glowing afterlife that must surely lie beyond the great metal doors. Such doors enclosed all of the secrets of wealth and fame and happiness, *no es verdad?* Holding the hem of her gown the color of stars, that *personaje*, whoever she was, swept past the *peones* in an instant of exploding light, trailing spangled laughter and lavender perfume, stirring the night air with her sweet red smile. Ah. Who was she? *Nadie.* Nobody. Just another actress with Chepito Andújar. Or maybe the *amiguita* of that banker. But *mira! Ahora!* The heads turned now as though on a string pulled by a master of puppets. *Querida!* whispered a voice like the cry of a soul. A woman crowned with white feathers, a woman streaming with golden ribbons, emerged alone like a tattered angel from the depths of a silver car. Regal and tall, with a small radiant head of white-gold, a head set so like a jewel upon her shoulders, one could easily mistake it for a carving of crystal in a *galería*. But who— Soledad! In the crowd one heard an intake of breath like a gasp of pain or ecstasy. That *estrella* of the cinema with the long bright eyes around which she painted iridescent shadows the color of bruises and sunsets. Soledad. She had vanished one day—was it months ago or years?—and still no one knew why; yet who had forgotten the shadows of the eyes, or the angle of the delicate chin, or the tilt of the pale head? *Querida!* she breathed over her golden shoulder to this one or that, striding through the gleaming doors with that enchanting walk of hers, one foot set so before the other, the march of a monarch. *Querida!*

At the round black table in the center of the wall of ivory satin, Señora Montero, surrounded by photographers and friends, stopped in the midst of a smile and turned toward the sound of that voice as a flower toward light.

The actress paused in her walk; her bright mouth made a smile of mischief, like the quick unfurling of a ribbon bow. *Por Dios,* she said. Rosa! But, *querida,* what have they done to your hair?

The jeweled white hand of La Señora flew upward like a startled butterfly; then it wavered, fluttering in midair as though caught in an invisible net. Soledad laughed; La Señora drew a breath and lowered the hand to her silver lap. Welcome home, Soledad, she murmured with a certain coolness. The actress held out her pale slender arms as though they were filled with flowers.

What a pretty ring, said Rosa, narrowing her eyes, making no other move. Like a shadow, Chulo Rubén Caso moved between them. I am delighted that it pleases you, he whispered in a voice of oil, and grasped the hand of Soledad that wore the pretty ring. *Perdóneme.* And with the practiced gesture of an old magician, Chulo slid the ring off the finger of Soledad and held it out to Rosa. It sat resting upon the white cushion of his palm, as an offering of peace between warring empires sits upon the plump pillow of velvet held by a royal emissary. Soledad had it made for you, said

Chulo, with a slight nod, a faint dismissing shrug, an apology for the modesty of the gesture. He whispered the name of the great jeweler in Paris, who had personally selected the stones. Soledad, he said, has flown here for this one night. Only to present this to you. *Verdad?*

Soledad inclined her golden head without a word. Rosa's face reflected nothing. She held out her hand, steady now as the hand of a pope. Chulo slipped the ring on her finger. It was a large amethyst the color of twilight or the eyes of Soledad, surrounded by a halo of small perfect diamonds, and worth perhaps a year of evenings such as this one. *Mira!* said La Señora, with a sudden smile of a child. She turned her fingers this way and that, so that the smoky light would dance within the stone. It is a perfect fit, she said.

Soledad laughed again, that miracle of a laugh. Of course, *querida,* she murmured with a wicked look. Did you imagine I would forget the size?

Two familiar spots of color rose on the pale cheeks of La Señora; she turned her head and resumed a conversation of nothing with the *señor* on her left. Chulo shook his head at Soledad, a warning. The music drowned his words, but one might see in the shadows his expression of a certain unaccustomed anxiety, and hers of a certain unaccustomed distress.

At the door of the men's room Señor R and Señor S exchanged stiff bows, each making a show to yield the right of way. They had recently patched up a quarrel stemming from the reluctance of Señor S to propose Señor R for another term in the presidency of the Jockey Club, on the ground that Señor R had been a trifle slow in divesting the executive board of his metal works of certain undesirable elements. *Hola,* Paco, said Señor S, arranging a smile of caution. The response of Señor R was that swift snap of the head which one may take as a wary salute. Roberto, he murmured, as though it might be a question.

Inside the men's room of black marble walls and plumbing fixtures of golden pipes, Señor R adjusted his starched collar and made a sound of clearing his throat. Had one heard, he said, the latest unfortunate news of their mutual friend Don José?

Señor S had heard a great deal, as who had not? La Señora—that *fundación* of extortion of hers—had held a pistol to the corporate head of Don José's *factoría*, where Pradera's most popular drink, Naranja Crush, was bottled. A "charitable contribution" had been demanded. Ten million dollars, was it not? *Sí.* An outrage of outrages. Don José had refused, no?

Ya lo creo; Don José is a man of courage.

But then the creature sent her army of inspectors—?

Ah. One has heard of that pestilence. The *infestación* of inspectors who look for insects. And they found—?

Señor R nodded with an expression of familiar distaste. Rats in the toilets, no? In the machinery? Filth under the bottle caps. A bubonic plague beneath the fingernails of the workers—

Señor S laughed a bitter laugh. And another under the armpits of the truck drivers—

How much? Señor S asked in a careful whisper.

Señor R shook his head as one in a shock of disbelief. Twenty-two million in fines and projected alterations. Don José filed for bankruptcy this morning. There is nothing— Señor R broke off into silence; only his shoulders rose an inch in the gesture of surrender.

Señor S sighed.

And now, said Señor R, in a new tone of fear, when the *fundación* man comes to one's office . . . His voice had diminished to the whisper of one who knows the walls are inhabited. The collector . . . carries in his briefcase an empty bottle of Naranja Crush. If *el señor* the director of the company does not have the checkbook open and the pen poised so, in his hand, the collector begins to sip. So, with a straw. As though to suck the emptiness in the bottle. Naranja Crush! Señor R made the noise of sucking on air. So!

As Señor R spoke, the face of Señor S had slowly drained of its ruddy color. What do they say becomes of all the money? I have heard—

Señor R laughed now, a bark of anger. Two hundred million dollars—can one not see it? On the fingers and the neck of that—he made the gestures of a *mujer sucia*—a slut showing off her finery. To show the spoils to her *peones.* Like one of those madonnas of the *pueblos*, all hung with bits of colored glass. *Mira!* she screeches at them. See what one gets for sucking the *miembro* of Montero!

Señor S was laughing now with a shaking of the head. She is like a disease with the people. I have seen the crowds—

Peones, said Señor R with a voice of contempt. Peasants . . .

Mujeres, said Señor S, with the same voice. Women . . .

The door swung open behind them and the two fell silent, each with his eyes straight ahead within his stall of black marble; each mindful only of the force and direction of his own stream.

Join us later for a whiskey-soda, Roberto?

Gracias, Paco, said Señor S, with the smile of a friend.

At three o'clock in the morning, a white telephone rang beside the pale satin bed of Juanita Ortiz.

Bueno?

Are you alone? A voice with the tension of a taut band, breathless as a runner. Rosa.

Sí, whispered Juanita Ortiz. Where are you?

I am there in fifteen minutes. Is it all right?

Sí, bueno. Juanita replaced the receiver and turned to kiss the sleep-filled face on the pillow beside her. You must go, she breathed, low as a sigh. Telephone me from the airport—or from where?

There was a faint stirring, as of a breeze; hair like bright petals curving into new patterns around a face with the shape of a heart. A slender arm rose at an angle from the knot of blue sheets. Who is coming? Rudi? The eyes of Soledad remained closed.

No. Juanita reached out to caress the slender arm, drawing the tips of her fingers slowly from the upraised wrist to the curve of shoulder. *Quiero* . . . she said. I wish—that I were going with you. Going. *Sin recuerdos;* never looking back.

Soledad yawned and smiled, the oblique smile of one who prefers not to reply. Was it Rosa, she said. Coming here?

Not what you think, said Juanita quickly. Why do you assume—

I? The bright shadowed eyes, open now, gleamed like eyes of a cat measuring the darkness. But her voice was still hushed with sleep. I never assume, she whispered. That is why you surprised me last night.

Juanita returned the smile of no reply. *Me siento*—I take it back. But you will call . . . from—?

Soledad was already unfolding, rising from the bed like a flower; deft hands fastening secret hooks within the gown of golden ribbons; slender feet sliding into sandals delicate as cobwebs. *Querida,* she said then. And bent to touch the soft mouth of Juanita Ortiz. She smoothed away a lock of hair that curled like the mark of a question over Juanita's delicate brow. You must tell your Rudi for me that despite the bad market, he is a fortunate banker.

Juanita frowned. Is it dangerous, what they have asked of you? Rudi and . . . that *cabrón* Chulo?

Not so very. Soledad made her voice light. Only to steal an old medical report. One that has been missing. But this is the last favor I will do; they have hounded me long enough for the few reckless moments of my life. Tomorrow I begin again to be as reckless as I please. After today I am no longer in debt.

They have agreed to finance your films?

What of that? snapped Soledad. They risk a few pesos; I risk my life. It is not a bargain.

Juanita sighed. If only I were going with you. We could—

Querida— Soledad's voice seemed far away now, as if it were searching for a note of sadness. No, she said softly. The truth is we could not. But let me hold you now—

Touch my breasts, so— Juanita held the hands of Soledad against her body. Are they like— Was it the same, with her?

Soledad shook her golden head. Why do you ask—for my pain, or yours?

I only wanted to know—if you felt a certain way with me. If it was different.

Soledad withdrew her hands gently and looked away, gazing over Juanita's slim shoulder at the little French clock on the wall, at the shelf of novels, at the round mirrored table cluttered with crystal bottles. Too many kinds of scent; the collection of a woman still searching for her own. Different, she echoed. Why does it matter? Have I asked what you do with Rudi?

Juanita's eyes filled with a sudden mist of stinging tears, No— because you do not care.

Soledad said nothing to this, but held out her arms. Juanita. For a moment they stood so, in a magic circle of embrace, both listening to the silence between them. Do you know, Juanita whispered then, we have spent all of the night talking of her?

Not all! Soledad laughed her laugh of mischief. Still, I have heard that now in San Luis one always ends the night talking of her.

And do you hate her for that?

Claro que no! How could I hate a woman I invented?

You never invented her politics?

Politics! That she prattles on the radio of women's right to vote? Of *aborción* and divorce, and "her" *pobrecitos* in the provinces?

No. Juanita shook her head. I do not mean those things.

Well, said Soledad with a tone of boredom. I hope that for her sake she has no other politics.

She does. I think they will destroy her for that.

You are serious! said Soledad. But who bothers to destroy a woman for such reasons? In any case she is already dying.

No— Juanita gasped with the sudden truth of it.

Ya lo creo, said Soledad gently. I saw it in her face last night. Juanita stared at her. This mission . . . this favor you will do for Rudi? Is it—to hurt her?

In Soledad's eyes a sudden cloud had formed; it hovered over the brightness like a veil. It is not for the messenger to guess what use will be made of a piece of *informes,* she said with care. I have said the business is not dangerous. I am only going . . . to find out a thing for your friends. There was only a slight emphasis on the word *your.* Juanita said nothing more.

Soledad stood now with her golden cape over her shoulders, the mantle of a warrior. *Por favor* . . . we will not say goodbye over the secrets of others. Rosa and I are strangers now—by her wish, or perhaps her need, to forget.

Not by yours?

Not by mine, murmured Soledad. At least I have never thought so.

Then will you tell me— Juanita began, and then stopped. No. I do not want to ask—

Bueno, said Soledad. I do not want to lie.

The last kiss between them was tender—the tongue of one slowly tracing the line of the other's mouth, like the sealing of letters.

THE yellow brightness of Juanita's hallway blazed at Rosa like an affront; she peered into it with the blank hurt eyes of one who starts at the play of shadows. My need of a friend—she murmured, as a shy child offers phrases of politeness. My need—seems always to come at such hours. . . .

Juanita rushed to embrace her; Rosa coughed and turned her head, as though to prevent the spread of a contagion. Sst! Juanita chided her, teasing. The best hours come when my friend needs me—

Rosa made her way unsteadily to the soft yellow sofa whose cushions gave a sigh of pleasure as one sank upon them. But when she opened her mouth to speak, a cry escaped—the faint fluting signal of a bird with an invisible injury. Juanita in her pajamas of water-colored silk curled up like a cat beside her, with a thoughtful nodding, a squinting of eyes, as though Rosa had uttered an ordinary sound and she must consider how to respond.

I am not afraid of life or death! Rosa exclaimed then, with a smile of mocking. *Recuerdas?* Juanita said nothing; *claro,* the mocking was not of her, but of a ghost they both remembered well: a Rosa of long ago, who had believed such a boast, made by a woman of reckless beauty with nothing to lose. Not a *mujer* of flesh, in truth, but an *estrella,* a star in a foolish romantic *cine* about spies and soldiers, in the danger of love. I am not afraid! Rosa said again, now with her head thrown back in weariness, her eyes fastened upon nothing. Did I tell you how certain I was that I would be—must be—that *estrella?* Such beauty, in that cape of black spangles, with that smile of the world. That smile—for the soldiers whose orders are to execute the whore. *Muerte a la puta, he?*

Juanita sighed and covered with her two hands the small cold hands that lay curled in Rosa's lap like fragments of carved chalk. I remember well, she said softly. My skinny *amiguita . . .* my little friend with the body of a child— *Por Dios!* who has ever known such a *pobrecita,* with bones that trembled aloud! *Claro,* my friend had a need to believe in that *cine!* It was— Juanita paused, frowning, then spread her hands wide, a gesture of knowing. A cape of black spangles—and a red smile to wave in the face of *la Muerte.* The bright uniform to make one brave, no? To disguise the small pale *muchacha* with no breasts—to show only the spirit that lifted her from a floor of dust! That was a good *cine—*

Rosa shook her head; a strange quick snap of vehemence. It was a lie, she said. Bravado was a lie like *esperanza. La madre* who weeps only for others. *La estrella* who never weeps at all. So many lies, and all the same. She sighed. Bright uniforms, for children at the circus! See here? This fine fur collar of small foxes whose heads bite their own tails? *Mira!* How they cover my throat with soft kisses; what a comfort they are on the long rides in dark cars. We have a special glass now for the cars, to seal me in, *sabes?* And special new drivers, have you seen them? With eyes like these—dead fox eyes to watch for the moments of my weakness. *Dios,* one cannot count the eyes. So many *zorros* watching for the weak moments—

No— Juanita made a fluttering gesture of protest. No—

Es verdad! Rosa's voice spiraled higher, as though she must chatter above the din of a gay party; above the iridescent laughter of strangers. *Sí!* But think what a favor I do them, Juanita! So many years they sat so, under their scowls, with only one another to hate. Now they sleep curled together, each with a fine fresh dream of what he will do to me, under the covers. And all his new *amigos,* his old enemies, shout *Sí!* Kill the whore! *Muerte a la puta! He?* Did you ever think it so?

Stop! Juanita's small face grew dark with anger. You and I—have we not carried such names enough in our lives? And have we not been weak before? I do not know you with this new voice of old bitterness. Where is the fire of my small friend? And the mocking laughter? *He*—Señora! Do you quench your own flames, to save them the trouble?

Rosa was not listening. Did you ever imagine, she went on, musing, as old women do . . . that hatred of your small skinny friend would rouse old men from their sleep? More than *amor* itself? Can you tell it from the look of me? Where does it show—here? My *magia negra,* my witch power? Do you doubt that I can raise all the tired *miembros* in the country? Only whisper my name in their beds!

Juanita rose to her feet and began a nervous darting about the room; the eyes of Rosa followed her with a curious detachment. Such a straightening of cushions, a touching of tall crystal vases, of small porcelain animals. Such a hasty stuffing of black cigarets into white lacquered boxes. *Black cigarets with tips of gold—*

Well, who are they who hate you so? Juanita called in a light voice, to make the pretense of joking. Those *militares* again? The old fools at the Jockey bar—their wives of the small silly hats? One knows they are all stupid, those tired old—but not to make plots against *los* Monteros! Without you their power explodes. Puf! Like one of those new *bombas* with the black cloud of mushroom. Do you think they do not know how badly they need you—with all their grumbling?

Rosa's laugh broke with the sharp sound of splintering crystal. Only one, she said softly. They admit the need of only one Montero —that one who wears their uniform. As for the *muchedumbre*—that crowd of wretched *peones* who say Montero and cross themselves— will they notice there is only one? They follow the leader I said was mine, no? Some of them—*pobrecitos*—still believe in *esperanza*. The rest—well, they have learned to obey. Certain things happen when they do not.

But Carlos! Carlos has no fear—

Carlos? Remember what he said once of his old rival Quiroga— the shark that was? We must file those teeth, he said. No need for *los tiburones*. No other sharks but me. So now . . . he sits, my *marido*. The President-to-be sits so, with his own teeth filed, chewing on soft food. Every day some *asesino* brings him a fresh secret wrapped in a roll of soft foreign money. From the dirty silver spoon of Baron von M—

Ah! She stared up at Juanita as though she had forgotten where she was. Well, she said then, with a careless shrug. These things live too long in our silences. Your handsome Rudi, and his not-so-handsome friends of the foreign banks. And now the *Yanquis. Conoces?* Do you know? All the silent partners of the new dirty deals—still pretending to be enemies?

Juanita said nothing; she stood so, on the opposite side of the room, with her head cocked to the side, as though listening. She stood so, before a mantel of carved white plaster, beneath a mirror of rose-tinted glass. With her head cocked at an angle, so that the rose-tinted glass need not reflect her thoughts. *Black cigarets with tips of gold—*

After a moment, Rosa spoke again, still in the murmur of one who muses aloud, only to herself. They sit so, she said. Deciding behind their blue smoke. How to tell Carlos what must be done to me . . . against me. My speeches are canceled. *Dígaselo.* Tell her it is arranged so, for this reason or that. Not another word this week. Tell her the doctor agrees that La Señora must rest. That La Señora has said enough. In truth, she has said too much!

She bent suddenly to her worn leather briefcase that bulged with ragged papers. Scribblings and notes; canceled speeches; old pleas. Both hands plunged inside the case, then emerged, tightened into fists, clutching papers, wadding them into balls, flinging them. *Toma! Vaya!* Too many words! Women who want things—more than is good for them. More than is good for business! They say I incite—who? Mothers of beggars in the streets? Whores and lazy *peones* who will not work! *Sí*—I incite—with my foolish talk of helping, of license and waste, as it is said. *Dios* knows what filthy ideas pass from my lips to the people! Sinful freedoms . . . handfuls of gifts to make them lazier still, no? So it is arranged. My promises are carefully broken. The money goes back and forth, to the same pockets—from the silent partners. And when I scream, when I cry, it is said—have you heard it?—she is *un poquito* . . . a little off! And if not for that doctor of hers, they say, with the wink . . . Well, but what did you expect of such a woman? One knows well that a whore has no need of a brain!

With a small pointed shoe, Rosa kicked hard at the heavy briefcase. It toppled with a dull sound against the leg of the lacquered table, upsetting a slender vase that held a white rose. Juanita made no move to right it. Thick blue folders slid from the torn mouth of the briefcase, pouring as from a fresh wound. Too many words! Rosa whispered again. Tell her . . . only the smile now. One more, for the *fotógrafos. Mira!* Rosa forced her mouth into a parody of the famous smile, turning her head now, full-face, profile—each of the poses one might see in the latest campaign posters. Look, Juanita! The smile without a voice. An *estrella* of the silent *cine!* At last —that little friend of yours is what she was meant to be.

Sst! Juanita twisted her face into frowns of disapproving. Even if you are right, this cannot last. Carlos is too wise for this. He knows well that he needs the voice of his *estrella.* I remember what that brother of yours used to say: Rosa will be the royal taster. Her tongue will test the words of danger, for the king's safety. It is so. When you speak, if the people are pleased, it is Carlos they praise. And if they are angry, who swallows the poison for him? Not Carlos—only the poor taster. It is—well they have said it, all of them. To be a royal taster is an important job—for a woman!

Rosa sighed. They have taught him new lessons, his *amigos.* Now they say I speak to stir the trouble. My mouth of a witch—my cauldron of *brujería!* Look, they say. The *peones* catch a fire of hell from that devil's tongue. This is what happens when one lets a little whore grow so big! Look—the *peones* write filth on your walls, on your *fotografías!* They riot, trampling each other in the plazas. They will set the torch to our houses and our cars! Whose fault is this? Who makes the makers of trouble? *Claro*—it is that devil of yours, that *puta* with a tongue! Listen—the bartender's men take care of the trouble. But who will stop the tongue of that *puta?*

Still Juanita shook her head. Can you not see? Carlos deceives them. He only pretends to hear such craziness. It is that game of the foils he plays with such skill. Let them think he moves the blade so—or so. While he tricks them—

Rosa smiled. He is changed, my friend. You cannot know. But when the time comes, he will do the new tricks, the ones they now

teach him. And this I tell only you. The time for it comes soon.
They will not wait long. . . .

Juanita's eyes glowed with agitated light. She held her hands like
cups, over the ears. Now I will not hear any more; you are exhausted. That is the cause of it. Too much of travel, of speeches. In
this they are right; I see it. Look at you, with such a briefcase full
of business, at this hour of night. You never rest; they are right in
this too. I heard your broadcast last week; that voice of a *trompeta*
fades with too much use. But still the people listen like children in
church. And the men in the *tabernas*—I have watched their faces.
You alone stopped those crazy transport workers this time. And no
one was hurt! Listen; you are wrong, imagining these plots. How
can they destroy the power you have? *Maravillas—*

Miracles. Again Rosa smiled with her mouth curled like a ribbon.
I know well what I can do, and what I cannot. A *mujer* of flesh
who can do miracles—she is a witch, no? One knows well to hurl
the stones! By now I have a thousand words of cursing for my miracles! Juanita—can you not understand what has happened to me?

Juanita laid a gentle arm upon the shoulder of her friend. *Déjelo!*
she said. You make yourself ill—

Sí, said Rosa. I am—

Sst, then! Juanita pulled her to her feet. Come—I know what you
need. Remember that night long ago when you were so pale, the
color of a terrible green soup? And shaking so, like a bare thistle,
like a rat in the water? Still I had to send you out, to find a job.
With the belt pulled tight as a noose around that skinny waist. And
I told you then, with my finger of warning, so! Never let them see
what shines behind your eyes. Show them this! And that! But there
is nothing there! you said. *Verdad*—I have only a little fire, here—
Remember? O Rosa, let us pull the belt tight again, and fix the
face of green soup! Are you coming?

Rosa smiled and shook her head no, but she rose and followed
Juanita into the pretty white bedroom that smelled of mingled per-
fumes and the faint pungent echo of black cigarets.

Seated before the small round dressing table, the altar where one
may pray to one's own images, Rosa stared at the thin face in the
mirror, touching with wonder the whiteness, the shadows. We were

only starving then, she murmured. Such an ordinary hunger we had—

He! Not you! exclaimed Juanita, dipping slender points of sable brushes into luminous powders, testing between the tips of practiced fingers a cream of lilac, another of rose-pink. Now she daubed lightly at the face which Rosa lifted toward her like a wan flower on a fragile stem. Juanita rubbed at the whiteness, restoring colors of life. Ah! she cried, seizing a thick black crayon strewn with stars, its fat white point round and luminous as a pearl. Rainbow of heaven! breathed Juanita. Close your eyes! Rosa obeyed; her lids fluttered with eager mistrust, that delicate seizure of faith in which the believer yields to certain magic. Juanita stroked the pearl crayon across her trembling lids, causing a mysterious glow of pink and violet, of opalescent blue and ghostly silver—a sweep of nascent dawn over eyes of midnight. Ah! said Juanita, smiling. Now, *dígame!* Tell me—when were you ever hungry in an ordinary way?

Rosa's eyes flew open; she smiled at the mirror; at those silver eyelids, pale and lustrous as little moons. She examined the crayon. Rainbow of heaven? From Paris, said Juanita. It costs the earth. Wait—and her fingers dipped again, now into tiny pots of silver, of bronze. With her thumbs she stroked away wine and purple, distilling, purifying. Here—she touched Rosa's throat—and here, just in the hollow, yes! Still the whiteness of Rosa defied her, gleaming through the vivid reds as though a blue warning light shone from within. Sst, Juanita said at last, standing back, squinting her eyes, appraising the work. Well. Shall we do something about your hair? Come on, say you want me to.

Rosa nodded, moving her head from side to side, touching, flirting with her reflection. Something—?

Small curls here, at the cheeks, like a gypsy?

Rosa turned again, swiveling on the little velvet chair. No—pull it back. Tight! No more curls—my face is sharp, like a blade. *O,* Juanita, look at me!

Rosa's eyes narrowed—dark slits in the blue-white shadow of

Again Juanita squinted; again she frowned. Rosa, have you got any money? I mean, in your own name?

heaven. There is . . . she said. Chepito opened two accounts, when we sold the radio station—one for Mama—

Well, but if you had to go away, suddenly?

Rosa shrugged. *Sabes*—men are squirrels, no? Always carrying the money so, in their secret pouches? First to one hiding place, then another. Carlos . . . Another shrug. Well, but in any case I have all these— She held out her thin arms, extending them straight out, the way a child does; the heavy bracelets on both wrists clanged together with a harsh sound. Juanita stared. Wide flat cuffs of platinum—blazing white metal, thick as shackles. Slave bracelets. All my fine *regalos,* Rosa whispered. My gifts, stolen from the people, *verdad?* Of course I am not paid for my services. In the government, at least, I am not—she smiled with sudden mischief—not a *puta* after all. Only a good housewife, a proper *señora.* I work only for my keep—

Juanita scowled. And why have they still not put you on the ballot? I thought it was settled. I thought he promised—Vice President—

Sí, he promised, Rosa sighed. In the way a man promises the heaven and its crown of shooting stars. *Esperanza*—

But I am serious! You have no— I mean, all that you have said— of the plots, the *espías?* They can do what they like. . . . But if you were Vice President, what could they do then? Who would dare then to cancel your speeches! Carlos? In truth, he trusts no one but you! I do not care who the others are—or what they say. Carlos is no fool; he knows—

He looks at me so, Juanita—with his eyes of doubt. Their poison words are in his head now. What does she really want, this *puta?* Vice President? Money of her own? What is this *monstruo* I have made? Perhaps it is as they say. She will kill me for what is mine. She will take my money—my manhood! Rosa sighed. Well, there is still too much we cannot say, you and I. *Verdad?* Rosa's gaze wandered slowly to the bedside table. *Black cigarets with tips of gold . . .*

Juanita felt a color rising to her own cheeks, a rose-pink that had not come from bright magic powders on brushtips of sable. She said nothing.

Rosa stood now to go, and touched her friend lightly on the sleeve of water-colored silk. *Me siento*—it is late—

There *is* something—

No. Rosa shook her head. No, *querida*. There is nothing.

I mean, there is something I can do to help—

Even if—Rosa smiled a smile of mischief—one had to give up the use of exotic cigarets?

You know I do not—

I know one who does. One who goes on a mission of secrets, no?

I did nothing to hurt you, I swear it!

You could have—

Then let me prove my friendship! As you did once, for me. Without questions. Rosa, let me—

Rosa's face was thoughtful. Remember that *demostracion*, when Carlos was in prison?

Sí—how could one forget?

Remember how difficult it was?

Not so difficult! It took—you said—only a few friends. And some money—

Rosa smiled. More than some—

Well, but we have more friends now, have we not? Even some rich ones? More than we had once! And that *muchedumbre*—those ragged ones with their foolish *esperanza*, those children who believe in *estrellas*? Would they not come again to cheer in the streets? If there were ways to help them come? As it was in that terrible time, for Carlos. Does *he* want it enough now—as you did then?

If those rich friends want it at all—

Juanita crossed her arms over her chest in the way of a wise mama. Are there not many ways, she said, to persuade a man who thinks he does not want what is right? *He?* Have we both learned nothing after all?

Rosa smiled. The dangerous game of *putas*—

The dangerous game of *políticos!* said Juanita. They are the same, no?

Sin duda, said Rosa, laughing. Of course.

And did I ever ask you how the money came—that night you saved my life?

Rosa shook her head. But I did not risk my life for it, my friend. Twenty dollars—

Well, we are both worth more now, *he?* How much is a *demo-*

stración for an *estrella?* For a Vice President? One million pesos?
Two?

Dear Juanita, said Rosa softly. You are still watching an old romantic *cine—*

*Sí—*and you are still that *estrella* who flirts with *la Muerte* in a
cape of spangles.

Rosa drew a long breath. What became of her, do you know?
What becomes of them all? Those *estrellas—*

Who knows, sighed Juanita. That one at least was paid well for
the smile. Those *putatitas* of the screen, of the radio. One knows
they are sometimes paid well for dying so young—

Tal vez . . . Rosa's mouth curled again in the pale mocking
smile. Sometimes.

Por Dios! Juanita cried. Well? Are we not going to try?

Of course we are. Rosa tossed her head in the old way of the *estrella,* moving with the light. She reached for one of Soledad's black
cigarets, and raised it so between two fingers, the gesture of a toast.
Was it like this she stood, that *estrella,* in that scene? Like this—
before the firing squad? And painted on her last red smile for
them? Was it for them? Juanita—is that still how you see your small
skinny friend?

Tears now cast a wavering silver light within the round dark eyes
of Juanita, beneath the lids that were colored like opals, like rainbow pearls, moons of heaven. *Sí,* she whispered, nodding in a way
to make the tears dissolve gently without falling. It is—how I see
you.

MARÍA Blanca has snapped on a heavy bracelet shaped like a
wide flat cuff; a slave bracelet, as it is called. The metal gleams like
a curved mirror; she makes a face at her image distorted in it, the

way a child discovers the magic of a feeding spoon. But what happened to the other? she says, with the suggestion of a pout. Carlos said there was a pair—

Quiroga closes the safe and smiles the smile that is not. We sold one, he says. Certain debts . . . certain enemies one had thought were friends, *sabes?* Now his fingers move swiftly, adjusting the small yellow painting of an arching bridge, which serves to conceal the general's valuables. Trinkets, he muses with disdain. Not worth what they cost.

She shakes her head, sighing. Did Carlos know you sold it?

Quiroga sighs in return, a heavy sound. It is the sort of day in which a man feels the weight of his years. La Señora—he pauses, allowing her to savor the sound—La Señora knows well . . . that the general has eyes within each thought. But in that time, things twisted many ways at once. Some payments still go on. . . . Well. Are you ready? Shall I tell them you are coming?

She nods, twirling before the tall mirror, flexing her feet so as to rise upon practiced toes. Her round skirt flares out in a wide circle, then subsides, clinging to her legs. Quiroga winces as though she has assaulted him.

Chulo is pacing in the hallway just outside. Quiroga assumes the fat one has heard everything, as always, including the click of tumblers within the lock of the general's safe. They exchange bows, and glances of knowing.

In a house of white stone in the sleeping town of San Marcos, the family of Juana Ibáñez gathered at the square dining table to keep a vigil without a meeting of eyes; figures of chalk that blinked in the morning light. Around them the scent of orange groves seemed to give off a faint color at the edge of gray silence; the air itself carried a weight of darkness against this morning, against this day that was to have brought a mood of fiesta to the town of San Marcos, and to the house of Juana Ibáñez.

Rosa, the youngest, was coming home. A brief visit, a pause in the long journey of La Señora's silver campaign train, time enough for a ceremony, the posing of the family in tearful embraces, yellow flowers in the arms of small shy girls, and the popping of little lights to record the moment for the newsreel.

But there was already news in this house, a piece of *informes* of a kind that could not be recorded with the popping of lights, but must be whispered in darkness with the tied tongue of fear. The husband of Catuja had disappeared on the night before this one; taken into protective custody, as it was said, for a routine questioning by the *policía federal*. The bartender's men.

Catuja sat now, twisting and twisting a white cloth in her lap, soundless with grief. Catuja who had always laughed too easily, whose body at twelve had swelled too quickly into a full roundness like her mother's, which gave her both shame and power over the rude boys of Montaraz.

Catuja had never conquered the shame or the habit of easy laughter; nor had she found a clever use for the power of her voluptuous body. At the age of fifteen she had convinced Lola of the foolishness of running away with their small fierce sister—that crazy Rosa who was scarcely thirteen, and who would surely come running back after a day of loneliness and fright in a distant city.

It was always Catuja who chose the safe course. Marriage at sixteen to a simple boy with a hard brown chest, a sly smile and a quick temper. Mama had helped her assure the safety of the first baby's birth in wedlock; after that, a life of *contento* was made with the help of gifts, money, and favors sent by the small fierce sister who somehow had made her way in the distant city. The husband of Catuja, Juan Bautista Saldias, was now, thanks to his marital connections, a postmaster general, with honorary public titles and a fine salary. But over the years the sly smile and the quick temper had led him to certain troubles, from which only the political *cuña* of his wife's connections had saved him. It was whispered that in politics he leaned too far to the left; it was suspected that he had befriended a Jewish radical; it was known that in the taverns his mouth had a looseness and his tongue a lack of caution. At last he had uttered a certain word in speaking of his brother-in-law the general, a word of *desacato*, of disrespect. *Desacato* was now a federal crime; Juan Bautista had uttered the certain word in the hearing of a man who coveted the job of postmaster general, and the honorary public titles, and the fine salary. A report was made. And though it was known well in the *distrito* that Saldias was who he was, the new clerk who filed the paper accepted a certain consideration in exchange for a small favor; he would obey strictly the order of his superior who had said that in the cases of troublemakers in the provinces, certain procedures were to be followed in the routine way, without exception.

Juan Bautista Saldias was given the treatment of an ordinary troublemaker, no worse. But in the first hour of this day that La Señora and her campaign train were to arrive for the brief joyous reunion in the town of San Marcos, the ruined body of Catuja's husband had been released to the family, with apologies for the unfortunate misunderstanding. Juan Bautista Saldias now lay silent on a bed in the *alcoba* that overlooked the orange grove; the ribs of his strong brown chest had been crushed against his lungs, and the remains of his sly smile were sewn together within a mask of white gauze. It was said by the surgeons who tended him after the release that even if he lived, it would not again be the life of a postmaster general, or even that of a simple man with a round wife given to easy laughter.

An *investigación* had been ordered; the clerk who filed the paper had been arrested, and despite certain alluring promises from the man who coveted the job of postmaster general, it was likely that the usual devices would elicit a confession from the unfortunate clerk before this day ended. In the meantime the family sat in silence around the radio shaped like the arch of a small church, listening to the hourly reports of the advances of La Señora's silver train in its triumphant journey toward her family in the quiet town of San Marcos. The eyes of Juana Ibáñez—those thoughtful eyes of a *viscacha* whose secrets are as hidden as its dangerous cave under the flat ground—shone now with the hard silver brightness of familiar pain. In her thoughts swam the echo of another time, when a child lay near death on the other side of a curtain, while another daughter spoke to her mama with the sad wisdom of one who already knows the rules of this world. Why does it surprise you, *Mamacita?* the daughter had said. Had Juana Ibáñez herself not taught them all the lesson? The *padres,* the *policía,* they all do what they must. And what they must do . . . must change from time to time.

Juana Ibáñez shook her head to dispel the sounds that she remembered, but she could not dispel this new sight of Catuja in silence twisting and twisting again these white cloths soiled with the blood of secret wounds that could not be named.

On the campaign train the advisers argued the merits of canceling the stop at San Marcos, of keeping the *informes* from La Señora until later in the day, when she had completed her speeches for the general and could be given relaxing medication. Dr. Ceballos had been consulted as to the wisdom of doubling the usual dose, in view of the unfortunate developments.

They had as usual reckoned without the efficiency of La Señora's own network of *informes*—those unofficial mouths that would pass a secret like a silver tray of *pasteles* between the cook and the maid, between the dresser of a woman's hair and the dresser of a man's wounds. The family of Juana Ibáñez in the town of San Marcos had no private *informes* that could be kept long from the ear of La Señora, even when she herself was traveling in protective custody aboard the silver campaign train.

Dr. Ceballos had been instructed to tell her that the train was running late, that the San Marcos stop could be made on the way back tomorrow, that she must conserve her strength now for the appearance tonight at the big dinner in Mendoza, for the *sindicatos* of railroad and transport workers.

Mientes! she said, pronouncing the word as one would spit a poison from the mouth. You lie. You do nothing now but carry their lies to me, like one of your drugs. I know that my *cuñado* is dying in San Marcos, and no one is to be blamed. Which means that *I* am to be blamed. As always! Because Carlos finds it easier to let them say what they like of me! He would do this—with my own family!

She refused to take the medication; she would as always confront them herself—burst in upon their deliberations in the smoking car. Those *cabrones*. No, said the doctor, finally. I will go. I will see to it that the stop at San Marcos is not canceled. *Bueno?* You will rest then?

She nodded wearily, gazing over his shoulder at the flat streaking countryside. Only when he had left did she permit the tears to form in her eyes; they would not fall.

Only the ceremony at the station was canceled; instead it was arranged that La Señora would make a brief private visit to the house of her family, without the *fotógrafos* or their small popping lights to record the tearful embrace for the newsreel. It would be explained to the *periodistas*, the newspaper men, that the mother of La Señora was ill; that the family wished to spare her the strain of a public appearance.

The children of Lola and Catuja had won permission to play outside while the family waited for the car of Tía Rosa. Not too far, and quiet play, without soiling the fine new clothes that were bought for the visit.

Within minutes the boys had scampered a quarter-mile down the road, to the copse of *ombú* trees, whose gnarled roots rise from the soil like the swollen knuckles of misshapen giants. Within minutes the boys were hanging from the topmost branches like wild young birds too crazy to know that an *ombú* is no place to nest, for at night its leaves are poison.

The little girls raced after their brothers, scolding and screaming; finally they stood transfixed beneath the trees, staring up at those mischief makers who could cling like a monkey with a single hand, or swing between the branches with screeches of fright and audacity. One little girl, Catuja's youngest, collapsed in a breathless heap apart from the others, and sat now playing with her new doll, whose dress of brilliant green material rustled when the child stroked it.

Hola! The sudden voice of a woman in elegant clothes; her face half hidden beneath the brim of a broad white hat, upon which a scarlet rubicola lay outstretched as if in flight. The boys stopped moving in the trees; the older girls blushed and said nothing. Only the youngest, Mircea, reached up to touch the feathers of the scarlet bird on the hat. *Mira!* she whispered.

Do you not remember Tía Rosa? said the soft voice of the woman, who smiled now and knelt to embrace Mircea.

The child shook her dark head. No. My papa, she added, is wounded. Maybe he will die.

I know, the woman murmured, but her face looked pale and strange, as though the child had accused her. She stood up quickly, and the brim of her hat brushed awkwardly against the child; the doll tumbled into the mud of the roadway.

For an instant they both stood staring at it; then the child began to cry.

I will send you another! said Tía Rosa, but the promise had a sharp sound, like a slap. The child's sobs grew louder. Rosa reached out a comforting hand, but Mircea shrank back and began to run, stumbling, toward her sisters, dragging the doll by the muddy hem of its elegant dress.

Rosa turned and saw, from the *ombú* tree, three pairs of round dark eyes watching her. Holding her wonderful hat with one gloved hand, she hurried toward the house. It had been a mistake, after all, to leave the limousine at the end of the road. But she had not wanted the driver to witness this homecoming. Not this driver; not this homecoming.

At the open doorway Rosa hesitated, in the listening way one stops to consider a danger. Her fingers held the hat with the scarlet bird, and her eyes searched the cool dim light within the house, for a smile of welcome, a movement of embracing arms. Then a man's voice—loud and harsh as a *trompeta*—blared a sudden greeting: La Señora! followed by the echoing howl of a throng, cheering, wild as animal cries. Rosa stumbled backward, a single step, as though the noise had struck a physical blow. But it was only a sound of radio; someone reached up to snap it off. She is here! cried the voice of Lola. But we thought—

Ah! Rosa's sigh escaped her like a breath held in terror. The plan was changed, she said quickly, in a voice too light and high, the voice of a guest with secrets, a stranger anxious to please. Chepito will come soon, she said; they—I—arranged it so because of . . . well, how is Juancito?

Their eyes shifted, one looking to another, furtive as conspirators. No one would gaze toward the door of the silent *alcoba*. At last Juana Ibáñez murmured the simple truth that could be said: *No sabemos.* We do not know. There is much bleeding inside him. She turned her palms upward in the way to invoke the will of *Dios*.

Catuja alone had not moved when her sister entered. Now Rosa ran toward her. O, Catuja—

No! The voice of Catuja was the piercing wail of a child who is lost. Never speak to me! Rosa stood frozen, swaying as though she might fall. Quickly the arms of Juana Ibáñez enfolded her. Catuja has not slept, she said. We are all— But come, sit down, we will have coffee with our talk. *Bueno?* But you are thin! The arms of a mother had made their swift judgment. Now her eyes studied Rosa's face with a fearful certainty. *Dígame la verdad*—you are ill! Rosa's gaze was level; with a shake of the head, No. Only tired. These long journeys—always so long. The crowds . . . And the news of Juancito—

Catuja sprang from her chair, eyes blazing. Talk like this! she screamed. The long journey—and with her hair done so, painted gold and swept into jeweled combs! While here is blood! She twisted the stained cloths; a wringing motion of two small fists made tight as claws. This blood of Juancito. Of how many Juancitos!

Sst! Juana Ibáñez hissed in alarm; Lola rushed to her sister and led her sobbing from the room. *Por Dios*, whispered Rosa, burying her face in the soft black warmth of her mother's lap. Juana Ibáñez tightened her embrace, as though her arms might yet protect such a child as once they had. Rosa began to tremble with dry wracking sobs; to Juana Ibáñez the fragile body seemed no more than twelve, no stronger than on the day she had lifted it from the dry dust of the Plaza del 16 Enero in a bloodstained dress of communion. The day Rosa had marched for the crown of *la reina*, at the risk of her life. *Niñita*, whispered the mother now, with a soothing voice that was a lie. Her daughter answered with bitterness. You blame me too, *Madrecita*. All of you. It is in your faces.

Juana Ibáñez sighed and nodded to Lola, who came quickly in silence and knelt to embrace her sister. Catuja stood watching from the open door of the *alcoba* in which Juancito lay silent in his mask of white gauze. Still she held the cloths against her body as though they staunched her own blood; her fingers glowed red where they touched the fresh stains. *Mira,* she said dully. *Mira.*

Stop this now, said Juana Ibáñez in a tone of commanding. Rosa comes to this house as a sister, as a daughter. She is of us, and not to be blamed for the mistakes of others.

Mistakes, echoed Catuja. *Los yerros.*

Rosa raised her head and stared at the hard white line that was Catuja's mouth. A sudden image lay superimposed upon the stricken face before her—Catuja laughing up at the face of Juancito; their two heads nodding up and down to the rhythm of the swaying *colectivo* on which they were riding to work—he at the post office, she at the grocery. Lovers in a tangle of dry old men and women with babies at the breast, children with round sad eyes and poultry in crates, shrieking. In Rosa's nostrils was the acrid smell of that car—sweat mixed with mother's milk; with chickens and dirt. In her eyes Catuja's shining curtain of black hair fluttered like a brave flag, as Juancito held her steady against the metal pole at the center of the rattling car. Their faces were so close that the space between seemed filled only with their longing. Rosa saw Catuja's hands touching Juancito's shirt, the buttons and the collar; small shy hands alighting here and there upon him, as though he must be covered with a sweet substance that would stick to the tips of her fingers. Sweet . . . Rosa moaned, shutting her eyes against the image, but it persisted. Juancito now touched her sister in this strange light way of awe and hunger; blunt fingers holding the edge of a thin sleeve of her blouse; a hand resting upon the fold of a skirt, inside a pocket, resting on the round bone of a hip as though he must steady himself with any covered fragment of her. And in their eyes, the yearning, like messages of light leaping across the narrow space between them. Catuja's laughing mouth, Juancito's sly smile beneath that soft mustache the color of chestnut. Rosa imagined the voice of that Catuja, a soft whisper. *Me gusta su camisa.* I like the shirt you wear. *A mi me gusta.* . . . And the little hand of Catuja reached again to touch the boy's soft collar, to make it lie so, to leave her mark upon it—and on the warm golden chest of Juancito. The boy's eyes shone with a pride, and the girl's shy foolish laugh rose in pleasure. O, Catuja . . .

But I did not know! she cried aloud to those phantom lovers. I know nothing of such terrible things. You blame me! Like everyone! For everything that is bad. As if I were God the Father—or the *Diablo* himself!

Juana Ibáñez murmured a sound of comfort and began to stroke with slow rhythm the slender arms, the shoulders that now shook without control, like those of a child wracked with fever chill. Carlos lets them blame me! Rosa whimpered. I know he does. He has only to give me a gift—anything—and someone will shout that I have stolen it—from the people! And he will laugh, with that shrug of his, saying nothing! Yet the wife of any rich man—everyone may see her covered with her jewels! With the skins of leopards and ermine! Who dares accuse them? Of what? *Madrecita*—how could I order the beating of Juancito? How could I?

Sí! screamed Catuja. You are to blame! The law of *desacato*—that is Carlos' gift to you! So that everyone will stop calling you filthy names— *Puta!* Whore! But they have only to look at you! She pointed an accusing finger at the hair of her sister, rolled like *pasteles*, like cakes baked of gold, held in place with glittering ornaments. Juancito pays for that, no? And that ring of a fortune? And the red *pájaro* that lies so still on your crown of straw? Juancito pays—

Basta! said Juana Ibáñez, and the screams of Catuja subsided at once into whimpers. Now leave us, her mama commanded, with a sigh of anger. Again Lola led her sister away, and Juana Ibáñez began to rock slowly, cradling Rosa in her lap. With two fingers she loosened the elaborate pins and combs that held the golden loops of hair; as the strands streamed, long and loose, over her fingers, she began to stroke them as one may play the strings of an instrument. In my village, she whispered, the old women would speak of evil . . . an air with the power to enter a body in sleep. *El aire de maldad. Recuerdo*—I remember how I would pray to the *Virgen*, just as you once prayed, my Rósula, to La Lloradora. Santa María . . . protect me from the air of evil. Yet I knew my life was small and poor, that it must be so forever, because *el buen Dios* had willed it. And the women of my village said that no young girl must dream of lifting her life, to make it large or fine. There was no way to rise against the will of *Dios* unless one allowed the *aire de maldad* to enter her. For it was said that only such a power of darkness could lift one's life—

Madrecita . . . Rosa looked up into the eyes of her mother. *Lo cree?* Do you believe this of me—that I am changed by an *aire de maldad?* Into a *diablo* who steals from people? One who tortures and kills like a *salvaje? Lo cree?*

Juana Ibáñez frowned. I believe, she said then, that *peones* go without bread, and then without the right to complain . . . and *puede ser* without the right to live in peace. Yet the statue of La Lloradora has worn a crown of gold for two hundred years. *La reina . . . la estrella* . . . there is always a woman with a red smile and a crown of stolen gold.

But I am not—

Sí, said Juana Ibáñez, with a slow nod of the head. She stared now at the strands of Rosa's hair twisted around her own gnarled fingers like rings of yellow silk. It is just so. *Olvidas*—do you forget —you? Who almost gave up your life for the crown of La Lloradora?

I loved her—

Sí, but you hated her too. Well I know.

Rosa was silent then, remembering her fear of the power of the statue; remembering her dream of Rosa wearing the crown of heaven with its rays of shooting stars. Remembering *esperanza* . . .

In truth, whispered Juana Ibáñez, in a soft voice of crooning. Who does not hate such a power, in a woman of real flesh?

But I never asked, I never wanted—

The wise *viscacha* eyes of her mother swam with tears that would not fall. *Sí, niñita.* You prayed that your life would be lifted. And I let you pray! To be an *estrella* of the *cine* . . . or of the world itself? La Lloradora heard the prayer. *Dios* protect all those who heard it afterward—and answered. *Su marido*—Carlos. And the *peones* who catch your fire and cry your name like a holy psalm. If it was the mother of *Dios* who blessed you first with the power to lift yourself so above the life that *Dios* willed for you, then you must accept what it brings. The love of those who see you so—and

with it their hatred. The rubicola that lies so, impaled on a crown of
straw for your head. And with it the knowledge that someone had it
killed for you. Rosa— Her voice faltered. You have lied to me. I
know you are ill—

Rosa now lay exhausted and silent. But after a moment she spoke
in the small voice of a child. Mama . . . they paint my name in red
letters of blood. Have you seen—written upon the walls that I—that
I have men beaten and burned. That I give orders . . . for *asesinos*
to destroy those who oppose me—

Juana Ibáñez said nothing to this, but went on coiling the fine
golden strands around her fingers. I have done none of these things!
Rosa cried. You must know! I have tried . . . so many things. I
have tried, but Carlos—

Carlos! said her mother, in a quick voice of reproach. It is Carlos
who has made you *la reina!* You cannot blame him now, no more
than La Lloradora.

But he blames me! For everything that goes wrong. Mama, I hear
things . . . how he lets them think, the *militares*, and the businessmen—lets them think *I* am their enemy. I, always I, who cause the
evil to be done. *La Señora quiere*—my wife wants! And raises his
arms to heaven.

Ssst! Juana Ibáñez shook her head now with anger. This is not a
thing for a wife to speak, not even to me. I know that my *niña* lives
in a place of terrible danger. The fear of this is in me always. This
marido of yours—I have known such men as this, believe it! And I
know the ways in which they may use the skirt of a woman. If he
wins, you may wear the crown of his victory beside him. But if he
fails, or an enemy seeks him, you may bear the blame of it. Especially if you have a strength, a *fuerza* that other men can see. *El
diablo, 'stá la mujer.* The devil is a woman, no? It is the way of it,
my Rósula. *Niñita* . . .

The fragile body at last lay perfectly still; Rosa had fallen asleep.
Salve María, murmured Juana Ibáñez, gently withdrawing her
fingers now from the coils of gold, to make the sign of the cross
over the face of her youngest child. So white a face, with its red
painted smile.

THE death of Juan Bautista Saldias, twenty-three years of age, postmaster general of the city of San Marcos, and brother-in-law to the Vice President, General Carlos Montero, was reported on the radio and in the press with detailed and poignant references to his lifelong struggle with the dread *enfermedad de los pulmones*. It was said that Saldias had first contracted tuberculosis during his impoverished childhood in Tucuman province. The certificate of death was signed by Dr. Ceballos, the personal physician of the Vice President and his wife, Doña María Rosa Andújar de Montero. The eminent doctor was said to have been in attendance throughout the final stages of Señor Saldias' illness. Funeral services were held privately in San Marcos, but it was said that Saldias' widow, Caterina ("Catuja"), eldest sister of Señora Montero, attended the services heavily veiled and supported on the arm of the Vice President and of her brother, José Bartolo ("Chepito") Andújar, confidential secretary to Señora Montero in her official duties with the Ministries of Education and Social Welfare, and also in the producing of her popular weekly radio broadcast, *Quince Minutos con . . .* (Fifteen Minutes with . . .).

On the night Señor Saldias passed away, La Señora devoted her entire broadcast to a moving tribute in the memory of her *cuñado* Juancito, and announced the plan for a new children's TB *clínico*, bearing his name, to be built near San Marcos. The Clínico Saldias would be financed with ten million dollars in donations through the *Fundación María Rosa Andújar de Montero*, the great charitable organization which La Señora had founded, and which had become such an important force for good in the life of Pradera.

One month later there was a small announcement of the appointment of Señora Caterina ("Catuja") Saldias to the post of Honorary Minister of Education. It was a post of ceremony; there were no duties, but the salary was approximately double that of a postmaster-general.

THE campaign train now had windows of a special dark glass, and opaque shades that might be drawn tight at the press of a button; from within the car one might see all that one wished of the beautiful countryside hurtling past, of the cheering *peones* huddled in crowds against the dark chill of early dawn, or at whatever hour the train of the general might be passing. It was said that in the towns where the train would stop, the crowds would assemble many hours in advance, strung out in small dark clots along the track for miles in either direction. When the cry of the train could be heard in the distance, the silence would break into melancholy chanting, a low rhythmic moan of *Viva! Montero! Viva! Señora!*

But the windows of a special dark glass had been installed after several incidents of disturbance—the pelting of fruit against the silver skin of the train, and twice, in the troubled provincial towns where labor strikes and student riots had increased both in number and in ugliness, there had been sudden hailstorms of sharp stones, bricks, jagged rocks. Despite—or perhaps because of—the vigorous efforts of the *policía federal* to contain the outbreaks, disorder and *desacato* continued to grow and spread like the strange wild fires set by farmers of the Pradal.

The windows were made with a thickness and weight to withstand the blow of any object hurled with force, even a bullet fired at close range. And so the passengers within might gaze with ease at the chanting *peones,* at the banners that bore the candidate's name and likeness, and that of his wife, at the shy small girls in smiles and white dresses holding yellow flowers in their thin outstretched arms. Unless one opened the window to wave, or walked to the platform at the rear of the train to stand and smile before them, the *peones* would stare only at the black mirrors of their own eyes. No one might catch an unscheduled glimpse of the passengers, or of the opulent fittings within the special cars of this train. It was said there were too many wonderful things inside—luxuries of a splendor which might arouse the envy of any *peón* deficient in the patriotic pride that ought to swell at the sight of one's leaders dressed in fine clothes and surrounded by trappings of *majestad*. Heavy draperies of velvet bound with braids and tassels of golden rope; a bar of black onyx furnished with goblets of crystal; heavy silver and delicate china and servants in uniforms of white, as though it were a palace on wheels instead of a train carrying a candidate for a free election, a man of the people who would appear tonight among them in his shirtsleeves, speaking the gruff simple tongue of the *tabernas*, trading stories of the old *vaquero* life. It was said that on this train were *maravillas* of electricity, to keep the general's cigars and wines at the desired temperature, and to keep the gilded hair of La Señora in the desired style.

The special window glass, imported from Germany, had lately been ordered for all government limousines as well. Now whenever a leader had need to journey through the streets of San Luis or the interior cities, there might be this same ease of mind, this same protection from the unpredictable moods of the people. In the limousine of La Señora, even the transparent sliding panel between the seat of the driver and the compartment of the passenger would be replaced by the new impermeable material, so that La Señora's eyes need never again confront a gaze that seemed to mock her in the rear-view mirror. When it was observed by the officer of *seguridad* that the driver's vision of the road behind would now be obscured by the dark barrier, large curved mirrors were designed for the front fenders of the vehicle. Although they hardly reclaimed the vision that was lost, it was decided that there was a greater need now for La Señora to feel that she rode in perfect privacy. Or at least in the perfect illusion of privacy.

In the paneled darkness of the smoking car, the general would remove his white tunic, open the collar of his shirt, and turn back the starched cuffs so, folding them with precision to the midpoint of his forearms. Those arms, it was said with admiration, were *muy sólido*, thick and brown, the hard arms of a strong man in the fullness of vigor.

At his right and left sat those *ayudantes* who continued to enjoy the general's trust, or who trusted that they did. He would sit so, between them, one polished boot resting upon the other, while he revolved slowly in the special chair of scarlet plush. It traveled a full circle, and also tipped forward and back, like the wise nodding of a statesman's head.

He wore an American cigaret at the side of the mouth, slanted upward so that the smoke formed an endless curling ribbon, in the way that a tape of *informes* issues from the mouth of a *telegráfico* machine, reporting the shifting values of the day. By now this plume of smoke seemed a natural part of the general's face; his softest and most expressive feature. He would light each cigaret from the glowing tail of the last, with stained fingers that sometimes trembled like those of a sick man, or an old one. It was said by the loyal *ayudantes* that this trembling was caused by the motion of the train, by the fatigue of travel, but each of them took care that the general did not observe them studying his efforts to control it.

Nor would their eyes dare linger on his face—that clear handsome visage which seemed afflicted now with signs of a troubled spirit. Darkness shadowed the eyes and lined the jaw; eczema that had plagued him in years past, when he was a young and anxious officer, returned now in angry splashes, like provocative slaps upon the cheeks of an aging duelist.

And in his eyes—those quick dark eyes—one might notice a glaze of inattention, the distracted look of a man who listens for be-trayals, and so misses the drift of talk. He kept a pair of powerful binoculars on the table before him, peering often at the distant sce-nery. But in the meetings of strategy his fingers would drum so on the glass, until a word displeased him. Then he would raise them to his face and train the great blind circles upon those who had spo-ken, until the subject was changed.

The celebrated smile would sputter then, like an electric sign powered by automatic switches. He laughed often, still with a fine resonance, but he had the habit now, when laughing, of rubbing the hands together, in the way of a *hotelier* who pretends a great pleasure in dispensing favors to transient guests.

Most of the time he would nurse his silences behind the plume of smoke, while the *ayudantes* droned or quarreled, one with another, over old troubles and new crises; of money promised and money stolen, of whether dead men in certain villages must be roused to vote for Montero, or whether one need only coerce the living with the usual persuasions.

It was decided so to arrange the victory for La Señora in the matter of the voting of women. There was a safety in this, it was agreed. Women would cast the ballot with their grateful hearts, for the husband of La Señora. For Montero who promised riches be-yond dreams, as he had promised his Rosa—and *claro*, as he had kept his word. *Mira!* Could one not see, from the look of her there, standing at his side, smiling up at him? The women could see—all but those witches of *sociedad*, the rich spoiled *doñas* of the little hats. *No importa*. The others, the millions, would fall to the strong brown arms of the general in the way of their heroine, their *es-trella*. It was a wise decision. The binoculars remained on the table.

But of other matters involving La Señora, no decision seemed so wise as one to avoid the mention of her name in any meeting of strategy, lest the general rouse himself to strike with a fist upon the tabletop, to make the glasses dance. The others would then ex-change looks, or avert their eyes to the carved ceiling, filling the pause with the lighting of fresh cigars and the thoughtful clearing of throats. Then they would begin another subject, a safer one, marking the moments until the crimson chair would embark on another circular journey; until the storm passed and the binoculars rose again, aimed this time at the window, at the hurtling landscape beyond. At last the general would be heard to mumble a word to El Tiburón, and the others could let go of the breaths they held.

Quiroga sat always at his right hand, so that the general's restless eye might catch his reassuring nod, his comforting grunt of assent, when the general wished to speak of change in the weather, or the look of the countryside, in the way *los adivinos*—the soothsayers—speak prophecy in riddles.

One must understand the woods in this region, he would say, gesturing with the binoculars. *Sí*, Quiroga would reply, with a frown of close attention.

Do you see the way these trees grow? Far apart, yet in regular columns, straight as the best of our troops, the ones trained by Germans? *Ya se ve*, Quiroga would murmur. It is so.

The trees in this region always march so, according to a perfect order. North or west, a man may ride straight through at a full gallop. And see there—how the young shoots rise with a modesty in the ranks? The seasoned ones flourish beside them, still in full vigor, no?

Ah, *sí*. Quiroga would shake his head, marveling at the lesson of geography.

Even the *viejos, mira!* The decaying ones still march in line with their comrades. Nothing mars the beauty, my friend. Nothing disrupts—look there! The end of a branch will break off clean as it dies. Then another—until nothing stands but the empty shell of the trunk. Yet even then, my friend, it stands so—hollow like that one, see it there? Upright still in its fresh uniform. It will not be stripped of its rank, its dignity. Leaves, green as any shoot. Sturdy twigs, bristling with life. A *majestad*, still, in its boldness, no? In the end, a new shoot will spring from within. Born in the embrace of old arms. See, that one there—how it rises strong and straight, full grown from the *viejo*? From its father?

Ah. Quiroga would nod. One understands.

The general would pause, and then resume, as though to reassure himself. The land permits no sign of decay, you see. *Mira*, my friend. The perfect order of a world when small men cannot interfere.

I have seen this region— Chulo Rubén Caso would lean forward with an eager nodding. In summer—when the thistles grow thick as armies. Thorns, crossed so, like the blades of swords, you know? I have seen the road here so barred with thorns that a battalion of tanks could not pass—

The general's chair spun rapidly, as though it were out of control. What does the doctor say of her mood this morning? Have you seen him? And what have you done about that peace prize? Those *cabrones* of the awards committee—are we never to have anything done as we ask?

Chulo rose heavily to his feet. *Ya voy.* I was about to go—

When the door of the car had closed behind him, Montero leaned back and sighed. *Bufón,* he said, half to himself. Quiroga sat straighter. General R has sent another message, you know. Another threat.

She will not cooperate this time, Montero said. She has more of the mule now than ever.

I know, sighed Quiroga. But so have they. And the *Yanquis* now promise carrots the color of guns—

I promised her—

Can one not distract her any more? A dragonfly of diamonds, like that of the duchess? They could rename a school for her in Córdoba. She always likes that. Or—I know: a journey of pleasure after the election? She wants to see Paris, no?

I promised her, my friend. Vice President—

Has she seen the blueprint for her monument? Does she know what it will cost?

She wants—

But what is really the matter? Quiroga said. Is she upset? Some *informes* of you? Not that last messy affair, with the two *niños*—?

Carlos shifted in his chair and waved an impatient hand. She cares nothing of those things any more. *Dios,* my friend, a man has needs. This at least she learned well from that *madrecita* of hers. No—this anger is of other causes. She—

Quiroga leaned closer. Does she want money? One could arrange a transfer—she knows of the new investments—?

What she knows! Montero laughed. Too much for a wife. But less than is dangerous. I am not yet an old fool, Manuel.

Quiroga nodded. Still, she gives you no peace with this craziness. We cannot afford it, Carlos. You know I am right. Not any more—

My friend, said the general, now with a harsh tone. *I* can afford what I want. Without Montero they are dead men—all of them. El Negrito most of all. *Yanquis!* Listen—do you think the *cabrones* will come through with that peace prize for me? *He?*

Quiroga sighed. Do you think the *Yanquis* will hold their hands up so, and let your bartender disarm El Negrito? Listen to me for once, Carlos. If she survives the campaign, you will not.

Montero said nothing to this, but swiveled in his chair and lit another American cigaret from the tail of the last.

You are still *infatuado,* my friend. Quiroga's voice now held a sound of fear. Your eyes are not watching the shadows that move.

Montero laughed. It is the first time, my old friend, that you underestimate me.

I hope so, my general.

No importa. Only know that I have not lost my eyes—or my reflexes—

Now Quiroga was silent for a time. The general spun his chair again, back to the window. The plume of smoke made a broken circle above his head. Like the mark of a question.

I suppose it is possible, murmured El Tiburón, then. A weakness may add to a strength. *Verdad?*

Carlos smiled. If the voice of La Señora grows faint. . . . You know that old poem, my friend? One may hold a dead bird to one's ear, and still hear its song. The song of the *pájaro muerte—sin duda,* it is the most beautiful.

El Tiburón smiled his smile. *Sí,* he said. One understands.

On the swaying metal platform between two cars, Chulo and Dr. Ceballos held a precarious meeting of business against the rattling chains that linked the private *coche* of La Señora to that of the general. After a time of struggling to hold their balance, maintaining *dignidad* and a proper distance, Chulo smiled at the doctor and said, So. You have studied the report from our friend the *estrella*? Is she still worth what she steals from us? And the old priest—?

The doctor's expression did not change. With the clanging of metal, the hot rush of air, he had perhaps not heard. Chulo frowned and began a fumbling business of relighting the cigar that he held so, between the teeth. Ceballos' elongated body rested lightly now—one would almost think with comfort—against the unsteady glass-paneled door of La Señora's compartment. In his narrow suit of Italian silk, the color of silver steel, he posed like a sleek guardian dog, ominously quiet, trained to kill with a precise snap of the jaw. He crossed his slender feet so, at the ankles, planting the tapered black shoes in a way to avoid the circling dust. He waited. Chulo lit one wooden match and another; he made a shelter of hunched shoulders, a cup of clumsy hands. At last the cigar glowed again with a pale light; Chulo hid his small pride within a grimace. Ah. Again he drew a breath. Again he said, So— Again the gnashing of metal swallowed his voice, as the furious air snatched away the pungent swirl of his smoke.

Ceballos smiled then. Interesting case, he said, in a way to suggest that Ceballos himself found nothing of interest. Of course it is as one suspected . . . since the first. Still, the details. . . . He spoke without bothering to raise his voice. Chulo's glistening brow creased with the effort of reading lips that scarcely moved. The doctor's syllables hovered like fitful insects trapped in enclosed space; then they escaped into the streaking white light.

. . . a puzzle of lost pieces, the doctor was saying. One can now assume—dead fetus retained in the body.

Retained? Chulo said. But how—?

. . . old woman's tale, said the doctor. *El niño perdido.* Dead baby never born—poisons the mama's blood, *sabes*? Such craziness, the superstitions of women.

Superstitions, echoed Chulo, now with a grave shake of the head. Women—

The doctor laughed as though he had meant a joke; and perhaps Chulo had been a fool. Such craziness, Ceballos said again. It is no wonder we take so long to learn they are right.

Chulo's frown dissolved; he smiled now, in confusion. Again he nodded. *Sí—sin duda!* And the pregnancy itself? Something irregular—

A conception outside the womb, said the doctor, with a sigh of boredom. Baby never survives. As I said, it is all of a piece. The anemia. The infection. The sterility, of course.

Dígame, said Chulo. Can one know how she came to have such— that is to say, how a baby is conceived, so? Outside—

Ceballos shrugged. Too much of force, he said. *Violencia . . .* in the fornication. The act of love, *sabes?*

Chulo shook his head, in the way of a man sobered by news of misfortune. Sst! he murmured. *Qué pobrecita, he?* And so it *was* a miracle, that miscarriage of hers?

The doctor made a sound of clearing the throat, as though Chulo had committed a rudeness. My friend, the girl should have bled to death on the spot. That she did not was the miracle.

Of course, said Chulo. I only meant— But why has there been no trace? All this time—one means, what could have happened to that *feto?* The report—the *abortista* herself—explained nothing?

Again Ceballos raised his shoulders, in the way one deals with persistent fools. He recrossed his feet; he gazed over Chulo's head, at a sudden grove of *paraísos* and pear trees that seemed to float like an island on a flat yellow sea. There are many explanations, he said. *Un feto . . .* tissues disintegrate. Or they will drift so, into pockets, hiding in the folds of skin. *Sabes? Tal vez*—sometimes the thing hardens to bone, *como . . .* like a fossil. One cannot discover the truth of it unless—

Unless—

If there is an autopsy. Ceballos smiled again. Of course in this case—regrettable. We may never— Well. But I have seen one not long ago, in Brussels. Remarkable. *Un monstruo*—perfectly preserved. A small grotesque figure, one arm extended so—a gesture, a beseeching—

Chulo shrank back against the swinging chain, as though the doctor's gesturing hands might cause such a *monstruo* to materialize before his eyes. In truth he wanted not to hear another word. But now the doctor's voice rose, perversely, so that every vowel hung in the air, like the beginning or end of a scream.

—while the other hand, glued to the face, so—the skin in loops like a patterned lace, streaming from the fingers. Remarkable—

Chulo gasped, choking on the stub of cigar. His eyes filled with red tears; he waved his hands; his feet slid dangerously under him; he grasped at the door handle, the chain, a metal loop . . . Ceballos waited politely, his eyes wide with faint surprise. Well, he said then, with a gesture of ending.

Wait, Chulo sputtered. With his balance nearly recovered, his hands moved to adjust his jacket, his tie, leaving traces of soot. What about—you said—the poisoning of her blood?

Again Ceballos gazed past him, now with a startled look of pleasure. A flock of blue-necked geese flew over their heads, sun glinting on feathers, setting off a blaze of iridescent light. He made no reply.

What does it mean? Chulo demanded. He thrust his streaming face closer, dropping his voice to a thick whisper. How much time? He would need only a little time; a man of many long thumbs can easily find a new way to close them upon the thing he wants.

Ceballos drew back, restoring the precise distance. He studied Chulo's distorted face, concealing distaste. *Quién sabe,* he said softly. Weeks; months. Perhaps—

Chulo coughed. You must, that is, can one not be . . . more definite? I—that is, the general will need—

Do you mean to say, said Ceballos, could one not interfere?

Chulo fought now to conceal his agitation. There was no room for it on such a small platform; no room for elegant pretense while one swayed like a monkey clinging to a dangerous branch. We are not—he drew a careful breath—not having this conversation. You understand.

Ceballos' head bent slightly; half a nod. *La Muerte* has a rhythm, he said. Like a train on a track. One may hasten a rhythm. . . .

Hasten . . . Chulo echoed, leaning forward. Then he remembered the doctor's preferred distance, and lurched back, with a smile of apology. To spare the suffering, *verdad?* A *pobrecita* in great pain—

Ceballos' face was a mask, of the sort Chulo preferred. If you like, he said.

Her body lay curved so, like an S, against the outer wall of her sleeping alcove, as though to embrace the shuddering train. She slept with one arm flung across her face, palm up, fingers curled, in the way a child shields herself from the blows of villains in dreams. For a moment Chepito stood holding his breath, listening to hers, shallow and steady as sighing. The white linen bedsheets clung to the sharp angles of hips and shoulders, blurring them into roundness. She had turned many times in the night, so that the covers now wound tight around her, like the swaddling clothes of babies, like *mortajas* of the dead. Rosa, he whispered; her breath answered him softly; her body did not move.

The brown velvet curtain had been thrown back to permit a cross-breeze to the bed from the open windows; a breeze stirred the curtain now, so that filtered light played across the folds, suggesting moving shapes—parts of animals, or women. Chepito smiled, remembering such games he had played once with another brown curtain, thin and ragged, hanging so near a restless boy and the sleeping body of his sister. Had he lain so, each night of his life, listening to this same breathing, peering through the darkness at silhouettes of her limbs that flashed like the limbs of wild horses running in a silent *cine*? Rosa, he whispered again; the sinuous S of her body glided now, unfolding; the arm that shielded her face fell away, so that now her eyes hid under the white crook of an elbow. Still the breath flowed from her in soft shallow sighs, like the sounds of a woman with a lover. Chepito stared at the curtain, remembering a thing he had long ago forgotten, a picture in his mind of their father with his hard brown hands on Rosa in the way a man touches a woman. How she had sobbed then to Chepito, her little brother. My fault, Chepito! she had said, in a voice of fear. And Chepito had lain awake in a fever, imagining the ways in which a man must learn to use the bodies of women, to know that he is a man. And had he not touched her then, with wonder, that same night, as though to share her with his father, in the way of a man? Had he not had the moist shock of her naked skin against him, beneath his fingers? With her breath upon him, and the white-

ness blurring as she moved? Was it so, the way she had lain, open
to him on her narrow cot, tempting him as she had Papa? Was it so
that she had wanted Chepito to touch her—there, and there, in the
places of women's secrets?

Chepito felt the sweat of his back trickling now like tears, rolling
in the hollow between his shoulders, spreading under the fine
starched shirt. Without thinking he reached out, seizing the edge of
the linen coverlet, sliding it gently down and away, exposing the
little bones, the small perfect breasts—buds of lilac, the breasts of a
child, and the torso gleaming blue-white, covered with a fine moist
film. So still, and the breath floating toward him like kisses, like in-
vitations. Ah . . . he felt his own heat rising. *Puta!* The sound exploded within him like a sharp pain, a tearing of flesh. *Puta . . .* the
silent, forlorn sob of a small brother, lost and afraid. Rosa, he said
aloud, with a fierceness to stifle the cry.

I am awake, Chepito, she said softly, moving to cover herself.
Has Tobalito sent word? And the others? Rudi?

Chepito's tongue scraped across dry lips. What is it? she said,
eyes searching him like skilled fingers. The money for the demonstration—? Carlos—? Her voice rose to a shrill cry. *Dígame!*

Nothing, he snapped. It is nothing. *Por Dios,* I am tired of your
screeching!

Sí! she cried. Soon I will stop! And then where will he be, my little brother? My handsome *niño bien* of a brother, with his stable of
fillies? His frisky *retozonas? He?*

Me siento, he murmured, but his eyes were sullen. I am sorry
. . . About the money, he said, taking care not to look away. It may
be that I must go myself—

She said nothing, but looked at him in the way of one who knows
well the symptoms of deception. *Sí,* she said softly. It may be.

MARÍA Blanca knows they are staring at her hands; have they recognized the rings, the bracelets jangling on her thin wrists? The hands flutter to her lap like exhausted birds; she tries to bury them in the folds of her skirt. Perhaps she has only imagined them staring. La Señora's hands were always so still; the fingers so long and pale with their curving painted nails like small brave enameled flags. La Señora had always left the moon of her nails unpainted, each sudden little crescent shining white and pure, like an exposed secret.

Señora! whispers the television cameraman. They are waiting. Blanca looks up with that startled expression of hers, as though she has suddenly awakened in a strange place and does not quite know what to do, what they expect. Of course by now she does know. Today, for example, they are to visit the *Pueblo de los Niños*, the favorite of all La Señora's good deeds on behalf of her people, her *pobrecitos*. A fairyland for poor children, filled with dolls and toys and the most beautiful little dresses in the world. In the time of La Señora, the only thing it had never been filled with was poor children. It was said, by unkind strangers, that La Señora did not like the sight of small dirty hands soiling her pretty clothes, breaking her fine toys. A few fortunate *niños* would be invited for the day, whenever La Señora and the photographers came. The children would be dressed well and fed party cakes, they would play with the bright toys while La Señora smiled, posing, holding one of the dolls with a white lace dress. When I was a little girl, she would tell the reporters who came with her, I dreamed of a doll like this. And now that I can give such things to the children of Pradera, it is as though my own dream comes true. She would hold the doll high, and with her other arm hugging a child with golden curls, she would say, I hope it is all right if I call this doll La Lloradora; see how it cries real tears.

It has been said that but for the will of *Dios*, Rosa Montero might yet have held her ground against those *militares*, those *salvajes*, those *asesinos* who plotted against her. Some still raise the palms to heaven and sigh for the sudden turnings of fate. *'Stá el destino*, they say. But for *el destino* she might have won the vice-presidency —and who knows? Perhaps without the need to raise up the dead; without the need to coax or bully the living into the voting place. There might have been no need at all for the usual persuasions.

In truth, it is also said that with the name of Rosa beside his own on the ballot, in the year of *Esperanza*, that year of the first voting of women, the general might have had the *triunfo grande* that he sought: an election victory greater than any in the history of Pradera.

But it is never said, at least not with a voice to be heard above whispers, that perhaps the will of *Dios* might have bent another way. If only the general had shed the money of Rosa's enemies, instead of the blood of her friends—

Still, in that time of trouble, there were none who could have said what was to come, not even by spying through the powerful binoculars of the general, or the skillful narrowed eye of La Señora herself. Just as there were none who could have followed the delicate threads of red and black that were woven so swiftly this way and that, through the sudden crossings and double-crossings of enemies and friends, on the eve of La Señora's *demostración*. The swift weavers of red and black threads made a dark tapestry in that single night, which came to be called *la noche de navajitas*—the night of small razors. On the eve of the *demostración,* it is said, La Señora slept too well—with the help of her doctor and the killers of pain—while the rules of the game changed around her, and players on both sides came to wear different masks.

La Señora slept well that night, having exchanged the promises of valuable favors for the vows of useful friendship, in the ways she had learned so well, and had practiced with such care, so many times on behalf of the general.

She had mastered the hundred fine new techniques by which a damaging secret might now be held above the ear of a *personaje* whose help was needed and slow in coming. She had saved the most valuable *informes* against this time, knowing well whose hand or tongue might be entrusted with certain truths—and for how long. She knew by the heart, as it is said, which loyalty, and which ambition, must not be doubted, if one were to win in the dangerous game.

But it was made certain, in that night of *navajitas,* that she did not know which rules were changed around her while she slept, or who gave the orders that changed them. It was made certain that she did not know the new loyalties and ambitions that flowered in that dark night, like the poison leaves of the wonderful *ombú* tree, under whose shade one must never sleep.

It has been said that somehow the secrets La Señora had saved were robbed of their power in the time of trouble. Or else that La Señora had not guarded them well from one so close to her that no one would dare imagine how his tongue might dart behind a fine new mask, or how his hand might clasp a thin slashing blade.

But when the dawn broke on the day of the great *demostración,* La Señora awoke with the scent of betrayal in her nostrils; wih the sound of *navajitas* in her ears. She woke in the way of an animal that springs to its feet trembling, all its senses filled with the startled knowledge of fire or storm; the certainty that somewhere a twig crackles beneath the foot of an intruder. The skin of such an animal knows well the temperature of danger, though it stirs a thousand leagues away, though the air in that distance has only begun to change.

Each detail of the *demostración* had been planned with precision, like the parts of a fine silver machine. The special trains, filled with *peones* from the outlying provinces. The *colectivos* and bullock carts, loaded with *pobrecitos,* with smiling *niños* and somber mothers waving bright banners that bore the rosy likeness of La Señora, the golden letters of her name. *Vice Presidente!* Students on foot would join the march from the universities, chanting, *Viva! Montero! Viva! Señora!* Parish priests, lured with promises La Señora herself would never have made, would lead their flocks in the *procesión* of new black automobiles lent by the church. One would deal later, it had been agreed, with the anger of La Señora when she learned which laws must soon be changed in payment for this fine showing of support.

Free lodgings had been promised for the poor who would come to fill the plazas with their bodies and their voices. Free milk would be given to the *niños,* and sweet raisin cakes wrapped in a stiff shiny paper imprinted with the *fotografías* of La Señora and the general. Even the troubled *sindicatos* of Manuel Quiroga had promised to send the usual messengers in the night, to collect the working papers of the *trabajadores.* Laborers by the thousand would march in the *demostración,* or never again hold their fine jobs in the *factorías.*

When the dawn came, La Señora knew that the people were pouring into the city, million upon million of them, as it had been arranged. Twenty thousand streamers had been set in place to fly from the public rooftops, and a hundred thousand white flowers had been laid in carpets upon the steps. The *policía federal,* in new white uniforms and polished black boots, had new guns to keep order in the plazas. The marching bands . . . the *fotógrafos* with their newsreel cameras . . . the wide scarlet ribbon of plush upon which she would walk up the center steps of the Casa Dorado to accept the nomination . . . the hand of Carlos, reaching for hers; the tongue of Carlos, tasting her name in a new way. *Vice President . . .*

And yet the acrid sting of betrayal assaulted her nostrils, and to her ears came the faint tearing sound—*Sst! Sst!*—of the *navajita.*

There was nothing to be done that one had not thought to do. There was no way to learn which role in the production had been played in a strange new key by the tango singer or his army of *limpiadores,* those cleaners of filth, censors of *desacato,* who had been the defenders of her name. Had there been a promise not kept by the Baron's mistress? Or was the payment stopped by that jealous wife, the baroness—or never delivered by the banker himself? Had some *negocio* proved too dirty for the boss of the unions, or for one of his *ayudantes* with teeth that had been filed too short? Which errand had not been run by the Minister of Finance, or the *niño bien* of a brother?

It should not have mattered who had the charge of certain arrangements, or who had given the orders from the Casa Dorado, from a secret office in an elegant night club, from the bar of the Jockey or the men's room of a dockside *taberna* filled with the smoke of *militares.* . . .

Perhaps after all it was only a coincidence, only a twisting of *el destino* or the will of *Dios,* that on the eve of the *demostración,* while the army of *limpiadores* unrolled the crimson carpet down the great stone steps of the Casa Dorado, and while the gardeners placed the white flowers in careful squares and circles spelling her name; and while the engineers laid twenty miles of black wiring for the microphones and loudspeakers, uncoiling it round the plaza like an endless snake without tongue or tail, another secret army of unmarked trucks and small black cars had rolled in silence through the city, delivering leaves of poison: three million copies of a forbidden *Yanqui* magazine of news, which carried on its blood-red cover a cartoon portrait of Rosa Montero . . . Rosa depicted as a witch, a *bruja,* a *monstruo,* dressed in the costume of a *reina*—a queen of evil. With a round face of empty eyes and a heavy crown of diamonds on her wild yellow hair. The *monstruo* wore the ragged shirt of a *peón,* hanging from her skeleton's body like cobwebs of lace, under the robe of royal furs—animals with the heads biting the tails. Through the holes of the torn shirt, a ransom of precious jewels winked like wise hard eyes. And under the blank eyes of the *monstruo* herself, two more jewels glittered like tears that would not fall.

Within the magazine was yet another portrait of La Señora, this one more shocking, for it was said to be taken from a secret *cine* made when she was only Rosa Andújar, a *muchachita* of fourteen years, with ambition to be an actress of the theatre. The *foto* showed this Rosa wearing only a *camisa* of transparent silk, and lying in the arms of a woman friend, an *estrella grande* of international fame. Under the *foto* was a phrase, Politics Makes Strange Bedfellows.

In the night of *navajitas*, before the *limpiadores* could be sent to cleanse the newsstands of San Luis, the secret army of *desacato*, in unmarked trucks and small black cars, had pasted copies of this shocking *fotografía* across the smiling portraits of Rosa that hung from the walls of every building in the Plaza Victoria, from every lamppost and street sign for seven miles along the route of the great *demostración*.

When the eyes of Rosa fluttered open, the general stood beside her bed, wearing his new white uniform and his new black polished boots, and in his hand was a copy of the *Yanqui* magazine.

He stood beside her, with his face of a mask, holding the magazine of *desacato*, saying nothing.

Recuerdas, she said after a moment, with a strange small smile. Remember, in the hour of your trouble long ago, when you asked me not to leave you? *Recuerdas, querido,* what you asked of me then?

The general shook his head, no; and his eyes shifted from her gaze. He dropped the magazine face down upon the bed, and lit an American cigaret.

You asked me if . . . I would have given up my life for yours in that night. And I said no. Rosa's hand reached now to touch the white sleeve of the general; it was so light a touch he barely felt it. I said no, she went on. And why not? you said. So I explained. *Claro*, I said. Your life has too much need of mine.

Her touch was light, but his arm had need of movement, and he shrugged to shake the hold of her fingers. Rósula, he said, in a voice of sharp edges. They are not going to let us have it.

Recuerdas? she said again, softly. The *demostración* that I bought for you, with secrets and promises—?

Sí. And with far more money than one can get this time. His voice snapped at her, like the razor against the strap. Money, *querida.* Still you refuse to count the cost of things! It is so, that women cannot understand the counting of costs. He shrugged again, and lit another American cigaret, though the tail of the first was not so short. Well, he said, sighing out the smoke. For the first time I cannot spare you. A man . . . a *man* must fight the secret wars alone. You see—

I see—

Listen! His hands struck the air with motions of slicing. Even if it fails, this *demostración.* If something goes wrong—for some reason—

For some reason, she echoed, in a voice of even tone. *Sí?*

What will it matter? he said. You have no need of a title—you are above these things. We will go on as we are. No one will stop us— we will have all that we want—the *Fundación,* and the good things you promise, the people know you will do them. The people believe—

Esperanza, she murmured, staring at him; the strange pale smile was still upon her face, like a ghost of another expression.

Listen, he said, pacing now around her bed, making circles, slicing at air. They will take away nothing—you are La Señora, *siempro lo mismo*—the same as ever. *Vidita!* You *will* be *la Presidenta.* Wife of the President, no? What does their anger mean, after all? Only that they fear you! So we will wait them out. We will stay with the old way of things. For another moment. Until—

Until—

Let them think we agree, *querida.* That it is not a time for thorns in the sides of those—of El Negrito and the others. We will let them have their way for now—

She smiled still, gazing at him with the wise eyes of her mother, of one who sees well under the ground.

They will have to deal with you—he was saying.

For what do I want it, *he?* she said then. Such a grand title? If not to betray you? Is that what you think, Carlos? You do not trust me now? That is the truth of it, no? You have taught me too well! Your art of the foil. Perhaps they were right to warn you. *Dios!* I see it now. Why would she want such a thing? Vice President? If not to use it in the way you have used it yourself! To build a great power —and then to push you out. Carlos! You— Have they said it so, my Carlito? That *puta*—that little whore of yours—wants now to be rid of you . . . of her *cabrón? He?* Is it what you think?

She sprang from the bed now, trembling, and seized his hand— *Vámonos!* Come on!—and began to pull at him with all her fragile strength. Running as though for life, in her thin tangled gown of a white transparent gauze, like the *camisas* of her childhood. Running from the bedchamber out into the dark corridor, pulling him along behind her, as a child in fright pulls a grown man who will not believe her. Shouting and crying *Aquí!* Come!—and she burst at last into the general's paneled library, that sanctum of the musty smells of *virilidad*—of cigars and leather, sweat and importance. The bare polished slab of desk gleamed in a shaft of silver morning light. She dropped his hand and slipped behind the desk, into the high-backed chair that faced the window, between the two flags of state. *Mira!* she whispered. How do I look, so? And slumped down, with her head turned from him, so that only the voice, disembodied, issued from the chair. Tell them—tell those *Yanquis* I want . . . one hundred tanks of advanced design. And *que hay?* What goes on there in Stockholm, with those *pendejos? Dígame!* She spun the chair around; two small fists lashed out, crashing upon the dark wood. The general flinched. Wait! she cried.

And pulled out one drawer, then another. Where are my binoculars? *Entonces!* Foot-long twin turrets, joined at the center. She raised them to her eyes and peered at him through the great blind circles. You! I said . . . get me that peace prize! Who is on that committee of awards? What? They have decided to give it to a poet? A *poet? Escuchan!* I want the name . . . of every *cabrón* . . . on that committee! I want to know . . . what their countries paid last year for beef! And the next shipment—I want the price doubled! No! Tripled! *Claro?*

Carlos was laughing now, so hard that his face had turned dark, like that of a man choking. His eyes streamed with helpless tears. *Dios*, he cried. How I wish Quiroga could see . . . and El Negrito—

Would they laugh, Carlos? she said, with a softness of rich cloth that conceals a weapon. Would they?

Por fin, it should not have mattered who had had the charge of certain arrangements, or who had given the orders. There were those who said one should have looked within the round blue office of the new *Yanqui* embassy, or under the bed of a lady of high *sociedad,* whose husband had been bled to death by La Señora . . .

There should not have been a suspicious fire in that night, at the elegant night club Los Pájaros; a fire that claimed one hundred famous lives, and whose cause the *policía* never found. Although they did find an empty safe with its door hanging so, like an open mouth from which a secret has escaped.

There should not have been a riot in the Plaza Victoria, claiming two hundred lives that were not so famous. The *policía* said that it started when students from the universities began to throw fruit and stones. There were others who said it started when the *policía* fired without cause into the crowd. . . .

A spontaneous *demostración* has a very great price, as the general had said. Sometimes the full cost is not reckoned by one who does not understand these things.

In the years to come, it would be whispered, and at certain times published, that *she* had somehow failed at the last to stir the people with her sweet red smile of promise, with her silver tears of rage. It would be said that perhaps the people no longer believed that shrill *clarín* of a voice that spoke still of hope for food and jobs, of *ayuda* for the hungry—for the idle? For the greedy? It would be said that the people no longer believed in sweet raisin cake, in cider and small coins, or in the year of *Esperanza.*

She stood in the blazing sun, in the center of the topmost step, such a tiny figure, like a *niñita,* a little child, all in white, and held her small trembling hands above her head, as though a pair of thin white sticks could hold the sky. She whispered—there was no *clarín* of a voice on that day, but a broken whisper into the microphones whose cords trailed like snakes twenty miles long beneath her feet.

Gracias, she said. I thank you. *Gracias a mis amigos.* For coming so far. I thank you . . . for believing in me. For your prayers. But I cannot . . . I cannot accept . . . I cannot serve you best from a fine office with official letters of gold upon the door. It is not my way. I am only a woman, after all. I am only one who serves her family, as women have always served. . . .

In the small ways of a sister, a wife, a daughter. I am fortunate . . . as our country is fortunate . . . to have a man at its head who is . . . who is a *salvador.* One who will save . . . all of us. For while I am at his side, you are at his side.

And this . . . is all one asks. This . . . is the will of *Dios.*

Viva! Señora!

It is said that they led her away sobbing like a child, supported on the arms of her brother and of that doctor who never left her side. While the crowd screamed, and the *policía* used the new guns to restore order in the corners of the square, Carlos Montero announced his selection of Brigadier General R—El Negrito—as his Vice President.

Viva! Montero!

CHULO! Blanca's voice is taut, exhilarated, like that of an athlete at the start of a dangerous game. Look! she cries, as he enters. Am I—? She twirls again, so that the circle of blue surrounds her body like a revealing halo. She is still raised up on her toes; the shoes have high thin heels made of dark silver metal, like toy weapons. Can you walk so? he says, laughing. She shakes her bright head. No! But see—I can dance a little.

He slides a hand under the flying skirt, touching the skin that has flashed naked just above her stockings. She wears stockings of sheer silk, very shiny, and fastened in the French way with a narrow belt of delicate satin garters, as one may see in the postcards sold to young soldiers. He laughs again; it is a mocking sound. She frowns at him. What? Do I displease you?

No, *querida,* he says, caressing her now with a voice of warm oil. I was only thinking of something—

Of *her!* she exclaims, pretending anger. In truth she does this often, to provoke him.

He protests with his eyes, and makes a sound to dispel her outburst, or his thought. *Basta,* he whispers, in a way of pleading. His hand on her now spreads apart; the moist palm presses harder against her thigh, as though he would fuse them together. She stands quite still now, patient under his touch. Enough of *her,* he says. His voice has thickened; she suppresses a smile at this, and instead gazes at him with eyes of reproach. Never, she says, but strokes his dark face with cool fingers, and then with her mouth; her tongue flicks at him like a small darting fish. Never, she says again. Never enough of her—

He makes a moaning sound, low in the throat. *Vidita!* he sighs. My little life; my love. We must begin—we must stop—

Chulo! She laughs when he is earnest, knowing he bridles at it. We must have begun; we must have stopped. Tell me, which do we do now?

He shrugs; he does not really care what she means.

Well, then. She sighs, moving closer to him. His huge hands seem to expand further with heat; the rings on his fingers are fiery, like iron tempered to mark the flesh. No one ever answers me, she says, and holds her arm out suddenly; he stares at it, imagining that it must be injured in some way. The bracelet, she tells him. What happened to the other one?

A girl died in a fire, he says quickly, without thinking. It was on her wrist.

Not Juanita Ortiz, was it?

No, of course not.

Blanca can never tell if he is lying. Still, he has pulled his hands away, distracted.

Juanita Ortiz died in a fire, she says, frowning to remember. At least it was thought so . . . At that famous night club? In the newsreel, a chandelier of forty thousand crystals exploded like a fall of water—

He reaches toward her again, seizing her now with a roughness. His fingers pluck at the buttons of the dress. She reaches up and guides them. Finally she stands before him so, exposed, smiling. He gazes at her until his eyes change. It was a night, he says then, in a hoarse whisper—many things exploded. A girl with a bracelet such as this—

Blanca sighs. Were her arms prettier than mine, *por ejemplo?* She holds them out, side by side, for his inspection: the pose of a slave girl with only one bracelet. The blue dress has fallen about her waist.

Whose arms? he says. His hands move over her, as though searching for something. Whose? Juanita Ortiz'?

Still you tease me, she says. Again her face wears the suggestion of a pout. Even you never tell me the truth of anything.

He glances at his watch. They are waiting, you know. Carlos is a sick man; and too old to stand long in this heat. After the ceremony you may command me to tell you any truth you like. And I dare not refuse. All right?

O, Chulo, she says softly. Do you promise?

He nods, with a wink of mischief. Who would dare keep a secret from a *vicepresidente?* From a *Presidenta?*

Presidenta, she echoes. He likes the slow way her lips and tongue move over the syllables. Think, he says, of how *she* would envy you this day. His fists crumple the dress as though it were a handkerchief. She makes no sound; he is bending over her, kneeling before her, against her, inhaling her. She closes her eyes, resting one slender hand upon his lacquered silver head, in the way a monarch rests the blade of knighthood. Ah. She hears the sounds he makes inside her, as though from a great distance. Ahh.

FROM the columns of news and the radio, one could not at once be certain whether Chepito Andújar—the *niño bien* who was brother to La Señora—had perished with the victims of that spectacular fire in the club Los Pájaros. The *policía federal* were investigating another possibility—for when Señor Andújar disappeared from the club on that *noche negra*, that black night of tragedy, so too had a fortune of secret jewels and money. One understood that Chepito had access to the safe in which they were kept, since he was a financial partner of silence, as it is said.

The safe from which the fortune had vanished was of a heavy steel, its massive round door embedded with twenty brass dials and locking gears that hummed like the interior of a giant's watch. It had been designed so to withstand any assault of heat or cold, of explosive devices or the light fingers of greedy *ladrones*, thieves in search of secret fortunes.

Yet on the morning after that *noche negra*, that dark night, the safe stood alone on a floor of ashes, with its great round door open wide like a mouth of surprise.

There was no doubt, however, of the body of Tobal Iribas, the popular singer of tangos who managed the club; one had only to look at the hand that had strummed the famous guitar, for on it were three unusual rings, ruined but unmistakable. They were of gold, and made in the shape of long curving talons, *uñas* of a powerful bird; they were fitted so, like sheaths upon the tips of those fingers that flew at the strings of his music. And he had them always attached to the hand, like bright deformities; one had seen them in all the *fotografías*. With strangers Tobalito had the habit of proffering the gilded hand so, in the sudden way of drawing a weapon. Then, with the wink of pride with which a man may boast of his *virilidad*, he would explain the rings. A gift of memory, he would say. From a rare *pajarita*—a small bird who had since flown to a perch far above him. He would raise the eyes to heaven and turn the palm up so, to show the words inscribed upon the curving metal. All three together made the message whole: "Olimpia Theatre/One Night/Only." The gold had melted in the fire of tragedy, so that it fused now with the remains of Tobalito's hand. Still one might see clearly the letters of "One Night/Only."

There were forty-three survivors of the terrible night. That golden cage of a room had been filled to overflowing; the door well locked and guarded against the great ragged crowd that huddled outside to await the glimpse of those birds of night—smiling *estrellitas* on the arms of rich *niños bien*—all those who could afford, in that time of trouble, to display the plumage in the ritual dance of mating; to take wing in a mock flight across a floor of black polished marble, beneath a chandelier of blazing crystal, within a locked cage of gold.

The night was nearly day, yet on they flew, wheeling and soaring between the golden bars, until the scream was heard by the ragged crowd outside, as the first tongue of yellow flame curled with a tender licking sound against the curtain of blue feathers. Sí, a curtain of feathers, iridescent blue, that had shimmered like a wall of living peacocks in the breeze. There had always been a breeze to cool the dancers in the cage of Los Pájaros; it stirred the air like a whisper of constant love; it came from the mouths of twenty mechanical wind devices buried deep within the walls.

At first it was thought that perhaps a careless spark had flown from the glowing tip of a cigaret held by a whirling dancer in a fine tuxedo or a gown of scarlet lace. But the shimmering curtain of feathers had many coats of a clear protection, so that no spark could burst so into a tongue of yellow flame. Only last month the inspector had made the test on a corner of the curtain, and granted a certificate stamped with a seal of red and gold.

It was thought then that the flame had traveled from the kitchen, with the spatter of grease or the combustion of a smoldering cloth that had soaked too long in a dangerous substance. But the *investigación* revealed no dangerous substance, and the kitchen had closed at midnight, three hours before the tongue of yellow flame whispered its fatal message to the curtain of trembling blue feathers.

In that time of money troubles, it was known well that the owner of a property might pay a secret fee to a wielder of torches, who would set an accidental fire for profit, in the way that farmers set their strange spreading fires on the Pradal, to burn off the land that has died. The owner of a fine property could buy the fire of profit, and then build a finer property for a larger profit; it was the latest thing.

But the *policía* found no proof for the support of such a theory in the case of the fire at Los Pájaros. Thus the claim of insurance, one hundred and twenty million pesos of gold, was paid without argument to the members of a small corporation—the new partners of silence behind the famous singer of tangos, that *pobrecito* who now at last was more silent than they.

Those who wink and lay the finger beside the nose, when speaking so of deals that are made in the shadows, began then to whisper of the *viento malo*—the wind of evil that blows a good fortune, like the breeze of a hidden mechanical device. *En verdad,* it was said that this good fortune blew into a certain private fund of trust, managed by a pack of *chulos*—and that those rascals were the close *ayudantes* of Carlos Montero. The arranger of these *negocios*, the Chulo of *chulos,* was the general's chosen Minister of Finance, Señor Elias Rubén Caso. In truth, as it is said, his friends had named him well: Chulo—one who may be a rogue, a pimp, a helper of the butcher, a rascal in charge of *negocios sucios.*

On the seventh day after the fire, the mutilated *cuerpo* of a young man in a fine tuxedo floated gently to the bright surface of the Rio Paraná, near the white pebble beach of Puerto Deseado, twelve miles downstream from San Luis.

Though the *cuerpo* was in a bad condition, the local *policía* traced the fine tuxedo to a tailor's shop in San Luis, where the suits of many *personajes* were made to one's order, and woven of the best imported cloth. It was then announced that the *cuerpo* could be identified with certainty as that of the missing *cuñado* of General Montero—that *niño bien,* Chepito Andújar.

In the columns of news and the radio, one could read and hear of the note that was found in the empty safe at Los Pájaros, preserved by some miracle from the yellow tongues of flame. The note was of *desesperanza,* of a terrible despair, written in the hand of Chepito himself. *Sí,* that one who had never lacked for the pretty *muchachita* on each of his strong brown arms, and the sly careless smile of the *niño bien* upon his smooth handsome face. Still, it was said, by the *policía* who found the note, that Chepito confessed his deep *desesperanza,* caused by the commission of serious sins, including an affair of adultery with a notorious *mozuela*—one who sold herself to many *personajes* of great wealth, power and political ties to General Montero. In truth—as it was implied in the columns of gossip—this *muchachita* was pregnant with the bastard of Señor Andújar. Thus the fear of her current protector's jealousy, of the public *escándalo,* of the shock to his family during the election campaign—all these had led poor Chepito to write the confession of his *desesperanza,* to fill the silk pockets of his fine tuxedo with heavy round stones, to mutilate his body, and then at last to hurl himself from the Puente Victoria into the Río Paraná, on the night of the terrible fire at the Club Pájaros. *En verdad,* it was said, the club which was the place of such serious sins had been burned to the ground by a judgment of *Dios.*

The missing fortune in jewels and money never floated to the surface of the Río Paraná. Nor did the beautiful *cuerpo* of that red-haired *muchacha* for whom (it was said) Chepito destroyed his foolish life. From the columns of news and the radio, one made the guess that she was the *manceba* of the international financier Baron von M. Did she really die in that fire? *Quién sabe?* The tongues that wag said that perhaps the *puta* herself had stolen the fortune and fled to the Continent with another fool of a lover.

But it was said, too, and with more of a truth, that she was too close a friend of Rosa, and so became the victim of *los asesinos.* A small pawn of sacrifice in one of those dangerous games the *políticos* play. After a while it was said, with a shrug and a yawn of what-does-it-matter, that she had merely vanished—Puf!—in the way such women do, those little radio actresses of no special talent. By what name was she called? Juanita . . .

THE Avenida de la Solana is a river of people four miles long, from the Catedral de Nuestra Señora to the Plaza de Paz. The police, who usually exaggerate these things, have estimated the size of this crowd at more than three million, over a tenth of the national population. For once it seems true. Traffic has halted throughout the city; public buildings stand empty—as though they had been evacuated; armed soldiers fight to keep narrow corridors open in the streets for the cortège to pass. Before the ceremony began, twenty-six persons were trampled or crushed to death; dozens more have been hospitalized. It is a vivid reminder of the old days; whenever the first Señora herself made public appearances, crowd casualties occurred routinely, like a royal train of human sacrifices.

Inside the cathedral, Blanca Montero stands pale and tense beside the body of her husband, as though they are still a pair of statues, one now within and one beside the glass coffin. Masses of red and white flowers, banks of candles, blaze around them like radiant nimbuses surrounding the heads of saints in medieval paintings. The hush is as palpable as the hunger and faith in the stricken, adoring eyes that pierce the solemn darkness at their feet. It has been less than a year since the first Señora returned to claim her rightful place among her people. And with her, the new Señora, claiming to incorporate the spirit of the first in her own living flesh. Now this new one stands alone before them, as though she has no more need of the hand that Rosa held in life, the powerful hand of Carlos Montero. She has only the name. Montero. This new *Presidenta*, this Blanquita, speaks now of her own holy missions, of the saving of their great country from strife and poverty; she speaks of love and faith and God and Montero, as though they were all one, and she were the one. The radio carries her message, and the reverent tears in her voice, to the people Montero had come home to lead. *Volvíamos!* she cries, *we* have returned. Her voice is a vibrant echo of another voice they prayed to so long ago, a voice they remember still. As she weeps, this Blanquita, it seems that her tears may wash away their pain, and with it the bitter years that have passed since they last believed a woman's love could save them. Montero is still with them, and La Señora too. This Blanquita, they whisper to each other, what do you think? This *extranjera*. This stranger. She is almost as young as La Señora herself was when she died. And from this angle does she not seem almost as beautiful? With her bright mouth, and the passion in her voice that makes her slender body tremble?

And there on the altar beside her, like a pirate's treasure, lies the crystal-domed coffin, lined with a pure white satin beneath the body of Carlos Montero, as magnificent as ever it was in life; the general himself, perfectly preserved as a symbol of living faith. Montero will never leave Pradera again. I am Montero, she says. I am La Señora. I am . . . *la Presidenta.*

Viva! Montero!

THE small private *clínico* in Entre Rios had been chosen for its remote location, the serenity of its gardens, and the ease with which it could be prepared for a convalescence of perfect seclusion and *seguridad*. It was announced only that La Señora would undergo a series of treatments for anemia and exhaustion, following a minor *operación*. The *operación* was unspecified; a slight disturbance, one understood, of the organs of *femineidad*.

One had heard many wonderful stories of the rich and celebrated *mujeres,* afflicted with such disorders, whose husbands had entrusted them to the expensive care of *el doctor* Ceballos. He had, *por ejemplo,* attended a royal duchess of England and two *estrellas* of Hollywood, as well as the young daughter of a Chinese millionaire who owned the patent of a miraculous medicinal balm. It was said that when the balm failed to cure the daughter, the millionaire had sent to Rome for Ceballos, in whose care she died at once.

En verdad, the doctor had remained in China for nearly a full year after the daughter's death; it was in that time that he perfected certain aspects of his remarkable specialty. The body of the girl had been restored to an appearance of perfect health, with the aid of one hundred and thirty surgical instruments, in a secret procedure which no one had observed. She was then laid to rest in a coffin of sealed crystal, at a shrine near her father's garden of medicinal balm. There too was the new private *clínico* of Dr. Ceballos, the first research center in the Orient devoted to the disturbances of the organs of *femineidad.*

It was known well that the *cuerpo* of the millionaire's daughter, six years after the death, had the fresh look of a living *muchacha* in a light state of sleep; as though her breath would float in a gentle fragrant sighing, and her clear flesh, the color of ivory cream, would give a scented warmth to the touch, if one dared caress any part of the *cuerpo.* It was this *historia* which affirmed the world reputation of Ceballos as a great *genio;* one heard him described so, in a hushed tone of reverence: *El doctor?* *Sí*—that one who creates *la vida en la muerte*—the life within death.

There were many who wagged the tongue over questions of how he performed his *maravillas;* of the nature of those surgical instruments, and the ways in which he used them. In truth, one might hear that he bathed the *cuerpo* for seventy days in a black salt from a waterless sea. And that he could, with two swift strokes of a curved silver needle, draw the brain and the heart of a woman through the *ventanas* of the nose.

It was sworn that the white-gold hair of one of his *estrellas* of Hollywood had continued to flow in abundant silken tresses requiring the constant service of a *peluquero*—three years after her death. She wore it now in three wide plaits, twisted up so from behind; it was the latest style.

It was said that the womb of another *estrella* had been hollowed and filled with a fragrant wine made from the leaves of a palm, a powder of crushed spices, and a fluid that had no color and could not be detected by any chemist. One had heard that—*puede ser*—this mysterious substance was nothing more than the *fluido* of *virilidad*, produced in the ordinary way, from the *miembro* of Dr. Ceballos.

In truth, if one listened well to the tongues of vulgarity, one might even hear of the method he devised to guard the virtue of the English duchess, whose husband, one understood, would have murdered her in a *pasión* of jealousy, had she not betrayed him by dying of that disturbance of the organs of her *femineidad*.

It was said that *el doctor* had removed those organs and covered each petal of the *flor dorado*—her treasure of woman's secrets—with a delicate layer of molten gold, before restoring the royal *cuerpo*. Once the *flor dorado* was sewn back in place, and the thighs of the duchess arranged in a pose of chastity, one could never guess that *el buen Dios* had not created her exactly so.

The husband of that duchess should have been released then from his *pasión* of jealousy, for *el doctor* had assured him that his flower of gold would remain incorruptible for a thousand years.

But the end of the *historia* was that his doubt would give the duke no rest. One month after the funeral, he desecrated the tomb, and set upon the *cuerpo* of his incorruptible wife. He deflowered her, so it was said, with a savage cry to wake the dead. *Puta del Diablo!* Whore of the Devil! And the petals of that *flor dorado* had bitten him like the teeth of a witch, tearing to shreds the poor flesh of his noble *miembro. Puta del Diablo!*

But in truth, who would believe such a *historia*, of a royal duke of England?

THE cot upon which Rosa lay could be raised and lowered to any angle, with a power of *electricidad*. She preferred to lie so, staring up at a ceiling blue as the sky, imagining an old silent *cine*, in which *la Muerte* was a sad handsome man who loved a girl too young and beautiful to die. Rosa remembered well the way of the story's ending—how the girl herself had chosen to follow him, with the gift of half her life.

Rosa sighed, remembering now another time long ago, when she had lain so, upon another narrow cot, with the same thought of that sad *cine*. It had been good, then, to dream of *la Muerte* in his fine evening clothes, with a tie of white and eyes of gentle pain. In that time, when her own *dolor* had come like the quick slashing of a knife within—as though to make a great hole for the flowing out of poison blood—she had known well what to do. One had only to pretend that the pity was for the girl in the *cine*, instead of for oneself. In that time Rosa had the certainty that La Lloradora—the weeping *Madre* of tears—would watch to see if Rosa's eyes too had the magic tears that would not fall. In that time she had known La Lloradora could save her, even if she had done serious sin, if only she wept in this way of the *Virgen*, holding the tears so at the edges of the eyes, never crying out for the real pain of the flesh.

This time it would not be so. A *mujer* of full years could not weep in that way, for an *estrellita* in an old *cine* who had to die for a strange dark love. *Claro*, the painted heart of a statue did not melt for a woman full grown, a *mujer* of flesh who had reached for a golden crown in the true *cine* of life. *Esperanza . . .*

Rosa felt the sudden cry rise in her like the fierce howling of the *niño perdido*—that child who has lost its *madre*, or the *madre* who has lost her child, which only the *Virgen* knows are one and the same. A cry that would tear the silence of the *clínico,* shattering the serenity and the *seguridad.* She turned her head so, to bury such a rage of pain within the pillows. Still it echoed in the hollow of her body, resonating through the bones, as though she had screamed aloud. *Madre . . . Ayúdame!* Help me!

Qué piensas? The whisper of Dr. Ceballos poured like the oil of a dangerous plant. Of what are your thoughts, *querida?*

Of you, she said, without raising her head. Of *la vida en la muerte.* He moved to bring his face close to hers, casting a shadow so that she must see the gentleness in his eyes. The touch of his fingers cooled her; his hands were liquid, like his voice—graceful as the caress of a woman, as the brush of a cool silken cloth against the skin. You are so beautiful, he murmured, and now she heard the thickness of a man's urgent heat within his voice; it was a familiar sound.

Mientes, she said, with a bitterness. But why should his lies be of a different kind? You are only the last *asesino,* she said; last of the assassins; last of the *padres.*

He shook his head but said nothing. Only the soft hands hovered, speaking for him, and then the sudden grazing of his mouth on her belly, on the sad little bones of her hips, that rose so, like the un-formed bones of a child. She cried out, but he held her down, mur-muring *Vidita!* my little life . . . and she softened under him, into a kind of sleep. There was only the oozing of dark blood between them, and the sound of his sharp quick sighs. Ah. Ahh.

After a time he gave her an injection of a clear fluid, and lifted her to adjust the bandage that held the swift flowing of poisons the color of rust.

Ayúdame, she whispered, but still she held the tears so, at the edges of her eyes. *Muerte—*

Do not speak so, he said, frowning, though in fact he liked to hear this. You and I have yet a long time together—

Sí, she said, in a small voice of far away. I have heard the *his-torias—* She spoke with difficulty, and the small hand that gestured had a pale gleam of iridescence; it moved with the lightness of air, as though it were nearly empty. He frowned again, with a sudden thought. Each of the fingers must be bound with a fine string, and the toes as well. Otherwise the nails would part from the flesh in the black salt bath of seventy days.

Qué piensas? she whispered, watching him now with her listening face, through her narrowed eyes.

He stared, but quickly smiled. Of you, he said. You . . . He rose then and touched the button of *electricidad,* so that the cot would rise; so that she might see her reflection in the large round mirror on the opposite wall. *Mira!* he commanded. Shall we fix your hair today? Would you like it so—and he held bright strands of it in his hands—in the new way? Three plaits twisted up so, from behind?

She said nothing to that, but reached toward the table beside the bed, seizing a small crayon of wax. She would paint a sweet red smile. I have heard the *historias,* she said again.

Historias—

Of your bodies of life. She drew the top of the red smile over her pale mouth. It is said . . . once you found a young woman of China. Buried alive in torture a hundred years ago. And you found her so . . . *Dígame* . . . One heard that her mouth was still open, so—in the scream of her silence. *Verdad?* She looked at him with her eyes narrowed.

You must stop thinking of these things, he said, looking away. Carlos worries—

She laughed then, but the sound was of a cry. I am still too full of blood, no? Carlos worries. He cannot wait long for this *angelita*—

Sst! he said, with sharpness. That mouth of a witch—that tongue of the devil. His face was dark with a thought of excitement. Might one not cover such a wicked tongue with leaf of gold . . . ?

I am not afraid of life or death, she whispered. But the tears at the edges of her eyes had lost the power to cling without falling.

Te quiero, the doctor murmured, and his eyes scanned her face for signals. He could feel the heat of his body as it rose again. *Querida*—

She smiled then, and whispered a thing he could not hear.

In the columns of news and the radio, it was said that La Señora Montero, spiritual leader of her country, died with a prayer on her lips for the people, and for the general, her beloved *marido,* who must lead them alone now in the year of *Esperanza.*

Yet there were some who knew well that she died in the old way of an *estrella,* moving with the light. She had only the bright uniform of her last red smile, and the brave whispered cry of the *mujer* of flesh. *Muerte . . . a la puta, he?*

THE general sat alone in his fine crowded rooms surrounded by transplanted treasures; loyal friends had saved the most valuable things during the crisis; when he left the Casa Dorado it was with assurances that at least the interior trappings would follow him across half a world, to be fitted precisely into his new temporary quarters. It was then assumed that his own exile would also be temporary. Fourteen years had passed, but in many quarters it was still assumed.

Meanwhile, they had done their best to recreate his Italianate palace here, in this unreal sunny playground off the Spanish coast. Certainly no one else here lived like this, guarded by replicas of Ming temples, heavy vertical blinds that shut tightly against the dazzling light. He sat in corners like a sullen bull, hemmed in by massive black bombé chests glittering with ormolu, mocking cartoons of his own chest swelling in its black tunic trimmed with gold braid—the immaculate uniform he still affected at home in the daytime, at least when receiving important visitors.

Too many carved chairs and damask sofas crowded like petitioners in the gleaming corridors; mantels bristled with the delicate skulls and horns of desert creatures mounted on crystal; the white walls were afflicted with eruptions of murky French landscapes the color of overripe avocadoes. Everything gave off a dark heat, a suffocating rich scent that sat like a curse above the cool stone floors within the silent glow of the green pool night-lit in the formal garden, on the fragrant breeze and behind the playful lights of the harbor below.

And the general would sit sullen on one damask chair or another, fretting to his aides about last night's dinner, about the boredom of the current season, about the insufferable parade of *personajes*—visitors from Pradera, from Germany, from the United States, offering useless political friendships. He would fret about the servants, the tourists, the boys from the military base whose favors his friend the colonel had lately been buying at a shockingly inflated cost. It was all an embarrassment, tiresome, unrelieved, like the weather.

The general's belly shone like a melon wrapped in pale linen; the large gold cross gleamed on his naked chest, like a flashing sign. He sighed heavily and went out for his evening expedition. Perhaps he would soon die of this boredom, he thought; meanwhile, he must plunge into the warm night, like an old animal hunting small game. Later, he would fret and shudder for an instant, in imitation of fever, like a sultry seven-degree temblor occurring miles away, distantly felt like an echo of passion, or the afterglow of a great power.

The night he first saw María Blanca dance had begun like this, like all his nights, with this restless promenade along the Calle Niño Perdido, flanked by bodyguards in casual resort attire, the slim bulges of their service revolvers almost hidden under their crisp white linen. The general's eyes flicked glances like scattered ashes across the curious faces and thin bodies of passing children. Every night, like this, his eyes performed their ritual dance, the dance of old men. Lighting briefly, like matches in the wind, on the sweet sad nipples of a twelve-year-old girl, or the wet lips of a boy of ten sucking the yellow juice of a flower carved of ripe papaya. A pale child with fine bones or a wide-hipped little dark one with a low forehead and the trace of an incipient mustache; it scarcely mattered. He would incline his head to one of the aides, and at the signal other heads would snap somewhere in the crowd behind them, a messenger would be dispatched, to make the necessary arrangements. The child or children would be brought later to the house, wide-eyed and giggling with fright. Sometimes the mother would deliver them, whispering harsh admonitions to behave well, to make no trouble, to touch nothing, to be silent, do as they were told. The following morning the mother would return, in her gray dusty skirt, to collect her child, as if after a small friend's birthday party. A servant or soldier would serve the woman a heavy white envelope on a carved silver tray. The envelope contained a crisp party favor, a souvenir, *una prenda de recuerdo,* from the general. The mother would hide it quickly in the folds of her skirt, licking her dry lips; her eyes would dart past the servant to the doorway where her child waited, trembling and solemn, its lips swollen, its face streaked with the tracks of semen and tears. The mother would not look at the child's face, but would rush to her angrily, seize her hand and pull her, stumbling and sobbing, out through the general's splendid marble hallway, down the steps and into the blinding blue-white sunshine, past the high walls of dark bushes bursting with crimson passion flowers, down and down the long treacherous curve of road into the steamy village, where the rest of her family huddled under the roof of tin patches, as if nothing of importance had happened.

The night the general saw María Blanca dance had begun like this; ordinary arrangements had already been made for a child or two to be brought to the house. On an impulse at 3:00 A.M. the general wished to stop at the Club 77, a new flamenco palace one flight up from the once popular strip joint irreverently called La Capilla, the chapel. The flamenco club had been designed to resemble a charming gypsy cave, a white fantasy grotto of thick looping stucco walls and niches, hung about with burnished copper braziers and leather wine bottles, embroidered shawls and bowls full of red carnations whose petals might be tossed in tribute to the dancers.

The general was not much of an aficionado; but he had heard there was a young dancer here who might amuse him, a girl who had lived for a time in Corrientes province and whose passionate movements, it was said, were almost as extraordinary as her body in repose. She was a protégée of the legendary dancer Manolo, who had discovered her in the United States and brought her to Isla de Perlas to disrupt his retirement. Manolo was past seventy, but his fans swore he could still dance with a velvet hat and transform it into flesh before one's eyes: it floated and sighed, it glowed and spun and yielded to him like a woman in love.

The girl, María Blanca Vargas, was not the star of this show, merely a featured dancer, an outsider in an all-gypsy troupe. The star, Gabriela de la Mora, was a proud veteran, with a noisy claque of fans. The general's weary gaze found her predictable and cow-like, a massive fertility figure encased in ruffles and flounces which she worked like a cape of an aging matador. Behind her a trio of amplified guitars pounded like the labored breathing of tired lovers; her enormous dress puffed and whirled about her as if it were the dancer. Above the red gauze frenzy her elegant head twisted on its swan's neck, sending haughty glances, but the woman's body merely curved like a tired, fat serpent, full of old menace but no surprises. *Zis! Zas!* Her hobnailed shoes attacked the wooden stage. The general yawned.

It was nearly four o'clock when María Blanca Vargas appeared on the stage. The general sighed; what had he expected, after all?

She was ordinary—medium height, medium hair color, thin. The costume was a marvel of night club flamenco vulgarity—white and shiny, covered with immense black dots, like flakes of perfect soot. He signaled to his aides to call for the check. He would stay for one number.

But when she began to move, he felt a change in the air, as if a door had opened. At first he thought it was only the silence—the rowdy fans of de la Mora had settled into their chairs, glumly silent. It was the policy among gypsies never to applaud or encourage foreigners. But in truth it was the girl who had wrought the change; she seemed to evolve as she moved, into a higher form of body, of being. Her limbs grew and softened, as though the bones inside them had melted into flesh; the fingers poured from her hands like slow liquid. Her face bore the intense joy of a religious fanatic, as if it felt her body being consumed by holy fire. One could imagine a phantom lover feeding on the blackness in her womb, filling her with strange-colored light. One moment she swayed like a drenched flower in a violent storm; then, suddenly, her fingertips and feet exploded in wild rhythmic spasms like pistols discharging, like ecstasy or ritual death.

When the dance ended, there was a fierce silence in that artificial cave; it echoed and filled the stucco archways. The audience of drunks and angry gypsies sat stunned, their *botas* halfway to their lips. If they could not celebrate such a foreigner, neither could they break her spell. At one table an old woman sat weeping, uttering no sound. Slowly the general rose to his feet to toss a solitary red carnation upon the stage. His eyes shone. María Blanca Vargas knelt to retrieve the flower. She curtsied and swept off the stage, looking like an ordinary woman in a gaudy costume. Medium height, medium hair color, thin.

The general made a brusque motion to his aide; he could not turn his head, or speak.

Moments later she appeared at his table wearing a black sweater and dancer's tights. Without the flamboyant dancer's make-up, those obscene gashes of red and black, her face seemed translucent, like a rare white tulip; she carried it carelessly as though she had no idea of its value. She smiled quizzically, with a secret-knowing look in her iridescent gray-green eyes, as if she could translate his fantasies into other colors. You see? the rounded corners of her mouth suggested, it is just as I told you in the dream. (There was, of course, no such dream, but only she suspected that.) Tomorrow you will think of me, her mouth continued silently, and this will create possibilities. The general was far too jaded to be seduced by the tricks of a face that resembled an imaginary flower. She was clearly no different from a thousand others, older by far than the girls he bought nowadays; she must be thirty, though when she danced her body was that of a child, a single sinuous curve of torso like a wisp of warm velvet smoke. But the impudent round corners of her pale mouth were another matter. As she spoke, he kept staring at this mouth, imagining the astonishing pleasures it must have invented, or perhaps had yet to invent.

I have been waiting for you, excellency, the creature was saying, in a voice full of sly mischief. I have probably sent you a hundred messages since I began my engagement. He frowned. Messages? Her laugh, low and soft, floated lightly toward him. He thought of the pastel balloons tied to the horsedrawn carriages that plied the Calle Niño Perdido, to show the tourists that Isla de Perlas was a continuous fiesta.

Not messages then, she confessed. Perhaps they were only prayers. He smiled uneasily.

I wanted to dance for you. Especially I wanted to perform the new dance which I composed in your honor. It is a *zorongo*—she smiled—called *La Nueva Vida*, the new life.

Ah, he said. I did receive that message.

And the other? She persisted, lowering her voice to a whisper. That I wanted . . . to be with you? She touched his sleeve lightly. His eye caught the amused glance that passed between his *ayúdantes de campo*, and he leaned away from her, extricating the arm. She rose at once, in a graceful arc, murmuring no excuse, sliding away. He shook his head and gave a small shrug of mock helplessness; his aides shrugged back. Beware of experienced whores who flatter an old man, *he*, Ramon? Frasco? They laughed politely. The general drained his *bota* and stood up to go. Beware of whores who kiss your mouth with olive-colored eyes. The general laughed again, alone this time.

At the door he turned and stared at the stage, as if some after-image of her might still be there, dancing. His body seemed to shudder slightly, an involuntary lurch, as though he were about to cough. For an instant there might have been an image on the darkened stage, but it was of himself, astride the body of that girl like some ancient risen god. He shook his head again to dispel it, then whispered hoarsely to Frasco, a change of . . . plans. Frasco did not smile; he nodded, Yes, my general, whispered hurriedly to the manager of the Club 77, and ran out into the Calle Niño Perdido in search of something the general had lost.

When at last she lay naked in his great carved bed, he bent over her solemnly, still in his linen clothes, the gold cross on his neck swinging between them to its own rhythm. He kissed her infuriating mouth as if he were searching it for her secrets, but he could not bear for his body to touch hers. Why are you afraid? she whispered. That is *desacato*, he said, with a crooked smile. *El libertador* is never afraid. She did not smile in return. It is that I remind you of someone, is it not? He shook his head no. Yes, I do, she persisted, teasing him now, balancing herself on one elbow, breathing warmth into his ear. I must remind you of her, she said, pouting. I remind everyone of her.

That is nonsense, he snapped. You are nothing at all like her. She smiled as if she had tricked him. Then could you just take off your boots and lie beside me?

He obeyed, groaning. In fourteen years he had not lain beside the body of a grown woman, he had only played with smooth children who could not look long into his eyes or stir his memories. For fourteen years he had been safe, and now this . . . cabaret dancer, daring him to undress his wounds for her, to let her tear at them with her glistening tongue, with her woman's smells. *Recuerdos*. Reminders. Nevertheless, he took off his shirt and let her cool fingers caress him. *Gracias,* she breathed, nuzzling, trembling against him. What are you? he said. What do you want?

She answered with her mouth on him, *Nueva vida,* my general. You knew what I was the instant you saw me. Her fingers slid down his body like trickles of rain. No, he said, without moving. No, she echoed, moving under him. No, no, no. He sighed and covered her with his body, like an eclipse. I told you, she gasped, I told you.

She wore a small teardrop of crystal on a delicate gold chain around her neck; it nestled in the hollow of her throat, as if a transparent finger were pressing gently against her pulse. Where did you get this? he asked. Is it like one the Señora wore? I had it made; there was a photograph of her. . . . Was it not just like this? The very same?

He closed his eyes, smiling. You were a child when she died. How could you care about such things?

She shrugged. I knew everything about her, she said. I prayed to her picture, don't forget. We all did. But only I knew I would be her when I grew up.

The general shook his head, dazed. This creature was not a grown woman after all, but a demented child. Still, his friends who had seen her at the Club 77 had been right; she did amuse him. So you want to be her, he said, making a joke of it. You are aware that even she could not survive long being herself. Blanca nodded gravely. Well, but it is different now. You are stronger.

I? What have I to do with it?

But everything, of course. How can I possibly be her without you?

He nodded, stroking her hair. Of course, he said. Stupid of me. He felt the warmth of her rising against him like steam; it seemed possible that he would dissolve slowly inside her, feeling only this softness, this warmth. Ah, he sobbed, filling her. Ah, *Dios*.

Frasco's knock at the door startled him, though he had been listening for it for half an hour. He motioned to her to stay where she was, and went out to meet with his staff. There was a visitor, Chulo Rubén Caso, owner of the largest airline, the largest shipping company, and the largest movie studio in Pradera; he was expected to pledge his substantial support to the general, should the general agree to stand for reelection in the spring. As they all knew, he had written, advising them of his vacation plans on Isla de Perlas, the present regime was in grave trouble. The unions, particularly the dockworkers, were about to demand a third extortionate wage increase within a fifteen-month period. The bankers feared . . . the men of business wanted . . .

Chulo swayed uncertainly upon his small pointed shoes, like a restless balloon. He paced as he spoke, repeating everything he had said in his letter, punctuating the worst news with discreet moppings of the back of his neck.

The general listened intently, though after a time he planted his elbows on his desk, clasped his hands and rested his head upon them, so that his eyes were no longer visible. Chulo's gaze shifted uneasily, but he went on talking. The mood of the people . . . Finally the general raised his head, sighed heavily, and waved a weary hand. But we know all that, Señor. What we still do not know, what we had hoped to hear from you today, is a concrete assurance, some tangible evidence that my old friends in the unions are ready . . . whether their famous loyalty can be trusted, assuming we were to undertake . . . Assuming we could *afford* to undertake . . .

Let me assure you, Chulo began, mopping strenuously.

The general held up his hand. Please do not assure me, he said. I am aware that while I am safely here on Isla de Perlas, my name remains on their lips like an anthem. Over the years I have found this most gratifying. But—

Chulo nodded excitedly. But you need *concrete* reassurances before you will commit—

Exactamento.

Chulo's hands, still holding the damp handkerchief, began fumbling in pockets. Permit me, he said, I have brought letters—

The general gave an almost imperceptible shake of the head. Frasco said curtly, We have read them, Señor. Our information is that they are filled with the usual lies.

Chulo withdrew his hand and bowed.

Well, said the general. If you will excuse me—

Excellency. Chulo bowed again.

The general did not move until Chulo had left the room. Then he muttered, Have Quiroga talk to him, when he gets back to San Luis. He doesn't seem to understand what's expected. Stupid man. My wife always— Well. The general coughed. Let us hope times have changed.

Yes, excellency, Frasco murmured. The six men in the room exchanged surreptitious glances, like discontented children idly passing a ball. The general paused at the door. I assume, he said, without turning around, that Quiroga at least knows what to do about the pledges. This time we cannot afford . . . surprises.

Frasco cleared his throat. El Tiburón understands, excellency.

Remind him anyway.

For some reason he felt better than he usually did after such meetings. Not that he had any renewed faith in Chulo. Like all the others, Chulo had failed to come through when it most mattered; so much for the power of past favors. Still, he had a longer memory than most, of the ways in which the general honored his friendships. Perhaps if the union problem on the docks worsened over the next several weeks . . . The general smiled to himself. Perhaps the threat of a job action, properly timed just before Quiroga's meeting with Chulo? Why not?

The general quickened his step on the staircase, remembering the woman in his bed, remembering the way she had whispered, with her mouth like a soft ring upon him, *Nueva vida*. Perhaps it was a sign.

Blanca had disobeyed him; she was up and dressed in her sweater and tights, the gypsy bag with her hobnailed shoes and ruffled skirt hanging down her back like the sack of a *bandito*. She was standing at the window, gazing down at the newest hotel, a rust-colored skeleton rising to block the perfect shoreline.

How did the meeting go? she asked. Tell me exactly.

He laughed. They want me to come home, he said. The country needs me. His tone was ironic. Where are you going?

And you agreed?

Of course, he said. I always agree. Unfortunately, no one is ever serious. Where are you going?

She made an impatient gesture with her hand. I have a dance class with Manolo. But you are teasing me about the meeting; I do not want you to tease me.

Blanquita, he said. And he took the string of her bag from her fingers. You must not go to your class. I want to make love to you now.

Tonight, she said. I will come back after the performance. I must go now; Manolo will be very angry.

And if Manolo is very angry?

She shrugged. I never make him very angry.

And what if I am angry?

You may punish me, she replied matter-of-factly, kissing him. You may even—she took his hands and placed them over her breasts, so that he could feel her nipples rising to him through the sweater, and the heat of her lower body pressing against his groin— you may even, she murmured softly, destroy me. He felt her shudder against him, a delicious shiver. He laughed delightedly, and delivered a medium-hard spank to her perfect rump. Blanquita, he said tenderly, you must not make me angry. Shall I have Miguel drive you to the class?

No. She swung the gypsy bag over the shoulder and blew him a kiss. I do not finish tonight until four o'clock. Will you be there?

He nodded, but with his back to her. Then he stood at the window, waiting until her figure appeared at a distance from the house, hurrying down the steep carved road, the bag with her heavy spiked shoes bouncing like a penance against her back.

SOMETIMES Chulo posts himself silently at the side of the room, watching her. Spying on me, she thought at first. But afterward, when he came to her, falling into step as she left the ministry, taking her arm, climbing into the car with her, he would say, Señora forgive me, you were perhaps too hasty with the woman from La Plata; you forgot to ask after the family of the young woman from Montaraz—the home village of Rosa Audújar. The young bearded fellow from Chaca needed urging that he come back to tell how it goes with his ailing father after the kidney operation. You must remember to look up at the camera after each transaction, and to favor the left profile, varying it occasionally with the head leaning slightly back, so—

At first she was furious with him, always watching, taking notes, criticizing every performance. Soon, however, she found herself gazing at the door, waiting for him to appear at his station. If he did not come, she could scarcely concentrate, she would become highly agitated, and finally send for him. Once he could not be found, and she canceled her appearance; a delegate was dispatched to announce that the dispensing of funds and assistance would proceed as usual, with staff aides assuming the Señora's customary role, but two-thirds of the waiting poor went away; they would come back the next time, when Blanca herself could see them.

In the afternoons Blanca tours the city visiting orphanages and schools, the new refuge for homeless women, the recently built office for the new society of women's rights. It has already been discovered that she has no natural talent for conducting meetings; she can deliver a prepared speech, in ringing tones, but she is not at her best answering questions. Her eyes do not meet the eyes of the questioner; it is a gaze that shifts; it seems to slide away, as though it wished to be somewhere else. It is said that, unlike Rosa, she has no gift for trust. She is *una extranjera,* perhaps it was inevitable.

You sent for me, Señora?

No, doctor, I merely asked whether you were still here. In case I . . . had need of you.

He smiles. Ah. And how is La Señora faring in the heat and excitement of these days?

Bien, gracias. Her glance is cool, matching her voice.

No more *cólico,* then?

You know of my stomach pain?

He smiles, studying her desk. He wanders about the room, casually, but it is as though he is memorizing it. I am your doctor, Señora. It is my business to know these things.

She watches him with mounting discomfort. You are not my doctor, she says then. You were Carlos' doctor.

If you prefer. He studies her. Let us say that I am the house physician. Let us say that the lady of the house suffers spasms of mysterious pain. Is it not my duty to *la Presidenta* which impels me to find the source of this pain? To treat it?

She sighs with a glance of impatience; truly she is weary of sparring. I do not need, she begins, then changes her mind. *Sí*, she says instead. I appreciate your concern. But I am perfectly well, I have always had a weak stomach, it is a misfortune of my family. The food here is too spicy, I must remember to eat more carefully, that is all.

Señora, I must remind you that your health is of great importance, to the government, to your people. I cannot permit you to jeopardize it. He reaches toward her with a sudden gesture of protection; she pulls away; the tips of his long fingers graze her white sleeve. *Perdóneme,* she says, not looking at him. I have a meeting now. Chulo knocks at the door and enters.

The meeting has been postponed, he says.

What do you mean?

He bows. Postponed, Señora. The Minister of Social Welfare was informed an hour ago; your secretary will confirm the change—he gestures toward the telephone—if you doubt me.

She makes no move toward the telephone, which causes the doctor to smile, not without sympathy. Then he reaches toward her again; this time she does not pull away. *La Presidenta* is not well, he says gently. The meeting to discuss the new *Centro por los Niños* will be held at a later date—as soon as she is well enough to preside.

Had it been held this morning, Chulo says, it would have gone on—regrettably—without you. It was assumed you would prefer the postponement?

Blanca feels tears rising in her throat; she cannot answer. Chulo and the doctor return her gaze of fury with smiles.

I AM here, Señora. The voice of Dr. Ceballos drifts from the doorway of the cabin. It is not a surprise; she has known that he would
come to this place of her "temporary" exile; someone would have
sent for him. Still, she did not suspect it would be so soon. She does
not turn; she knows, after all, how he will look, a tall figure in
black, sinister, with the long white face of *la Muerte*. I am here,
Blanca, he says again softly. If you have need of me. Have you?

Blanca makes no reply. She stands at the window that has no
bars, gazing out upon the gardens of the prison island of Santa
María. She is wearing a suit of heavy silk pajamas, the color of ripe
plums in the orchards of Santa Rosa. And underneath, the stockings
of net that the dancing master, the legendary Manolo, once gave to
her saying, Wear these when you practice. They give the illusion
that the feet are a pair of captive birds, who must beat with their
wings to set themselves free.

She stands so, at the window in her hobnailed dancer's shoes,
and begins to move. At first her feet strike the wooden floor like the
steps of someone running, someone pursuing, pursued by, a
shadow. The rhythm slows now, crackling like the sounds of rifle
shots fired according to a given signal, as though for the celebration
of a royal birth, or an execution. Her body tenses and releases; the
center seems to knot and then unfold, like the center of a woman in
ecstasy, or laboring for the birth of a child. At last her angry toes
are still; she rocks now only on her heels, on the backs of her feet.
She rocks, softly, slowly, into silence.

About the Author

Lois Gould's previous novels are *Such Good Friends, Necessary Objects, Final Analysis, A Sea-Change,* and the fable X: *A Fabulous Child's Story.* She lives in New York City with her family.